CJ West

Gretchen Greene

[handwritten inscription and signature]

22 West Books, Sheldonville, MA
www.22wb.com

i

Requests for permission to make copies of any part of the work should be mailed to the following address: Permissions, 22 West Books, P.O. Box 155, Sheldonville, MA 02070-0155.

The following is a work of fiction. The characters and events are of the author's creation and used fictitiously. This book in no way represents real people living or dead.

Cover design by *Sarah M. Carroll*
Author Photo by *David Ciolfi*

ISBN 10: 0-9767788-3-1
ISBN 13: 978-0-9767788-3-7

Acknowledgements

Special thanks to Russ Cohen, author of *Wild Plants I Have Known... And Eaten*. Russ provided a guided tour of edible wild foods in conjunction with my local library. The tour and the information in his book inspired Gretchen's foraging. My children and I thoroughly enjoyed the tour. I recommend participating if you can find a similar outing through your local library or your department of fish and wildlife. We have eaten Autumn Olive from our yard on several occasions.

Thank you to Dawn and Brian Fitzgerald, owners of the Admiral Fitzroy Inn, who opened the inn to me for research. Randy, Gretchen, and Cassie spend a day at the Admiral Inn, which closely resembles the Admiral Fitzroy in Newport, RI. Thanks also to Angela Craig for providing insight into the facility and the surrounds. The Admiral Fitzroy Inn will be a stop on the 2010 book tour and may become a regular stop if all goes well.

Thanks to Kyla Bennet for her insight into energy conservation, recycling, and land preservation. Much of Gretchen's knowledge of the environment stems from my discussions with Kyla and the material she directed me to.

Thanks as always to my pre-release readers Jady Sarno, Kerilynn Newman, and my wife Gloria.

For Natalie & Sydney,
two small miracles that shine brighter with each passing day.

Gretchen Greene
Age 8

The really big boat hit a rock
I wish daddy never left the dock

Now there is lots of black sticky goo
it's on my clothes and the duckies, too

Fish can't swim, birds can't fly
we brought tears to their eyes

Covered with gunk they can't get off
oily birdies lay and cough

Kids in school say its my fault
oil drilling has to halt

I'm too young to stop it now
someday I will, that's my vow

CHAPTER ONE

Gretchen Greene stretched her arm out into the cool morning air, silenced the rattle of the antique alarm clock, then pulled it under the wool blankets and wound it precisely four turns. Wound tighter, it would run too fast. Looser, it might run down before she wound it again at bedtime. Modern clocks offered precision, but they burned electricity all day to provide one minute of early-morning service. Gretchen would never abide such waste.

She shivered, unhooked the wool blankets that covered the windows, and folded them as the sun began warming the apartment.

"Cold enough?" her roommate, Sonia, called from beneath her synthetic blankets. Sonia didn't complain about the sudden burst of sunlight at 6:00 A.M. because it was their primary heat source on clear October days. Gretchen's offer to pay the heating bills in exchange for control of the thermostat must have sounded generous, but had Sonia known she never intended to turn the heat on, Sonia might have petitioned her parents for more money—or found another roommate. Gretchen knew Sonia resented her maniacal focus on conservation, but living alone was more wasteful than heating the apartment for the two of them. She hoped that after they lived a year together Sonia would reduce her carbon footprint out of habit. She'd already realized that the room warmed surprisingly well when the sun was welcomed in. Together with the heat from the surrounding apartments the sun kept them comfortable except for the first few hours of the day. Sonia had made good progress in their first month together.

Gretchen smoothed the cotton comforter enough to display the sturdy beech spreading its branches to the edges of the bed and the fawns and rabbits curled up underneath, but not enough to chase away every wrinkle. She hurried to the bathroom where she stripped off her sweats, turned on the shower, and stepped in. The water in the pipes had cooled overnight. Another resident would have waited while the cold water ran down the drain, but Gretchen stepped right in. Dripping wet, she stood out of the spray and shivered as she scrubbed the bar of homemade soap over every inch of skin. When she stepped under to rinse, she ignored the goose bumps and lathered her long brown hair with the homemade bar. When her hair was rinsed, she closed the valve and stopped the flow of water within two minutes of stepping in. Briskly toweling her hair got her blood flowing. She felt much warmer as she left the bathroom without flushing.

Dressed and in the kitchen, she gobbled a muffin with a glass of water. Other college roommates fought over food. Gretchen simply told Sonia the muffins were made from white oak acorns foraged on trips home. Sonia didn't believe her at first, but once she saw the barrel of acorns on the balcony and watched Gretchen grind them into flour, she was convinced. The muffins remained until Gretchen ate them.

Finished with breakfast, she took Sonia's leftover coffee grounds out to the balcony where the bee box lay still in the chilly morning air. She spread the grounds over the top of her worm farm, then sprinkled some water over them and covered them with damp newsprint. On her way back inside, she pinched off a sprig of peppermint and ground it between her teeth. The channel number glowed on the cable box. She detoured over, flicked off the surge protector, and headed to school.

Living on the fourth floor protected her balcony garden from nosey passersby, and the stairs added a bit of exercise to her commute. Most residents waited for the clunky elevator, leaving Gretchen a clear path up and down. Pacific Street was yet to be clogged with the usual knots of exhaust-spewing traffic, but the air still tasted gritty and metallic, unlike home where the air carried the scents of life bursting forth from Mother Earth. Unburned diesel and a host of other pollutants whooshed in and out with each breath, coating her lungs with carcinogens and shortening her life expectancy. Cities were full of greedy Energy Fiends who bumbled around without an inkling of the damage they caused in the name of comfort, convenience, and entertainment. She avoided these Meccas of pollution whenever possible. She'd only come here for a chance to help Dr. Whitney change the world. They were on the verge of a breakthrough and Gretchen was rushing to the lab to be first to see the latest results.

Halfway down the block she spotted a box truck idling in front of a convenience store. The driver made two trips inside, pushing a cart piled high with bread and other baked goods while his truck spewed filth into the air. She stopped to watch for three full minutes, though the urge to beat Whitney to the lab was strong. She'd never seen him so excited by a test. Even more worrisome was his conversation with Lyle Ashton, an executive from Proctor Energy. They funded the research, but they didn't deserve to profit from the sun's power after polluting Earth's atmosphere for decades. She needed to beat Whitney to the lab, but it was early. Another minute wouldn't hurt.

She reached inside her backpack for a round bumper sticker. The black EF printed in the center blended into the hot red background, but her activist friends spotted these stickers by their location and color more than their lettering. She pressed the sticker low behind the passenger's door and walked on. With luck one of her friends would spot this truck when it was parked for the weekend and toss a dead fish into the cab. EFs like this guy deserved a few slashed tires or some nasty graffiti, but retribution only exacerbated the problems Energy Fiends created. Better to give him an appreciation for foul air.

Gretchen had matching stickers with hot green backgrounds for the Earth Friendly people she encountered. Unfortunately, she'd only given away two of those and they went to students she'd sought out knowing who they were and what they were about.

Ten minutes later, Gretchen arrived first to the lab. She sat at a console, awed by the astounding efficiency of their latest work. This discovery would make fossil fuels obsolete for anyone who could afford the changeover.

Solar panels would give way to an unobtrusive collection technology installed on any surface that received sunlight. Developed countries would celebrate energy independence. Cars and houses would be the first applications, but this technology could even be applied to clothing. Gretchen imagined a jacket powering an MP3 player, phone, watch, anything that needed to be plugged in. She didn't own any of these things, but if she generated the power herself, why not?

How had Whitney done it?

He was a booze hound who did barely enough to protect his grant money, but in three days he'd cleaned himself up and produced a historic discovery as if he were following a recipe. There was intense pressure from Proctor Energy, but bullying didn't produce this breakthrough. There was something else at work, but Gretchen couldn't understand what. The discovery she'd dreamed of since reading *Silent Spring* was now before her eyes. In the jumble of feelings about Dr. Whitney, Proctor Energy, and their discovery churning inside her, the worst was knowing how little she'd contributed. Dr. Whitney allowed her ideas. He'd welcomed them more than she'd ever expected, but the expertise and the insight that spawned the final product were his alone. Her ideas had been heard, but they hadn't been helpful.

Her fingers tapped out commands, quickly capturing the designs, the formulas, and the results on a tiny thumb drive. Gretchen sealed the drive in an impervious, egg-shaped carrying case of her own creation.

What she did next frightened her.

This discovery would destabilize the world economy. Middle Eastern countries that depended on oil revenues were about to be plunged into squalor. They squandered their oil wealth for decades, thinking that as long as oil rose up from the ground they'd have a line of energy junkies desperate to buy. When they saw this technology, they'd recognize their mistake and understand they were about to be shuttled to the bottom of the economic food chain. Without the constant influx of easy cash, chaos would ensue. War and famine were inevitable. Only the order of these catastrophes was in question. These plunderers of Mother Earth deserved no less.

As she erased the professor's work, Gretchen mourned the innocents.

Global warming was unstoppable. The people of Western Europe deserved this discovery's power. The spring of energy would give them a chance to stay warm when the Gulf Stream petered out. Technology exports would become an economic engine to spur them on in the face of the frozen world that was about to engulf them.

Gretchen replaced the test results with a failed set from a week earlier.

Third world populations couldn't afford conversion. She held the formula for abundant, clean energy that would revolutionize the industrialized world, and yet millions of people would be shut out. They deserved her help. These were places where solar energy radiated most strongly, where the discovery could be best utilized, and where economic stimulus was most desperately needed. Surely they deserved the seed of prosperity she held in her hand.

Gretchen erased the backup tapes from the previous three nights.

She stood, pressed the formula for boundless energy deep into her vest pocket, and wondered about the changes to come. People's energy appetites were insatiable. They'd forgotten how to do and make things for themselves. They craved plastic-packaged, hormone-injected, preservative-ridden food that poisoned their bodies. They couldn't survive without hundreds of electronic devices that guzzled power. Somehow they didn't notice their homes glowing even on the darkest nights. This discovery would spur new needs until the Earth was covered in Whitney's Nanopanels.

Gretchen rushed out of the lab with a source of unspeakable power, unsure where she was headed or who deserved it most.

CHAPTER TWO

Gretchen slithered from Whitney's office, turned the corner out of the energy department past Jeanne who was just settling into her desk, and rushed alone down the hall for the exit. She couldn't avoid Dr. Whitney if he stumbled in early. She hastened as fast as she could walk without moving jerkily. If Whitney saw her leaving and got suspicious about the results, he'd know exactly where to go for an explanation. As she reached the midpoint of the hall, she knew that today Whitney wouldn't be stumbling, he'd be energized and ready for action. He was expecting great things. Gretchen didn't know how he could be so positive, but he was going to be very disappointed when he saw what Gretchen left behind. He'd be furious when he searched his desk for the notes she'd hidden at the bottom of a recycle bin several offices down.

A large man appeared at the glass doors when Gretchen was fifteen feet from freedom. In thirty minutes she could have taken the subway to South Station, hopped a southbound train, and spent the long ride home thinking about what to do next. A patent would block Proctor Energy from exploiting the discovery, but she knew nothing about the application process. She'd be in a legal mess if she signed the application herself, but there had to be a way. There were many people in the world more deserving. The huge conglomerate coughed up so much pollution, it should pay to set things right. Climate change was going to touch off wars over disappearing coastlines and scarce resources. Gretchen held the key to helping the most impoverished get their share. She couldn't decide if the Africans or the Western Europeans deserved it most.

Ty Summers marched through the glass doors right into Gretchen's path, blocking her exit. He had the doughy face and mid-section bulge of a guy who gorged on steaks and burgers. His extra-wide Hawaiian shirts fell straight from his broad shoulders, but no matter what he wore, he couldn't convince Gretchen that he was a vegan. She could smell the meat from his pores when he stood close. Unfortunately, he'd singled her out as his first campus friend. He'd been at school just two months and already had been accepted onto Dr. Whitney's research team, which made it easy for him to stay close to her, sometimes late into the night. It had taken Gretchen a year to impress Professor Whitney, and this hick just strolled out of the pumpkin patch and found himself in the middle of the biggest discovery in decades.

"Check results yet?" Ty drawled a long hesitation between words as if he'd been taught to suppress the 'ems and ma'ams from his speech, but couldn't trim them from the thoughts that drove his oration.

Gretchen leaned left in an unconscious attempt to detour around the wayward cowboy and continue her quest. She was still thinking about patent applications until Ty mirrored her and snapped her back to the present.

"Dr. Whitney's mighty proud yesterday," he challenged.

Slow as he talked, Ty was no fool. He'd caught her leaving. There was no denying she'd been in early to check their work. Her only concern had been beating Whitney to the lab. She didn't expect students this early, but Ty seemed infected by the professor's excitement. She cursed herself for tagging the delivery truck. If she hadn't stopped, she would have been gone before the curious cowboy arrived. He wasn't sharp enough to understand the theory behind the discovery or even to be surprised when she told him it didn't work, but the lie refused to form on her lips.

Ty touched the brim of his hat as if it was his fault she hadn't answered. The combination of the suede hat and the Hawaiian shirt looked ridiculous. On colder days he wore a long leather duster and gave new meaning to the term *surfer dude*. Her own wardrobe wasn't leading-edge fashion. She chose versatile and durable pieces so she could buy as little clothing as possible.

What she did buy came in shades of green or brown, earthy colors that made her look ready for planting. She layered shirts underneath her brown vest to suit any weather. Fashion sense wasn't a requirement to join the alternative energy research team or neither of them would have made the cut.

A black Suburban pulled into the parking lot behind Ty and the movement snapped Gretchen from her fashion musings. The school was waking up. The grounds would soon be teeming with students and the fewer people that saw her on campus the better. She needed to get away from the meaty cowboy and get home before the professor saw the results.

Ty was still standing there with a finger on the brim of his hat, frozen, waiting for her response.

"The results weren't good," she blurted. "Sorry I can't explain them. I've got to go."

Shock registered on Ty's face faster than she believed possible. His hand dropped from his hat to the door handle. He gripped it firmly, holding it closed.

"Don't seem right. You sure?" His drawl was friendly, but his eyes were narrowed, his grip strong. He hadn't acted this forcefully in the two months she'd known him. Her heart rate quickened. She glanced around him for anyone headed inside, but no one was there to force Ty to move aside.

"It's not the first time. He's tried hundreds of experiments and he hasn't gotten it right yet." She stepped right up to the door, but he didn't move.

Ty scrutinized her from twelve inches away and she fought the urge to step back. He knew she was lying even if he didn't call her out. Did her expression betray her? He rarely understood their lab work, but he seemed positive that this particular experiment should have worked. Gretchen had seen the results. The only other person this optimistic was Whitney himself.

Before Ty could speak, Gretchen gestured toward the door as if blocking her way was rude. When that didn't work, she patted his arm. His hospitable demeanor returned with the contact. He opened the door and followed her through.

The Suburban had been joined by an identical vehicle parked in the next space. The two drivers were clearly visible. If there were passengers, they were hidden by the tinted glass of the side windows. A Hummer pulled in the far end of the lot, its chrome face mocking Gretchen with a hungry grin. On another day she'd have detoured far out of her way to tag this monster. She'd gladly slash four tires to keep this glutton off the road regardless of the wasted rubber. If the professor's parking space wasn't at that end of the lot, she would have gone over even in her rush to jump the Red Line and get out of there.

She cut across the parking lot with Ty trailing right behind.

She turned to send the rube on his way, but just then the professor's convertible swerved into the lot with its tires squealing and zipped to a stop in his reserved spot. Gretchen bolted in the opposite direction without an explanation. Ty grabbed her arm and wouldn't let go.

"What the Hell's going on?" For an instant the drawl disappeared and the biting clarity of his words alarmed her as much as the pressure on her arm and her desperate urge to hide from Whitney.

The lie flashed to mind unbidden.

"My dad's sick. I've got to get home, but I just realized I need to go back to my apartment to get cash for a ticket."

"Terrible day for that to happen." Ty slightly loosened his grip.

"It is," Gretchen said without realizing what she'd admitted.

"Can I help ye?" Ty slipped back into his drawl and released her.

Taking a car to the apartment then over to South Station didn't seem like a big thing, but Gretchen shunned personal automobiles. She hated burning all that fuel, but keeping Ty away from Whitney was her best chance of getting out of Boston with the data. Maybe in an hour he'd forget the encounter and she'd be home in New Jersey before anyone connected her to the failed experiment. "Where's your car?" she asked.

As soon as Ty pointed opposite Whitney, Gretchen was off and he had to hustle to keep up. The walk took them right in front of the two Suburbans and the suited men seated in back.

"Where d'your parents live?"

As she told him she lived in New Jersey she noticed he didn't nod to the men in the Suburbans even though they appeared clearly through the windshields. She wouldn't have noticed if it was anyone else, but for Ty it was odd. She'd never met someone so polite. She told herself he was distracted because he was so interested in her, but she didn't believe it. Ty nodded to everyone he passed on campus. She'd mocked his bobbing head many times and she wasn't the only one.

"I'd be glad to take ye."

Gretchen's head snapped around. "Are you nuts?"

It was more than four hours there and another four hours back. The horrible waste of gasoline aside, what sane person would spend his day chauffeuring a girl who'd never shown any interest? Something about Ty Summers wasn't right. She knew he was attracted to her. He'd practically shadowed her the day he arrived on campus, but he wasn't the type to do anything gross. He was sweet, just a bit simple. She'd make a break from him as soon as she got to the apartment.

CHAPTER THREE

The BMW Z4 bucked to a stop eight inches from the curb. Whitney smoothed his hair, then licked his finger and dabbed a nick under his chin that refused to stop bleeding. The crisp autumn day was perfect to show off what he'd accomplished. He left the top down, as if he welcomed the sun into every corner of his life, hopped out, and hurried to his office. Along the way he passed three students who hurried to keep up. He didn't understand why until he saw Josh heading to the lecture hall. When he turned for his office, the disappointed students clustered behind Josh and headed for another lecture from the grad student. Whitney had appeared twice this semester and after today, he'd never appear again. He'd heard the complaints from the students and the administration, but he didn't have patience for undergrads unless they were attractive young women eager to adorn the passenger seat of his Z4.

He stopped in his own doorway and held up his fingers to frame the photo he'd pose for later. The sunny courtyard behind his desk would send exactly the right message. The scattered coffee mugs on the credenza befitted a hard-working researcher, but not if the press sniffed dried whiskey. Whitney shuttled the mugs out and returned. The stacks of paper everywhere made him look hands-on, but on closer inspection most of them had yellowed because he hadn't done new work in years. Every photo taken today would be scrutinized by his peers. He couldn't give them reason to suspect he was a fraud. He'd earned the recognition and he wouldn't let anyone or anything mute his applause.

He rushed out to Jeanne, a thick middle-aged woman who'd been in the department for ten years. She usually viewed him with contempt, but she rose quickly to his request for a recycle bin, probably owing to the suit, the shave, and the early hour.

They stood with the wheeled bin between them and dumped heavy stacks of yellowed papers from the desk. He had used and reused the failed experiments to keep the research team energized, but that was over now. Whitney set aside a single three-inch stack of notes from the previous night's work. There wasn't time to reprint the curled pages, but their age spoke of a mammoth multi-year effort.

They also kept a bright stack of student papers Josh had graded but Whitney would never find time to approve. Otherwise only a few mementos remained. Whitney straightened the photo of him and the Institute president and adjusted his chair so the picture would be over his shoulder when the photographers came. Jeanne wheeled the bin away and promised to return with something to get rid of the dust.

Whitney squeezed an eye drop in each eye and as he leaned back, his head pounded from the early activity and the dust. Instead of reaching for the bottle in the bottom drawer, he headed to the lab to collect the results he planned to showcase to the world. Dr. Wenham and Dr. Nelson snubbed him as he left the energy department. They'd be looking for endorsements in a few weeks and they'd get exactly what they'd just given him.

The students worked in the lab as if it were any other day. He couldn't hint at what was about to happen without risking his secret, but soon they'd learn that this was a historic day for the Institute. Whitney printed the results. He shuffled the pages as he left, browsing the numbers and considering how he'd work them into his speech.

He halted four steps short of the door.

"Shit!" he screamed. The numbers were all wrong.

Heads swiveled toward him as he rushed back to the console. It had to be a configuration screw up, but he'd prepared the tests himself. He'd been meticulous. He'd done everything himself and he'd done it twice before.

He pounded the keys, praying he'd printed the wrong result set, but he found last night's timestamp exactly as he expected.

The bright red Nanopanel mocked him from behind the Plexiglas. Impossible it hadn't produced any current overnight. He could accept low efficiency if he'd screwed up a connection, but he knew he hadn't. The panel was good. The connections were good. So what was happening?

Whitney scanned the faces around the room. Several were still watching, expecting another outburst. The students knew what Whitney was trying to accomplish, but it was all hopes and hypotheticals to them. He hadn't given them reason to believe this test was different from the last hundred.

"Demitri," he yelled to the most senior assistant he saw.

A young Mediterranean man with perfect hair trotted over. "What's up, boss?"

"Gretchen been in today?"

The kid shook his head.

"Seen anyone on this machine?"

He said he hadn't. He'd unlocked the lab for the other students fifteen minutes earlier. Demitri and Gretchen had been there late into the night when Whitney set the experiment to run unattended. Neither of them would meddle with it and none of the other students had credentials to enter the lab without supervision.

Whitney dismissed Demitri, picked up the papers, and rushed back to his office. He was muttering to himself and fighting the urge to scream a string of obscenities when his cell phone rang.

"Good morning, Doctor."

"Morning, Lyle. When will you be on campus?"

"We're here outside the lab. Just waiting for you to blow the trumpets."

Whatever time Whitney thought he had to recover had just disappeared.

"Don't tell me you're surprised?" Lyle Ashton led the research division of Proctor Energy. Whitney fell under his reign even though he was technically an Institute researcher. The bulk of his funding came straight from Ashton's office. Ashton cold stop the flow anytime he wished.

"Did you do this to me?"

"Do what? What are you talking about, Whitney? You've been dying for this day. Don't tell me you couldn't get your shit together."

"I've got it together."

"We both know you can't live on your Institute salary. The house in Newport, the booze, the women, that fancy car you drove here today, you don't earn all that giving four lectures a year."

"Screw you, Lyle. You know what I'm worth."

"I need you to prove it. We're out of time. If we don't go public, it's just a matter of days until this thing crops up across town. I'm not going to be shut out. I've got too much invested. Do you hear me?"

"You're probably feeding them my ideas," Whitney mumbled.

"We both know who's shooting off their mouth. Now get it together, Whitney. The press will be here at ten."

"Ten?" Whitney squealed.

"You want a show, don't you?"

Whitney cursed Ashton and hung up. He wished he'd never taken the grant money, but his discovery would have been impossible without Ashton's equipment. If Ashton had waited before calling the media, this glitch would have been no problem at all, but once the students saw what he'd done there would be no containing the news. Ashton was right. An official press conference was the way to go. So what if he didn't have the data? He could reproduce it. He would get up to the podium and tell the cameras what he'd discovered. It wasn't technically a lie. It was just a matter of timing. He imagined himself standing in front of the entire Institute with Dr. Wenham and Dr. Nelson demanding to see his data.

Whitney checked his watch. He had less than an hour.

He flipped open the three-inch stack to see where he'd gone wrong. What he found was an experiment he'd invented to keep Gretchen and Demitri busy. He flipped back to the cover page. He'd saved the right stack, but the notes didn't match the cover. He hadn't trashed them with the recycling. No! He hadn't been that careless. Someone had switched them before he arrived. What was Lyle Ashton doing to him?

CHAPTER FOUR

Randy Black held open the neck of his flimsy hospital gown. Cassie slipped her hand inside and touched the bubbled skin where Heather Lovely's bullet had burrowed in. He'd suffered tremendous pain, but the doctors touted his recovery as miraculous. The bullet had missed his lung, his shoulder blade, and even passed through the narrow space between his ribs on the way in and out. A quarter-inch variation and the long thin bones would have been shattered, sending fragments tearing through his heart and lungs. When Randy explained that ribs were angled differently in front and back and that the bullet had to enter at a precise point and at an exact angle to make it through, Reverend Simmons grinned. "Remember the fan in Westport. Anything is possible for you, Randy. Anything."

Cassie's smooth fingers traced circles on his chest, toying with his slow-growing stubble. He felt the pressure jittering in his stomach rather than on his skin, like a little lighting storm sparked by the electricity between them. Randy had longed for her as she pursued his story, but he'd kept his distance, expecting her to leave when her writing was done. Her stories were long printed. She'd told the world about the men he hunted, but she'd written even more about those he saved. No one would know the entire truth, but Cassie knew more than anyone, and here she stood with her hand on his bare chest. The reverend looked on, completely at ease with the romance blossoming on the hospital bed. Randy found Cassie's left hand and squeezed it to keep her close.

"What happened that day, Reverend? There were sixteen people inside that building and over a hundred outside. The explosion was massive." Randy couldn't help smiling when he thought of the whole outside of the building falling away. He wished he'd been outside to see it come down. "That was the biggest explosion I've ever seen, and I've seen a few. How could everyone walk away?"

"You didn't mean to hurt them."

They both knew he didn't, although with Heather Lovely and the imam it had been a close decision. They both received the ultimate punishment but not by Randy's hands. Randy had killed before. He was undoubtedly capable, and the chaos of intense action gave him a high he couldn't get anywhere else. But since his audience with God, Randy Black was bound by a new set of rules, rules that made living with his skills and his circumstances exceedingly difficult.

"Clever what you did. And brilliant." The reverend reached over and patted the blankets above Randy's knee to congratulate him. "You knew you'd never get out of there with those CDs. Getting the evidence to the authorities, the trustworthy ones, made a difference. You figured a way to let the world in and Cassie here did the rest."

Cassie squeezed his hand. He'd almost died delivering the evidence to her. The stories she'd written made her a celebrity and he knew she felt undeserving of all the accolades. Together they'd ended a rash of corruption in New Bedford politics. They'd unseated numerous corrupt politicians and cleansed the police department of dozens of compromised officers. In the process Cassie had seen a different kind of killer up close and when she showed that man to the world, a nationally syndicated column followed. That column ended her battle with Walter for control of the newsroom. He might still be fighting, but no one at the paper listened to his babble. Randy caught her glance at the stack of newspapers on the chair. All the big papers carried her stories. She'd read dozens of them to him as he recovered. She still came to see him even though his reasons for being in the bed were more political than medical.

"I wonder sometimes," Randy began.

"Why you survived?" the reverend asked. "What do you think?"

"I think He's still giving me a chance."

"Maybe you've already redeemed yourself. Maybe He needs you here. Think about it, Randy. You've got rare skills. Young people are being tempted to embrace all forms of evil. Drastic action might be exactly what's needed. Could you imagine me triggering a blast like that one?"

The image made Randy chuckle.

"You are in a very small minority, Randy. You don't need blind faith. You've seen. Very few people on Earth can be as confident as you are about the life to come. You knew the risks, yet you looked evil in the face and risked your eternity to destroy it."

"Maybe I just like blowing stuff up."

"That's for sure." Cassie's joke carried a hint of concern.

"It takes a special man to risk himself for others when he could just as easily walk away. God has plans for you, Randy Black. Big plans."

"I know someone else that would like to make plans. When are you getting out of this bed so we can go on an actual date?"

Randy waved them both closer.

"I'm fine. I could get up and go for a run, but they don't know what to do with me. I've been told it's in my interest to stay here and keep quiet. If I call attention to myself, the governor can't help me."

Cassie's head swiveled the length of his body and then fell on the guard outside the doorway. She didn't complain because she knew how delicate his situation was, but she looked angry and cheated. Randy wondered if she realized what dating an accused murderer could do to her credibility. Her competition would attack. Walter Macedo would take the lead. It was the wrong time for them to be together. She was just getting established and her star could fade as quickly as it had been lit. The tougher the newspaper business became, the more ruthless the competition for the remaining jobs. Randy couldn't be responsible for her losing the work she loved.

"The governor can't help after all you've done?" the reverend asked.

"He has the power. It's the will that might be a little shaky. He believes I killed two people. Most people who watch the news do, too."

The Marstons had been on every news broadcast and the front page of every newspaper, but when Randy and Cassie broke the scandal, the good people of Massachusetts moved on. The judge trying Randy's case had been murdered, the defense attorney had been fired, and the prosecuting attorney was in prison. With all the upheaval in the justice system, it would be easy for one case to fall through the cracks while awaiting prosecution. The governor was taking the cowardly approach. He wouldn't pardon Randy even after all he'd done, but he'd let the case sit idle until someone complained, or so his minions had said.

"He's not going to put you on trial?" the reverend asked incredulously.

"As long as my former lawyer keeps his mouth shut and the media doesn't make a fuss, I think they'll let me disappear." It was the first time Randy said it out loud. Most of the information he got from Art Wallace, who stood by his door on the day shift. Whether Art was feeding him a line of bull to keep him from breaking out or the governor was really grateful for what he'd done, he couldn't be sure. Selling his house and moving away from Cassie was a horrible idea, but Randy had bigger problems. He had a mission to fulfill. If he failed, he'd be facing a scaly demon for all eternity. He believed fate would deliver him where he needed to be. He just needed to follow the signs and do whatever was necessary.

"Disappear?" Cassie's fingernails dug in.

"There are lots of powerful people who want me out of the spotlight."

"They want you to put your life on hold? Are they that afraid of the media?" Cassie's peers were stunting her plans.

"Why can't they stand up and do the right thing? Obey their moral compass for a change?" the reverend asked.

"You don't understand, Reverend. There were thousands of CDs in that vault. They were knee deep after the explosion. I only had seconds to decide which ones to take."

"And the rest?"

"Vanished. They searched the building. They found cash and guns, but the CDs were gone."

"You think Tom Gold paid the cops to look the other way?" the reverend asked.

"Hard to tell. The cops on the search team could have been *on* those CDs. Heather was running a big business. She caught hundreds of people on video. They didn't want their wives and their children to know what they'd done. That's why Heather was so successful in the first place."

"So where's all that evidence now? Destroyed?" the reverend asked.

"Not sure. I was taking a very long nap when it disappeared."

All three of them laughed.

Cassie hadn't known there was more evidence until Randy regained consciousness three days later. She had investigated, but by then the CDs were long gone.

"Tom Gold is hiding behind attorney-client privilege. So far nothing's stuck to him. I'm the only one who knows how deeply he was involved. The only one who'd be willing to talk about it, anyway."

"So that's why you have the big guy in blue at the door?" the reverend asked.

"It's not for the service. He hasn't brought me a single beer."

CHAPTER FIVE

Demitri waited for Whitney to disappear, then jumped behind the console and read the results that had made the professor scream. According to the data, the collection panel behind the Plexiglas hadn't captured any energy from the intense lights mounted above. The lights had drawn enough electricity to have been on all night and a few clicks brought them on again so brightly the other students turned away. Demitri knew the Nanopanel worked. The lights worked and the three of them had painstakingly checked and double-checked every connection the night before to make sure everything was perfect for the test. Whitney hadn't smelled of booze in four days. Even if he had been drinking, Demitri and Gretchen had assisted his every step. They all left the lab together with the experiment running. Whitney wouldn't have come back and sabotaged his own experiment unless he was afraid.

Demitri let himself inside the enclosure and checked one last thing. He connected an electric motor to the battery that the data said would be completely dead. When he switched the motor on, it hummed steady and strong. He let it spin until he was sure the panel had done its job. Back at the console, he clicked through every parameter. When he reached the end, he realized the experiment had worked perfectly, but someone had replaced the configuration with garbage because they didn't want Whitney to know.

Demitri popped his phone from its holster and started down his contact list until he remembered Gretchen didn't own a cell. She shunned the entire technology as a bunch of babble that distracted people from what was important. He remembered how she'd gone on and on about cell phones giving every person in America another way to burn two watts of electricity all day long. Demitri hustled out of the lab and scanned the crowd for the long brown pony tail and matching vest.

He couldn't remember where her next class was. If she'd already been in the lab and done what he suspected, she might run. He couldn't let her take off with their data. Not today. He dodged around groggy students, bumping those too slow to get out of his path, and burst through the double doors to the wide courtyard.

The cowboy hat tipped him off. No one but that rube from Texas wore a hat like that in Cambridge. At his height, Ty stuck out everywhere he went. Gretchen was just ahead, both of them rushing for the cars.

Demitri sprinted across the grass and caught them on the sidewalk short of the far parking lot. They were leaving campus together. The rube wasn't smart enough to doctor the results, but Gretchen was and there was no denying they were leaving campus early on a very special day.

Demitri pulled to a stop, breathless, and looped his fingers through the shoulder of Gretchen's vest.

Gretchen startled and spun around like she'd been attacked.

Ty clutched Demitri's wrist almost without seeing it. His boots shuffled on the sidewalk as he planted his feet. His fist was clenched, cocked, and ready to strike so fast Demitri released Gretchen and jumped back. Ty recognized him before he struck, but didn't release him right away as if he were trying to decide whether he'd plant his knuckles on Demitri's thick eyebrows, the deep dimples on his robust cheeks, or the cleft in his chin.

Demitri couldn't believe the Texan could move that fast.

"Seen Dr. Whitney this morning?" Demitri asked, catching his breath.

Demitri was addressing Gretchen. They were both on the team, but Ty knew almost nothing about energy. Somehow he'd talked his way past Whitney, probably when the professor was hammered. Demitri snubbed the rube at every turn, knowing he couldn't fight back for fear of being exposed. Demitri dominated every interaction when Gretchen was around, and Ty was forced to suffer in silence and compete for Gretchen's attention in non-scientific ways.

"No," Gretchen answered. "How'd the experiment go?"

"It bombed. Not enough juice for a nightlight."

"Nothing? How'd that happen? He was so fired up for this. And we were so careful."

The test was big enough for Whitney to clean himself up. Gretchen hadn't seen him explode in the lab, but she had to expect he was on the verge of losing his funding or his professorship. She denied knowing what happened, but she didn't ask Demitri's opinion. The rube tensed when Demitri confronted her. He knew. They both did. Demitri couldn't force her to tell him anything out here, but he wasn't going to let her leave campus until he found out who tinkered with that experiment.

Gretchen reviled Americans and her prejudice gave Demitri surprising control over her. His dark skin and accent were an instant attraction. The mere sound of his voice made her forget her rush to leave. He knew if he could keep her talking, she'd go back to the lab with him. Ty wasn't so enchanted. Demitri couldn't tell if it was jealousy that had him standing back with his arms crossed or if Ty was feeling pressured to get off campus and away from the professor.

"I don't know," Demitri lied. He gave her a story about the connections being loose or the lights malfunctioning, but they both knew this wasn't a glitch. He mesmerized her with his voice and she didn't seem to suspect how badly he needed to keep her on campus. It was a critical day for Demitri and he couldn't let Gretchen screw it up no matter how much she fawned over him.

Her eyes shifted upward and she started talking about the final coating of the panel and how the formulation must be blocking energy absorption.

Demitri kept his eyes on her but listened to Ty as he answered his cell phone. "I'm here," he said, then, "No, not yet... Will do."

Demitri grabbed Gretchen's arm and tugged her toward the lab. "Come on. Let's go take a look."

Gretchen took a few steps. Ty followed even while he was on the phone. When she stopped short Ty barely avoided bumping into her.

"I can't. I really can't," she said pulling back toward the parking lot.

"Why not?" Demitri protested.

"My dad's sick. Ty's driving me home."

The excuse took Demitri by surprise. That's why Ty was being so snappy. He thought driving her home would give him an in. Such a sap. Gretchen hated everything Ty stood for. He wouldn't get anywhere.

The click of approaching heels sounded behind them.

"It won't take long," Demitri said. "A few minutes, max. You should have seen Whitney in the lab. He was out of control."

Mary Stewart from the campus information center pushed her way up to the group and came to a sudden stop, drawing everyone's attention to a flowing skirt that was too light for the cool morning air. Her feathery blonde hair was tussled by the wind. "Just the two people I was looking for."

Even Mary excluded Ty out of habit.

"What can we do for our favorite hostess?" Demitri asked.

"I've got a dozen reporters expecting a tour from Dr. Whitney, but he's barricaded himself in his office. Even Jeanne can't get him out. I can give a basic tour, but I won't be able to answer the journalists' questions. I was hoping you kids would help me out."

Truth be told, Mary didn't have access to let herself into the lab.

"I'd be glad to help," Demitri volunteered, "but I need Nature Girl for the really technical stuff."

Mary didn't wait for Gretchen's answer. She grabbed both of them and turned for the lab. "You kids are a godsend!"

Chapter Six

The Institute scheduled tours twice a day so prospective students and their families could come and be awed as they stepped inside the revered buildings lined up along the Charles River and north into Cambridge. While they imagined any manner of experiments going on behind the brick walls, highly polished students reminded them that they were touring the number one scientific research institution in the world and that more practical applications were launched from this campus than its nearest three competitors combined. Tour groups weren't permitted outside common areas because the disruption of the twice-daily circuit would be too great, but the restriction only added to the mystique.

These weren't parents filtering into Dr. Whitney's lab.

Gretchen recognized Lyle Ashton with his silver hair and black overcoat. The handful of bodyguards taking positions outside the lab seemed like overkill. Two particularly vicious-looking men, one blond and one dark, the yin and yang of personal protection, came into the lab but stopped just inside the doorway. Ashton worked his way to the front of the crowd where he could control everything said about the project he financed. These were the men who had parked outside in the gas guzzlers laden with bullet-proof glass and armored panels. No wonder Ashton needed protection. He and his firm were responsible for twenty percent of the pollution drifting over North America. His slick advertising convinced Americans to burn fossil fuels simply for the joy of motion. Whole classes of vehicles sprung up. Dirt bikes, snow mobiles, jet skis, they entertained people too lazy to take up a sport that involved exercise. These same people would idle endlessly in parking lots to get a space fifty yards closer to the entrance. Inside, shopping malls burned electricity fifteen hours a day running escalators to transport these slugs from floor to floor. No wonder half the country was obese. Gretchen had to look away.

Elsewhere in the crowd, she spotted a reporter from Channel 4. Mary had forbidden cameras from the lab on orders from Dr. Whitney, but Gretchen had seen three cameramen setting up outside the building, so there were at least two other television reporters in the crowd. Gretchen didn't care much for the glamour of television news or the incessant drone of inch-deep stories, but she appreciated the efficiency of the medium. The other two television reporters were intermingled with a group of people Gretchen loathed almost as much as Lyle Ashton.

The gall of newspaper people to print dribble most customers didn't even read. Sure, it was more thoughtful than television news, but the papers piled up in living rooms everywhere, waiting to be thrown away. Some customers recycled. Thinking about the mammoth rolls of paper streaming through a grimy machine that printed, trimmed, and folded them made Gretchen shudder. Motoring their products all over the state was nearly as bad. At least these companies were finally being shuttered by Internet competitors. News delivery was important. But stories about inner-city thugs maiming each other, drunks plowing into other cars, and airplanes crashing to the ground were of no real use to anyone. The spectacle of the gruesome and dangerous succeeded only in lowering spirits and wasting precious natural resources. She hoped the era of sensationalism would soon fade and that common sense would have its day, but she wasn't optimistic. People didn't know how to do anything for themselves anymore because they were fed a constant diet of superficial mush.

Malcolm and Kylie huddled by a computer behind the crowd and whispered warily, intent on their work. When Gretchen talked about the tall data storage cabinets Proctor Energy provided, Malcolm and Kylie would be in the middle of the tour. They'd seen tours before. They knew an awkward moment was coming, but they kept working.

There were others in the room Gretchen didn't recognize, probably bloggers here without an invitation. They'd rush back to dorm rooms or apartments and spread the word on the Internet. If it were up to Gretchen, this was the group she'd be speaking to.

Mary slipped through the crowd and stood beside the console Gretchen had used to take Dr. Whitney's results. Behind Mary, the Plexiglas cube held the panel that could make Whitney famous. Gretchen wished she'd taken it earlier, but given the change in plans, the oversight was fortunate. Mary waved Gretchen and Demitri to join her up front, introduced them, and then launched into an overview of Dr. Whitney's nineteen-year career at the university.

"As you all know, Dr. Whitney has some groundbreaking news to announce today."

Demitri twitched. Was he angry for not being credited in the same breath as Whitney? Surely Whitney would thank them later at the press conference, but Demitri couldn't think he'd contributed that much to the effort in the two years he'd been on the team. Whitney had been working on this for over a decade.

"I'm not going to steal Dr. Whitney's thunder," Mary continued, "but I wanted you all to see where this important work was done even if we can't allow you to take photos."

Ty melted to the back of the crowd by the door, disconnected from the throng that stood ready with notepads, their heads turning in unison like a school of fish, flashing glances at equipment they would describe later based more on its appearance than its function.

During their walk to the lab, Gretchen had suggested technologies to highlight and students to compliment. Comforted by the preparation and the students at her side, Mary gave a first rate tour with a little help from Gretchen and Demitri when she needed a technical term. Mary asked Gretchen if she had anything to add. She really didn't, but the crowd was waiting for her to say something.

"On a clear day the sun radiates enough energy to supply all our *needs*. Add to that wind and hydro-electric and there isn't a *need* to burn fossil fuels that pollute our air and water. Someday we will be able to live in cities without breathing harmful fumes."

Feet shifted in the crowd. A few snickered.

The overdone woman in front was the first to bark out a question. "Are you saying we pay billions pumping oil and refining it for nothing? Certainly we don't enjoy giving our money away? If the answer is so simple, why haven't we done it already?"

Gretchen pointed to the shiny black phone the woman had been using to send a text message seconds earlier. "That's a very nice phone. Is it new?"

"Could you answer the question?"

"How much energy do you think it takes to create a phone like that one? How long did you keep your last one? Six months? Less? That's why we burn fossil fuels. Because we can't imagine a world where we use something for its entire serviceable life."

"People have to live."

Mary pressed forward to deflect the angry questions, but Gretchen couldn't let this go. "Live! Will you die without a new cell phone? We're working hard to create clean, renewable energy, but that isn't the entire equation. There must be a limit to *your* appetite for power. Technology can only do so much. What are we going to do when fossil fuel sources run out? Cover the Earth in solar panels so you can go home to an electric back massager?"

Mary leaned in to rescue the journalist, but Gretchen saw a young man in the second row who had tuned into her message. He looked like he'd actually tell the world that energy independence was as much about conservation as it was about alternative means of production. Gretchen pointed in his direction to Mary's dismay.

"What would you have our readers do?" the young reporter asked. "Without remodeling our entire lives, that is."

"First, get in touch with nature. We spend vast resources heating and cooling our homes. When it's sunny in the winter, open the shades on the south side of your house to take advantage of the sun's power. When the sun goes down, close the shades and keep the heat in."

"You can't be serious?" the overdone woman asked.

"I live here in Boston and I have my thermostat turned off. My heating bill so far this term—zero. Nature will work with you the same way in the summer. Open your windows at night when it's cool and shut them in the morning when the day heats up. You'll have a few hours where your house is a bit too warm, but you won't burn electricity on air conditioning."

The television reporter sighed and turned to Mary for help, but Gretchen wasn't budging.

"I suppose you can't live without air conditioning either. This is New England. How many really hot days do we have each summer? Five? Six?"

The woman didn't respond.

"I bet some of you turn on your AC in June and run it until September. Don't you know how ridiculous that is?"

The young man goaded her on. "What else?"

"Do we ever think about the energy we waste in transportation? What if we had to walk? We wouldn't go to the grocery store in the morning and then run out to the dry cleaner in the afternoon. Not if they were close together. And we'd be darn glad to catch a bus or a train, wouldn't we?"

The woman up front rolled her eyes. She was above the need to conserve. The world had been created so she could squander its bounty in service of her whims. Gretchen wanted to reach out and slap her. She extended a finger and an angry scowl instead.

"Funny, isn't it? It won't be funny when the planet goes dark. All that time you spend burning the lights on your makeup mirror, running your blow dryer and curlers, spewing aerosols everywhere—that's going to end. Then we'll value ideas over boobs and hairdos. What'll you do then?"

The room fell silent.

Mary gasped. She clamped down on Gretchen's bicep and pulled her back from the crowd. Even in the face of Mary's scowl, she heard the air sucking in between the reporter's teeth. Mary flushed. Gretchen's retort had tainted the coverage of at least one television station. If the print reporters knew what she thought of them, the devastation of Dr. Whitney's announcement would have been complete.

The reporter stormed out. As Gretchen watched her go, she saw Lyle Ashton grinning over Mary's shoulder. Ty also enjoyed the spectacle from his post by the door. A buzz rose among the crowd, but Gretchen couldn't tell if they were applauding her ideas or sympathizing with their colleague.

The young man interested in conservation tips stepped forward and asked to get a photo of the students in the hall. His piece was taking a turn toward Gretchen. Mary scowled.

"Thank you all for coming," Mary said above the din. "We'll be assembling on the lawn in ten minutes for Dr. Whitney's announcement."

The reporters filed out of the room. The student assistants followed.

"We need to talk," Mary whispered in the angriest tone she could snarl and yet not be heard outside.

Gretchen ignored her and joined the group against the wall. The reporter arranged Malcolm, Kylie, and Josh behind Gretchen and Ty, then shifted Ty and his cowboy hat to the back and centered Gretchen in front with Kylie by her side. His photographer snapped five quick shots. Others joined in, assuring that this photo would be in several morning papers.

Demitri talked to one of the other reporters, but broke away in time to capture a shot of the group with his cell phone. He was unfazed that he'd missed his chance at immortality.

When the group broke up, Mary directed them to the courtyard to stand by Dr. Whitney as he made his announcement. Malcolm and Kylie told Mary they had an important deadline and asked Gretchen to buzz them back into the lab. When Gretchen turned, everyone was gone except Mary, who was closing in for the inevitable scolding. Fortunately Mary had no academic power.

CHAPTER SEVEN

Art tossed four chips onto the bedspread and said, "One thousand," in a low, steady voice. It was about a third of his remaining stack, few enough so he could still fold if he had to.

Randy studied the man who'd been sitting outside his room for weeks. When he saw the sign he expected, he said, "All-in."

The guard immediately flicked his cards into the muck.

"How do you do that?"

It was the fifth time he'd done it in twenty minutes. He knew Art was bluffing. He didn't have anything in his own hand, but that didn't matter. When Randy raised all-in, the trooper could only fold.

"I know you didn't see my cards. I dealt. You can't have the nuts every time. How do you know?"

Earlier the guard had wanted to play for money. He'd been disappointed when Randy suggested playing for chips from the gift shop downstairs, but fetching them saved Art a lot of money.

Randy waved him closer. "You're giving me a classic tell."

"What tell?"

"When you bluff the turn or the river, you stare blankly at the board. It's almost as if you're cursing the deck for missing your ace-jack."

Art's face slackened.

"Check out Caro. There's a whole list of tells in his book with pictures and everything. It'll keep your buddies from robbing you blind."

The trooper reached down on top of the discards and turned over the top two cards: the ace of hearts and the jack of spades.

"It's a gift," Randy said. He wasn't positive it was an ace-jack, but it had to be a big ace. Not a king or queen because both were on the board. Having a pair would have given Art confidence he wasn't showing. It could have been an ace-ten. It was a bit of a lucky call, but Randy was proud of the read all the same. He tossed his unsuited seven-six facedown on the pile and packed the cards into the box. Art helped stack the chips, shaking his head the whole time. When they finished he walked back to his post.

Randy was glad to have a trooper stationed outside his room, but he would have felt safer with the SIG tucked in beside him. The gun would never be as useful as it was against the Marstons, but he'd missed its toothy grip ever since he lost it in the rubble of Heather Lovely's stronghold. The scandal Randy broke that day ended dozens of careers. There were dozens more men Heather Lovely had blackmailed. Any of them would pay to see Randy silenced. The most dangerous was his former lawyer.

Randy wondered if God kept him alive because he failed to see Tom Gold punished. Randy hadn't had a vision since his premonition of the mosque attack. That could mean he was on the path. Saving so many people had to be good karma. God had seen what he'd done, but He didn't reveal whether Randy's future had changed. His name still hadn't and that was the clearest sign he'd been given so far. The instant someone called him Oliver Joyet he'd know he'd earned salvation.

Not everything had gone well since God challenged him to turn things around. Sebastian had been murdered on the courthouse steps. Randy's plot put him there and that made Randy responsible even if he hadn't pulled the trigger. Forgetting that Tom had Randy's fingerprints on the rifle that shot Sebastian and the implications of another murder trial, Randy wondered if there were other consequences his rampage had set in motion. Could he be expected to intervene? Impossible. How could he manage the effects on Deirdre and Charlie living in different states, not to mention Elizabeth at the winery in Piolenc and Monique's lonely husband and his two boys on the Deudon family farm? Randy had more to do. Otherwise he would have died

31

in the rubble on Coggeshall Street. But did his future depend on those he'd already harmed or those he was yet to meet?

Seemingly in answer, a slight man stepped through the doorway in a hundred-dollar suit. He hefted an overstuffed computer bag that looked more like a carry-on than something he'd lug to work every day. Art allowed him to step inside and close the door, so whatever he had in the bag wasn't likely dangerous. Still, Randy thought it was about time to trade the hospital gown for street clothes in case he needed to get moving in a hurry.

The man introduced himself as an aide to the governor and shook Randy's hand. That was the most official acknowledgment of their meeting the young man would make.

"You've provided a tremendous service to the commonwealth, Mr. Black," the young man said. He reached into his bag and retrieved a compact phone and set it on the table at the bedside. "There are some people very interested in what you say and do over the next few months."

"And you want me to do it in court?"

"Not particularly."

How had one of Tom's thugs gotten through the door? Where was Art? And why had the young guy pulled out a phone instead of a gun?

"Relax. We have everything we need."

Randy was anything but relaxed. His heart pounded underneath the flimsy gown.

"We're prosecuting fifteen government officials and almost as many corrupt cops. The stories all intersect. Revelations come rolling out every time we do a deposition. The DA's office has more work than it can handle right now. That's without considering the cluster going on in superior court. Not only was the senior judge murdered, but we learn that he's been fixing trials. Every defense attorney in Massachusetts is lining up appeals."

"So what do you want from me?"

"Not a thing. I'm here to show our gratitude."

"And?"

"And nothing." The bag opened to reveal banded stacks of cash.

Randy threw up his hands and moved back. "What's that?"

"Your reward."

Finders fee, reward, no matter how he phrased it, that much cash in a bag looked like a bribe. Randy hadn't asked for a reward, but there was one thing he really needed from the governor: a pardon. Judging by the pile of money and the unofficial delivery, the governor hadn't done the paperwork. Randy doubted any paperwork had been done on his reward either. The aide brought a tiny fraction of the cash seized in Heather's vault. The reward could be legit, but wouldn't a reward be a check with a framed citation? Neither was present in the aggressively sanitized room.

"What exactly is this?"

"The governor's utmost thanks." The guy couldn't have been older than thirty-five. He offered no proof that he even worked for the government. What he did have was an air of confidence, a bag full of money, and eventually an explanation.

The governor couldn't offer a pardon. It was within his power, but it was political suicide to pardon a murderer. "The public has a long memory, but a short attention span," he said. "Superior court is in a shambles. They won't notice your file is gone for years. As long as you stay out of the news and don't make the governor look foolish, there will be no prosecution." The deal offered no guarantees whatsoever.

"So he's going to leave me in limbo?"

"You'd prefer prison?"

"No."

"It's not forever. Depending on the next election you could be high on the list for a pardon. Until then, take a long vacation. Stay out of the spotlight and God help you, stay out of trouble."

"I'll be sure to vote against him."

The young man cracked a smile as he handed Randy a business card with Adrian Fitzgerald centered in bold letters. There was a single telephone number underneath with no indication of the governor's title or whether the number was a cell or a landline. Nothing else was printed on the card.

"Hang on to that. We don't print many of those."

"Thanks."

"Art will stay to the end of his shift. After that, you're on your own. I suggest you go somewhere you won't be recognized and stay there."

Before Randy could ask, he produced the only official paperwork he'd ever give, release papers signed by Randy's doctor. "Just go. You don't have to say anything to anyone. Better if you don't."

The man zipped the bag and left it on the chair in the corner.

"Thanks. And good luck," he said, then disappeared.

When the door closed, Randy went for his jeans and boots. He wanted to rush out right behind him, but his situation hadn't improved. He was still in line for judgment here and in the hereafter. If anything, his situation was more difficult. He had the freedom to go where he wanted, but once he left the hospital, Walter Macedo would badger him for a story. Tom Gold and dozens of others tainted by Heather Lovely would see Randy as a threat to be neutralized. The best way for Randy to stay alive was to take the young man's advice and stay away from New Bedford. Unfortunately, that was exactly where Randy planned to go.

CHAPTER EIGHT

Mary didn't wait for the doors to close. "What were you thinking?"

"You asked *me* to help. They asked questions, I answered."

"What do you think Channel Four is going to broadcast? This is the biggest discovery at this school in fifteen years, maybe ever."

"How do you know? Did Dr. Whitney even tell you about it?"

Mary shied for an instant then barked at Gretchen again. "You better not say one word during this press conference. Get up on stage with Demitri. Let Dr. Whitney thank you publicly. But not one word."

"You're welcome for helping with the tour."

Mary stormed off.

Gretchen slipped into the women's room.

She paced in front of the stalls, her image appearing in each mirror then leaving unexamined for the next. How could Whitney announce his discovery after what she'd done? The Proctor executives were here to take credit. They hadn't even seen the results, but they were ready to whisk Whitney's panel away so they could wring out every last cent in secret. A fortune. Money they didn't deserve. Gretchen fumed, thinking about the gas-guzzling Suburbans. Maybe Whitney would tell them. Maybe the press conference would fall apart. She faced herself in the mirror and understood how she could make that happen.

She crossed the hall and let herself into the lab, heading straight for the console. She slipped two texts from her backpack and stashed them in the bottom drawer before Malcolm and Kylie looked up from their work.

Around the corner, she opened the Plexiglas enclosure. When she did, Malcolm came trotting over like she was breaking into a bank vault. He was too close for her to get the panel and rush out, so she calmly loosened the clamps that held it in place.

"Hey," he said. "Prof called while you were out in the hall. He said he didn't want anyone touching this experiment."

"That means you, not me. He wants this for the press conference."

"It's your head." Malcolm watched her disconnect the wiring and lift the panel out of its Plexiglas home.

She moved past him and he closed the door for her, leaving his prints along with hers. They wouldn't need prints when Whitney returned to investigate. Malcolm would tell anyone who asked that Gretchen left with the panel. Her story about bringing it to Whitney wouldn't hold up long. She wouldn't hurt anyone to protect herself, nor could she. She'd run.

He stood by as she packed the panel into her backpack and cushioned it with a sweater.

"What's with the big announcement?" Malcolm asked. "Did he finally do something?"

"I guess. I haven't seen the results myself, but he's really been different the last few days. Something's definitely up."

"Hard to believe," Malcolm said.

"What are you guys working on? Why aren't you outside?"

"Our lab project is falling apart." His voice trailed off and his eyes begged for help, but Gretchen wasn't staying in the lab a second longer than necessary. She was leaving campus as fast as she could.

"Bummer," she said. "I gotta go. Whitney needs this yesterday."

Gretchen rushed out of the lab. Malcolm went back to his doomed project rather than follow her to Whitney's conference.

Demitri leaned up against the warm bricks, sheltered from the wind with his eyes in a chemistry text. He flipped pages back and forth as if he were studying for an exam or puzzling out a riddle, but his attention was focused on Lyle Ashton as he spoke into his phone.

"We know it works, Patrick. What exactly do you think the press is expecting? They're not scientists. They'll write what we tell them to write."

Demitri wasn't close enough to hear Whitney on the other end.

"Forget the results. We'll rerun the tests later."

Lyle Ashton was sounding angrier with each delay.

The crowd was unimpressive in terms of numbers, but the prerequisite journalists were in place. The story would burst into the public consciousness by the evening news. Tomorrow, Proctor Energy and Dr. Patrick Whitney would dominate the headlines. The bodyguards around Lyle Ashton wore smug looks, mocking the professor's arguments as nonsense without hearing them.

"Who in Hell is going to know, Patrick? Really!"

Lyle Ashton looked toward the platform. Mary was standing by the podium chatting with Josh, the only lab assistant in attendance. Demetri could see Ashton's blood pressure rising. He couldn't let the journalists leave no matter what. Lyle Ashton was going ahead with his show and if Whitney didn't come out soon, he'd send his goons in after him.

"Get your ass out here," Ashton barked.

Demitri closed his book and disappeared into the nearest door.

CHAPTER NINE

Mary nervously watched the antsy journalists milling about until Professor Whitney finally emerged from the building, trudged across the lawn shuffling papers, and took his seat next to her. She could feel her boss, Dr. Kent, scowling behind her as she stepped up to the podium, as if his expression could reach out and poke her in the back of the head for fouling things up. She welcomed the journalists and faculty again, thanked them for their patience and wondered why her boss had chosen today to oversee her work. She'd pulled this meeting together with only a few hours notice, but all he would say afterward was how poorly the smattering of empty chairs reflected on their prestigious institution. Even the six chairs lined up to honor the student assistants went empty save one. Gretchen, Demitri, and Ty were nowhere to be found. She had seen Malcolm and Kylie go back into the lab and didn't have the time to drag them out to their seats. She wished she'd gone back to fetch them. These kids were missing out on history, history they'd had a small part in bringing about.

A few faculty members dotted the seats, testament to Dr. Whitney's secrecy. If they'd been told privately about the breakthrough, they wouldn't have braved the chilly air to listen in on a press briefing. Was it curiosity or funding rivalry that brought them out? If Dr. Whitney's boasting was more than hype, there would be a realignment of the pecking order in energy research. She sensed a realignment in her future for bungling such an important announcement, regardless of how little control she was given.

Mary tried not to think about the personal implications. She spoke strongly to reach the handheld recorders all along the front row. Now that Dr. Whitney was seated, the first six rows of folding chairs were filled. Even passing students were drawn in, forming a semi-circle that blocked some of the wind for those seated in the audience. As Mary recounted a story about superconductivity, one of her favorite Institute discoveries of the last several years, she saw Gretchen slip outside the building and skirt the edge of the crowd. She couldn't stop her introduction to call Gretchen to her chair, so she wrapped up, shook Whitney's hand, and stepped aside. Her boss straightened his green tie as if to say he'd have done a better job introducing the professor.

Looking past Dr. Whitney, Mary saw Ty emerge from the crowd and stop Gretchen from reaching the parking lot. The two of them stood on the lawn and started talking, with no regard for Dr. Whitney's opening. Distracted as Mary was, the next several events melded together. She was frozen, standing amid utter chaos as her brain replayed what it had seen and seized her with a warning that she was in dire peril. The intensity of the messages overwhelmed her ability to comprehend them, so her brain could not command her body to action.

A breeze lifted three typewritten pages Dr. Whitney had set on the podium. The uppermost fluttered out of reach. Flustered, Whitney lurched after it.

The green tie twitched beside Mary. Dr. Kent desperately clutched his abdomen as a spasm gripped his entire body. He went rigid then shook with a wave of tremors. He weakened and folded lower and lower.

A nick appeared on the top edge of the podium, sending splinters flying. Simultaneously, the brick wall between Mary and Dr. Kent exploded to life. Shards of brick pelted Mary's face. Later she'd realize how close she'd been to being killed and how fortunate her next act was. She clutched her boss by the shoulder, stepping right through the path the last bullet had taken to ease him down to the grass. The next bullet whizzed by Mary's head, fluttering strands of hair trailing behind her. The proximity and the velocity struck her with a primal realization that she was under attack and needed to get moving. The entire crowd scrambled from their seats and rushed in every direction. The fortunate ones at the back had a clear path to cover behind cars in the parking lot.

Mary turned away from her stricken boss and ran along the brick wall deeper into the courtyard. She passed Josh slumped in his chair, his hair soaked in blood. Dr. Whitney ambled in a low crouch. Bricks exploded in front of her as she caught Dr. Whitney. Something deep inside her recognized the situation even if she couldn't grasp it consciously. She dug in her heels, stumbled, and fell to the grass. She reversed direction and clambered on hands and knees back toward the safety of the podium. There the bullets stopped tracking her. Alone, with her head sheltered inside the wooden base, she heard her own screaming voice above the clamor of the terrified crowd.

Whitney ran for the door he'd come through earlier with bullets chasing him. Without cover, they'd find him and leave him bleeding like her boss and the poor student in his chair. A commotion on Mary's right distracted, or maybe relieved her from watching what her brain was telling her would be Whitney's ultimate death.

The men from Proctor rushed toward the podium and fanned out, the blond and his dark counterpart at the fore, guns barking upward toward the rooftop. Mary peeked out from behind the podium and she could see dents and holes appear in the aluminum duct work. If the Proctor men had returned fire earlier, they might have saved Josh, but they'd gotten Ashton to safety first. He was their priority.

She wondered then why they'd been allowed on campus with guns. Even as they were saving her and what remained of the crowd, she thought it was too dangerous for them to be armed.

The screaming was gone now. The entire crowd had found somewhere to take shelter from the bullets. Several people had dropped to the grass, staining suits and dresses as they hid among overturned chairs on the lawn, but most had run for shelter behind the parked cars or fought their way inside the building. Mary crouched low now, hearing for the first time the rapid-fire spitting of the automatics on the roof and the corresponding collision of slug and brick or wood or turf. The metallic slide of magazines being dropped and replaced surrounded her as the Proctor men battled the attackers above.

A pair of cowboy boots and two canvas shoes rushed away through the parking lot. Gretchen and Ty made it to safety. Mary turned on her hands and knees looking for someone to tell. Later she'd wish she'd screamed for someone to follow them, but her throat was too hoarse to be heard and she couldn't know what they were headed into. She spun around looking for someone to come and take her away from the killing field, but the only people nearby were either firing upward or cowering for their lives.

At the far end of the courtyard, Whitney reached the door and burst inside, apparently unharmed. The gunfire stopped as suddenly as it began, as if Whitney's escape signaled the end of the game and victory for the Institute. Mary didn't move until one of the security guards lifted her up by the arm and helped her out of the main courtyard. She found shelter against the brick wall around the corner. Being guided away on wobbly legs felt nothing like victory.

CHAPTER TEN

Malcolm's vision flashed to black when he saw the results pop up on the monitor. He smashed his fist on the desktop and the water in his glass rushed from every edge toward the center, forcing a single drop to jump up above the surface and hover there separated from the rest for an instant. It plopped back down, sending ripples outward until they reached the edges of the glass and bounced back together, neutralizing each other's energy until all were diminished. A dozen papers hopped a fraction of an inch off the desktop. Kylie snapped to attention.

"Shit," Malcolm hollered.

Class started in thirty minutes. The results were all wrong and another extension was not going to happen. The tour had set them back even though they had worked through much of it. He couldn't blame their failure on Whitney and his publicity. Whitney hadn't offered any guidance, but he hadn't made any major demands either.

The door burst open as if the lab were bugged and the faculty was rushing in to deal with his foul language. The men who marched in weren't stodgy professors. Clad in black with black hoods and duffels, each carried a pistol with a bulging silencer mounted on the muzzle. The first three ignored Malcolm and Kylie. They spread out to different corners of the lab and quickly went about their work. They set their heavy bags on the floor, unzipped them, and manipulated something inside.

"You can't be in here," Malcolm said, still standing, but backing away as he realized the absurdity of his warning.

The fourth man didn't carry a bag. He stepped to the center of the room and wheeled around to take in the entire space.

Malcolm wondered how they'd gotten past the hand scanner Proctor Energy had installed on the lab door. Lots of students wanted to use the equipment. Sometimes Malcolm let his friends in, but as smart as these Institute kids were, they couldn't defeat the biometric scanner. These men had come through seemingly without effort. Malcolm should have understood then that the guns and the confident intrusion meant these men were not to be interfered with. He should have run, though even if he had darted for the door the moment they came in, it wouldn't have substantially raised his chances for survival.

Kylie screamed when the fourth man raised his gun.

The man stood directly between them and the door. Malcolm's feet still hadn't shifted when he felt the burning slug rip through his intestines. The gun spat out three more bullets. They folded him, but he kept his feet in some grandiose idea about escaping, as if he could run past a trained killer in spite of the pain.

Kylie was still shrieking.

"Go," he begged her.

He stumbled forward, picked up the water glass and heaved it at the gunman. The water sprayed everywhere and the gunman was forced to cover himself. The glass hit his raised forearm. Kylie finally started running.

Malcolm grabbed a stapler and cocked his arm.

Kylie slipped on the slick floor, but the gunman was more concerned with Malcolm and his projectiles.

He fired. The fifth bullet slammed Malcolm back against the desk. He hit the floor on hands and knees and watched through glassy eyes as the gunman swung toward Kylie.

He fired three times, prompting screaming gibberish from a man in the far corner. One of the bullets had missed and whacked the outer wall very close to where he was working. Malcolm collapsed flat on the floor and watched Kylie flailing over the slippery tiles. The gunman's feet stepped into view and Malcolm heard a series of spitting sounds. The gunman jumped back, apparently from a point-blank ricochet off the floor, but when his feet left Malcolm's view, all he could see was Kylie lying still.

If he were standing, he would have seen the blood pooling around Kylie and known she was killed instantly. He also would have seen the three men placing blocks of explosives all around the lab. One man worked the computer servers and storage area, packing enough explosives so that nothing stored there would survive. There would be no evidence of Malcolm's failed experiment, or any other performed in the lab that year. The work benches were also laden with charges to obliterate anything stored on the individual computers around the room. One man rushed around the outer wall planting charges on the support beams, apparently in the hope that the room would collapse.

Malcolm's hands grew too weary to keep clutching himself.

He fought dizziness and nausea to keep up the pressure and slow the warm fluid escaping between his fingers, but it was flowing faster.

Loud gunshots erupted outside. This spurred another sputtering of gibberish. Footsteps tracked around Malcolm. He closed his eyes, expecting a bullet, but the men rushed past him and out the door.

Suddenly he was alone and the room was quiet.

Someone would come.

Malcolm folded himself toward the door to wait.

Seconds passed and he realized what the men had been doing all around the lab and why they had rushed to leave all at the same time. His right arm was still strong and he used it to pull himself toward Kylie. His legs refused to kick him forward. They lay limp behind him, a dead weight anchoring him to his failed experiment and the useless data.

The first explosion triggered and sent fragments of countertop cartwheeling over Malcolm's head. The desk between him and the explosion sheltered him from a torrent of plastic, metal that had once been a desk, and the hundreds of objects collected on top of and inside it. Debris slammed outward in every direction.

The concussion was deafening.

Malcolm covered his head and tucked his torso under a desk. When the other charges triggered an instant later, the whole room, Malcolm included, was converted into a hailstorm of debris firing and churning at the mercy of the incredible power that propelled it. The mass met in the middle of the room, like the water molecules charged inside the glass. The swirl of debris slammed together in the center. Individual chunks of metal, brick, and plastic collided, deflecting again and again until the inner wall gave way and the entire mass pressed outward to escape.

Chapter Eleven

Randy was glad to be rid of the flimsy hospital gown. He felt sturdier in jeans as if the denim could protect him in the heat of battle. When he pulled his shirt down over his head, he flinched at the tension in his arms. His clavicle had healed months ago from the crack of Pinto's nightstick. The bullet wound from Heather Lovely's gun hadn't hurt in weeks, but the phantom pains reminded him how close he'd come to death and how important it was to follow the path. The vision of the hazy cavern, the hideously long teeth, and the oozing lines of parallel whip marks on T.J. Lynch's soot-covered body would never fade. Salvation was paramount. Every time he faced a rudderless moment, vulnerability nagged him.

He laced up the Doc Martens Cassie chose for him and thought about how much things had changed since their first meeting at St. Luke's. She'd snuck into his room, planning to make a name for herself by exposing his innermost secrets. He'd turned things around, showing her the evil in a man other reporters praised. Somewhere on their journey she saw his humanity and they saved each other. His story launched her career and her articles convinced the governor he was worthy of leniency. Other reporters saw him differently, but the dissenting voices couldn't compete while the spotlight shined on Cassie. If those voices knew what Randy and Cassie were thinking they'd rise up again, this time screaming about ethics and bias.

He imagined driving to New Bedford and spending a few weeks in Cassie's apartment downtown. He needed time to figure out what to do next, but being near Cassie was risky. One article from Walter Macedo or a public scuffle with Tom Gold would put Randy back in prison to face murder charges he couldn't beat. Ten years chasing Charles Marston had stolen his chance for a normal family life. His future was one kids dreamed of after watching old westerns. He'd always be running from those murders and fighting to secure redemption in the next life. He was doomed to wander the country to escape notice. Ironic now that he'd welcome a regular job it was impossible for him to hold one.

He kneeled at the bedside, something he'd done more in the last six months than the last sixteen years. "Thank you for this day, dear Lord," he whispered aloud. An echo of sadness rippled in his thoughts, an echo he couldn't conceal from the Almighty. Being alive worried Randy. Being alive meant he hadn't accomplished what God required and so he risked eternal damnation with every misstep. In a few minutes he'd venture into the chaos of Boston and beyond. Once he did, he wouldn't be able to shake the feeling that he was on God's stage. "Help me to find your path, dear Lord, and help me to do your good work here on Earth."

An explosion rumbled in the distance. Randy's first thought was a terrorist attack at the Hancock tower, but the noise was too distant, like artillery fire across the river. He lost his train of thought. He knelt a few more seconds with his head bowed, but the urge to look outside was too great. He quickly whispered, "Amen," and rose to the window.

The crisp autumn sky revealed nothing of the devastation across the river. There were no planes overhead and no smoke to be seen, just rows of low-slung brick buildings with people and cars scurrying between them. Randy didn't rush outside toward the ominous rumble. Regardless of who might need his help, Randy had a sudden urge to play cards. Maybe it was leftover buzz from destroying Art. It felt blasphemous, but there was no denying a few hours at the table would take his mind off things and help him keep his distance from Walter Macedo and Officer Pinto. He could splash around with the governor's money and think about where to go next.

A tap on the door brought Art inside. When Randy told him he was leaving, Art produced a parking stub and told him where to find the McLaren. Randy thanked him and turned for the door.

"You can't leave those," Art said, pointing to the newspapers stacked on the chair. "You can't ever get those reprinted, hero."

The pile reminded Randy of the frantic days he'd spent with Cassie and the chaos they'd created in New Bedford politics. Randy didn't consider himself heroic. He'd been desperately trying to save himself. Earthly deeds were his path to a pristine white robe. True heroes were inspired by an innate desire to save others. Randy had been shoved.

Randy turned away, but Art grabbed him by the arm.

"I've been doing this a long time. I've pulled people out of car wrecks and I've taken drunks off the road, but I can't point to someone and say that I saved them. You saved forty people." Art grabbed a handful of papers from the stack. "It's not something to walk away from."

The headline of the uppermost edition proclaimed, "Disaster Averted."

Art poked a photo that showed a crowd of Muslim worshipers on Coggeshall Street surrounded by a swarm of journalists and cameramen. "These people think of you every morning when they wake up."

Art handed Randy the papers and shook his hand. He grinned when Randy left him with the poker chips and reminded him to read Caro so he had a chance against his friends. The nurses didn't pay any attention to Randy in his street clothes until he passed Sheri, who'd been his nurse for months. She winked as he passed her at the double doors.

He walked anonymously the rest of the way to the garage.

Randy tossed the papers on the passenger's seat and covered them with the briefcase. He wound his way down to street level and crawled along with traffic until he reached the expressway. At 10:11 A.M., he found three open southbound lanes. The northbound lanes were still packed with commuters as they had been for three hours. Randy had never had a job, but he hoped someday he'd find himself trudging along nose-to-tail with thousands of other drones on the way to the office. He was better suited to catching bail jumpers and collecting bounties, but that would put him in the sort of situation he was trying to avoid. He imagined himself drifting from place to place and doing chores for his dinner like the heroes of the old west, but they ended up in more than a few gunfights.

Randy merged onto Route 24 and sped down the open road. Fifty minutes later, he swung around and parked in front of the bank two blocks south of Cassie's apartment. Randy hurried through the glass doors and approached the information desk. His haste alarmed the guard, who stiffened and followed him and his heavy case across the lobby and around back to the safe deposit area. Randy wasn't sure why he was in a rush. He didn't have anywhere particular he needed to be, just an urge to get to Foxwoods and play some cards, but every moment since leaving the hospital he had a clear idea of his next task and an urgency to see it finished.

The briefcase wouldn't fit in his box, but it only took the manager a few minutes to reassign him to number eleven, a larger box close to the vault doors. He paid five years rental in advance and moved the contents from his old box to the new one. He stood and admired the deed to his Dartmouth house. He couldn't stay there, but it was a terrible time to sell. He wouldn't know for a long time whether it was financial savvy, gratitude or love that inspired him to remove the front door key from his ring and leave it inside the box. The manager helped him authorize Cassie to open the box even though he didn't know her exact address or social security number.

He could tell himself that she'd just be watching the house for him, but it was deeper than that. If he came home unexpectedly and found her with a man, he'd be crushed. That was exactly what he set himself up for, but he knew it was the right thing to do.

He hustled down the block and caught a neighbor who let him into Cassie's building. He picked the lock on her mailbox and left a note with a deposit box key taped to it.

Cassie would take care of his house. Even if he couldn't live there himself, he'd have a base to return to, if only sporadically.

CHAPTER TWELVE

Mary followed the blond bodyguard toward the mouth of the courtyard, but stopped to watch one of the other guards working methodically on her boss. He pulled off Dr.Kent's tie, tore open his shirt, and applied pressure just below his ribcage. The man who called himself the window to the Institute lay shattered on the turf. She hadn't noticed the blood when he fell, probably because she scampered away to escape the bullets, but now she saw the blood steadily staining his shirt and draining the color from his skin.

Mary turned toward an approaching engine that was too loud and too close to be a student using the parking lot. The chrome-plated grin of a Hummer bounced over the curb and tore up the grass as it wheeled down the walkway and skidded sideways to a stop at the building entrance forty yards away. An identical vehicle trailed behind, skidding to a parallel stop like the mate in a pair of hockey skates. Four men burst out the glass doors from the direction of Whitney's lab. The first stopped and unleashed a wild spray of bullets across the courtyard.

Mary stood tall, fully exposed, and as sure she'd die this day as she'd been grateful for being spared moments earlier. Bullets struck the turf at her feet. Some whizzed past and hit the brick wall behind her and others zipped over her fallen boss and the man working to save him. Still others missed the building altogether and streaked alongside, ready to strike down anyone unlucky enough to step through the doors at that moment.

Three men climbed into the Hummer from the protected side.

Another two repelled down the side of the building to the protection of the second vehicle.

A pistol boomed by Mary's head so loud she imagined the guard was sheltering behind her. She was too frightened to move, terrified that if she did, she'd walk into the line of fire. She imagined that she couldn't hear the report of the guns fired at her because her ears were too frightened to register the danger, but she knew on some level that the weapons were silenced.

A distinctive click. A soft drop on the grass, a metallic slide, another click, and then the shots continued.

Doors slammed. The vehicles turned and sped away in the direction they'd come. The shots stopped and slowly Mary's muscles thawed. She patted herself and learned she hadn't been hit. The ground rumbled as she finished checking herself for blood. The combination of sound, vibration, and terror sent her tumbling to the grass.

Window panes shattered. Dust billowed out and blanketed the courtyard like a foggy coastline. She couldn't imagine where the dust came from. The research area was immaculately kept, but soon she realized the dust was the pulverized remains of Professor Whitney's lab and the walls that once contained it. Someone desperately wanted to keep Whitney's discovery out of the press. This was much bigger than collegial competition. She was simultaneously curious about Whitney's announcement and glad she didn't know enough to become a target for the madmen with silent guns.

A timid campus policeman poked around the corner and took a few hesitant steps onto the grass, ready to dodge back behind the bricks at the first hint of trouble. He saw Mary kneeling in the open and stepped cautiously to her, embarrassed by his hesitancy.

Mary relaxed when the first police cruiser zipped to a stop. The officers rushed from the car, surveying the scene with their heads low and guns drawn. They were followed by a parade of fire trucks and three ambulances. Firemen rushed into the remains of Dr. Whitney's lab. Police officers kept the gathering crowd back. Mary was stranded inside the crime scene between the men working on her boss and the students straining for a look.

A policeman squared off with the blond bodyguard and Mary heard him say there were two men on the roof firing into the crowd. When the guard said he and his colleagues had returned fire the mood became serious. Careful notes were taken. The bodyguards' guns were unloaded and bagged as evidence. Mary wanted to say that these men had saved her and countless others, but she could only watch as the officers subtly herded the bodyguards away from the onlookers. While the police scrutinized their identification, one of the Suburbans backed up slowly, turned, and disappeared behind a fire engine.

Mary moved deeper into the courtyard for a better look at the shattered windows. Her steps attracted an officer who stopped her and asked where she'd been during the shooting. When she told him she'd been standing behind Dr. Whitney, he led her back to the podium and the nick where the first bullet deflected and struck her boss. They had already marked the spot with a plastic marker numbered "1." More than a dozen similar markers were attached to gouges in the bricks behind the podium.

"Not exactly a surgical strike," the officer joked.

Mary was too shaken to appreciate the joke and the officer looked apologetic for his insensitivity. He changed the subject by asking for any other details Mary could remember.

She described the breeze, Whitney's fumbling for the papers, and the wood flicking off the podium. She then described her panic to get away and how the bullets followed her as long as she stayed near Dr. Whitney.

The officer indicated Josh lying on the ground with his leg still up over the seat of his chair and asked how close Whitney had been to him. She showed him where they'd passed four feet behind. The bullet had struck Josh squarely in the forehead. The officer mused that Josh had been targeted and asked if Mary thought that made sense. Josh didn't deserve to die for becoming Whitney's apprentice. Clearly they'd been after Whitney. They fired at him. They destroyed his lab. Josh's death had to be an accident, a stray bullet meant for Whitney, but the officer was convinced he had been deliberately shot.

Mary turned to the five empty chairs and was suddenly glad she hadn't forced the students to attend. Their noncompliance saved them. Two of the students were in the lab. An hour later their remains would be pulled from the rubble. The remaining three, Gretchen, Demitri, and Ty, were alive.

"We've got to find the others," Mary said, now urgent.

"Who?"

"The other students. They were targeted. They were all targeted."

The officer didn't understand.

"The press conference. Dr. Whitney called the conference to announce a major discovery. Someone didn't want the news released. First Whitney, then the lab; they're destroying every shred of his work including the kids."

Mary wished Whitney had told her his news. It might have made her a target, but at least she'd understand what the gunmen were after.

The officer wondered aloud if they could have stolen Dr. Whitney's work before demolishing the lab.

Mary hadn't seen them carrying anything as they rushed from the building, but some of them had been blocked by the Hummers. She had no idea what she should have been looking for, but she knew Whitney, Gretchen, Demitri, and Ty were in grave danger.

Mary remembered the photo taken in the hall outside the lab. She pointed out one of the cameramen and the officer rushed to him and quickly came back with his camera. Most of the people in that photo were already dead. An artist arrived within thirty minutes to translate her description of Demitri into a sketch. They downloaded Whitney's image from the school's website and within an hour, the four faces flooded out to police departments and news stations all over Massachusetts.

CHAPTER THIRTEEN

"Where are you?" Whitney barked over the phone. He huffed as if their race were physical and not intellectual.

"I'm almost to my lab," Dr. David Lee replied as he stepped from his Spectra Blue Prius into the parking lot of the Westborough research facility.

"Turn around. Get out of there." Whitney sounded frightened, his voice fading in and out as if he were running to his own lab to try and keep up.

"I'm sorry, Whitney. You can't take back what you told me."

"It's not about that."

"Come on, Whitney. What do you take me for?"

"My lab exploded. Get out. I'm telling you. Turn around. Go somewhere safe."

Lee walked up to the outer doors, pressed his ID badge against the reader, and stepped inside. Cell reception weakened inside the reinforced walls and Whitney's voice came and went. No matter what he said, Lee wasn't turning around. He was on the cusp of a breakthrough and every hour in the lab counted. His wife had to beg him to sleep at home. He'd been in the lab ninety hours a week for a month, but most of his progress was thanks to Whitney. Lee had been stuck for a year and a half. He'd gone for drinks with Whitney and posed his problem. Whitney had a ready answer and that one formulation pushed Lee years ahead.

"Haven't you seen the news?" Whitney asked.

Lee hadn't. He'd been in his car for thirty minutes listening to Brad Paisley's, *Mud on the Tires* CD. The twangy songs connected Lee to the heartland America he sought years ago when his parents brought him here. Unfortunately they'd dumped him in Lawrence, Massachusetts. Growing up he'd always pictured himself a cowboy, catching strays and branding calves. His excellence in science had gotten him only to the suburbs, far from the Wyoming pastureland he dreamed of, but he did have enough land to raise a cow if he ever really wanted one.

"I haven't," Lee said, closing in on the lab entrance where he knew the call would be dropped. "We don't need to be enemies, Whitney. You can come work in my lab when I go into production. You'd do the same for me. It'll be like old times back at school."

Lee chuckled to himself as he opened the door.

He didn't wait for the call to disconnect before snapping his phone shut.

For the first few steps everything in the lab looked normal, but when he reached the bend where the computer equipment was racked, he saw one of his assistants sprawled on the floor with a halo of blood pooled around her head. He rushed toward her, which proved to be his last earthly mistake. Two other assistants lay still behind the workbench.

When Lee turned, he saw the gunmen who'd been hiding inside the door, waiting for his arrival. He hadn't practiced the quick draw. Even if he had, he was armed only with a pen and a telephone. Before he could move, the first three bullets hit in a flurry. His muscles seized as the slugs tumbled through him. He was alive when the fourth bullet whacked into his forehead, but he never felt the impact of the mushrooming forty-caliber slug.

Lee didn't see the men run. Didn't see the explosives mounted under the work surfaces and inside the computer racks. Didn't see the blast that scattered his work to oblivion. His competition with Dr. Whitney was over.

CHAPTER FOURTEEN

Gretchen skirted the crowd with the corners of Whitney's panel poking out the top of her backpack. She watched for signs of recognition, but all eyes were focused on Mary Stewart as she introduced Whitney. Gretchen followed around behind the arc of curious students toward the parking lot until Ty stepped out and blocked her way. His aggressive stance convinced her he'd seen the panel. She considered bolting around him, but his lips hinted at a smile and she couldn't outrun him with the heavy panel weighing her down. She hid the pack behind her legs and wondered why Ty wasn't on the platform, basking in this much-needed boost to his academic reputation.

He didn't suggest going up on stage. Instead he asked if she still needed a ride to New Jersey. The heavy bag strained her shoulders and students kept bumping into it as they jockeyed for a view of Whitney. She needed to get out of the crowd before the panel dropped out on the ground, but she couldn't hide the panel on the four-hour trip home. She was about to tell Ty she'd made other arrangements when the crowd around them gasped and dropped low, seemingly all at once. People scampered every which way and the two of them were left standing with a clear view to the podium. Whitney fumbled with something. Josh jolted upright and slumped over. Whitney dove to his left then got up and ran. Mary stood erect, looking stunned.

Before Gretchen could process the chaos unfolding around them, Ty had hold of her bicep and jerked her into the frenzied mob and through to shelter behind a few wide oaks that lined the parking lot.

Ty whipped open the passenger door of the nearest car, pressed her head down, and shoved her into the seat of his Malibu. He flashed around the other side. The tires spun backward, then forward, jolting the car from a stop to a swerving exit in less than three seconds. Cars and busses rushed by in a blur. She barely noticed that he reached fifty on Memorial Drive. That was Josh back there on the ground and the force that slammed his head back had to be a gunshot. Josh was dead and whoever shot him was gunning for Dr. Whitney. Did they blame him for tampering with the results? How could they know already? Gretchen imagined the Proctor men were angry when Whitney tried to back out of the press conference. Who else could know?

Ty turned off onto Massachusetts Avenue and then Landsdowne Street. Traffic slowed and they stopped and waited to make the corner onto Pacific Street. Ty didn't have the radio on. She hadn't thought about it, but the absence of hicks singing about their trucks, dogs, and lost girlfriends seemed strange. The car smelled new, the aroma of chemicals plied to color the interior and the seats several cows had given their lives to cover. The engine hummed, quietly polluting the air even though they were making no progress on their journey.

Gretchen was thinking how wasteful car travel was when the ground shook and a powerful rumble reverberated past. The tremor came from campus and she immediately knew it was the panel between her knees the bombers were after. Ty snapped a look at her, not a look of fear, but interrogation, as if he knew she triggered the terror unfolding at the Institute. But he couldn't.

Ty turned the corner and pulled to a stop in front of her apartment. He found it without prompting even though she'd never brought him there. A chill rippled through her. He followed her around campus, but did he also sit outside and watch her window?

Ty's phone rang and he answered briskly.

"Thanks for the ride," she said, intending to part ways.

He held up one rigid finger. "I've got it with me," he said into the phone. Then a pause. "I'm in my car. No, I'm fine." Another pause. "Yes, sir. Will do."

Sir? Gretchen looked back from the first step and wondered who Ty would call sir. No one from campus would call now. "Thanks for the ride," she said, backing up one more step. "I can make the train from here."

"I can't leave you alone after what happened."

As he pocketed his phone and rushed to catch up, she noticed he'd lost the Texas drawl and the wobble in his walk somewhere between the tour and the gunshots in the courtyard. She assumed it was adrenalin, but she couldn't help thinking she was holding the door to let a stalker into her lobby. She hustled up the stairs.

"Something wrong with the elevator?" he called from below.

"Yeah. It's a massive waste of energy."

She pushed herself to jog up all four floors. He lagged an entire flight by the time she reached her apartment. She left the door open and rushed for her canvas duffle, glad to have a moment to shift the panel without being seen. She laid the heavy plate on the bottom and packed clothes all around it. At first, running home had been a cover. After seeing Josh get shot and hearing the bomb go off, she wanted to get as far away from Whitney and the Proctor Energy henchmen as she could. She was warming to the idea of going with Ty regardless of the waste. As long as he didn't know about the panel, it would be the fastest and safest way out of Boston.

Ty shut the door hard as he came in, then walked across the kitchen to the balcony slider, pulled it open, and stepped out. While he was checking out the view, she was packing clothes to make sure the panel would stay hidden deep in the bag.

"How long you been keeping bees?"

She didn't bring many visitors back to the tiny room, but none of Sonia's friends recognized the wooden frame for what it was. When she told them she collected her own honey, many of them doubted bees could survive here in the city. She had more in common with Ty and his down-home upbringing than most people, even if he embraced the fossil fuel economy and funding from those Proctor plunderers.

Ty stepped back inside with an expectant look and she realized she'd been too busy hiding the panel to answer him.

"Since I was ten," she said.

She tried not to strain as she lugged the bag into the kitchen. He watched her every move as he had since he worked his way onto the research team two months earlier. She couldn't be sure, but he seemed more interested in her than Whitney's research. It wasn't about sex. If it was, he'd have chosen a girl who spent more time on clothes and makeup. Ty was keenly interested, but what was behind that Texas hospitality?

Gretchen packed the remaining muffins into a paper bag and filled a large plastic bottle with filtered tap water. The oversized thermos was one of the few legitimate uses of plastic because it would outlive any container made of natural materials. She'd already had it ten years and expected to use it for twenty more.

"Hungry?" she asked when she saw Ty drooling over the muffins.

She tossed him one. He spun it around twice, looking to peel off the paper cup before realizing there wasn't one. When he bit into the muffin he made a pained face. He chewed and swallowed. He didn't enjoy it, but he didn't spit it out like Sonia and her friends had.

"What's in this?"

"Acorn flour."

"Bitter enough?"

"You get used to it."

Before they left, Gretchen detoured back for a bar of homemade soap in case they had to stop overnight. Ty finished his muffin and washed it down with several big gulps of water he took by bending over and catching the stream from the tap with his lips. He insisted on lugging the bag downstairs and he didn't complain about the muffin, the stairs, or the weight the quarter-inch steel panel added to her bag. She wanted to protest when he hefted it into the trunk, but there was no logical explanation for wanting to keep the bag up front. She let him pack it away and then she let him open the car door and close it behind her.

Gretchen set the bag of muffins and the water bottle on the floor between her feet. Ty shook his head in that direction as he started the car.

He wouldn't ask for another muffin for a long time, but if he knew where they were headed, he would have carried them himself.

The Malibu swung onto Memorial Drive, rolled along for half a block, then traffic came to a dead stop. Ty kept checking the mirrors and swiveling his head from side to side even though both westbound lanes were stalled. He had an intensity about him that Gretchen had never noticed. He'd been shadowing her all morning. He'd done it before and she'd assumed it was misplaced romantic interest, like he was working from the bottom of the dating food chain up to avoid competition. Why didn't he understand she couldn't be with someone like him? Earlier it felt awkwardly inappropriate, but now he was more interested in what was going on outside the car. Did he think he had her now and didn't have to work for her attention?

"What's up with you?" Gretchen asked. "Relax."

Ty's swiveling stopped. He focused straight ahead as if he'd been caught doing something he shouldn't. "Terrorism doesn't make you nervous?" he asked without looking.

"What would terrorists want with the Institute? It's thieving capitalists that stopped Whitney's press conference."

"What thieving capitalists?"

"Proctor Energy."

"That's ridiculous." He turned and looked at her like a child, a look she'd given him plenty of times when they were working. "As long as I'm helping you," he said, as condescension turned to cold determination in his glare, "I need you to level with me."

"Ok." She drew it out, holding the "A" while she considered her myriad deceptions that morning.

"You told me the experiment failed. Then you told Demitri you hadn't been in the lab. Which is it?" Every word was bitingly clear.

He didn't know what she'd done. He couldn't. If he did, he would have called someone at the Institute by now. Trapped in the car together, there was no way to get away from him. She couldn't explain and, no matter what, she couldn't risk him taking her back to campus.

"I went to the lab." That much he knew because he'd caught her leaving. "I knew if I told Demitri about the experiment, he'd want me to go back and work with him, but I have to get home."

Ty nodded and turned back to the road.

He knew she had more to tell, but he didn't press. He let the lie sit on the leather between them. She needed him to take her away from campus and he wanted her beside him. All the warnings about getting in a car with strange men came flooding back. She knew almost nothing of Ty and it was clear he'd been planning this moment a long time. The car was barely moving, but Gretchen couldn't jump out and leave the panel. She focused on his every movement as he kept watch on the danger outside.

Twenty minutes later, they exited onto the Boston University Bridge and found the source of the problem. Flashing blue lights blocked the outer lanes and police officers stood in the roadway and inspected each car as it passed. Gretchen ducked her head. Ty snickered, then rolled down the window and smiled at the Boston cop who let them through with a wave. They zipped across the bridge and on to the turnpike heading west, away from the chaos surrounding the Institute.

CHAPTER FIFTEEN

Walter stormed into Bart's office and slammed the door. Bart checked the square cuff on each forearm where he'd rolled up his trademark white shirt precisely three turns, but that was the only sign he'd noticed the disturbance. Walter steamed from behind the twin guest chairs and waited for Bart to look up from the piece he was reading. Walter knew better than to interrupt. Bart reigned in the newsroom, but if he thought Walter was going to slink away now that Cassie was syndicated, he was dead wrong.

The instant Bart lifted his eyes, Walter snidely asked, "Where's *she* going?"

"Who, she? Lots of women work here, Walter."

They both knew who Walter meant, but Bart was toying with him, mocking his complaints to make him sound childish. Why wouldn't he listen? And why did he insist on catering to Cassie Corcoran when she was running around with a murderer? Didn't he care about justice?

"We both know who I mean. She's not going to Boston?"

"I still assign the stories around here, Walter."

"Since when do we cover Boston? And what about seniority? If anyone should be going up there for a story this big, it's me. You're not sending her because her derelict boyfriend is at Mass General?"

"Cassie is a fine journalist. If you don't trust my opinion, take it up with one of the fourteen other papers who carry her stories."

"She wrote one good story. One!"

"She wrote dozens of articles, Walter, and I seem to recall you reported on that same story." Bart luxuriated over his words. "Something about a rampaging menace. No redeeming value to society, I think you said. You lost a lot of credibility when that rampaging menace got himself shot saving forty people."

"I wasn't the only one—"

"Exactly," Bart stormed. "You rehashed the same tired history everyone else reported. Cassie saw what you didn't. She showed the entire country that sometimes there's a lot more behind a story than we realize. Sometimes we get it wrong. Sometimes people surprise us."

"She's dating the guy!"

"Her personal life is her business. Regardless of what she does with her time off, her stories put us on the map. I don't care how she gets her stories. What I do care about is readers. Cassie's got them."

Walter nearly choked. "How do you expect me to get read? I've got seniority and you send her to cover the biggest story in years. How can I compete with that?"

Bart pulled his glasses down to the end of his nose and looked over them. Walter expected him to launch into one of his rants about life not being fair, hard work winning the day, or this not being a democracy. Walter couldn't understand why he always sided with Cassie. There was nothing going on between them. He was way too old for that. Walter refused to believe it was her writing. It had to be a father–daughter thing.

"I'm not putting you on this story," Bart said. "If you need to take some time off, that's your business."

About the time Walter left Bart's office, Cassie stepped through the glass doors into the lobby of her apartment building and turned right toward her mailbox. The trip to Boston was the first of its kind for a crime writer from the *Standard Times*. Like most local papers, they took their regional and national news from the Associated Press and ran it as is. As she made mental preparations for her trip, she worried that her new readers would be disappointed with the story she delivered. This new piece wouldn't compare to her Randy Black story. That had taken nearly a month to research, and Bart had only approved three days for her to scour the streets of Boston. Sure, her Randy Black investigation spawned dozens of stories and won her national syndication, but then she had a connection with the man at the center of the story. Bart had assured her his deadline wasn't pessimism. He was just being realistic about the situation.

She turned the key and reached into her box, thinking more about what she'd find in Cambridge than the day's mail. The police were working hard to catch the bomber. If they had him locked up, there would be a long line to interview him. If they hadn't found him, she couldn't imagine finding him herself and interviewing him in three days.

The folded sheet of paper was a surprise. There was no slot for mail to be inserted by a friend or neighbor. Only the postman could open the box, but there was Randy's handwritten note on top of her electric bill. She'd been in his hospital room that morning. How had he gotten released and visited her mailbox before she did? And why didn't he tell her he was coming home? She'd have been angrier if she wasn't so intrigued by his message. She detached the key from the page, feeling the adhesive residue in her fingers as she reread the note.

She dialed the new cell phone number he left.

"Hey. Got my note I take it," Randy said.

"Yeah. When did you have time to change your number?"

"You never know who's listening. You remember what they found in my sneaker. Those friends of mine aren't any happier."

"Speaking of criminals, did you know tampering with a mailbox is a felony?"

"I don't spend time reading Massachusetts law. It's kinda dry."

"It's federal, actually, big boy prison."

"I take it you haven't opened the safe deposit box yet."

"I can't just walk in there and open your safe deposit box."

"Sure you can. The paperwork is all done. All you have to do is sign. You'll find your new house key in the box."

"My what?"

"It's not *your* house really and it's not exactly new. It's a few years old. Technically it's still mine, but I'm hoping you'll stay there for a while and keep your eye on things."

"What about my apartment?"

"The house is six thousand square feet. Anything you're keeping in that apartment will fit just fine. Feel free to move stuff around."

Walter would see this as the payoff for repairing Randy's reputation. Walter's credibility was minimal, but if he started yelling about *quid pro quo* journalism someone would eventually listen. She couldn't claim to be objective about Randy when she was living in his house. If this was an invitation to romance, it was the strangest approach she'd ever heard. Still, she'd seen the house and the offer was appealing. It was in a great neighborhood and she could walk to the beach.

Randy had been silently waiting for her to consider as if he knew she was weighing the ethical implications.

"The house key is in the box. There's a garage door opener in the kitchen and there's a power of attorney in the bank box all notarized and signed. All you need to do is sign to make it official. There are checks in the box so you can pay the gas, electric, taxes, whatever comes up."

"What are you, hiring me? Why can't you do all that stuff?"

"I'm not going to be around."

"Why not?" she snapped. Her face flushed and she didn't want to consider the reasons.

"Someone from the governor's office came to see me. Some young kid. He suggested I disappear for a while."

"So there's no pardon?"

"Not yet."

"Coward." People like Walter would run the governor out of office if he pardoned an accused killer. Nothing Randy did after killing Charles Marston mattered to Walter and his ilk. They wouldn't forgive him no matter how many people he saved.

"Listen, it's going to be chaos up there in Superior Court. The governor wants to let the new guys settle in and clean up Heather's mess. They'll forget about me as long as I stay out of the public eye. That means staying away from Walter and my dear friend Officer Pinto. Best way to do that is to stay outside their jurisdiction."

"How long?" She was embarrassed by her needy tone, but she could hear the longing in his response.

"I won't be far. I'll be back once in a while, but I can't risk walking around the city every day. I can't explain away another explosion. Everyone down there thinks I'm a pyro."

"And you're not?"

He laughed, but she could tell he was serious. Tom Gold wanted to silence Randy forever. And there were others. Even winning a confrontation with them would send Randy back to prison.

"So where are you now?" she asked.

He told her he was having a late breakfast and heading down to Foxwoods. From there he'd find a place to lay low for a while and figure out what to do next. He might even get a job.

Cassie told him about the explosions in Boston and her assignment to cover them from Cambridge. She couldn't believe he hadn't heard about them yet. They'd been on the television news all morning. She couldn't promise to move into his house without thinking about it, so they agreed to share dinner over the phone and talk it out then.

Cassie packed a bag for a few days and rushed downstairs to get to Cambridge while the on-scene investigation was still in progress.

CHAPTER SIXTEEN

Cassie turned off Memorial Drive. She knew she was in the right place when she saw crime scene tape stretched across the lawn, but she felt like a cousin invited at the last minute to a "friend" birthday party, arriving late to find the cake eaten and the presents opened. There were a few people watching from outside the tape, but most journalists had gotten the facts and headed off to write their stories. A reporter sat in the front seat of a television news van. Cassie assumed she was keeping her hair out of the wind until it was time to shoot a noon feed.

Cassie followed the tape, stepping around the few onlookers still watching the technicians work methodically back and forth. The sheer number of markers on the grass was startling. The news reports had shown two victims being removed from the area where the markers for spent casings lay. With that many bullets flying, it was a wonder there weren't a dozen victims. She made a note to get an official count of the shots fired. The damage from the explosions didn't make a spectacular photograph. The lab must have been in an interior room. The outer walls contained the damage, but she snapped several pictures of broken windows anyway. She wondered if she could get inside for a photo, but the entrances were all sealed inside the ring of tape. She'd have to get an escort to get in and unfortunately she didn't know a single Cambridge officer.

Three investigators huddled on the grass. One pointed toward the roof and Cassie noticed several holes in an air-handling vent. She zoomed in and snapped a few photos. The ducts overlooked the press conference and the ruts in the grass where the getaway cars tore up the lawn. The rooftop attack was coordinated to strike victims in the crowd and provide cover for the bombers to exit the building. It seemed the shell casings on the ground were fired upward at the attackers as if the victims had retaliated.

Who was shooting at the perps? The police hadn't arrived until after the bomb went off. The men on the roof were gone by then. Someone in the crowd had fired back before the explosion, but who? Students? Professors? Journalists? Not likely. This was a good angle. Too bad the shooters were gone.

Cassie left the courtyard and followed Massachusetts Avenue north to the wide pillars of the information center. When she approached the counter, she hesitated to speak. The whole area had the suffocating air of a funeral home. Two women huddled in a corner whispering to each other with tissues clutched like prizes in their fingers. Neither woman responded to her presence.

Cassie cleared her throat and slowly one of the women rose to meet her, first extending her arm to her friend, not wanting her duty to interrupt their time of consolation. The deep lines around the woman's eyes were swollen and red. She lifted her glasses and dabbed away tears as she reached the counter.

Cassie barely needed to introduce herself before the woman launched into the remarks she'd given dozens of journalists already. She spoke rapidly and stoically as if repetition had drained the emotion from the words. Dr. William Kent, their boss, had been shot at a campus press conference that morning. He was at Boston City Hospital in critical condition. Three students assigned to Dr. Whitney were killed in the attack. She wouldn't name them, but she went on to describe the press conference and the bombing of the lab. Hearing this reminded Cassie that her writing had to be superb to be recognized. There were dozens of reporters on scene when the shots rang out. They *were* the story in a sense and that put Cassie at a huge disadvantage.

All the information this woman was giving her was available through other reports, but Cassie couldn't write her story by borrowing from other outlets. The woman behind the counter knew this and generously answered a few questions in spite of her grief.

When Cassie returned to the courtyard, she had the basic facts for her story, but no angle. The attack was far beyond any school prank, but terrorists, or even crazed, homicidal students would have inflicted more casualties. The shooters passed over rows of reporters and shot a single student. They targeted his professor but missed. If Cassie could find the professor she'd have a story, but every reporter in the city was looking for him. Campus information gave her only his name. She walked back for one more spin around the crime scene before finding a quiet place to connect to the Internet and hunt for him.

A big guy in a two-toned state police uniform broke away from a gathering of officers just outside the overturned chairs on the lawn. He headed for the crime scene tape as if to leave. Cassie was lost, wondering about the professor and his work, and wouldn't have recognized Art Wallace, the man who'd let her into Randy's room at least a dozen times, if he hadn't stopped directly in front of her.

"Hi, Art. What are you doing here?"

"This is a little out of your territory, too, isn't it?"

Cassie shrugged.

"I know, you're big time now." He hesitated then whispered, "Hungry?"

Cassie nodded and he suggested they meet around the corner in five or ten minutes. He didn't want to appear too chummy with a reporter. Later she'd learn that Art had no assignment when Randy left the hospital. When the call went out for the bombing, Art left his post and rushed over. He had no authority, but he'd been helping out for two hours and he knew far more than Cassie would learn from outside the tape. She pretended to study the crime scene as his car disappeared around the corner.

Cassie paced the length of the courtyard, watching the investigators work and wondering what Art would tell her. She scribbled notes and waited as long as her patience would bear, then drove the Corolla in the opposite direction Art had gone. She ended up parking farther away from the diner than if she'd walked, but Art's cover was intact when she spotted his tall hat in the corner and joined him in the booth.

Art's coffee was half empty.

"Thanks for meeting me," Cassie said as she sat down.

"Don't thank me yet. I haven't told you anything."

"But you're going to?"

His eyes locked on her. "This is completely off the record."

"Deal." She wanted to reach over and shake hands to show how serious she was, but Art didn't move. She wondered why he was helping her and how much he was likely to share. They barely knew each other from her visits to Randy's room. Art was married, happily he'd said. She decided he was helping a friend and to take whatever he offered.

"I'm stuck for a motive," she said.

"Aren't we all? The press conference is the key. Problem is, the professor didn't have time to say anything."

"You think that was by design?" Cassie wondered aloud.

"Looks that way. They tried to kill him. They destroyed his lab and they burned what little he had in his office. There was a huge bin of papers he sent to be recycled this morning. They've got other researchers combing through to see if any of it is worth killing over."

Something was bugging Art. He grimaced when he spoke, as if he was angry at himself for understanding the true nature of the attack.

"What do you think is going on here?" Cassie prodded.

"This thing smacks of someone faking his own death. The guy has a big announcement to make, but he's interrupted at the last second. His lab and all his work is destroyed. His notes are burned. And now we can't find him. There's no way to prove what he did or didn't do in that lab."

"What's he running from? Is there really that much pressure on these college researchers?"

Art didn't share his suspicions. Instead he gave her the picture the local cops had been circulating and identified the two students who were killed in the explosion and the one on the lawn. He identified Professor Whitney and Demitri Mangas, the two heads added at the margins. The police were also looking for Gretchen Greene and Ty Summers, who stood one behind the other in the group photo. Any one of the survivors could explain what was happening. Art didn't name the students who were killed and Cassie knew better than to ask.

Cassie didn't say so, but she'd start her search with the professor. "So, you have a problem with Whitney getting off the hook?"

"Something like that. Soon as we find the professor, we'll know what's going on. Until then it I'm not ruling anything out."

"But it's not terrorism." Cassie was sure it wasn't.

"Not enough casualties. There were dozens of people in that crowd. A few bursts from an automatic would have mowed down fifteen people at least. Everyone who got hit was associated with Professor Whitney. Three of his students were killed. The only casualty not on Whitney's team was the unfortunate William Kent, head of the campus information center. He chose the wrong place to stand—directly behind Whitney."

"It bugs you that Whitney got out, doesn't it?"

Art bristled at this. "He ran the length of the courtyard against a brick wall," Art said. "They've identified dozens of impacts against that wall, but not a single drop of blood in the hallway where he ran. They missed him completely."

"Some pretty poor shooting."

"Too poor."

CHAPTER SEVENTEEN

The shots chased Dr. Patrick Whitney out of the courtyard and into the building. The bullets stopped once he was inside, but he ran straight through and exited the doors at the far end of the hall. He kept running down the sidewalk, away from his speedy Z4, but each stride took him farther from the men who'd been shooting from the roof. He was two blocks away when the lab exploded and that's when he knew he couldn't reproduce his results. Half a block further his lungs were burning, his legs aching, when a cab swung around onto Massachusetts Avenue. He darted in front of it and doubled over. The cabbie slammed the brakes and the cab squealed to a stop. Whitney rushed to the back on wobbly legs and jumped in.

"What the hell you doin' man?"

"Just drive."

"You trying to get killed?"

"Hear that explosion? That was for me. If you don't get moving we're both going to be dead."

The cabbie whipped around and eyed Whitney. He saw the dread in Whitney's face and snarled, "Get out."

"I'm not going anywhere," Whitney panted. "You want to live? Drive!"

The cabbie eyed the sidewalks and the surrounding buildings. He didn't see a threat. He wanted Whitney out, but he could move the cab faster than he could drag Whitney out of the back seat. He hit the gas and asked, "Where to?" as he maneuvered down Massachusetts Avenue.

"Get over the river. Fast as you can."

Whitney whipped out his cell and called his friend David Lee. David gloated about how close he was to a breakthrough. He wouldn't listen to Whitney's warnings. He thought it was a joke or Whitney trying to slow him down. Nothing Whitney said could keep Lee from his lab. Whitney hoped he wasn't marching to his final moments, but when the call dropped, Whitney knew Lee wouldn't live to enjoy his daily burger and fries.

The cabbie relaxed once they were over the bridge and across Storrow Drive. He kept on through tight neighborhood streets for a few blocks, but then he slowed as if he felt safe hidden among the brownstones. Whitney wondered how many times he'd gotten requests like this.

Whitney folded his phone as the cab stopped for a light.

The cabbie pointed to a spot along the curb. "How's this?"

Whitney couldn't go home. Anyone could find him there.

He couldn't go back to school or to Newport.

He wished for a place without guns and it hit him. He barked the destination to the cabbie and they were off.

Fifteen minutes and five miles later, they emerged from the tunnel. He picked Southwest Airlines, hoping they'd have the most people bustling through the terminal so he could blend in. He hadn't noticed the SUV that followed them through the tunnel to the terminal. Whitney paid the cabbie sixty dollars and hopped out at the departures area empty handed. He focused straight ahead, rushed inside, and passed over the Southwest counter for a smaller carrier without a single passenger in line. When he stepped up to the counter he realized he hadn't checked flight information. He didn't know anything about this airline, including where it might fly. He wasn't planning to board a plane, he just wanted to get into the secure area where no one could gun him down. Then he could think.

The young woman noticed his lack of bags and eyed him skeptically. "Can I help you, sir?"

"I'd like a seat on your next flight to LaGuardia."

The woman clicked some keys and frowned.

"I'm sorry, sir. All flights are booked until seven P.M."

"That's fine."

The woman asked if he wanted a round-trip and grimaced when he asked for a one-way. She expected a complaint. He'd agreed to wait eight hours much too readily and he didn't have a single bag. If he tried to pay cash she would keep him there and press a button to call for help. But he hadn't done anything wrong. Nothing they'd uncover. Let her call. Whitney paid with his credit card and turned from the ticket agent as soon as he had his boarding pass. He imagined she was reporting him as he hurried for the security check-in.

Eight metal detectors combed the passengers for anything deadly they might try to smuggle onto their flight. Whitney was herded together with hundreds of other passengers and for forty minutes he inched toward the row of detectors and minimally-trained men and woman running the checkpoints. The uniforms made him feel safe. Anyone carrying a gun into this line was assured a quick trip to prison.

When he finally reached the head of his line, Whitney emptied his pockets of change and keys, took off his shoes, and sent them through the scanner. The TSA officer waved and he stepped through the portal into the secure area. He breathed deeply the air of safety as he laced up his shoes and dumped the change back into his front pocket. Two hundred fifty dollars had purchased him as much time as he needed to think about what he'd done and where he could go to be safe.

Fifty yards down the carpeted hall Whitney spotted the ideal spot to kill some time. He pulled open the wooden door and stepped inside the darkened lounge. CNN played on the television by the bar. He hoped a baseball game would come on soon. He couldn't sit there for hours and hear the same stories repeated every thirty minutes. He noticed a heaping plate of onion rings as he walked toward the back corner and picked a booth. The only people behind him were a couple dabbing fries in ketchup and feeding each other across the table. They barely noticed Whitney sliding into the booth.

A Middle Eastern man entered the bar less than a minute after Whitney. He had no bags, but took no interest in Whitney as he followed the bar to the restroom in back.

74

A stumpy waitress stopped to take Whitney's order and as she did, the smoldering lab appeared on the television behind her. He ordered a beer as his face filled the screen. The two-year-old shot from the Institute's website was recent enough for anyone to identify him. Fortunately no one in the bar was paying attention. Gretchen, Ty, and Demitri flashed onscreen next. When Malcolm and Kylie failed to appear he hoped they'd been found and questioned and not trapped in the lab as he feared. He'd seen Josh shot squarely in the forehead and knew that was no accident. The Nanopanel would cost them trillions and they'd spend that much to suppress it. Their reach was unfathomable. The students were beyond his help.

"Can I get you something to eat?" the waitress hissed.

He ordered quesadillas. He'd pace himself until he decided what to do. Turning himself in to the police would only make him easier to find. Blending in with the masses seemed like the best idea, though if he were running, this is the place they would look for him.

The Middle Eastern guy returned from the restroom and took a seat facing the television with his back to Whitney. He spoke loudly enough to be heard ordering a thick American steak and a beer. Whitney got his food first. He took a few bites and a big slug of beer before he heard the guy at the bar complaining that he couldn't cut his steak with the knife they'd given him. The waitress slipped him a steak knife.

Whitney knew he was in trouble when he saw the man's firm grip on the wooden handle.

CHAPTER EIGHTEEN

When Cassie finished the last bite of her salad, she couldn't ignore the wafting aroma of pepperoni anymore. She picked the thinnest slice, broke it free, and savored a large bite of spicy sauce and warm cheese.

"Now you're talking. All that bunny food wouldn't satisfy a hamster."

Pizza and chocolate were her weaknesses. She'd walk an extra half mile tonight to make up for this slice, but keeping Art here for pizza had been a bonanza. He told her about the tap on the professor's phone and that the press conference was hastily pulled together that morning. She made a note to find the woman from the Information Center who'd been caught in the gun battle. Art also told her that the professor had been in the office more in the last few days than the previous month. He'd made a dozen calls to Proctor Energy and to a Dr. David Lee in Westborough. His office line hadn't seen that much action in a long time.

The situation was still evolving and Cassie was right in the middle of it, thanks to Art. Another day of research and she might have a great piece. It was time to pay for the pizza and get back to campus, but she could tell something about the attack wasn't sitting right with Art.

"What's bothering you?"

"I keep coming back to this press conference. Why the urgency? The thing is pulled together last minute and then it's scuttled by gunshots. If you weren't invited, how could you know it was going to happen?"

"You think it was someone on the team?" she asked.

"A student? No. But someone didn't want him talking to the press today. If they weren't invited, how could they react so fast?"

"It's not another professor. It's way too extreme," Cassie said. But compared to Heather Lovely, the attack was businesslike. "And it's not his sponsor. They wouldn't—"

Art's grimace stopped her mid sentence.

"If it was bad news..." she offered and studied his response.

He wanted to say something. She couldn't get what he was hinting at, so she tried again. "You think they were trying to stop it? Proctor? They were right there on the ground, weren't they?"

Art didn't answer.

"What?" Cassie asked.

"Proctor's men fired eighty-one times and didn't hit anything."

All those shots had to hit something. Cassie imagined where those bullets landed further out into the city.

"Some of that is training," Art said. "They need to get their boss to safety, so they throw lead down range and keep the bad guys' heads down. But their boss was only fifteen feet from cover."

"Then what happened?"

"Hard to say. But there was no blood on the roof or by the Hummer where the bombers jumped in. None of the Proctor shooters were hit either."

"Someone should have hit something."

"With eighty-one bullets? Hell yeah."

The attackers hadn't done much damage either. They hit one student and accidentally shot William Kent. If their goal was terror, why didn't they fire into the crowd? From an elevated position it would have been impossible to miss that many panicked people scurrying away.

"Anything else I should know?"

"Check into the good professor's lifestyle."

"Financial?"

"Financial, personal, all of it. From what I hear he was living well beyond his means, dating a bunch of college girls, and drinking like a fish.

A few professors noticed he's cleaned up his act lately. He's been working hard. He's been sober. The perfect scholar."

"You think he knew this was coming?"

"He knew something was up."

The police had his phone records from campus. If Art knew who the professor was afraid of, he didn't share. Even so, Cassie was glad she'd made friends with Art while Randy was unconscious. She thought about how well things worked out and left Art to finish the last slice of pizza while she went to the register and paid the bill.

On the sidewalk, Art suggested she talk to Sergeant Douglas, the communications officer for this investigation. He'd already briefed dozens of reporters and he had a thing for blondes. Art hinted that if she were friendly, she'd get everything the other reporters learned and then some.

Cassie walked back to campus to burn some of those pizza calories and to give Art a chance to get back to the crime scene on his own. She wondered what Randy would have thought if he saw her unclip her hair and let it fall to her shoulders. The sight of it might get more information from Sergeant Douglas. Randy would be jealous. He'd make a joke, but he'd be jealous.

Art drove away in the opposite direction. In a twinge of fright, she imagined Art was playing a joke, that she'd return to find everyone gone, but they'd be investigating for hours. Even after that, there would be someone watching over the courtyard to make sure no one contaminated the evidence. She turned the corner and found the cruisers right where they had been, but the camera trucks were gone. She was the only one chasing the story from this far behind.

Cassie stopped at the tape and called for Sergeant Douglas.

A solid guy craned his neck and turned back, not recognizing Cassie at the tape. But an instant later he was completely turned, excusing himself from a group of uniformed men, and walking in Cassie's direction. She fingered a handful of blonde strands and laid them over her shoulder to hold his attention. When he reached her, she introduced herself as a reporter and he stiffened. Was he expecting a cop groupie or something? Who else would ask for him on a crime scene?

Douglas gave her half the facts Art detailed in the diner without a trace of his insight. He refused to say anything about the professor's whereabouts or even how many officers were out searching for him. When he refused to talk about the guest list for the press conference, Cassie decided she'd be better off randomly dialing into the Institute's energy department. She wasn't frustrated with Art for sending her back. He may have been covering his tracks. No harm in that.

"What happened to the security guards who fired from the courtyard?"

A younger officer trotted over. Distracted, Douglas didn't answer.

"Are they being held?"

The younger officer whispered something about Whitney's credit card. Cassie asked another question to keep Douglas close enough so she could overhear. "Are you going to charge the bodyguards with discharging a firearm within city limits?"

Douglas turned his back and she heard one of them say they needed to close something down. Whatever it was, it was big. They went back and forth and Douglas agreed to call the captain. The younger man stepped back and said, "Do you know how many people fly out of there?"

"We'll see," Douglas said. He turned back to Cassie and apologized. Something had come up and he needed to make an urgent call.

"Logan?" she asked.

Douglas didn't flinch, but she knew Whitney had been to Logan. Maybe he was running. Maybe Art was right, he was trying to fake his death and disappear. Cassie turned for her car. As she did, she ran straight into a uniformed man who'd been waiting to talk to Douglas.

CHAPTER NINETEEN

Pinto sat in the garage tapping the steering wheel and staring blankly at the concrete wall. He dreaded going upstairs to meet the criminal, hat in hand. His wife had been hounding him to come here for weeks. It was the right thing to do. This conversation could save his job, but Pinto wasn't much for apologies. Just thinking about what the hoodlum had gotten away with made Pinto angry. How could he stand at Randy Black's bedside and say what they expected him to say?

Pinto hadn't made a mistake.

Looking at it from the outside, most people would say Pinto was wrong. It was against policy for sure, but the man he'd found duct taped to the banister was the most dangerous he'd ever met. Smooth and calm, he'd relaxed Pinto into slicing away the tape. Pinto never saw a threatening move. He only felt a rush of air before his windpipe slammed closed and he blacked out. Someone that dangerous needed be dealt with severely and that's what Pinto and his team did. No charges were ever filed, but anytime Randy Black decided to talk, the hospital records would speak clearly. His brother officers couldn't defend him then.

Twelve years on the force taught Pinto that men like Randy Black didn't change. It pained him to think the punk could steal his livelihood on a whim. That was before he became a damn celebrity. Randy might have saved those people from the mosque, but if he did, he had an angle. Pinto had worked with good men who Randy sent to jail. The chief called it fabulous police work, better than anything his own men had ever done. The more the chief praised Randy Black, the more the cops wanted to haul him in. If Randy Black crossed the line, Pinto would be there to close the cuffs.

Pinto remembered how long it had been before he could talk without pain. He opened the door and headed upstairs to tell the thug he was sorry for hitting him with his nightstick, but anyone who took his gun and cuffed him with his own cuffs deserved exactly what Randy got. Pinto would do it again. He left his nightstick in the car so he wouldn't be tempted.

Off the elevator, everyone was walking somewhere. He crossed the lobby to the information desk and was directed down a long hall to another bank of elevators. Pinto had to ask directions two more times before finding the ward on the seventh floor.

An empty chair sat outside Randy's doorway. Pinto stepped up to the threshold in his crisp uniform, ready to put Randy's babysitter at ease about the intrusion. There was no trooper to protest when he stepped inside. All he found was an empty room and an unmade bed.

Back at the nurses' station, Pinto cornered a young nurse who checked the computer half hidden on the arced desktop. She told him Randy Black was still assigned to the room. He could have gone somewhere for treatment, though the nurse couldn't say if anything was ordered.

Pinto took the chair from outside the door and shifted it around to the inside. He sat in the dark not wanting to warn Randy that he had a visitor until it was too late for him to run. For the first five minutes Pinto rehearsed what he'd say when Randy walked into the room. After fifteen minutes, he started thinking about the way the nurse had looked at him. The wrinkle in her lips could have been a lie, but why would she help a thug from Dartmouth? Pinto imagined Randy had jumped the trooper and ran, just like he'd done to him in Westport. He couldn't call the state police and ask who was assigned. They wouldn't tell him anything.

When he gave up waiting he scowled at the nurse on his way out. Halfway back to his car he decided to take a chance. He'd driven all the way up here to talk to Randy Black. There was a bombing over in Cambridge that morning. There would be dozens of officers over there. Maybe if he got lucky, he could find one who knew something about Randy Black and where he might have gone. If not, at least he could take a look around the scene.

When he parked sixty yards from the crime scene, he thought he noticed a familiar figure. There were too many people in the city to believe it was her, but when she turned around and came rushing down the walkway, Cassie Corcoran almost ran him over.

"What are you doing here?" Pinto asked.

"Working. You're a long way from your jurisdiction, Officer."

She brushed past and hurried down the walk. Pinto saw a similar scramble from an officer behind the crime scene tape. Corcoran knew something. Where Pinto found her, he'd find Randy Black.

The damage to the building was nothing like the blaze in Westport or the office building he'd demolished in New Bedford, but Pinto immediately connected Randy Black to the destruction.

He opened his phone and dialed Walter Macedo.

"You're not going to believe what I just found."

CHAPTER TWENTY

Ty didn't react to the buzz of Gretchen's zipper. He didn't even look as she wriggled her arms out of her vest and tossed it on the back seat next to his hat. His eyes scanned the road ahead then switched from mirror to mirror and back to the windshield. She didn't own a car and never intended to, but she'd ridden in one enough to know his obsession with the road was weird. Few things commanded a man's attention more than a woman removing clothes and he hadn't even peeked. He could have been brooding over her lie, but more likely he was plotting a way to get the panel for himself. She wasn't particularly attracted to Ty, but his indifference was unnerving. What kind of a woman was she if a man wouldn't watch her strip?

Gretchen didn't wear makeup. The brown T-shirt over the white long sleeves wasn't flashy, but she wasn't trying to attract attention. If anything, she'd been pushing Ty away since he arrived. Until now he'd always come back. He joined the research team to be close to her even though his eyes glazed over when they discussed technical details. Why did he pick her? Other guys avoided her, but Ty was always there. He was the first person she saw at the lab that morning and he was there in time to pull her out of the crowd at the press conference. His attention had saved her, but now he motored down the left lane oblivious to her in the passenger's seat. She felt a tremor of uncertainty. She was always pushing people away. Ty, Mary, the television reporter. If Ty wasn't even looking at her, there was definitely something wrong. Would she end up alone?

They accelerated past a group of cars then swung across the middle and right lanes in a wide open space ahead of the cluster they had just passed. The needle slowly drifted below ninety.

"Hungry?" Ty asked as he took the off-ramp in a blur.

"Rush much?" The car hunched forward as the brakes dragged it down from eighty on the downhill ramp. He wasted enough energy to carry them two miles. Ty flashed her a puzzled look and snapped back to the intersection ahead. Gretchen braced herself against the dash to make her point. Ty tried to stop smoothly, but he was across the white line when the car finally came to rest.

"Heating up the brakes doesn't help anything." She couldn't resist. Why was she always looking for a fight?

He looked at her dumbfounded. She wasn't sure if he didn't understand what she was saying or didn't care about wasted energy.

"You have a preference?" He pointed at two fast food restaurants across from each other.

Gretchen picked up the paper bag and gave the muffins a shake. "Yeah," she said.

The car swooped into the joint on the right and idled in the drive-through while a woman hung her head out a blue minivan and talked to the speaker. When it was their turn, he ordered two massive burgers, fries, and a drink, a lunch with enough calories for an entire day. She didn't comment about what these gargantuan chains did to food production with their ultimatums to farmers. They squeezed every penny while polluting the environment and their customers' bodies with equal disregard. The blitz of flashy advertising reeled in passing zombies whenever they saw the glowing signs on the side of the road. Fast, easy poison, next exit.

At least they'd stopped using Styrofoam.

Gretchen helped fit the extra wide cup into the holder as Ty swung onto the road and raced up the on-ramp. Within four minutes of turning off, they were speeding south again and Ty was stuffing a huge burger in his mouth with one hand and steering down the left lane with the other.

The car had cooled while they waited at the drive-through, so Gretchen reached into the back and put on her vest. She firmly zipped up and then rustled the paper bag as she took a muffin. Ty didn't even glance. Instead he took another huge bite out of a sandwich she couldn't fit in her mouth.

"What did cows ever do to you?"

He was defenseless with his mouth stuffed. The car was going eighty, wasting loads of gas. How could he be so ignorant? Didn't he care what he was doing to himself and his world? She took a sip of water and gave him time to swallow.

"Cows wouldn't exist if we didn't eat them," he said, not quite finished chewing. He transferred the hamburger to his lap and picked up his drink without taking his eyes off the road.

"It's no life what they're subjected to."

"You'd rather we let them go extinct?"

"They're not extinct in India," she said.

"Yeah, and they live like rats." He worked the soda back into place and held her eyes until she worried they'd drift off the road. He held steady and she managed not to look away. "Do you really believe Americans would let cows tear up their perfectly manicured lawns and eat their shrubs? There'd be one hanging in every garage out in the 'burbs. What's left, the wolves and mountain lions would eat in three years."

She'd picked a bad example. People even got mad about deer eating their bushes. Her hunting protests were forgotten once the deer started wandering into people's yards in February. Fortunately, people were more and more disconnected with the land and hunting was fading on its own. Animal populations were climbing and it was hard to get people excited about protecting animals that jumped over their fence every day. Ty was right about the landscaping damage. Hunting was gaining support in the suburbs as the deer learned to hide at the fringes of larger properties. Overgrown bushes provided ideal food and cover. Hunters were in demand. Birth control for wild animals just couldn't gain popular support. Why couldn't people see that saving the animals was worth the money? Ty would attack that idea as ridiculous, too.

People were filling the Earth and trampling everything beneath their feet. Humans needed a predator far more than the deer or cows did.

Ty drove on and munched his burger, unaffected by her comments. If she told him what she was thinking he would have laughed. He'd worked hard to get close to her, but he didn't need to impress her now that she was in his car. She tried to forget the whole exchange. He'd saved her that morning and she should be grateful. He was driving her to New Jersey where she'd be safe. Who else would do that?

Ty crumpled the hamburger wrapper and tossed it in the back seat. At least he didn't throw it out the window. He picked up the cardboard container of fries with one hand and stuffed them in his mouth with the other. He braced his knee against the wheel and kept them centered in the middle lane. Even stuffing himself, he cycled through the mirrors to the windshield and back, though not as militantly as before.

Gretchen held her breath when he took the soda from the cup holder and took a long drink. Fries in one hand, soda in the other, he kept the car perfectly centered with his knee. He reached over to replace the oversized cup without looking.

Gretchen reached out when he fumbled, but before she had hold of the cup, he let go and grabbed the wheel with both hands. The plastic top popped off and black soda splashed all over the console. It fizzed and foamed as it ran down on both sides, soaking the muffin bag and her shoes. Fries bounced on his lap and she fell toward him as the car swerved right. Her ribs smacked the console and her head bounced off his meaty shoulder.

He yanked the car left to keep it on the roadway.

"What the hell?" She righted herself in the seat.

Rather than answer, Ty gunned the engine with his eyes locked on the rearview mirror. She turned and saw a Hummer closing in from behind. The Malibu swerved left and passed a woman talking on her cell phone. The Hummer swerved into the breakdown lane to get around on the other side, then it cut back across the highway. The cars behind them slowed, creating a logjam of traffic behind them, but the people ahead had no idea what was about to come weaving through. The Hummer caught the bumper of a

Mustang and threw it into a spin. The driver must have panicked and yanked the wheel the wrong way, because the car came perpendicular to the roadway then flipped up into the air and rolled over four times. Sheet metal crunched and twisted in slow motion, mashing every corner of the vehicle as the Malibu zipped by on the other side.

The Hummer came even on Gretchen's side, and just before it rammed them Ty slammed on the brakes and let it rocket ahead. Ty stomped on the gas pedal and tried to maneuver around the Hummer to the right, but the driver moved over and pinned him to the guardrail. Sparks flew. The crunching sounded like the guardrail and the Hummer were eating the car from the outside in.

"What does he want?" Gretchen sounded desperate even to herself. Somehow she guessed it was the panel in the trunk, but she couldn't imagine how they found her or even how they knew she'd taken it.

"We're going to find out."

Ty locked the brakes and the car ground to a halt.

The Hummer came free for an instant, but it turned and rammed its nose into Ty's front tire, as if the big SUV could plow the front end of the Malibu through the guardrail and down the embankment. Now that the vehicles were perpendicular instead of side by side, Ty had room to get out and run, but his door was jammed shut. Through his cracked window he saw the driver jump down and rush around the back of the SUV into traffic.

CHAPTER TWENTY-ONE

The McLaren streaked down the left lane twenty minutes from Foxwoods. Randy's thoughts were meandering somewhere between poker strategy and the governor's uncertain offer when the first car flashed broadside and cut him off. The ABS pumped it down from 60 mph to a stop. In a blink the McLaren was closing at 70 mph. Randy swerved for the center of the roadway and all three lanes lit up with brake lights.

Someone up there had made a nasty mess. Randy didn't want to stop and get jammed up waiting for tow trucks to haul away the wrecks, so he stayed off the brake and surged ahead. Every other driver seemed to be standing on his brake and swerving to avoid slower cars ahead. Randy zigzagged to the breakdown lane for the grass, but a heavy guardrail detoured him back toward the center. He slalomed around half a dozen stopped cars and slowed to fifty as he squeezed down the line between stopped lanes of traffic. He was down to forty when he squirted around a spinning wreck and out into the open like a NASCAR driver risking his life to keep his position on the track.

As he broke free, he saw the beginnings of the carnage. A single car stopped sideways in the right two lanes. The woman at the wheel covered her face with trembling hands. Randy pressed the accelerator as a Mustang took flight and went tumbling sideways down the roadway. He squeezed around behind just inches from hitting the rear end. Another tangle of stopped vehicles blocked the road. The McLaren swerved to the median, passed them, and Randy fought hard to get back up on the open roadway. He was panting when his tires reached the center lane.

He saw the problem then. A Hummer clapped together with a Malibu, and the two vehicles ground to a halt in an open stretch of road. The cars ahead continued on. The cars behind were clogged up around the Mustang and no one but Randy ventured closer.

The Hummer rammed its front end into the Malibu, pinching it against the guardrail. The wreck blocked the right two lanes. Randy's first thought was to pull ahead out of the way and walk back to help. He didn't want to have his name reported. He'd help quietly and move on.

When he angled to pass the Hummer on his right, three men ran around the back end of the SUV out into the center lane. They carried AK-47s with silencers attached, headed for the pinned Malibu.

This was no accident.

The Malibu driver sat dazed behind the wheel. The passenger, a dark-haired woman, frantically struggled to get out, but her door was wedged against the guardrail and her window wasn't working. The McLaren veered closer as if to pass the Malibu and ram the Hummer broadside. The gunmen stopped directly in Randy's path, but their attention was on the occupants of the car and not oncoming traffic.

Randy yanked the wheel left and slammed the gas pedal to the floor, spinning the rear wheels and slinging the rear end around in an arc, so the rear bumper narrowly missed sideswiping the Malibu.

Bullet holes appeared on the hood of the Malibu. Spidery cracks skittered across the windshield as Randy reversed the wheel to slow the skid. The two occupants ducked for the floor as the right side of the McLaren slammed the gunmen between the low-slung sports car and the high, tank-like SUV. The impact threw Randy out of the driver's seat and sent him flying headlong into the passenger's door. The gunshots ceased. The occupants of the Malibu were safe, but Randy had no idea who they were or why they'd been pursued. The men with the AK-47s weren't cops. Cops didn't come out shooting on the highway in broad daylight and they didn't carry silenced weapons. The split-second decision had been the right one, but the bleeding face pressed against the passenger's window gave Randy pause. He had an urge to help the man on the other side of the glass. He needed to get out, check the injuries, and then get moving before the cops and reporters arrived. Any damage to the McLaren was superficial. He could get it fixed on his own.

A car door squeaked open. If it was the Hummer driver, he could have an AK-47 of his own. Hands thumped in agony against the McLaren's side panels. At least one of the gunmen was alive. Randy untangled his legs from the console and yanked the parking brake. As he pulled himself up, his neck felt like it had been wrenched in a direction it wasn't made to go.

The Malibu driver nodded his thanks through the cracked glass, then he kicked his door open and was ready to climb out, but snapped his head back in the direction of traffic and jumped deep inside the car. At that instant, a chrome grill flashed. A glossy black blur ripped the Malibu's door from its hinges like the wing from a butterfly. The McLaren jolted and flipped up on its side so the driver's door faced the sky. A horrid crunching of bone, flesh, and sheet metal met the asphalt roadway. The rotating McLaren crushed the three gunmen as if they were cigarette butts beneath a giant's foot. Randy bounced upside down. As he righted himself, he saw a bloody arm pinned between the cracked passenger's window and the asphalt. The steering wheel, the bucket seats, and the console provided a ladder straight up to the driver's exit.

The second Hummer came to rest at a sixty-degree angle with its body resting on the rear end of the McLaren and its front wheels rotating free in the air. Gasoline fumes rose from a puddle building underneath the cars. Randy jumped down to the roadway and found the bulky driver of the Malibu crawling through the puddle of gas, his shirt soaked through, eyes watering. Randy helped him squeeze between the cars and get back to the guardrail. The girl appeared there by the trunk. Her window was still closed and her door was still jammed shut, but she was out and unhurt. The guy was limping, but he moved well enough to get over the guardrail and onto the grass.

The hand on Randy's chest took him by surprise. It wasn't a blow but a shove backward. Randy recovered after a stutter step and saw the SW99 come out from underneath the Malibu driver's gas-soaked Hawaiian shirt. The girl looked stunned. They both followed the barrel toward the Hummer and saw a guy clad in black hanging out his door to aim an AK-47 at them. Randy could only watch and hope the Malibu driver was quicker.

The report blared.

The impact met the Hummer driver square in the forehead and he collapsed. His lifeless body fell six feet and splashed into a shallow pool of gasoline.

The three of them faced each other there on the grass. Randy's decision was becoming murkier. The Hummer driver and the other three wanted this guy badly. That one shot with the four-inch-barreled Smith & Wesson showed this guy had talent. There wasn't time to find out how he planned to use that talent before Randy decided what to do about the other men climbing out of the Hummer.

CHAPTER TWENTY-TWO

The look of surprise told Randy the woman didn't known her friend had a gun. The look of disgust said she didn't appreciate him shooting even to save her life. There wasn't time to ask how they knew each other, but if she didn't know about the gun, she didn't know this man well. It took significant training to make a shot like that and it took balls to do it with an automatic bearing down on you. The Malibu driver was the kind of guy who attracted trouble and could handle it when it came his way. This was news to the girl.

The woman screamed, "Stop shooting!" as if the guy would stand there and let himself be killed.

"You want to die?" the man hollered back.

Randy stood stranded and unarmed in the middle of a gunfight with a couple who couldn't decide who was in charge. They'd probably tear each other apart when the shooting was over. He flashed a look at the McLaren. There was no moving it with the Hummer perched on top like an eagle clutching a silver fish. If he could get into the trunk, he could grab the governor's cash, wave a fistful of hundreds at the passing traffic, and get a ride, but it was doubtful he'd make it that far. Even if he could, the twisted sheet metal wouldn't surrender its treasure without a pry bar.

There were no coincidences. Randy had been sent to help the girl. There'd be time to find out why later.

A dark head leaned out of the Hummer then jumped down onto the hood of the crinkled Malibu. The woman kept yelling at her friend while a second gunman cleared the door. She was going to get the three of them killed. Her boyfriend stood his ground and fired again. He should have run for cover, but he stayed with the girl. Was it love or obligation? There was no time to stand out in the open and wonder. The man didn't need saving, but he sorely needed help controlling his friend.

"Stop it!" she screamed, hitting him and ruining his aim.

A wave of panic hit Randy. How long had he been standing there watching? How many suppressed shots had they fired at him while he was deciding what to do? He snapped back toward the roadway in time to see the two men split. One rolled away, over the hood of the first Hummer and jumped down behind it where he could use the engine for cover. The other disappeared beneath the leaning Hummer and worked his way to its rear tire. They were flanked with no cover, but somehow the man kept the assailants pinned. He was going to run out of ammunition soon. He couldn't keep her occupied, change magazines, and return fire—all while she pounded his chest.

Randy reached them in two long strides. He thrust his arm between them and grabbed her nearest hip. He threw his other arm around her shoulder from behind. He let himself fall backward, yanked, and she spun and fell on top of him as he cradled her to the ground. They rolled away from the gunfire toward a steep slope that dropped away from the highway. He expected a flurry of slaps when they stopped rolling. There hadn't been time to place his hands precisely. He wasn't sure what he'd grabbed in the fall, but hadn't felt anything he shouldn't have. Her arms came free for a second and she didn't swing. He grabbed both elbows to be sure she didn't.

Randy worried the maneuver might earn him a bullet if Lover Boy considered him a threat, but he seemed glad to be free from the girl. Lover Boy dropped to a crouch and alternated careful shots, one at each assailant, keeping them pinned. "Go," he yelled, gesturing toward the slope even as he lined up a one-handed shot.

Randy kept hold of one elbow and dragged the girl to the bottom of the slope. He let her go when they were out of sight from above. Lover Boy hustled down after them. Once he stopped shooting, the gunmen crested the ridge, stood in the open, and took careful aim. Slugs whizzed overhead.

Lover Boy seemed to expect this. He dropped to the ground and fired three wild shots, but the gunmen didn't flinch.

Randy and the girl broke into the woods with slugs whacking trees all around them. They plunged in without fear of snakes, briars, or the swampy muck that grabbed at their shoes as they ran. The bullets tracked the girl in spite of the target Lover Boy offered out in the open. When Lover Boy ducked into the trees, he stopped behind the widest oak he could find and fired back up the slope. That discouraged them from coming further down the hill where they'd be exposed. The two men shouted gibberish to each other and retreated back up to the roadway.

Randy wondered what was going on up there. Cars were crawling by the wreck. Would the drivers see the gunmen? Or their friends lying dead on the asphalt? They'd be entranced by the twisted metal. Someone had to have called the cops by now. The guy in the Mustang would still be up there. Would he tell the cops Randy had been going 95 mph and then wrecked the McLaren intentionally? Would the skid marks betray his acceleration into the slide? Would the cops come after him for murder?

Randy didn't want to go back up there even if the cops chased the gunmen off. Unfortunately, all he could see ahead of him were trees and swamp.

The governor had said to keep it low key. He'd be pissed if he knew Randy was doing 95 mph and weaving through traffic. That alone might sour the governor's offer. Never mind that he'd wrecked a four hundred thousand dollar car with the governor's hush money, or whatever it was, in the trunk. Maybe someone would get careless and flick a cigarette into the puddle of gas. That would burn even more explosively than Charlie Marston's sawdust. That would stop the questions about the McLaren, the money, and the men underneath. If only he could be so lucky.

The damage wasn't entirely his fault. The second Hummer had rammed him on purpose. Still, he felt guilty about the insurance claim he'd file, but he couldn't replace the McLaren otherwise. He might not be able to find another one anyway. Maybe he shouldn't try. Maybe he should let go of that last remnant of the old Randy Black.

Lover Boy backed his way through the bushes and brought the smell of gasoline from his crawl under the Hummer. He huddled with them in the low bushes, but his attention shifted back and forth along the slope. Their view was mostly blocked by thick groupings of trees and the bushes that sprung up at the edge of the forest. They couldn't see the gunmen, but they hadn't given up, not after wrecking four cars and losing four comrades in the fight. There would be no easy escape up the slope.

"Think the cops are up there yet?" the girl asked.

"I hope they don't show up one at a time," Randy said. The firepower in a state police cruiser would be no match for two automatics. A single cop might not even have time to radio for help.

Movement off to the far right confirmed Randy's suspicion that the gunmen weren't giving up. A patchy figure worked his way to the bottom of the slope and positioned himself by a wide river that lazily floated by. He blocked them from crossing the river or using it to sneak under the highway. He stood there and watched, like he was waiting for help. He couldn't be waiting for the cops. The man and woman weren't fugitives. They just didn't have the vibe.

Could the gunmen be some sort of commandos? Ridiculous. Commandos wouldn't have bunched together and gotten pinned by the McLaren. Commandos would have dropped the three of them before they got out of their cars. Lover Boy was better trained than the men chasing them, but the woman was completely raw. She was his girlfriend or his mission. Even she wasn't looking hopefully up the hill. Either they weren't expecting to be rescued, or they didn't want to be found.

"That was way more than road rage," Randy prompted.

"Yeah," he whispered and left it there.

What had they done?

Randy hadn't seen his SIG since he dropped it outside Heather Lovely's vault. Finding salvation would be easier without it, but he'd just proven his car could be lethal. Right then he'd trade the fifty K in his trunk for a P229 and three loaded clips. God had selected him for his special skills. Maybe everyone Randy was sent to help would be as desperate as these two. Saving them would mean harming someone else. Randy was no preacher. He wasn't sent to help with an emotional crisis. He told himself he was here to take drastic action, but that rationalization was dangerous. He couldn't justify killing. Not even to save the two people huddled next to him.

The man didn't need saving. He was an excellent shot and by the way he crouched under cover, he was trained to survive. The woman lay bunched at the foot of a mountain laurel in the only dry spot around them, her white sleeves tucked underneath herself. The brown vest camouflaged her well against the dead leaves on the ground. She was completely unafraid of the creepy crawlies among the leaves. She knew how much trouble she was in, but she was keeping it together even if Randy couldn't understand the fit she'd thrown when Lover Boy started shooting.

"Who are those guys?" Randy asked her.

She shook her head solemnly, afraid to make noise, but she didn't hesitate. She didn't know.

Randy tapped Lover Boy on the shoulder and indicated a path parallel to the river that led deeper into the woods. Lover Boy nodded then pointed to himself and the ground. He'd stay behind and cover them. He had the only gun so his staying behind made sense. By the way he looked at the girl, it was clear she was the target, not him.

CHAPTER TWENTY-THREE

The third Hummer fought its way out of snarled traffic, through the breakdown lane, and onto the shoulder. Hisham wasn't worried about dents and scratches and his driver's aggression won them quick passage onto the grass. Stalled drivers honked and gestured, not knowing who was behind the tinted windows. They bounced over the grass at 40 mph, passing three cars at a time until Hisham ordered the driver to stop three hundred yards short of the wreck. Angry drivers honked on their way past. Until the police arrived to set out cones and sort things out, it was everyone for himself. The cars fought for every inch. Fools.

Up ahead, a young guy paced behind an upside-down Mustang with a crushed roof. He went front to back, protected from the oncoming traffic by the wreck. He kicked the front quarter panel and muttered curses no one could hear. The fool should have been glad to be alive. Traffic parted around him, one lane getting by on each side, then the drivers rushed to capture the center lane beyond.

The laptop inside the Hummer displayed a terrain map of the roadway and the surrounds. Four red dots appeared bunched on the interstate ahead of them. Another two dots were stationed at the far left of the map. One held steady by the bridge at the near edge of the river, the other held at the edge of the woods at what looked like a high point well back of the wreck. None of the dots were moving, but Hisham assumed only the dots on the roadway were injured. Four more dots appeared in a cluster at the top of the map. Hisham, at the keyboard, wasn't represented. He didn't venture into the field often and even if he did, he'd never allow them to insert a tracking chip under his skin.

"Do we have them?" he asked into the miniature microphone dangling from his ear.

The other men in the Hummer rushed to insert their earpieces so they could hear both sides of the conversation. Automatics ready, the three men in the rear eyed the door, eager to bolt out and join the fight. The pit bulls longed to bite, and for once Hisham was glad to have them along.

"No. They're in the trees between us. We're blocking their path back to the road."

He couldn't believe it. Six men with automatic weapons couldn't stop one man and a woman in a tiny American car. How had they let them escape into the forest?

"Police?" he asked, wondering what else could go wrong.

"Not yet."

"Good. Let's finish this before they arrive."

"There's another man involved."

"Not a policeman?"

"No. He didn't have a gun, but he led the girl into the woods."

"Leave him in the forest next to the other two."

The men in the Hummer welcomed his pronouncement. This would be no surgical strike, not that their training allowed for such precision. They were about to be turned loose against two men and a woman. Only one of the men was armed and he only had a handgun to defend himself against six men with AK-47s. The job wasn't without danger, but the likelihood of the men in the Hummer getting seriously injured was remote.

Hisham ordered his men to flush them away from the highway and into the woods. He wanted to be sure the girl never returned to the road. A prolonged search for her body would give them time to leave the country.

A few clicks on the screen formed a grid from the river north to their position and west into the swamp. The men piled out of the Hummer and trotted down the slope, according to Hisham's orders. Three of the dots formed a line near the top of the grid and moved west, separated by fifty meters. The fourth dot reached the corner of the grid and moved south. The man adjacent to him moved farther south to equalize the distance between the three men guarding the roadway. This last man moved slowest of the squad as he was closest to their quarry. When the six of them were in position, Hisham opened his mic again and said, "Go."

The three dots along the roadway moved slowly forward, squeezing the fugitives between the gunmen on two sides, the river, and the swamp behind. They wouldn't last long. Hisham didn't wait for the shooting to start. He climbed down and walked toward the wreck to make sure they hadn't left anything in the car.

CHAPTER TWENTY-FOUR

Randy put his finger to his lips and gently pulled the girl down flat on the ground facing him. She wanted to turn and look, but she understood that rustling leaves would attract trouble.

Two men hustled past on a path parallel to theirs. At eighty-plus yards, Randy saw only flashes of dark clothes through the brush, but he heard leaves crunch heavily under each deliberate step. They had to be on a well-worn path because they moved quickly without breaking branches. They kept fifty yards between them, maximizing the distance they could cover with their rifles and minimizing the chances of anyone rushing between them and surviving to reach the other side of the path.

Instinct told Randy to turn to the river and he knew he was being flushed like an animal. In a minute, the men would start sweeping the bushes and pressing them toward the river or, more likely, the men from the roadway would wait for their friends to get in position and then press in, simultaneously hiding themselves from view and pressing their quarry toward their comrades deeper in the forest.

"What did you do, sweetheart?" Randy whispered.

The third man stopped in the distance, blocking any escape to the north.

Her eyes widened. "Don't call me sweetheart. My name's Gretchen."

"I'm Randy. So, tell me, Gretchen, why do these men want to kill you?"

"I'm a college student on my way home. I don't know what they want."

She was college age, but that wasn't the whole story. She'd done something to make these men want her so desperately. She didn't have a bag, so if she was carrying something valuable it was very small. He imagined a diamond the size of a meatball. More likely she'd seen something she shouldn't have and made someone powerful very angry. Randy couldn't help her until he found out who wanted her dead. There wasn't time to argue. They needed to get moving, but Gretchen wasn't fooling anyone.

Lover Boy crept up through the bushes so quietly the man on the path didn't turn. Randy shook his hand and learned Ty was also a student, though he looked thirty. He was pudgy and covered himself with a bulky Hawaiian shirt that smelled of gasoline. He was a heavy guy, but stalked through the woods like a predator. The way he wielded the gun, Randy would have pinned him for a Ranger or a SEAL if he was in better shape.

Ty eased the magazine from his SW99. There were two shells visible at the top, but he replaced it with a magazine from his belt.

"Low?" Randy whispered.

"Down to one mag, plus three rounds in this one." He kept his eyes back in the direction he'd come. "We're not going to win a firefight."

Gretchen gauged the way deeper into the woods against the path Ty had taken to reach them. Her eyes settled in the direction of I-95.

"Forget it," Randy said. "Running isn't going to work. They're waiting for us back there. You'll never make it up that hill."

"There's only two of them," Ty said

"No," Randy whispered. "We saw three more." He pointed toward the path and where he assumed the men would be waiting for them. "We need them to come in after us, so we can take them quietly. Otherwise we're going to be perforated."

Randy told Ty and Gretchen to stay put until they saw the first man coming. Then they'd head off in the direction Randy plotted, deep into the center of the trees, staying between the river and the three men on the path.

Randy motioned for them to get low. "Whatever you do, don't break cover," he said, ready to sneak off.

They both looked at him strangely.

"Don't step out onto a road and don't try crossing the river." They understood, but he could see they didn't grasp the danger. "They're waiting up there to shoot you. Stay under cover. They'll wait for a clean shot rather than give up their position. Stay in the thick stuff, understand?"

With that, Randy worked his way forward, bending branches slowly to keep the leaves from rattling. He nestled himself deep into a thick clump of bushes and watched as Ty tried to calm Gretchen in their hiding place.

A minute later, a black-clad torso waded toward him, sweeping an AK-47 from side to side as he scanned the vegetation. His heavy boots tangled in the undergrowth and his hips struggled to pull his legs through the tangles. He stopped every ten steps and listened for anyone trying to sneak out of his path. Gretchen and Ty crawled far ahead. The gunman heard the rush far ahead and angled to cut them off. He ran the first twenty steps, slashing through the undergrowth to get in position. The burst of speed left the men on his flanks well behind and sent Gretchen and Ty scrambling in the direction Randy had told them to go.

The next time the gunman stopped he was faced with a thicket of head-high bushes. Rather than push inside and blind himself to anything beyond, he skirted it and stopped again just four feet from where Randy lay hidden. The man could have spotted Randy easily, but he was too intent on the spot where Ty and Gretchen were hiding.

When the man pushed ahead again, Randy sprung up behind him. The rush could have been his own legs slashing through the undergrowth. By the time he realized the commotion was closing in on him it was too late. Randy caught the gun barrel in his left hand. Using his left for leverage to keep his man from turning, Randy came around with his right and clobbered him over the back of the head.

The man wilted and fell.

Randy dragged him deep inside the thicket and propped him up against the lone tree. A long boot lace made the perfect restraint for his ankles. Even if he got untied he wouldn't move fast without boots. Randy belted his hands together behind the tree, so when he regained consciousness he couldn't see how the belt was fastened. Randy stuffed a dirty sock in his mouth and secured it with the second boot lace. The man didn't resist. He'd be disgusted when he woke, but Randy planned to be long gone then.

The scuffle netted Randy a fully-loaded automatic with spare ammunition and a Taurus handgun. He didn't recognize the model, so he dropped the clip and counted fifteen 9mm rounds. The AK-47 was silenced. The Taurus had been holstered. Randy didn't need a silencer for the Taurus, so he didn't bother searching for one, but he did find a radio clipped to the man's belt with a single wire that led to a microphone and an earpiece. Randy transferred the radio to his own belt and went to look for another target.

Pushing out of the thicket and back into the open, Randy spotted the man walking the river's edge. He'd heard Randy moving and was looking for him in the brush. Randy dropped low and crept closer, then motioned for Ty to attract his attention. As soon as Ty moved, the man turned and took several hurried steps. Ty's break was perfectly timed to convince the gunman that someone was running out of the woods, but instead of chasing, the man reached for his radio. A jumbled rush of consonants fought each other in Randy's headset. A similar string of gibberish was shouted in reply.

When the gunman was done telling his partners what was happening, he took up the chase, running wildly through the brush. He passed too far from Randy for an ambush, so Randy let him go and took up pursuit from behind. The gunman's feet made so much noise he was deaf to anything behind him. When he slowed to look for Ty, Randy barreled into him shoulder first and slammed him to the ground. The brush swiped Randy's automatic away, but he quickly had the Taurus pressed against the man's temple. In spite of the language barrier, the man knew his options were to be quiet or dead.

Randy hadn't counted on the radios.

The men would know each other's voices. They were organized enough to know who was where. The call pinpointed the trouble and told the others to move in. Randy and Ty had a clear path to the highway, but Gretchen was sixty yards away through the brush. Randy might have made it if he bolted, but if Gretchen started running, the soldiers would gun her down.

Ty appeared, stalking back toward Randy and the man he'd tackled.

Randy nodded to let Ty know he had control without taking his hand off the man's throat or lifting the gun from his temple.

Ty froze and Randy heard footsteps crashing toward them.

Hidden as they were, low in the brush, the third gunman rushed up within twenty feet without seeing them. He didn't spot them until their captive squealed. By then he was close enough to see the Taurus aimed at his comrade's temple. Randy assumed the threat would force a standoff, but the gunman leveled his AK-47. Another man would have fired the Taurus and made it two against one, but Randy hesitated.

The AK-47 flashed and bullets whacked a tree behind Randy and ricocheted toward the river. For a moment, he was stunned the third man had fired. Randy should have pulled the trigger and killed the man he straddled, but instead he lifted the gun toward the new threat. As he did, the man beneath him bucked and Randy momentarily lost his bearings.

Another bullet whizzed by. The hair on Randy's neck stood erect.

Randy clamped down on the first man's windpipe with his thumb, simultaneously stabilizing himself and neutralizing his captive. He whipped his head around to line up a shot, but before he could find the sights, a booming report sounded. The third gunman's head snapped hard to the left. For an instant it looked like he'd been beheaded, but his face snapped back into view as he collapsed into the scrub.

Ty scrounged the automatic from the dead man. Randy realized there would be others and he needed to get his man tied up. Ty scowled as if Randy was wasting time. Ty's method was faster and permanent. Randy rushed to secure him as he'd tied the first gunman. He felt foolish belting the man's hands knowing that he'd free himself within the hour. He knotted the laces so tight around the man's ankles, he worried they'd cut off blood flow to his feet. He should have backed away and let Ty shoot him, but he couldn't.

Ty rummaged both men for ammunition and equipment. His easiness about the corpse said he'd done this before. His focus was on escape. The consequences of his shots had been considered long ago and now he dismissed them as swiftly as the slugs left the muzzle.

Gretchen hunched low and scurried to them through the brush.

Shouted gibberish rattled out of the bush where Randy left the first gunman. He'd already managed to spit out the sock and now he was yelling instructions to his comrades. Randy guessed they'd captured or killed half the gunmen. There was an automatic for each of them now, but Gretchen refused to touch hers. If she picked it up, and if she could shoot, the odds might have been even.

Randy considered firing low through the brush to shut him up. When his comrades found him, they'd untie him and he'd rejoin the fight. Randy knew where he was at the base of that tree. He could make the shot, but he didn't lift the gun to aim. If it were up to Ty, the men wouldn't have belts around their wrists. They'd have bullet holes in their foreheads. Ty's approach made them safer, but Randy couldn't bring himself to shoot the man bound to the tree even if he couldn't see him die.

The assailants approached more carefully after the warnings from their comrade. Two circled back toward the highway to cut off any escape that way. The other remained hidden somewhere ahead. The river was a clear path out, but the water was cold and deep. They wouldn't last long soaking wet in the growing darkness. It was going to get cold overnight and Randy was starting to think they'd be trapped out here until morning.

He opened his phone and dialed for help.

CHAPTER TWENTY-FIVE

The honking horns signaled the arrival of the search team from the girl's apartment. The Hummer stopped at an angle across the two right lanes, blocking both. As traffic worked its way around the overturned Mustang, the right lanes cleared so Hisham could see the remainder of his team. One man stayed behind to direct traffic into a single lane. The others piled into the Hummer on the grass and wheeled down the breakdown lane to the wreck.

They parked at an angle that blocked the Malibu from passing drivers and readied the Hummer to zip into traffic when it was time to go. Three men clad in black exited. A driver in a blue Chevy stared at the group as he puttered by. Four black Hummers in such close proximity stood out, especially when two of them were slammed together in a jumble of twisted metal. Fortunately the bodies were too hard for the motorists to see. After seeing the man directing traffic, the onlookers would assume they were policemen in special uniforms. Hisham hoped this would delay a call to the authorities. His team worked for several governments, but the United States of America wasn't among them.

Hisham turned his attention to the men facing him. "Anything?"

"No. She left nothing behind."

He glared. Could this boob even know what he was looking for? "How could you finish so fast? Do you know how small this thing is?"

"Yes, sir. She had barely anything in the room. We searched her roommate's share of the apartment, also."

Hisham stepped up into the Hummer and retrieved the laptop from its mount. When he launched the video feed from that morning, he waved the man over and showed him Gretchen Greene downloading data onto a removable drive not much wider than a pen. He paused the replay with the blue plastic drive clutched in her fingers.

He glared at the man again. "Did you search well enough to find this?" He tapped the screen for emphasis.

Hisham saw a glimmer of self-doubt in his soldier, but the girl had probably taken the data with her. Why else would she flee? The roommate would certainly call the police when she found the mess they'd left. There was no going back.

He ordered them to search the Malibu. The first man into the car gingerly leafed through papers in the glove compartment. Did he have to teach them everything? Hisham yanked a black duffel bag from the Hummer, stormed over, and ripped the man out of the car. He climbed in, grabbed everything from the glove compartment, and stuffed it into the bag with a flourish. He grabbed the bag of muffins and jammed it in as well. He even dumped the water bottle to be sure nothing was hidden inside.

Hisham shoved the bag into the man's chest and watched as he hustled it into the Hummer. The others sparked to life.

A tire iron appeared and in seconds the trunk popped open. The men converged. The girl's clothes were strewn all about. They found the panel at the bottom of the girl's bag and Hisham smiled for the first time that day. After seeing his work up front, the men took everything from the trunk except the spare and the jack and heaped it all in the back of the Hummer to be sifted through later. They even picked up her clothes off the asphalt and the cowboy hat off the floor in case she'd hidden the miniature storage device.

Now that they had the panel, the girl wasn't needed. They could retrieve the stolen data and return home.

The team leader brought Demitri out to face the devastated Malibu.

"Why did she run? What does she know?" Hisham demanded.

"She doesn't know anything. The shooting must have spooked her."

"She sabotaged the lab an hour before the press conference."

The boy looked shocked.

Hisham considered showing Demetri the video and watching the boy squirm, but before he could decide, a single gunshot rang out and the headset erupted with chatter. What should have been six men converging for the kill turned into something entirely different. His men sounded panicked. One of them was killed. Worse, two others didn't report in.

The team had heard the transmissions as well. They rushed for the Hummer and came out armed and ready to plunge into the forest as soon as the order was given. Hisham turned, half expecting to see the girl and the two men break for the highway, but saw only trees. The reports ceased, but the conflict could rage on in silence if his men had given up their weapons.

Someone announced over the radio that they had blocked the path back to the road, but they were almost evenly matched. Hisham waved two more men into the forest. They trotted off down the slope, neither of them hiding their weapon. When they radioed to announce their arrival, the others sounded relieved.

When Hisham turned back to the wreck, he saw a dark blue Ford pickup move out of the single lane and park beside the Hummer. The driver wore dirty jeans, work boots and a T-shirt. He walked with his hands on his hips, pectorals clenched.

"Where did you assholes learn to direct traffic?" the driver yelled.

"Get back in your truck and move along," Hisham said dismissively.

"Screw you. You can't keep us sitting back there single file. What the hell are you guys doing?"

Sirens sounded. The state police were here to clean up the wreck. It was fortunate they'd taken this long. Hisham opened his mic to order the Hummer to come up from the rear, but when he did, the construction worker stepped up angrily like he was ready to take a swing. Hisham cut off his transmission and held out his hand with his fingers splayed. The guy kept coming until he saw the muzzle of the Taurus aimed at his chest. Then the construction worker's demeanor completely changed. He lifted his hands as a show of compliance, but Hisham didn't hesitate. He dropped the first round dead center in his sternum and the big guy stumbled backward and hit the asphalt with a thud.

He opened the mic again. "Let's get off the road."

The flagman choked off the single lane, so all traffic behind him came to a standstill. This stymied the police and allowed the roadway to open up for a faster getaway. When the road was clear for half a mile, the flagman scrambled into the Hummer and raced south, forcing his way into line with the cars that zoomed past his abandoned his post.

As the two remaining Hummers raced away, Hisham checked the laptop and saw a ring of six men surrounding a patch of forest beside the river. The girl and her friends were blocked from the police. If he'd had more time, he would have ignited the spilled gasoline. The roar of the fire and the secondary explosions would have covered the gunfire in the woods and given his men time to deal with the girl.

When they were two miles away, the red dots disappeared from Hisham's map. He wished he'd done more to occupy the police, but by the time they found a more discrete route into the woods, the girl and her friends would be dead and he could pick up his men and get out of this godforsaken place.

CHAPTER TWENTY-SIX

"If you pull the trigger on that thing, lead comes out the other end and punches holes in the bad guys." Ty snickered at his own joke. Randy didn't find it funny; neither did Gretchen.

Huddled together as they were, it was obvious who was doing the shooting. Ty had burned through three magazines while Randy still hadn't emptied his first. Ty couldn't know why Randy was hesitant to shoot, but it was clear that while he'd kept an escape route open deeper into the woods, the six men had tightened the semi-circle on Randy's end, completely blocking any escape to the highway. Randy could have hit them as they rushed between trees, but he'd passed up several easy shots. Randy didn't want to go back up to the road and talk to the police about the men crushed underneath his car, but there was something more that kept him from shooting—something that wouldn't be resolved today. Backed up against the riverbank, his reluctance to take a life could get them killed.

An upper arm protruded from behind an oak as one of the men signaled his comrades. Randy fired. The man dropped behind the tree and wailed.

"That's what I'm talking about," Ty applauded.

Two men rushed over. One kept the escape sealed off. The other attended the wounded man. Shattering that man's upper arm took two men out of the fight without killing either of them.

Gretchen wasn't doing anything to help. A commandeered rifle lay in front of her, but she refused to touch it. If she'd taken it up, they'd only be slightly outnumbered, though she was unlikely to hit anything.

The steep riverbank provided excellent cover. The cold water prevented the gunmen from getting behind them, but the risk of hypothermia also prevented them from swimming to safety. Randy's hope of escape dimmed as the light faded from the forest. Soon the dark-clothed men could move unseen. The threesome needed to get out of there, but the only clear path was into the water and Randy wasn't going swimming, not in October.

Ty fired two quick shots and one careful one, then a dark figure retreated from the swamp and dove for cover. Ty dropped the magazine and replaced it, barely taking his eyes off the forest. After the metallic slide of the action snapping forward, a new sound fluttered in the distance. The noise intensified over the traffic until the drumming of rotors became clear. It had been thirty minutes since Randy's call.

He flipped open his cell, redialed, and left the speaker on.

"Sir, good to know you're still with us. Hold while I patch in the captain."

"Captain Wolfe here in State One, go ahead."

"We hear you over the trees. We're west of I-ninety-five. On the riverbank. Five hundred yards ahead."

"Roger that. Coming to you."

The emergency operator broke in. "Can you describe the situation on the ground for the captain, sir?"

"We're surrounded by five men with automatics at about eighty yards. If we were any closer to the river we'd be wet. They're scattered around us in the trees."

"Sir, we've got three state troopers on the scene of that crash. Can you get to them?"

"Negative. We're facing assault rifles. Even if we could get up there, three Glocks aren't going to do much against those AK-forty-sevens."

"Can you confirm those assault rifles, sir?"

"They are AK-forty-sevens. Say again, A-K-four-seven."

"Hold tight, sir. I'll put canine and SWAT units en route."

The rotors steadied overhead. Randy waved to the men above.

"We've got you, over." Randy could barely make out the voice above the beating rotors. He pointed out the attackers as accurately as he could, but the captain's response was completely drowned out. Randy pressed the phone to his ear, but the sound he heard was from a speaker mounted on the helicopter and not the telephone.

"This is the Connecticut State Police. Canine and SWAT units have you surrounded. Throw down your weapons. Clasp your hands over your head and walk to the river."

None of the men in the forest moved.

"We can't see them," Wolfe said over the phone.

"They're not buying it." Randy hollered into the phone, but couldn't believe Captain Wolfe could hear him with the helicopter hovering so close.

"This is your final warning." Wolfe repeated his command and at the same time, the blue helicopter with yellow stripes dipped below the tree canopy. The craft hovered twenty feet above the water in a space so tight that a jag to either side would have the rotors trimming branches along the riverbank.

A rifle barrel poked out the rear window of the copter.

The reaction from within the trees was horrifying.

Before the sniper in the helicopter could get himself situated and get his eye in the scope, three men rushed the riverbank and took cover. Randy screamed that they were too low, but it was too late.

Automatic fire erupted from all three gunmen. A meaty hand grabbed a handful of Randy's shirt and yanked him in the opposite direction. The force pulled him from the mossy bank and almost sent him tumbling into the frigid water. Gretchen scurried along the river's edge ahead of them. She ran as fast as she could manage, hunched over with her head below the level of the bank. Ty followed as soon as Randy understood his plan.

The copter darted from side to side, impacts hitting every square inch around the door and the windows. The rifled spilled out of the open window, bounced off the skid, and splashed down near the center of the river.

The automatics emptied magazines into the craft, seemingly without concern for aim. "Taking fire. Taking heavy fire," was the last thing Randy heard before he closed his phone and ran.

Randy followed the others up and over the bank. They broke into the swamp where their footsteps began to splash and the mud sucked at their shoes harder and harder with every stride.

Behind them the copter banked hard toward the forest. A rotor sliced into the first treetop with the metallic ching of a sword beheading its victim. The impacts of rotor against wood came faster and faster until the noise jumbled together in a rolling crash through the treetops and down to the forest floor where the copter smashed to the ground and caught fire.

Gretchen led the way into a marshy area that seemed to go on without end. Clumps of brush grew alongside established trees anywhere the soil rose above the waterline. For Randy, every step required planning. Every patch of dry earth was guarded by briars. Movement was slow and if they were caught, there would be no place to hide. Gretchen hopped from clump to clump, grabbing the smooth trunks of young maples and the larger branches for support as naturally as if she were walking down the corridor to class. Ty seemed comfortable as well. He directed them forward and hung back to make sure they weren't being followed.

"You seem pretty at home out here," Randy said to Gretchen as they slowed their pace and bunched together, hopping from hummock to hummock. Most women he knew would be so freaked out by insects, they would have gotten themselves killed three times over.

"This is where nature intended us to be," she said.

"I don't know if nature has intentions, but I'd prefer my living room about now. Most women I know would prefer anyplace to a swamp."

"The women you know are out of touch. Nature provides everything we need. Like the riverbank back there that let us get away."

"Forget the riverbank. If I were you, I'd be thanking God, Ty, and the Connecticut State Police. In that order."

"God, sure, tell me another fairy tale."

Chapter Twenty-seven

Traffic on I-95 stalled for thirty minutes. Carl watched his partner's strong dark forearm tense on the wheel and bristled his own blond hair in a show of solidarity. Eight state police cars passed them on the grass, five from Rhode Island, the rest from Connecticut. The cruisers were followed by three fire trucks, five wreckers, and a parade of local police cars, some of them unmarked. Drivers in all three lanes turned their cars off and waited it out. When a SWAT van rushed past, they knew Ty was involved in the multiple-car wreck reported on the radio. It was a nasty one to clog traffic this bad.

"Keep those guns down in back," Carl said. He'd already surrendered the .45 his father had given him. He wouldn't get it back until they'd run ballistics tests to be sure he hadn't shot the kid or the suit. He didn't want to lose his backup, too.

"Man, these pricks are making a mess."

"We should've taken them out back at the school."

"Not with Ashton there," Carl answered.

As soon as the cops were done questioning them that morning, they'd made a run to the airport and put Ashton on a plane back to headquarters. Ashton was a big time exec who liked to be down in the details, but there were some jobs Ashton needed distance from. Most of the time he listened to Carl, but this time the bullets had done the talking for him. Ty and the girl were somewhere nearby. Carl was glad for the room to operate.

He had no authority here on the road. They had to wait like everyone else. When the mass of red lights finally stopped glowing and the cars started moving again, Carl heard the whoosh of rotors in the distance. When they reached the accident scene they saw the Speedy Dry the firemen had sprayed over the clump of cars. The Malibu was crunched against the guardrail, its trunk popped open. One of the men in back confirmed the plate number matched Ty's. The wreck didn't look that serious even though one of the Hummers balanced on top of another car. Carl knew who'd been in the Hummers and why they'd chased the girl across two states.

Carl signaled the driver to pull around the accident scene onto the grass.

The nearest cop trotted over. "You can't stop here. Keep moving."

Carl explained that a relative was in the Malibu, and they weren't going anywhere. The cop told them to stay put and went off in search of a more senior opinion.

An explosion rumbled in the distance. Carl assumed the helicopter had dropped down to extract Ty and the girl and been shot down.

He opened his phone and dialed, hoping they hadn't been on board yet. He sighed deeply when Ty answered. "Well, you're alive."

"For now." The voice was so faint, Carl could barely hear, but he knew better than ask Ty to speak up.

"What was that?"

"State police helicopter."

"That explains the scrambling up here."

"Where are you?" Ty asked in a whisper.

"On I-ninety-five looking at a crushed company car."

"Shit. Don't tell me they're going to come stomping in here."

"You don't even want to apologize for damage?"

"Funny. What's happening up there?" Ty asked.

"They're lining up. Heavy weapons, dogs, about twenty men."

"That's not good. They're going to push the bastards right back into me and I've got my ass hanging out in the open. Any chance of getting a boat up this river to bail us out?"

"Not likely. Even if I could bribe the cops to get one, there'd be a lot of questions when you came motoring down river."

"What do you suggest I do? Climb a tree?"

"Or dig a hole. Whatever works."

Carl tapped the Suburban's nav screen, broadening the map until it spanned the forest. The river cut a fairly straight path about two miles to a sparsely-populated wooded road. "Follow the river straight through," he said into the phone. "We'll be waiting for you on the other side. One more thing. What about the girl? Will she play ball?"

"She doesn't even know the teams."

"She knows something's up. Otherwise she wouldn't have bolted."

"She's not a big fan of the firm. That's for sure."

"She's not working for them?" Carl asked.

"Nope. They're trying pretty hard to kill her."

"What's she thinking?"

"I don't know, but she took the panel."

"So it didn't go up? Great news. Where is it?"

"In my trunk."

"Correction. It was in your trunk. Looks like the cops popped it open. How could you leave it behind? You know how important that thing is."

"Did you see the two monsters that ran me off the road? And the bullet holes in my car?"

"Wah, wah, wah. Get yourself through the woods and get the girl to join the team."

"If she won't?"

"Make sure she will."

"See you in an hour."

CHAPTER TWENTY-EIGHT

Randy hopscotched along Gretchen's trail into a soggy flat where the river fanned out and leveled the landscape, killing the mature trees in its path and letting sunlight spur growth on the ground. They hugged a swath of cattails and picked their way among grassy clumps and over narrow channels of deep water. A mature maple sixty yards ahead had lost its footing and been uprooted by the wind, creating a bridge over the frigid water. The far bank was marshy, but rose up above the water line within a few dozen yards. Crossing would be risky. The waterlogged earth meant slow progress and nowhere to hide while they hopped toward the tree, but once across the river, they could defend themselves easily.

Randy hissed to get Gretchen's attention then pointed to the tree.

She gestured back, mocking him for pointing out the obvious. She glanced in Ty's direction then turned and zigzagged forward.

Was she abandoning Ty? Or trusting him to find them?

She stopped on a thick tuft of grass surrounded by murky water. Randy caught up and she whispered, "See? Nature provided our escape."

Long ago the reverend had said there were no coincidences, but did God manipulate circumstances at such a minute level? Nature wasn't scheming when it dropped that tree. Water washed soil away from the roots. The tree grew taller and more top heavy, and the wind took hold and toppled it. The tree and the river didn't care about saving them. Nature's tools were equally available to all, but fate had a way of leading Randy to what he needed.

Gretchen hopped onto the next grassy island. Thump. Splash. She canted heavily to her left and the muck slurped and sucked as she hauled her leg out of the soggy peat. The mud blackened her jeans up to her thigh.

Exactly what she deserved for mocking God.

Randy swallowed his laughter. His mother would say, "That's God punishing you," when karma avenged a minor injustice. Gretchen would scoff. She'd call it superstition. Memories of his mother were too precious to risk, so Randy kept his memory to himself.

Gretchen didn't get angry for her plunge into the cold mud. She didn't curse the heavens, probably because when she looked up she saw only atmosphere and galaxies. She did embrace the natural world with vigor. He couldn't imagine who she thought "Nature" was or how she could explain the known universe creating itself.

Randy caught up and offered a hand to steady her as she brushed off her jeans. She refused with a stern shake of her head.

"Do you like thinking it's all just one happy accident?" he asked, unable to help himself any longer.

"Truth is truth. Nothing to be happy or sad about. It just is."

"So all the complexities that make life possible just fell together?"

"They didn't just fall together. It took millions of years of trial and error. Natural selection chose the winners and losers. Every characteristic, every instinct is the result of millions of generations. It's not like someone could sit down and sort it all out in a week. That's lunacy. Look at how little we can do with bio engineering."

"We're not very powerful in comparison. And your theory about the universe? Random events created everything? That's insane. God planned creation. Instinct, traits, knowledge, they all work because He made it so. He could have made dogs red if he wanted to, whether red was a good color for camouflage or not."

She turned toward him, bewildered. "What's a red dog going to eat?"

"Colorblind prey." His quick answer surprised him.

"Your red dog would starve or be eaten in a week."

"You can believe anything if you try hard enough," he said. "It still doesn't make it right."

She eyed her next step then turned back. "You show me a red dog and I'll go to church with you."

Randy thrust his hand out and said, "Deal," louder than he should have.

They shook and she nodded at the gun. "Maybe I should be holding that."

"You'd think an atheist could pull the trigger."

She clenched her teeth then turned in a huff for the tree. She hiked as fast as she could without risking another dip in the water. Why couldn't she shoot? Didn't morality stem from religious teachings? Not in her case. Her stance against violence would be the first of many values to confound him. He wondered what an atheist feared. Was it karma or Humanism that kept her in line?

The trip to the leaning tree dead-ended twice. They changed leaders and camouflaged their contempt for each other by focusing on getting across the river. Randy continually scanned the darkening brush behind them until Ty emerged. They were just ten yards from the tree when Ty waved them back across the marsh. A confused series of hand signals followed as Ty urged them to come back and Randy asked why he wanted them to. Hollering over the distance would have been suicide.

Randy indicated the tops of several heads then opened his hands to ask where the gunmen were. If they'd crossed the river already, Randy would have abandoned the crossing and headed back into the swamp, but Ty didn't understand the signal. Randy then gestured with the gun.

Ty gestured emphatically parallel to the river—on his side of the marsh.

Randy wanted to get into heavier cover and he could see Gretchen eyeing the thick brush on the other side of the river, too. Together they signaled toward the tree. Ty shook his head stubbornly, but when they turned and began hopping forward, Ty rushed to catch them, bouncing from hummock to hummock at a reckless pace.

The inevitable splash came quickly.

Ty sank in muck to his knees and dragged himself out onto solid ground only to fall back in six yards later. With both legs wet, he gave up on the tiny clumps of land, trudging through the water instead. Without the need to pick his route, he quickly gained ground and reached the tree as Randy gave Gretchen a ten-finger boost so she could pull herself up.

Ty dragged himself out of knee-deep mud and whispered urgently, "We need to stay on this side."

"There's nothing but swamp back there." Randy gestured to the rising terrain on the opposite side of the river. "That's where we should be headed." In thirty minutes it would be too dark to move quietly and there'd be no way of telling who they were about to stumble into. They needed to find a place to stop—preferably a dry place.

"There's a road out there somewhere." Ty gestured parallel to the river on a path that meant trudging through swamp as far as they could see.

"There's a road everywhere if you walk far enough. I'm not going back through that." Randy couldn't imagine why Ty wanted to, either. Had Ty been here before? Randy's own orchestration of the events in Piolenc flashed to mind, but even Randy couldn't plan a six-car collision.

Ty desperately wanted to turn back, but they'd be a lot safer with neck-deep water between them and the gunmen. It was too cold to swim across, so unless the gunmen found this tree in the dark, they'd be safe until morning. The cold seeped in through Randy's wet pants and he wished he'd been carrying matches.

Gretchen crossed the tree like a balance beam, using branches to keep herself steady. The treetop bent lower as she crossed until it was low enough for her to jump down. Relieved of her weight, the tree snapped skyward. Branches whooshed and leaves rattled, calling out their position. Randy instinctively ducked behind the upturned roots, but they couldn't stay separated. He climbed up, used the gun and the branches for balance and had Gretchen grab hold of a sturdy branch to muffle his dismount. Ty followed. His weight sent a great crack through the upper part of the trunk as he reached the far bank, and his dismount was barely three feet.

The three picked their way through the last few yards of flooded terrain and they reached dry ground before anyone emerged into the marsh.

Randy convinced them to sit in the brush and watch for anyone following. They hunched together, turned their attention to the swampy clearing they'd just crossed, and listened to the rushes of the forest at dusk. Several minutes after they quieted, the mice and the squirrels went to work collecting the evening's food. The scampering of the tiny animals was much louder than their size suggested. A group of ruby-crowned kinglets chirped signals to each other as they rushed from tree to tree prospecting for insects. Nothing heavy enough to be a human footstep sounded nearby.

Gretchen was getting antsy when Randy caught the glow off in the direction Ty had wanted to take. When he tapped Ty's shoulder and pointed out the light, Ty stood up.

Randy tugged him back down.

The light broke into two distinct headlights and made a slow trek down a wooded trail far across the swamp. The vehicle angled away and stopped deep in the forest. Ty urgently wanted to go and meet the car's occupants.

"Not a good idea," Randy said.

"I called a friend for help," Ty said. "That's got to be him."

Gretchen looked nervous about going back. Randy wasn't sure if it was the marsh or Ty's friends she was afraid of.

"Why don't you call him again?" Randy asked.

CHAPTER TWENTY-NINE

The security checkpoint at Logan stopped Cassie cold. She couldn't get through without a boarding pass, so she couldn't follow the hordes of state, TSA, and Boston police officers scouring the airport for Professor Whitney. They searched the area ahead of the checkpoint quickly and then swept further into the terminal. She promised Bart that Whitney had been here, but he wouldn't sign off on an airline ticket to get her past the checkpoint even though she was the only reporter who knew what was happening. She waited half an hour, but not a single officer left the terminal. She stayed on, hoping a cluster of blue uniforms would escort the professor out, but they never came. They could have used an employee exit, but there would have been a celebration if they found Whitney. She couldn't print her instinct, so after another fruitless half hour of waiting, she decided to check in with Bart and write a story that would sound pretty much like everyone else's.

Halfway back to the departures curb, a television displayed an aerial shot of a multiple car crash. Police officers and firemen surrounded a jumble of vehicles. She wouldn't have stopped, but the car at the bottom had a wing-like door that reminded her of Randy's McLaren. The news chopper panned over a group of police and dogs lined up to search the surrounding woods. She assumed a fugitive escaped from the crash, until the camera panned to a raging fire in the forest.

How did a car accident start a fire that deep in the woods? She couldn't hear the audio with all the commotion around the ticket counters. She almost gave up when she saw the graphic reporting that a state police helicopter had crashed at the scene. When she saw I-95 on the monitor, she panicked and called the Rhode Island State Police.

Interstate 95 was the only convenient way to get from New Bedford to Foxwoods, so Randy would have traveled that stretch of road. He was an incredible driver. If anyone could avoid an accident, Randy could, but she had a queasy feeling as she waited for a dispatcher to pick up. He confirmed Randy's car had been involved in the crash, but he wouldn't comment on Randy's injuries. She told the dispatcher she was Randy's girlfriend, but he wouldn't tell her more. Did that mean he was dead? Had they opened the door to pull his body out? She asked if anyone was hurt. Pregnant silence. She didn't wait for an explanation; she hung up and hustled across the skyway to the garage, dialing Randy's cell as she went.

Cassie redialed Randy's number every five minutes as she raced out of Boston. She sped up every time he didn't answer. The side trip might kill her article about the explosion at the Institute. Would Bart print it a day late? She pictured him pounding his fists on her desk. Her writing time was slipping away. There was precious little she could do that all those police officers could not, but she had to see what happened for herself.

Traffic snarled fifteen minutes south of Providence, shortly after the I-295 interchange, and that was where her piece on the Institute died. She could have opened her laptop there in the triple-lane parking lot, but her thoughts were abuzz with what she'd find on the roadway up ahead.

It took two hours to cover twenty miles. A news helicopter circled a column of smoke rising from the forest. A line of cones and a blinking sign herded traffic into the left lane, as if cars moving 3 mph couldn't move over without a huge blinking arrow pointing the way. The mechanical clicking measured the time slipping away while she was trapped in her car.

Inching ahead, she passed glass fragments scattered across the roadway and a group of highway workers tasked to sweep them up.

The rear half of the McLaren had been crushed and mounted by an amorous Hummer, but the passenger compartment survived fairly well. Seeing it in person gave her hope Randy had escaped the wreck on his own. She drove past the cones that outlined the crash area and parked beyond a line of emergency vehicles, immediately drawing the ire of the nearest officer who wore the blue uniform of the local police.

She identified herself as a reporter and asked to speak with the officer in charge. The man in front of her didn't budge.

"Where's your vest?" he challenged.

When he shifted, she saw a coroner's van that had been blocked from passing traffic by two ambulances. Seeing it, she froze. She pointed at the black van but couldn't speak.

"Are you ok?"

"The McLaren belongs to my boyfriend." She stumbled over the last word like a foreign object too big for her mouth.

Sympathy broke on the officer's face. He turned toward a group of officers clustered around the back of an SUV.

"His name is Randy Black," she offered, hoping he wasn't planning to desert her there by her car.

"Get your vest," he said and went to the cluster of men, tentative about interrupting. Cassie retreated to her trunk and pulled out the yellow reflective vest the paper had issued her. She'd never worn it at a crime scene. There was no real danger with the traffic accelerating to 15 mph, but without the vest, she would have been sent away. As it was, she was left standing between her Corolla and the ambulance for a full fifteen minutes before the officer in charge, a brisk lieutenant who eyed her like he had much better things to do, walked over and introduced himself.

As he faced her on the shoulder, a wispy ribbon of smoke rose from the forest behind him. Voices shouted. State troopers from Rhode Island and Connecticut mixed with firemen and local police officers at the edge of the woods. The lieutenant side stepped to capture her attention.

"I'm sorry," she said and introduced herself. "You've got about everybody represented back there, don't you?"

He brushed off her insight and launched into the details of the accident, seemingly frustrated by his liaison responsibilities. There was only one other news team on site, a camera crew parked further down the highway, broadcasting a wide shot of the scene.

Cassie should have noted the details the lieutenant rattled off. Somewhere during his speech she realized this, but didn't take up her pen. She dreaded news of Randy and until she heard what she was listening for, she couldn't concentrate on mundane descriptions of the vehicles involved and the likely time and cause of the accident. She tried to reason out the result herself. There were no victims standing around and no patients inside the ambulances. Where were the people from the cars? And why the coroner's van?

"Any injuries?" she finally asked as much to draw herself into the conversation as to get the answer she dreaded.

"Five fatalities."

The answer stole her power to respond.

When she looked up again he said, "We're not releasing names pending notification."

Aside from the McLaren, the damage didn't look serious. Only one windshield was splintered. Certainly no one had been ejected. All of the vehicles were upright and except for the McLaren, the passenger compartments had little damage. If he hadn't said five people died, she'd have assumed the injuries were all minor.

"Can you comment on the causes of death?"

"I can't speculate. When the coroner releases his report, we'll give a briefing to the press."

"This crash didn't kill five people?"

"Not by itself."

"Randy Black wasn't among them?" she asked hopefully.

"We can't be sure."

"What do you mean you can't be sure?" How could he not know? What were all these cops doing? She'd been calm and professional until then, but his ambiguity brought an edge to her voice.

"We have a number of—" he began.

"That's his car back there." She pointed angrily.

"Please relax. I know that's his car. Get control of yourself and maybe we can help each other." The lieutenant gestured toward another officer. "Can you describe him to me?" he asked as the other man trotted over.

"He's six feet tall, thin, brown hair, and he's usually wearing jeans and sunglasses."

"How about his complexion?" the second officer asked.

"He's white. Tan, but white. What's going on?" Cassie asked.

"We have four deceased without identification, three vehicles that we can't trace ownership on, and a dead man lying in the street whose car doesn't have a scratch on it. The situation is fluid, but the good news is we don't think your boyfriend is a victim. If you'd stick around to confirm that, it'd be a great help."

If Randy wasn't here, where was he?

"If you're looking for a perp, he's a good place to start," a voice chimed in from behind. Cassie turned and saw Officer Pinto and Walter Macedo.

"What are you doing here? A little out of your jurisdiction?"

"As are you," Pinto said. "I went to Boston to see your boy and apologize of all things. I found his room empty and a bombing not two miles away. I saw you at the bombing, too. Now we find his car in the midst of this mess and, surprise, here you are again. It's just too good to be true. Who could imagine he'd get out of the hospital and freak out so soon?"

"You don't believe that."

"Don't I?"

"He saved forty people. If—"

"I've got work to do," the lieutenant said, but there was no doubt he'd listened to Pinto. "You three continue your spat, just keep out of our way. Ms. Corcoran, we'd appreciate it if you waited for the coroner."

The lieutenant turned and walked away, leaving Cassie, Walter, and Pinto on the roadside with the junior officer to keep them away from the wreck.

Cassie wanted to yell to the lieutenant that she could call Randy on his cell, but he hadn't answered his phone in three hours of trying.

"Give it up, Cassie," Walter said. "You can't keep following this guy around like a puppy dog."

"You couldn't be more wrong, Walter. He saved those people in New Bedford. You're going to find out that's exactly what he was doing here."

"Just like he saved Charles Marston. Saved him from a life of sin."

Gunfire erupted somewhere beyond the helicopter crash. The search team ducked for cover at the edge of the woods. Cassie rushed around the coroner's van and held her head low. Walter and Pinto beat her there. The faraway shots continued in heavy bursts that overlapped each other.

Hiding behind the van she realized where Randy was and prayed he was safe.

CHAPTER THIRTY

Randy took the cell phone out of Ty's hands, pressed the send button twice, handed it back, and said, "Nice and quiet. Let's not call attention to ourselves until we're ready."

"I could have done that."

"But I wouldn't know who you called, would I?"

"Where's all that Christian faith?" Gretchen asked, her voice too loud.

Randy hushed her and whispered, "I might be short on trust sometimes, but it keeps me alive."

In the stillness Randy heard the phone ringing in Ty's ear. The three of them faced the headlights from their vantage tucked in a clump of bushes. Something rushed past the marshy bog they had crossed. The man had been close and rushed off toward the ringing phone. If he wasn't focused on the truck way out in the woods, he might have heard them talking and closed in. Gretchen hadn't seen him, but Ty peered into the darkness, watching for him to reappear.

"He was close," Ty whispered.

"There'll be more," Randy said, readying his rifle.

"Is that you over there?" Ty breathed into the phone.

He held it away from his face so Randy could hear what was said in response. "Of course it's me. Stop whispering and get over here."

Randy gestured for him to flick the lights. Ty relayed the command and in a few seconds one of the headlights went out and came back on. The man was standing in front of the truck and had covered the light with something.

Randy took the phone. "You've got company. Forty-five degrees right of where your truck is headed. These guys are none too friendly. If I were you, I'd put the high-beams on him and back the heck out of there before his eyes adjust."

"We're not going anywhere without Ty and his friend. Who the hell are *you* giving me orders?"

"I'm a friend. Turn the truck or you're going to have an ugly surprise in about forty seconds."

Cloth brushed the speaker. In the distance a figure moved in front of the headlights in the direction of the cab.

"When he gets blinded, we get the hell out of here," Randy said "Let's get up higher, behind something solid. If they start shooting, run. The noise will cover us."

Gretchen looked puzzled. Ty didn't move.

"Your friends are armed, aren't they?" Randy asked.

Of course they were.

"They can't see us," Gretchen said.

"It doesn't matter if they can see us or not. There's going to be a lot of lead flying and this bush isn't going to protect us. We can't wait to see what happens. We've got to go."

Ty rocked forward. His pants were soaked and he moved robotically, like the Tin Man with his joints rusted. Randy gripped his hand and helped him up. It was ice cold. "We've got to dry you off."

The vehicle in the woods turned and stopped with the man centered in its headlights. He dodged upriver, flanking Ty's friends. Randy warned them of this in a whisper. He didn't get a response and assumed the phone was lying on the seat of the truck. There wasn't time to wait. Randy signaled and they turned their backs and hurried away.

The three trudged off in a jerkily-moving line as they tried to avoid the branches that came out of the dark to swipe at their faces. They climbed a slight incline where the tree trunks grew thicker. Taller trees meant thinner undergrowth and easier passage.

Behind them machine-gun fire rattled to life. Shouts followed and a series of single shots rang out. Then, seconds later, a more potent weapon started ripping off rounds in their direction, the barking of the automatic more urgent, the muzzle aimed in their direction. They only heard half the battle because the men chasing them were using silenced weapons. At least now those weapons were aimed at someone else.

A slug knocked into a nearby tree and ping-ponged through the forest. Randy grabbed Gretchen and pulled her down on the other side of the incline. They lay together with their heads covered by the crest of the slope, hair resting on leaves and pine needles, arms and legs sprawled through low-growing bushes.

More guns joined the fight in a stuttering cacophony. Randy heard something from the cell phone speaker and pressed it to his ear. "Give me a left flank. Now!

"Johnson, get somewhere you can get some perspective!

"Keep his head down damn it!

"Beautiful, now we've got him."

Reports punctured the gloom.

Randy didn't dare lift his head over the rise, but the commanding voice on the cell phone came from a well-trained soldier. If the men from the Hummers had been as organized, Randy, Ty, and Gretchen would have died before the helicopter arrived. As the gunfire settled into short bursts, Randy imagined the men from the truck getting the upper hand. He couldn't be sure whether this was insight or just wishful thinking and he wasn't going back to find out.

They hugged the slope and listened to the action across the river. After several exchanges, the shots slowed. They were surprising when they came, like the last few kernels in a bag of microwave popcorn as you pick it up.

A man screamed in pain and a second later two authoritative shots boomed with a pause between to allow for careful placement. The recipient was sent to Judgment. Several seconds passed in silence.

"Let's go," Randy whispered and helped Gretchen to a crouch.

Ty pointed back in the direction of the shots.

Randy wasn't going back there in the dark. They couldn't know who won the gun battle. Only Ty knew for sure what his friends wanted and Randy wasn't crossing the marsh at night.

Randy urged Gretchen past Ty. Ty huffed and waited there on the hill, but Randy knew he wouldn't leave her. Eventually, he followed them down the slope and deeper into the trees.

"Who were those guys chasing us?" Randy asked Gretchen when they had a little space from Ty.

"I don't know."

"They were pretty pissed. What did they want with you?"

Her feet shuffled in the leaves and stopped.

"That was an ambush back there. That wasn't road rage. They want something and I can't help you if I don't know what it is."

Even in the dark he noticed the flinch of her right hand. She was nervous about something she was carrying. Something small enough to have in her pocket. Ty caught up enough to hear their conversation but didn't interrupt. If he was driving her south and was willing to kill to defend her, he knew what she was hiding. Maybe he wanted it for himself. He was aware of her every move. His interest could have been romantic or professional, but there was no way of getting the truth out there in the dark.

"Where did you come from?" Randy asked.

"Boston," she answered and told him about the Institute in Cambridge.

Randy asked if they had heard the explosions that morning. Terror painted Gretchen's face even before he finished his question. She wouldn't tell him where she was when the bomb went off or how she was connected to it, but she was involved somehow. She wasn't the bomber. More than likely she was a target and she'd been chased all the way across Rhode Island to the state line. Randy had been praying for guidance at the moment of the explosion. He and Gretchen had been across the river from each other and from then on, events conspired to bring them together seventy miles away.

Randy was brought here to protect Gretchen. He was sure of it.

Ty seemed intent on protecting her, too, and quite capable of doing so, but there were no coincidences in this second phase of Randy's life. Gretchen wasn't an easy woman to stay close to. She had some strange ideas about right and wrong—none of them flexible. Her stubbornness could get them all killed and it made perfect sense that Ty needed help. Ty would make a strong ally, but his insistence on meeting up with his friends was worrisome. Randy couldn't be sure if he was called to help Ty protect her or if Ty was just another enemy she needed protecting from.

CHAPTER THIRTY-ONE

When the guns had been still for three minutes, Randy heard barking coming from the highway. Voices shouted instructions and the rush of leaves and cracking branches sounded like a bulldozer pushing in toward the crash site. Police dogs. And behind them, plenty of cops. If the dogs scented them on the highway, they'd tromp through the marsh and swim the river right to them. The cold water would slow the handlers, but the dogs would run straight to their hiding place. They couldn't outrun dogs—definitely not in the dark. Ty might shoot them, but Randy couldn't. His only hope was for the dogs to fixate on the gunfighters, so he led Ty and Gretchen slowly up a rise to a boulder with a generous wrapping of mossy vines. They sat in the leaves directly behind it, where the boulder trapped their scent and deflected their voices deep into the forest.

The dogs kept coming, barking and thrashing through the woods somewhere near the helicopter crash. The dogs would smell gunpowder, the gunmen, and the two college kids. Which trail would they follow? Randy hoped the handlers would lead the dogs away from the river, but they kept driving in, closer to the tree crossing and closer to the gun battle that raged in the woods. Ty's friends and the remaining gunmen would be forced to run. With any luck they'd all stay on the other side of the river, and the cops would find enough bodies to keep busy until morning.

Ty hunkered down at the near end of the boulder where he could cover the path they'd followed up the hill. He fingered his phone but didn't dial. The ring would give away his friend's position. Instead he ejected the clip from the AK-47 and counted the shells. Randy picked out another boulder at the crest of the hill thirty yards away. If someone came upon them, he'd run there. Together he and Ty could defend the hill against anyone climbing through the brush.

An oddity struck Randy as he watched Ty silently work the weapon. What college kid could pick up an unfamiliar rifle and handle it expertly without a moment's hesitation? He moved like a trained soldier. He had killed at least two men—one point blank. Wouldn't a college kid be having flashbacks about now? Did he serve in Iraq or Afghanistan before college? The plumped-out features could conceal a few extra years. That might explain his comfort with combat, but not his pre-occupation with getting Gretchen to his friends. What did he know about these two?

Gretchen looked ordinary, huddled against the smooth rock in her brown vest. Randy wouldn't have guessed men would kill for her secrets. Beyond her, Ty visibly shuddered. Now that the sun was down, his wet pants were conducting the cool night air right through him. The flimsy Hawaiian shirt wasn't helping. Gretchen was wet up to her left knee, but she seemed comfortable even pressed against the cool rock. Randy was somewhere between. The heavy shirt he'd warn for the ultra-cool casino air serviced him well, though his Doc Martens were soaked and his toes were numb. As soon as the dogs were quiet they needed to get warm.

He remembered feeling the bomb blast from his hospital room and wondered how Gretchen and Ty were connected to it. He prayed he wasn't helping the bombers escape. He turned toward Gretchen, determined to get some answers. The next time he pointed a gun at someone he wanted to know who they were before he decided to shoot or hold his fire.

"What happened at school this morning?" he whispered to Gretchen.

"At the press conference?"

Randy's stomach gurgled. He hadn't eaten anything since lunch. It was dark now and dinner was desperately in doubt. He nodded.

"These men climbed up on the roof and started shooting."

Randy prompted her through the story of the bombing and her escape with Ty. According to her, Ty was a classmate and lab partner, nothing more. They were talking when the chaos erupted and he helped her get away. She wasn't in love and she didn't seem appreciative of what he'd done. There was more anger in her story than anything. She didn't like her professor or the reporters and she seemed barely able to tolerate Ty in spite of all he'd done. Randy decided she was a bitter young woman and that he shouldn't expect much thanks when this was over.

"They blew up the lab and chased you all the way here. Why?"

She paused, puzzled by a question she should have long considered.

"What were you working on? What was the conference about?"

"Solar energy. Our professor was going to announce a big breakthrough. Our sponsors were there, TV reporters, newspapers. It was big."

"Where's your professor now?"

"Missing."

"Let me guess. The rest of the team is missing and all the research went up in smoke. You and Ty are the only ones left?"

"Me more than Ty. He just joined the team." Before Randy could ask about the coincidence, Gretchen told him Ty had been on the team for almost two months. Randy wanted to believe it was good fortune that someone with such military skill happened to be with Gretchen during the attack, but the little yellow warning lights kept flashing on the dashboard of his brain. But if Gretchen hadn't known the discovery was coming two months in advance, Ty certainly couldn't have known.

"Did you work on this discovery?"

"Yeah." She instinctively looked down at her vest pocket and Randy knew she was carrying something from the lab. "Professor Whitney created a way to miniaturize solar panels. The transmission facility is woven together in a miniature fabric that delivers energy though a grid from the exterior of a surface to a battery housed on the inside."

"Is that worth killing for?"

"Not in itself. But we created a panel of incredibly thin layers. It can be applied to any surface and it looks like paint, energy-producing paint that is amazingly durable."

"Paint that harnesses the sun's energy. Cool."

"Very cool. Imagine if the entire south side of your house collected energy every sunny day. You could sell electricity to your neighbors and still use as much as you want."

"But what if the *paint* gets scratched?"

"The fabric routes around dead cells. A huge scratch might disable a sizable collection area, but the rest of the cells would go on working like nothing happened. The efficiency was the big news. These panels were going to be so small and so effective you couldn't afford not to use them. They'd be on every building and every car in three years."

Randy sat back against the boulder and gazed out into the dark, imagining a car that ran on solar power and a house that heated and cooled itself. Someone would have to find a way to store all this new power, but once they did, there would be some big losers. Nuclear, coal, and big oil would be marginalized. Oil companies would disappear. They might remake themselves into pioneers of this new technology if they discovered it soon enough, but more likely the executives would hold on to their old ways and go down fighting.

The biggest losers would be countries built on oil economies. Some didn't have other natural resources or high-tech workforces, but they did have masses of people dependent on a flow of virtually free money. Those countries would come completely unhinged when their astronomical wealth vanished. Massive social welfare programs would cease. Horse farms would wilt in the desert. Palaces would crumble.

If they knew the potential of this discovery, these entitled few would spend billions to protect their wealth and power. There would be no limit to the devastation they would inflict to keep the secret from surfacing, no end to the men they would send to destroy Gretchen and Ty. At that moment Randy felt incredibly small. He was glad to be hidden in the forest even if he didn't know why Ty had attached himself to Gretchen.

"What's in your pocket?" Randy asked.

Her eyes flashed down and he knew.

CHAPTER THIRTY-TWO

Cassie shuffled her overnight bag onto the console and rested her laptop there while it hummed to life. If she was going to be stuck sitting in her car, at least she could get some work done. The ambulance shielded her from the headlights and she didn't register the rush of traffic anymore. Cramped as it was, she was a lot more comfortable in her car than Randy and the two college kids were out in the woods. It wasn't cold enough to die of hypothermia, but she had to keep the heater running to stay warm. She wondered how the three of them had come together. Unlikely he'd known the girl from New Jersey or the guy from Texas. If they met during the crash, how did they convince him to come along? Had they escaped the gunshots together? And what were they doing out there? Were they lost or running for their lives?

If he'd answer his phone, she'd tell him what she'd learned.

Professor Whitney was on the run, too. She wondered if he could be alive since hundreds of people were looking for him and not a single sighting had been reported, not even during the search at Logan. It seemed she was the only journalist who knew about that. She could have capitalized on that knowledge with an article, but she'd missed deadline. Her next story wouldn't be printed for over twenty-four hours. By then the professor's condition could be all over television.

The bigger question Cassie pondered was what to report about the professor's discovery. She'd jotted a few hundred words about the press conference so the paper wouldn't be shut out of the story, but she'd learned quite a lot after leaving campus. She'd called a few faculty members of the energy department, and the bizarre story of Dr. Patrick Whitney had unfolded.

The first professor she spoke with tried to convince her that the press conference was a farce. For years Dr. Whitney had been a philandering drunk who came to work hung over and unshaven, then hid in his office while graduate assistants delivered his lectures. She detected jealousy in the assessment, especially when he bemoaned the lifestyle Proctor Energy financed for Whitney. She didn't think much of the sporty BMW and the Beacon Hill apartment until another professor mentioned the same things. Neither of the men thought Whitney capable of a newsworthy discovery, not with the pitiful effort he put forth. The second professor supposed Whitney was faking his own death to run off with an undergraduate and an armload of embezzled grant money. Wouldn't that be a delicious twist?

The explosion stopped the press conference and freed Whitney from making an announcement, but if Whitney was faking his disappearance, could he really blow the second lab in Westborough and kill those students? He'd have to be pretty sick to do that. Whatever his problems with booze or money or coeds, Cassie couldn't believe he'd go that far.

A third professor had a more upbeat perspective. He said Whitney had cleaned himself up recently. The last few days he'd been coming to work sober and working long hours in the lab. Maybe Proctor had heard about his carousing and threatened to cut him off, or maybe, even in his stupor, he'd discovered something so monumental that the thrill prodded him to clean himself up for the spotlight.

Cassie turned on talk radio. The host characterized Whitney as a drunk. A student called in to say he was incompetent and to blame him for the explosion. Idiot. How does a solar panel explode? Others talked about his Beacon Hill apartment and the cops waiting for him to return. She remembered one of the professors saying Whitney had a house in Newport. If she could be the first one there, she might find something worth reporting, but she couldn't get inside, not without help.

She called Randy's cell phone again and got no answer.

They could be in Newport in less than an hour if he would only answer.

There was another call she'd been putting off since the cop asked her to wait in her car until the coroner was ready. If she believed Randy could be in one of those bags, she wouldn't be able to think of anything else, but she knew Randy was out there in the woods. The call would be almost as unpleasant as looking in the bags.

She dialed Bart's office, let it ring through to voicemail, and left a message. Then she dialed his home and he picked up on the second ring. She apologized for disturbing him, but the real affront wasn't the timing of her call but what she had to report.

"A little late for deadline."

"You got my story earlier?"

"Four people killed, three missing, two buildings destroyed and you send me three hundred words? Don't they deserve a hundred apiece?" Bart groused. "What do you expect me to do with that? Run it on page one with nothing behind?"

"I'm working on something bigger."

"Not the accident on I-ninety-five?"

"I'm down here now."

"Great. I've got two crime reporters and they're both fifty miles outside our coverage area playing tug-of-war over the reputation of a hoodlum."

"What?"

"Walter's down there."

"I know. I saw him earlier. But he left."

"He knows your friend was involved in that accident. He's trying to link him to the bombing and right now, his timeline fits."

"Randy was in the hospital this morning."

"He was out before noon. Is it coincidence that the building blew right after he was released?"

"He didn't have time to plant a bomb."

"Tell Walter that," Bart said.

"You're not paying him to chase that crap, are you?"

"Like I'm paying you to find your boyfriend in the swamp? I'm sure our readers are dying to know how he makes it out."

"That's not fair."

"I'm not paying for Walter's trip either."

Either? She hadn't checked in with Bart before calling the hotel. If the story was good, Bart would pay. She couldn't leave Randy alone down here and it was starting to look like he'd spend the night in the woods. She was staying until he came out whether Bart paid or not. "I'm working on another story."

"I hope so. When people see smoke and dead bodies on page one, they expect a follow-up. I hope you're not going to submit it telepathically like the follow-ups you sent in today. That makes it really hard to get the layout right."

He had a right to expect more, but she'd been chasing Whitney and then Randy half the day. "I'll get your story and it'll be bigger than Heather Lovely."

Bart huffed on the other end. "I'm not going to wait that long again. If that's your plan tell me now and I'll put Walter back on the clock."

"Walter couldn't write this story."

"Try telling him that."

CHAPTER THIRTY-THREE

The stainless-steel egg cupped in Gretchen's hands looked like something a wealthy Easter Bunny would leave behind. Randy watched Gretchen unscrew it. The inside was padded with foam. A plastic capsule cushioned in the center held a thumb-sized flash drive. She handled it with such deference he knew it held the last remaining copy of the professor's work.

Gretchen screwed the two halves back together. "I invented it myself. It's waterproof, shatterproof; heck, you can run it over with your car and the data will survive."

"Do you always carry it around?"

The accusation shocked her. Wasn't it an obvious question? Two groups of gunmen desperately wanted the data inside that egg. Why did she have it? Did she cause the catastrophe? Is that why they chased her all the way from Cambridge to the Connecticut woods?

Randy tried again. "If the lab was destroyed this morning and all the data with it, how'd you get the information on that flash drive?"

Gretchen didn't answer.

"You downloaded it beforehand. You knew they were coming!"

Ty peeked in their direction. Gretchen didn't blink.

"If you want my help, you're going to tell me why you made that copy."

Ty looked away, but he was completely still, intent on her response.

Randy re-gripped the AK-47 and Gretchen tensed. He couldn't shoot her, but panic flashed across her face.

"Whitney's been different lately. We ran an experiment last night and I think he knew it was going to work. Don't ask me how. I didn't really believe him, but I went in early to check the results. And he was right. It worked. The Nanopanel is ready for commercial production, theoretically anyway."

Ty snapped his head around. He didn't know what was in the egg until then and Randy could feel his anger at the betrayal. She'd lied to him. She'd almost gotten him killed and Randy threw her deception out into the open. If Ty decided the data was more important than the girl, Randy could wake up to find the girl dead and Ty gone. If he woke up at all.

It was too dark to walk out. Ty had been shivering and it was only going to get worse. Randy needed to keep himself warm and he couldn't make noise while doing it, so he stood with his torso erect and his knees bent and let the strain on his quadriceps silently warm him as he listened for dogs in the distance. When the searchers had been quiet for twenty minutes, they hiked in the opposite direction to settle in for the night. Going to the cops would have gotten them safely out of the woods, but Randy wasn't ready to be interrogated about the crash. After stealing her professor's work, Gretchen wasn't eager to talk with them either, so they each carried their secrets deeper into the woods.

Randy stepped over to Ty and put a hand on his shoulder to test his ease. Ty agreed to guard the rear with a sturdy whisper, his hostility to Gretchen apparently dissipated. Randy led Gretchen south into a dry section of forest. He wished he hadn't happened upon these two. The discovery was important, but she didn't seem particularly worth saving. He might have overlooked her theft more easily if not for her vendetta against God.

They continued slowly in the moonlight. Randy cracked several branches underfoot, but Gretchen seemed to sense the pressure and shift her footing, moving almost soundlessly over the forest floor. Ty crashed loudly enough so they always knew where he was, but not so loudly it was obvious he was signaling his friends. It may have been a mistake leaving him back there, but Randy didn't trust him alone with Gretchen.

When they were two hundred yards farther from the river Randy asked, "So why did you take it?"

He couldn't see her face, but clearly heard her whisper, "They didn't deserve it."

"Who?"

"Proctor Energy. They don't own the sun. Why should they make billions when other people need the money more?"

"They funded the research, didn't they?"

"So? We did the work."

"Your professor received a salary, didn't he? And you got equipment and tools to help you learn about energy research, didn't you?"

"That doesn't change anything."

"If it was your work, you would have paid for the lab equipment."

"I couldn't afford that."

"So you couldn't do it without their investment." She kept walking without acknowledging his argument. "I'm getting pretty hungry. Does that mean someone is going to come walking out here and feed me?"

Ty closed in from behind and for the first time Randy felt uneasy not being able to see him. Ty walked quietly enough to monitor their conversation and Randy hoped that was all he had in mind. Gretchen didn't appreciate Randy's take on individual responsibility. Ty didn't pick sides.

"If we let people lie around and do nothing, then pick them up and give them everything they need, that's not helping them. Don't you get that? If those oil guys weren't paying for this research, your discovery never would have happened."

She pushed ahead of Randy into the dark.

She probably hated airplane manufacturers and pharmaceutical companies, too, but she'd fly across the country for a life-saving medical procedure. She wouldn't think twice about the people who'd invested themselves in making that possible. She'd resent their fees even as she breathed oxygen she never would have tasted without them. No matter what he said, she wouldn't see how foolish her position was.

Randy couldn't help thinking about how the work of these hated capitalists changed the world. The capital needed to build jumbo jets was immense and yet they made people's lives so much more convenient. The hours and the technology spent to research and test new drugs amounted to astronomical costs, many of which would never be recouped. He wondered how Gretchen would respond to these ideas. Could she really despise every sort of investment? Would she be happier if some ubervirus like AIDS wiped out half of the world's population? The burden would be easier for the Earth to bear. She'd be happy about that. He wondered if she cared about people in general or just those who were too lazy or too stupid to fend for themselves.

Ty shivered as he came even. When they stopped walking for the night he was going to risk hypothermia. Randy was thinking about the risks of building a fire when Gretchen angled over to a thick stand of pines at the base of a hill.

She snarled at Randy and went to work plowing up the thick bed of pine needles and stacking them in a semi-circle. The men helped and soon they had a wall to shield the flames from view. She piled dry pine twigs in the center of the cleared area, then arranged them, beginning with the smallest of twigs leaned together to support each other. Above this she allowed a fair amount of air space and stacked increasingly larger branches. She produced a box of stick matches from her vest and with one match, she ignited a few oak leaves beneath the twigs and the whole construction sparked and crackled to life.

Ty was most thankful for the fire. He stood close, heating his pants until it hurt and then turning to heat the opposite side. Randy worried about the gasoline that had been on Ty's shirt earlier, but it had evaporated. He smoothed his pants, warmed his hands, and he never did catch fire.

Both men were voracious after hiking through the woods for hours. Neither expected to skip dinner and find themselves cut off until they made it out of the woods. Gretchen was nonchalant about going without food and water until morning and her attitude put a cap on the men's grousing.

When they were warm and resigned there would be nothing to eat until morning, they settled in around the fire for the night. Gretchen braced her back against a pine and heaped pine needles over her legs and up to her chest. It looked foolish, but when Randy tried it, the insulation warmed him almost immediately. The two men faced her across the fire, all three covered in auburn needles. The four weapons lay within reach.

Well past midnight when Ty was snoring and Gretchen hadn't moved in an hour, Randy slipped his hand over and pulled Ty's SW99 to him. He wasn't sure what he expected to happen, whether he thought Ty would turn against them and take the egg for himself, or if he expected some wild accident along the trail, but Randy gently eased the magazine from the gun and emptied it bullet by bullet. He unloaded the chamber, replaced the magazine, and hid the bullets deep inside his front pants pocket where the tight fit would keep them from jingling as they walked.

Randy closed his eyes again and listened to the sounds of the forest, expecting a deer or raccoon to wander into camp.

All night he wondered what bound Ty to Gretchen. The egg provided the clearest motivation, but it could have been something sappier that had Ty trudging after her. A glimmer of romance could get some guys on a fool's errand like this. Surely he could have ended things by now if all he wanted was money. Still, Randy kept his AK-47 within reach and tuned himself for the slightest shift in the pine needles next to him.

CHAPTER THIRTY-FOUR

Randy didn't hear the rustling until Gretchen had brushed off the pine needles and melted into the stand of young pines. His eyes popped open. When he couldn't see her, he braced himself to jump up and follow, but she pushed her way through the branches headed toward the swamp, parallel to the river. If she'd decided to run, she would have headed toward the highway, not into the deepest part of the woods. He relaxed and a moment later heard the telltale zip and rustle. When the stream of liquid pattered down on the needles, he was glad he hadn't rushed after her.

The sound awakened the same need in him and he gathered himself, waded into the scrub, and leaned against a tree trunk where he could hear Ty's movements and Gretchen's return. She came back to her pine needle bed while he was clearly in view. He didn't turn around and she didn't complain about his choice of trees or the lack of civilized amenities.

Back at the remnants of the fire, Gretchen looked the same as she had the night before. Her hair was still neatly pulled back. She'd leaned against the pine tree all night and must have had globs of pitch in her hair, but she didn't fidget with it even once. She looked well rested for a hunted woman who'd stolen a multi-billion dollar technology and spent the night on the forest floor. He wondered if her conscience nagged her at all.

Randy stepped on the barrel of Ty's AK-47 with one foot and kicked the lump of needles with the other. Ty reached for the weapon before opening his eyes. When Ty realized it was Randy's foot on the barrel, Randy stepped off.

"Morning, Sunshine."

Ty bristled his whiskers against the grain and lingered over the sandpapery friction. Then he squeezed his cheeks together with both hands as if the pressure would force life into his elongated face. His cheeks plumped out again and he scanned the ashes and the pine needle beds. Randy could see the reality of the day hitting him. They were still in the woods. It was still cold. There was still nothing to eat. Ty shook off the needles and wandered in the direction Randy had gone, though several yards further. He didn't look like a cold-blooded assassin, but Randy didn't consider giving him his bullets back.

The dawn light sliced in among the trees to reveal a series of hills that climbed steadily to the south. The shortest path out of the woods was across the nearest hill toward the sun, but if they followed the sun they'd come back to the highway within sight of the crash. Someone would be waiting there. If the police had called off the search and gone home, the gunmen or Ty's friends would be parked nearby. It would be safer to go south a mile or more before they came out of the trees. They were alone in the woods and they'd stay that way as long as they moved quietly and stayed under cover.

When Ty returned, Randy pointed out a stand of mature trees toward the base of the next rise. The going would be fairly easy, but Gretchen insisted they head further west down to an overgrown clearing crammed with head-high bushes that would fight them at every step.

"I'm starved. You don't have any more of those muffins, do you?" Ty asked as they started downhill.

"I Didn't think you liked 'em." She seemed to enjoy their desperate hunger.

"I'd eat a dozen about now."

"Don't worry, we'll find something."

"Find something?"

"Guess where those muffins come from?"

Ty was baffled. Randy's hunger made him curious, too.

Gretchen pointed to a wide oak, then stepped over and picked up a freshly dropped acorn from the ground. She tossed it to Ty and then plucked a leaf. "See these lobes here?" She indicated the rounded edges. "These rounded lobes are from the soft oaks. They're less bitter."

"So you can eat 'em?" Ty asked.

"That's what I put in my muffins."

Gretchen walked on down the slope toward the bushes. She had to be hungry, but she ignored the acorns. Ty grabbed a handful and stuffed them in his pockets. Randy picked one up, cracked it open, and gave it a taste. Nuts pack an incredible amount of energy, but the acorns were so bitter he couldn't scrape the remnants off his tongue fast enough. Ty ate three before giving up, but he didn't dump them from his pockets.

When they caught up with Gretchen, she was bent over the base of an oak tree with a knife in hand. She sliced up and down along the base and came up with a thick red mushroom that was marbled like a slice of beef. It looked much more appetizing than the acorns and it was much bigger.

"You sure that's all right?" Randy asked.

"Positive. It's a Beefsteak Mushroom."

Randy held out his hand for a piece.

"There are some mushrooms that are harmless if you cook them but will kill you if you don't. Knowing that, I cook all my mushrooms," Gretchen warned.

Randy withdrew his hand and followed Gretchen further along. She trimmed three more mushrooms off nearby trees, handing them to Ty as she did. The red coloring stood out from a distance. Ty and Randy spread out and checked the neighboring oaks with no success. Three mushrooms wasn't much of a breakfast for a woman and two men who hadn't eaten dinner the night before.

Gretchen found something among the bushes and whistled for Randy and Ty to come down. She was stripping tiny red berries off a bush that was loaded with them.

"How do you know this stuff is ok to eat?"

"I'm a forager," Gretchen said. Randy knew what foraging was, but didn't believe Americans roamed around picking food from the wild. "About twenty percent of what I eat, I find in nature. This is Autumn Olive.

It's highly invasive. You can't kill the stuff without digging it up. It spreads like wildfire, so we're actually doing some good by eating the berries and tossing the seeds back under the plant where they won't grow."

Randy popped a few of the red berries with three light speckles in his mouth. The seeds were half the size of the intensely sour berries, but Randy leaned the AK-47 against a tree and stuffed his mouth full. They surrounded the bush, spitting seeds as they chewed.

Gretchen ventured further into the clearing to try berries from another bush, which she reported tasted even worse. A stirring at the edge of the clearing caught Randy's attention. He lifted the rifle and watched. Ty saw his movement and stood perfectly still. When Gretchen shifted to yet another bush, a cottontail scampered out of the brush and froze beneath a fallen tree.

The bead settled just inside the rabbit's ear and Randy fired, the zip from the muzzle barely audible. The rabbit flopped once and was still.

Ty tossed his berries on the ground. "Now that's breakfast." He high-fived Randy and ran over to collect the kill.

Gretchen pushed out of the brush. When she saw the brown carcass and Randy with the gun, she scowled at him like he'd just killed a relative and she was plotting her revenge.

"Bastard," she hissed. "What did you do that for?"

"Quiet," he whispered harshly. "You'll give us away."

She seethed at him from just outside the bushes. "How could you?"

Randy stepped closer. "Maybe you can live on berries and a couple of mushrooms, but we're starving."

She glared and Randy could see tears welling in her eyes. The death of the rabbit, a creature she'd never seen alive, had a huge impact. He was glad then that she'd left the AK-47 behind back across the river. She still had the knife she'd used to cut the mushrooms. She was so upset over the rabbit that she might have hastily fired a shot at him, but she couldn't look him in the eye and stab him. She muttered a string of obscenities, took the mushrooms from Ty, and headed for camp. They needed her knife to clean the rabbit, but they let her get far ahead before following.

"Dude. If there's a way to piss off Nature Girl, you just found it."

"Seems I've found a few."

"Killing one of her furry friends. You won't top that."

"Why don't you go beg for the knife. She might want to stick me with it if I get too close," Randy half joked.

Randy lurked at a safe distance while Ty convinced her that she needed them to get back to civilization and that they wouldn't make it without something to eat. She gave up the knife grudgingly and set about rebuilding the fire.

Ty hovered over the rabbit while Randy made an incision from the anus to each ankle, and around each foot. Then he began peeling back the fur. Ty held the feet to give Randy leverage. He sliced and pulled in turn, peeling off the fur, like removing a sweater that had been glued on. Each slice allowed a bit more play and soon they had the fur pulled up to the neck.

Randy made a final cut along the abdomen and removed the organs, careful not to contaminate the meat.

"Farmer?" Randy asked Ty as he scooped the organs aside.

"My dad is," Ty answered.

Farm living explained why Ty hadn't wretched during the process. Charlie Marston had lost his lunch the first time they'd done this together, but that was the point. Randy had been establishing for young Marston who was the pupil and who was the master. This was entirely about breakfast.

The fire crackled behind them. Gretchen turned her back to them so she didn't have to see what they were doing, but they weren't going to eat a wild rabbit raw. Fortunately, Gretchen was adamant about cooking her mushrooms. Randy didn't have matches and he would've bet Ty didn't either.

"What's up between you and Nature Girl?" Randy asked.

"We're friends."

"Where are you taking her?"

"Home."

"Where's home?"

Ty hesitated. "Somewhere in New Jersey."

Randy looked up from his work. "Let me get this straight. You're not getting any, but you're driving her to New Jersey and in the process you're out here dodging bullets?"

"Not a very good bargain on my part." Ty focused on the carcass.

"Don't shit me. What's your story?"

"We were standing together when these guys opened fire from the roof. People were screaming and running everywhere. I shoved her in my car and here we are. What am I supposed to do? Leave her on the side of the road?"

What a bunch of crap. No one drove four hours to be a nice guy. Then four hours home. The lie made Randy angry but he tried not to let it show. "Where'd you learn to shoot?"

"Army. Four year hitch."

Randy had never enlisted. He knew nothing about the military, so it was another dead end. Ty had business with Gretchen. He was protecting her for now and without him, Randy might make her so angry she'd stomp off on her own and get killed. They needed each other. Randy didn't need to trust him. He just needed to keep the group together until they could walk out. After that, would he send them on to New Jersey? It seemed like a dangerous idea, but he didn't have a better one.

They shaved saplings and fashioned a rotisserie over the fire. Gretchen averted her eyes and made a show of eating her mushrooms without offering them any. When the rabbit was finally cooked, Gretchen walked away while they tore into the hot flesh with hungry fingers.

CHAPTER THIRTY-FIVE

While Randy was hiding deep in the woods that night, the lieutenant kept Cassie on the highway for the chance she could identify one of the victims. She tried to write while waiting in the Corolla, but she couldn't help watching the coroner in the rearview mirror. When he moved to the other side of the wreck, she took some notes for her story, but kept wondering who caused the wreck and why Randy ran off into the woods. She waited for what seemed like hours before the lieutenant appeared and brought her over toward the crash.

Five man-sized black bags were arranged in a line at the roadside with enough space between for the coroner to open the bag and display each body. The first guy was an American, a big guy with a surprised look on his face. Cassie told the coroner she didn't recognize him and he zipped the bag closed.

The next three men were Middle Eastern. She didn't recognize them either, but their faces were contorted, bruised, and battered. She barely glanced at the third man, but that was enough for the gashes to imprint themselves into her memory. The fifth victim had a hole in his forehead, but it wasn't as gruesome as she expected a gunshot to be.

When the last bag zipped closed, she was thankful Randy wasn't in one of the bags, but she was bitter that he'd made her look at the graying skin and ghastly expressions. Randy was too smart to end up in one of those bags, but she'd seen him fall not long ago with a ragged exit wound bleeding through his fingers. He was obsessed with his mission. He'd sacrifice himself to accomplish it. He was as fanatical as any suicide bomber. His methods were entirely different, but how many of these zippered bags would she see if she moved into that house? How many nights would she pace the floor praying he was alive? The house was too far from the sea for a widow's walk. What Cassie needed was an overlook of the highway because the road and not the sea would bring Randy home.

Finished with her grizzly task, she chose a hotel ten miles south of the accident, barely into Connecticut. It was a low-rise, populated by habitual gamblers trying to save a few bucks by avoiding the on-site accommodations. Cassie picked it because it was just off the I-95 onramp and she could get back to the accident scene in minutes.

She indulged in her second pepperoni pizza of the day and spent the night nibbling and waiting for her cell phone to ring. Sipping bottled water made her feel better about her diet. A Coke would have helped her stay alert, but she couldn't concentrate on writing anyway. The chatter from the cable news garbled her thoughts and kept any coherent ideas about the professor and his discovery from gelling into publishable form. Mostly she stared at the screen and typed random questions to herself, none of them strong enough to spur a burst of activity on the keyboard. She was more interested in the breaking news updates that repeated themselves every fifteen minutes. In spite of her distraction, she developed a workable headline, "Cloud of Suspicion Overshadows Solar Breakthrough."

Eventually she fell asleep with the lights on, the laptop humming on the threadbare bedspread, and the news anchors blathering away on the television. The pained Middle Eastern faces haunted her sleep until finally she saw Randy's lifeless face in one of the bags and heard the zipper closing. She flung her arms wide to keep the bag open and pull him out. Her knuckles smacked the keyboard. Cradling sore fingers, her eyes opened to a hint of daylight at the shades and an annoying voice in the room.

"... he's a train wreck. It was just a matter of where he'd derail."

"So, you're familiar with this man?"

Cassie blinked. The woman on the screen wore a bright red jacket and shared a microphone with Walter Macedo while cars rushed past in the background. The smashed cars and emergency vehicles were gone.

"Familiar? Familiar enough to know he's a menace. I'm a newspaper reporter from New Bedford and I authored a series of stories about a family he attacked in Westport."

"And you think he's come here to the Connecticut / Rhode Island border?"

"I know he has. His car was towed from this scene last night." Walter pointed to the ground emphatically. "And the police found over forty-thousand dollars cash in his trunk."

The woman looked embarrassed that she hadn't gotten that information herself. "Anything else you'd like to share with our viewers?"

At this point Walter seemed to realize he was giving his story to the competition and that Bart was going to scream at him the next time they talked, but the camera lens mesmerized him. His story flooded to half a million people all over the country without an editor cutting it down or softening his claims. Walter's true voice was being heard and he was power-drunk with the microphone in front of him, even if some part of him understood the editing was for his own good.

"You should know he's incredibly destructive. He demolished a two-hundred-foot barn and two houses in Westport. He put an established winery completely out of business for eighteen months. And just a few months ago he used military grade explosives to destroy a one-hundred-year-old building in downtown New Bedford."

"Are you suggesting he's connected to the bombing yesterday?" The reporter couldn't believe her luck.

"Don't do it, you asshole," Cassie yelled at the television.

"...was in Boston yesterday at the time of the explosions. The forty-thousand dollars cash is more than enough for this lunatic to destroy the campus lab and shoot those people. He lives for this kind of thing."

The reporter eased away from Walter slightly and it looked like she was getting ready to cut him off. Her eyes shifted as Walter talked. Cassie assumed someone was telling her through her earpiece to end the interview. The reporter turned around for an instant then dashed three steps to her right. The cameraman moved along and kept her in frame as if the two had choreographed the maneuver to get Walter off the air.

"We've just learned that police have recovered an undetermined number of bodies in the forest behind me."

Right on cue, two paramedics came out of the forest towing a sled with a body bag strapped on top. As they broke free of the brush and into the grass, a police officer came up behind the reporter and warned her not to get any closer. The cameraman kept her in half the frame and the men climbing the slope behind her in the other half. She went on about a series of gunshots heard there after sunset.

She rehashed the helicopter explosion and showed the rescue vehicles parked on the roadside. The police hadn't released the names of the crewmen or their condition, but several news stations had broadcast footage of the helicopter burning. She reminded her viewers that no one was taken from the woods by ambulance and advised them to expect the worst. The studio host asked a few questions about Randy and a student named Gretchen. When she said they were seen running into the woods together, Cassie stood up on the bed. The police believed Gretchen had been kidnapped. Randy Black was a person of interest in the case.

One day after talking to the governor's man, Randy was back in the news. What was he doing out there? Why would he risk going back to jail?

She grabbed her phone from the nightstand and clicked his name from the list of contacts.

"Hey," came the familiar reply.

"Where the heck have you been? I've been calling you all night."

"Swamps aren't famous for good cell coverage. I'm trying to find my way out right now."

"Do it quick. The cops think you kidnapped a girl named Gretchen. Tell me she's with you and she's ok."

"She's fine. We could use a ride. Neither of us is anxious to talk to the boys in blue. Could you help us manage that?"

"You have a thing about getting picked up in the woods, don't you? Should I look for the tight lumberjack shirt and baggy pants?"

"Funny. You in the area?" he asked.

"Ten miles from the crash. Where are you?"

"Southwest of the crash. Trying to avoid the highway."

"Hang on," she said and pulled up a Google map. "If you head southwest, you'll come to a road in about a mile and a half."

Cassie told him the police had found the money and impounded his car. She also told him what Walter said on television and that the police were looking for him. She thought she had the bad news to deliver, but when he told her not to park on that back country road, she wasn't sure.

Randy told her to drive back and forth every ten minutes and to avoid anyone but him or a young woman with straight brown hair and a brown vest. Cassie skipped her shower and pulled on her pants and shoes as fast as she could. Randy didn't say it, but she knew whoever had killed the men on the roadway was still out there. She packed her things and started her Corolla three minutes later.

Chapter Thirty-six

"We need to go this way," Randy said, pointing 120 degrees away from the sunrise. Ty stepped up with his AK-47, casually matching Randy's stride and asking what they'd find there. Gretchen was already thirty yards ahead in the right direction. She hadn't looked at Randy since they'd eaten the rabbit, and she didn't look back then. Randy told Ty about Cassie loud enough for Gretchen to overhear.

"Your friend's more trustworthy than mine?" Ty challenged.

"My friend is a woman."

Gretchen turned.

"She's a newspaper reporter," Randy continued, "and she's going to meet us in broad daylight. She doesn't carry automatic weapons. I'd say we can take a ride from her." He gestured back the way they'd come the night before. "She's much less dangerous than the alternative. Do you disagree?"

Hearing this Gretchen turned her back and picked up her pace.

"Smartass," Ty said and nudged him with the butt of the AK-47. "My friends would have had us home by now."

"Those of us who survived."

Ty laughed it off, but there was no doubt he was anxious to find the men behind the headlights the night before. What did they want with Gretchen? Would Ty slip away and call them while Randy wasn't watching? Ty still hadn't checked the SW99 at his back. Randy had no idea what he'd hoped to accomplish by unloading the gun. He didn't expect to encounter anyone on the walk out—as long as they were quiet. If Ty was going to shoot anyone that morning, it was going to be Randy or Gretchen. So even though he felt guilty, he didn't tell Ty what he'd done. With luck they'd get out of the woods, meet Cassie, and part company.

At the base of the slope they pushed through the thorny Autumn Olive bushes and Randy's luck turned for the worse. On the other side of the thicket, the ground rose steadily off to the east, but in the southwest where Cassie planned to meet them, it slid lower into a swampy tangle of brush and muck that stretched as far as they could see. Solid footing was spotty, and deep water could force a dead end anywhere along the way. Rather than risk teetering out where they could be trapped, they turned east and stayed with the solid ground. They angled south as much as possible, but the terrain was determined to squeeze them back toward the interstate, the police, and the cameras that would be waiting.

They climbed into a thick stand of trees where the canopy blotted out the sun, stunting growth on the ground and making foot travel much easier.

"What's your deal?" Ty asked when they were free of the briars.

Randy trudged on without answering. The truth would be impossible to believe while he was carrying two guns.

Ty kept on. "I never thanked you for what you did on the road last night. That was no amateur move taking out three of them with your car. You drive professionally?"

"I'm not a stunt man or anything. Just a regular guy looking for work."

"What do you do?"

"Same as you."

Ty's eyes swept to Gretchen. He nodded and fell back. Randy felt like they'd come to an agreement, that they were both protecting her, but Ty was hiding something and Randy didn't like having his back to him.

Randy trotted ahead and caught up with Gretchen on a small crest that overlooked a spreading plain of soaked earth to the right and a series of low hills to the left. The land seemed determined to squeeze them back to the highway and they had to change plans if they wanted to stay dry. He opened his cell phone to dial, but had no service. He'd try again somewhere higher and nearer the interstate.

Gretchen snickered as the phone snapped shut.

"You have something against telephones?"

"You really need to make a call now?"

The girl sorely needed a backhand. He waggled the phone in front of her. "I'm not in the mood to get wet. If my friend meets us far enough south, I thought we could come out on the highway without being seen. If I could get some service, this would be a damn nice piece of gear."

"Just another piece of silicon crap that sucks power twenty-four-seven and then ends up in a landfill, leaking nickel cadmium and concentrating toxic elements that were fine until we pulled them out of the ground and refined them."

"Speaking of toxic, you should try bottling that. I'm just making a call. I'm not dumping sludge on the poor forest creatures."

Gretchen went white at the mention of sludge. Randy shook his head. Why did she get so fired up about the smallest things?

He led her down the slope just outside the bushes that thickened at the water's edge. Ty allowed himself to fall further behind. Randy wasn't sure if he was avoiding Gretchen's nagging or getting ready to call his buddies.

"So, you don't have a cell phone?" Randy chided.

"Absolutely not," Gretchen said. "I don't need movies, Internet, and music everywhere I go. That's what's wrong with this world. No one is happy unless they're sucking power a hundred different ways at the same time. No one can just sit and think anymore."

Maybe entertainment technology was a waste, but Randy wouldn't agree with her out loud.

"Think about this," she went on. "How much do people spend on gym memberships? They pay money to stand on a treadmill and go nowhere while they're exercising. And then, to top it off, they watch television and fill their heads with mindless babble. We spend millions of dollars running to get nowhere when we could stay home and climb some stairs or go outside and enjoy a trip around the block and maybe see our neighbors. Is it worth all the metals we mine, the plastics we concoct, and the electronics that go into these contraptions?"

"Yeah." Randy laughed out loud. "They should just come with us, get lost in the woods, and eat some berries."

Gretchen's face soured, probably at the thought of the rabbit. She said nothing for several minutes as they pushed through waist-high brush.

"So what got you into energy research?" Randy asked.

"All the fossil fuels we're burning. We're choking the atmosphere."

"So you wanted to save the world?" Randy saw her shrug and corrected himself. "I know, the world will be fine, it's the people who are at risk."

"The people are the problem. We're pushing so many animal species to extinction. There's no helping them once they're gone. People will survive. There's too many of us not to. What could possibly kill six billion people?"

She said it like she was looking for ideas. AIDS was Randy's first thought, but people learned to cope. An epidemic would thin the population, but never endanger it. Gretchen rooted for man's predators, microscopic and otherwise. She was the angriest person Randy had ever met.

"So what did you do before you became a researcher?"

"I helped preserve South American jungles from encroachment."

"By people?"

"What else?"

"I'm guessing the banners and community meetings didn't cut it?"

She gave a knowing smirk that piqued Randy's curiosity.

"Ok, spill. What'd you do down there?"

"We burned them out." She saw his reaction and backtracked. "Rallies and lobbying didn't work. The government puts its hand out and looks the other way, so we did what we had to."

"What exactly did you burn?"

"The development."

"Doesn't burning houses cause more pollution than it prevents?"

"The settlements were delayed for years."

"At what cost?"

"We didn't hurt anyone but the developers."

"You can't burn millions of dollars of property and expect to get away with it."

"We didn't at first. We held rallies. We spray painted warnings. We flattened tires, fouled engines, cut power lines. We did everything to stop them, but they wouldn't listen." Gretchen's eyes sharpened as she told her story.

"They had a right to be there. Didn't they fight back?"

She grimaced.

"That's why you left."

"They tried to kill me."

"Now I get it. You have the data because you like being chased."

Gretchen whirled around. "Every member of our team is dead. If I hadn't taken the data, the Nanopanel would be gone forever."

Ty caught up from behind. "Keep your voice down. It's going to be ok, Gretchen. It really is." Ty seemed sure of himself for a man on the run.

When Gretchen relaxed and they started walking again, Randy sidled up to Ty. "Thought more about where you're taking her?"

"She wants to go home."

"That thing belongs in Cambridge."

Ty walked ahead.

Randy imagined a billion-dollar discovery sitting on Gretchen's kitchen table while fifty armed thugs hunted for it. These two seriously needed a better plan. Maybe Cassie would know who was investigating. Maybe she could help change Gretchen's mind and get the egg where it belonged.

A chainsaw moaned in the distance.

"Sounds like they're coming for the helo," Ty said.

"Let's hope that keeps them busy while we slip out of the woods."

CHAPTER THIRTY-SEVEN

The AH-64A Apache settled over the river where its defenseless law enforcement cousin had hovered ten hours earlier before crashing to Earth and bursting into flames. The Apache brought its 30 mm M230 chain gun to bear on the surrounding woods, ready to unleash over six hundred rounds per minute as it rotated in place, but the gunner couldn't identify a single target. They had hauled over from Otis knowing that State One was shot down, but not expecting the responsible parties to stick around overnight to get lit up. This was New England. Helicopters didn't get attacked here. In three years at Otis they'd never fired at a live target. It was nothing like their buddies in Iraq who launched Hellfires, destroyed tanks, and came home heroes. Protecting America at home might be important, but it was hopelessly boring. Getting out for a hop was a treat.

The investigators worked a grid over the crash site, identifying parts, labeling them, and hauling them away for reconstruction. A platoon from Otis surrounded the investigators and faced the forest with M4 Carbines at the ready. The gunner could see the charred circle where the fire had raged the night before. It was out now and the hunt for the men who took down State One was just as cold as the soggy, blackened earth, but he wouldn't let himself get cocky. If it was a shoulder-fired missile that took out the copter, he'd need every second to get on his target if one was pointed his way. Later, the investigation would discover small-arms fire had crashed State One. The craft was barely bullet resistant, but it was an open window that allowed the shot that killed the pilot and brought them down hard.

The pilot took them up for a tight circle directly above the site. They watched the trees crashing down to open a corridor from the highway into the woods by the river so the heavy equipment could haul out the remains of State One. Six green Humvees lined the highway along with as many state police cars, a bunch of local police cruisers, and almost a dozen civilian autos. There was a swarm of activity between I-95 and the crash site. There were no bad guys anywhere in the vicinity, but it was a great day to fly. They made a wider circle that produced nothing but a patchy green view of trees and swamp, exactly what the guys flying over Vietnam must have seen before the bullets started flying.

They kept making circles and the gunner kept his eyes on the ground ready to zero in on anything moving among the trees. Finally, after a half hour of circling, the platoon on the ground spread out and started working the brush. They formed a line straight across, looking for bodies or the lost college kids who'd been out all night. If they were going to make contact from the air, they'd do it out ahead of this group.

The pilot swung out a hundred yards ahead and they scanned the ground for anyone retreating into the swamp.

Chapter Thirty-eight

The second time the helicopter flew overhead, Ty and Gretchen dashed for cover and stayed hidden well after it disappeared. Their zeal worried Randy and he wondered what brought these two out here. Gretchen was an energy researcher. That much he believed, but he couldn't understand how she could sacrifice so much for the environment and then pollute it by burning houses. And how could she risk losing a technology that promised to save so many of her precious animals? Ty was even more difficult to gauge. He acted more like a soldier than a college kid. Ty may have been innocent, but it was more than quick thinking that had paired these two together.

A movement down the slope distracted Randy from his thoughts.

A hunched figure climbed out from behind a boulder. He wasn't wearing black like the men from the highway, but if he was hiding from the helicopter, he was trouble.

Randy clenched a fist. Ty understood the signal immediately and remained motionless, except for his head, which swiveled toward the danger and back to Randy for direction.

Gretchen looked confused, but when Randy signaled Ty to find cover downhill while he went uphill, she skirted a tree and hid from the intruder.

Randy nestled in at the hilltop and looked down through the trees at the man climbing toward them. Ty moved well down the slope and braced against the base of a massive pine with his AK-47 aimed at the ground.

The intruder was too close not to have seen them move, but he kept walking right to Gretchen's hiding place as if he were alone in the forest.

His slick, jet black hair was pulled back on top of his head, and his eyebrows and nose were big enough to stand out from thirty feet away. The Institute sweatshirt belied his purpose. He wasn't bumbling into their midst. That was an act, but he didn't appear to be armed.

Randy pointed the AK-47 at the man and bellowed, "Close enough."

The intruder stopped abruptly and raised his hands in mock confusion that didn't fool Randy. He'd been aware of them since the helicopter passed.

"I don't want trouble. I'm just looking for a friend."

The deep baritone prompted shuffling leaves under Gretchen's canvas shoes. She ran to him so fast that Randy's rifle was aimed at the center of her back. When he saw her arms around him, Randy raised the muzzle skyward and stepped away from cover, but hesitated where he could easily dodge back.

The man looked embarrassed by Gretchen's clinging. He wasn't Gretchen's boyfriend. They didn't kiss and the man only touched her high on her back, but she was glad to trade Randy and Ty's protection to be with this wanderer.

They stood with their feet interspersed.

Randy stepped closer and heard her say, "Thanks for finding me."

Ty lowered his weapon, but didn't leave cover. He grimaced from behind his tree instead. Clearly he knew this guy from the Institute and didn't like him. Was he on the losing end of a love triangle? Or was it something more? She'd never thanked him for being shot at, getting wet, and sleeping out in the cold. Why was she thanking this guy? All he could do was bring her to the highway. Anyone could find it by following the sound of rushing cars.

What was so special about this Middle Eastern guy? Knowing Gretchen, he was probably a foreign-born, vegan socialist.

"How'd you find us?" Ty barked.

The man shifted his head around Gretchen's. "I heard shouting and headed over. It was mostly luck, I guess."

Randy adopted Ty's caution. "You heard us from where exactly?"

Demitri introduced himself and explained that a group of students heard about the accident on the news and shuttled down to help find Gretchen and Ty. They had started at the crash site about an hour earlier.

It wasn't even seven o'clock. Could they really get college students out of bed and all the way down to Connecticut this early? Randy noticed Demitri's pants weren't the slightest bit wet. Could he have crossed the swamp and stayed dry? Could he have gone around? And where were the other searchers? Randy paused to listen and couldn't hear a single trampled branch or calling voice.

Ty still hadn't moved away from his tree. Randy wondered if Ty just didn't like Demitri, or if he shared Randy's suspicion that there was more to Demitri's trip to the woods than a search for a college friend.

Randy craned his neck back and forth in exaggerated fashion and asked, "So you stumbled out here all alone and walked straight to us?"

Gretchen rolled her eyes.

Demitri replied coolly, "Like I said, I heard yelling." He sensed Randy's skepticism and turned his attention to Gretchen. "The highway's about a half mile this way."

He pointed in the direction Randy had been avoiding since they started moving. Randy wasn't walking out onto the highway unless they went further south, but Gretchen swooned at Demitri's suggestion.

"It would be safer to follow our original plan," Randy said.

Ty left his tree and moved to the center of the group. He knew Gretchen would go with Demitri and he made clear that he'd choose Gretchen's company over Randy's. Demitri eyed the AK-47 uneasily.

Ty could protect Gretchen from this one college kid. Randy wished he hadn't emptied the SW99 hidden at Ty's back, but it wouldn't come to that. Demitri was no match for Ty's training, wherever he'd gotten it.

"I'm not going down there if I don't have to." She indicated the swamp.

"Where are you going to go?" Randy asked.

"We'll be fine," she said.

"The highway's not far," Demitri added. "There's a bus waiting."

Ty's expression begged Randy to come along.

CHAPTER THIRTY-NINE

Logic told Randy that Gretchen would be safe with the two men, so why didn't he want to let her go? Ty could protect her and she was obviously infatuated with Demitri. The terrain was wide open and they could easily follow the rush of cars to the roadway. It was the coincidences that bothered him. She'd stolen the data on the day the lab was attacked. Ty conveniently appeared to help and now here was Demitri volunteering to guide her from the woods. The discovery was worth killing for and Gretchen Greene would be a willing victim. Randy didn't trust any of them.

He called her over. "Are you sure you feel safe with them?"

She was annoyed by the question. "It's over. We're going back."

"I hope you'll make the right decision when you get there."

She spun and stomped back to Demitri like a ten year old.

She wasn't giving the data back. Should he care? God didn't put him here to save money for some oil company. Would He? Was that company supposed to save thousands of people by giving them free power? Randy had done all he could. Hadn't he? She hated Americans and capitalists and he couldn't change her mind. She'd be sure to give the discovery to someone who was neither. That someone might use the discovery against Americans, even bleeding-heart liberals like Gretchen. He should have been proud to see her headed safely back to school. What she decided then was beyond his control.

Randy's phone buzzed, startling him. He leaned the rifle against a tree and answered while Gretchen, Demitri, and Ty huddled several feet away.

"It's drier if you come more south than southwest," Cassie said.

"That's what we've been doing."

"So the three of you are almost out?"

"Not quite. Looks like you're only going to have one passenger."

"What happened?"

"They met a friend from school."

"Out there? That's strange, isn't it?"

"A busload of kids came down from Boston. They'd rather follow him back to the bus than follow me through the swamp. Can't really blame 'em."

"What about you?"

"I don't really have a choice."

"Not after what Walter said on TV. I wouldn't risk it."

"Where are you?" he asked.

"The breakdown lane. A mile north of the crash. I'm making some calls while I wait for this hot guy to get his butt out of the woods."

"Learn anything?"

"The professor didn't have a lot of friends on campus," she said. "Adult ones anyway."

"What are you saying?"

"He spent all his time boozing and chasing college girls. The other professors think he faked his disappearance. They say he didn't want to lose his funding so he staged the press conference and the attack."

"How can a college professor afford to hire mercenaries?"

"How does he afford a BMW Z4 and a second house in Newport?"

Randy flashed a look at the three students edging away from him and wondered what they'd say about their professor. Gretchen believed in the discovery, but could the professor have fooled her?

Cassie was still talking in his ear. "... no way he discovered anything. He was drunk most of the time and he was almost never in the lab."

"Let me check on that from this end," he said.

Cassie agreed to meet him in about half an hour and clicked off.

Randy took two steps forward. "Gretchen. Can we talk a minute?"

Demitri minimized a sneer.

Gretchen huffed over. "What?"

Ty and Demitri kept a polite distance and pretended to open a conversation, but they both did their best to eavesdrop.

Randy nodded to the pocket of her vest. "You sure that thing works?"

"I saw the results myself. What do you care? We're leaving."

"Some of the other professors think Dr. Whitney faked the results and staged his disappearance."

"I'm telling you it works," she said loud enough for everyone to hear. "The blood was real. That wasn't a show back there. I saw Josh get shot and I felt the ground shake when the bombs went off."

"So you believe the professor?"

"Lucky bastard."

"Lucky why? Because of the discovery or because he got out in time?"

"Both. He didn't deserve this." She patted her pocket. "He was wasted most of the time. Sure, he gave directions on what he wanted us to try, but we did all the work. He hid in his office and drank himself silly."

"But he pointed you in the right direction."

Gretchen drifted away into thought.

The men stopped talking in the background.

"Something change in the last few weeks?" Randy asked.

"He was frantic. Sober and frantic."

"Think the sponsors put a gun to his head and he finally came through?"

"It doesn't work like that. You can't make a discovery like this in a week. This is a decade of work."

She was right. Randy was out of his depth. He couldn't understand the data. So why did he care about a professor he'd never met and a woman he couldn't stop arguing with? He convinced himself to let them go as the helicopter made another pass, lower this time. Gretchen and Ty made no attempt to hide, but Demitri sidestepped behind a tree.

"We better get going," Demitri said. "The longer we stay, the further apart the search team gets."

Strange no one from the team had stumbled into sight. From their position at the crest of the slope, they had a great vantage down through the trees on either side. If anyone passed within a hundred yards, they would hear and see them. But no one had come. Demitri wouldn't have been tasked to search an area this big all by himself.

"Why don't you call them and let them know you found her? They can pull the search party back together right here." Randy pointed to a clearing on the hillside.

Demitri withdrew his phone from its holster and dialed. He could have been calling anyone, so Randy wouldn't take whatever he said too seriously. What worried Randy was that he hadn't made the call on his own and he hadn't been very excited to find them. It was like he knew where to look.

Ty had been eying Demitri suspiciously since he found them. Until then, Randy had assumed it had more to do with competition for Gretchen's affection than anything else, but then he wasn't sure.

Demitri's phone connected.

"I've got them both." He waited several seconds.

"We're a half mile in. South of the river. Can we meet here?

"Ok. We'll be out in ten minutes." He hung up the phone and turned to Randy. "They want us to come out. They're calling everyone back."

Ty stepped up and shook Randy's hand. "Thanks for what you did yesterday. We would have died against the guardrail if it wasn't for you."

Gretchen waited for the two to finish shaking hands then turned and fell in step with Demitri. She never thanked Randy for saving her. She never even looked back. They trailed away and relegated Ty to rear guard.

Randy turned south, down the opposite hillside.

He didn't feel like he'd just saved two people from certain death and he felt no closer to saving himself. Gretchen was destined to give that technology to someone who hadn't created it and didn't deserve its benefits. No amount of arguing would change that, but he couldn't shrug off the defeated feeling that bogged him down as he descended into the wetland.

Could he really expect to change her views in such a short encounter? Even if he could, should he?

CHAPTER FORTY

Hisham huddled in a shallow crevice between two huge boulders and watched the boy's progress on the monitor. Perched high above the clearing, he was ready if the boy would only get moving. That the boulders were left behind by retreating glaciers meant nothing to him. He ignored stunning greenery that could only grow on palace grounds in his homeland. He fumed instead. He was tired of over-indulged Americans and the incompetent fools he'd been given as assault troops.

The young student was no exception. He was paid well for achieving admission to the prestigious school, but the boy lacked commitment. Why couldn't he stop the girl from escaping the city? He was soft from the easy American life. A better man would have shot her on the campus lawn, gathered up the evidence, and been done with it. Hisham should be stretched out on a jet headed east instead of folded in among the dreaded rocks where the cold sapped his body heat. He'd cursed the boy numerous times before his phone call and several times since.

Finally, the red dot moved toward him on the monitor. He craned his neck and checked on the Hummer parked on the narrow path leading to the highway. No one could have taken it without him hearing, but seeing for himself put his mind at ease.

Back to the monitor.

He checked the positions of his three remaining men. Three stationary red dots formed an arc ready to envelope the incoming dot. The boy kept leading them toward Hisham at the center. Soon he'd see all four of them.

The Proctor man and the man from the highway who'd caused so much trouble would pass right below the boulders. The boy was about to earn his pay. Pity if he was caught in the crossfire, but there would be little backlash.

Hisham whispered into his radio for the men to pay attention. The group would be stepping into view any second.

Demitri kept a torrid pace down one slope and over another with Gretchen close at his side. Ty fell back. He knew they were walking into trouble. What would she do if he dropped Demitri without warning? She might scream and attack him or she might turn and run right into Demitri's friends. She'd never believe the kid was a spy for the cartel.

Demitri angled down toward a wide clearing when it would have been shorter to stay with the high ground. The boulders and trees along the ridge made the clearing an ideal ambush. Ty was out of time.

"Ah," he wailed. He folded over and clutched his ankle. "Hold on!"

Demitri didn't stop until Gretchen came back to help.

Ty hopped to a tree and sat with his legs extended and the rifle across his lap. He scanned the ridge for Demitri's friends until Gretchen arrived.

Ty whispered, "You can't go down there. It's not safe."

"What are you talking about?" she asked incredulously. To Ty's dismay she spoke loud enough for Demitri and even his accomplices to hear.

Ty clutched his ankle as if he were in serious pain. "It's killing me," he said, but the ruse didn't work. Demitri stormed back.

"Don't do it, Gretchen," Ty urged. "All he cares about is the data."

Her head swiveled from Ty to Demitri and back. She stepped down slope toward Demitri and stopped. Ty shouldered the rifle and leveled it on Demitri's chest. "Stay back," he ordered.

Gretchen's first instinct was to run to Demitri, to protect him, but she locked eyes with Ty for an instant and held fast. Ty could drop him if he went for the girl. Demitri respected the rifle and stayed where he was.

"Don't listen to him, Gretchen," Demitri said.

Ty took his eye from the sight. "If I wanted to hurt you, I would have done it long before now. Without me, you would have died yesterday."

"Sure, he's keeping you alive because he wants to lock you up in his laboratory. Did you tell her who you work for, Ty? Did you tell her which cause she's been fighting for?"

From her first rant against capitalism, Ty knew this moment would come. He'd kept his feelings to himself not for the good of the assignment, but because she'd never understand what he stood for. The truth was in her interest, in America's interest, but Gretchen was too angry to hear it.

"I'm here to help you, Gretchen. If you go with him I can't protect you." He shifted his eyes toward the ridge, then in a wide semi-circle behind her. If she understood what he meant, she didn't check the perimeter herself.

"Big oil doesn't have your interests in mind," Demitri challenged.

Gretchen gasped and jumped straight back from Ty, not directly toward Demitri, but closer.

Ty settled the sight on Demitri's left eye. Even as he did, he knew the gun wasn't helping him convince her that he was the good guy. He wasn't a practiced liar, particularly not where Gretchen was concerned, and the truth disarmed him. He was here to protect her, but she was so stubborn she'd spurn his help because she despised his employer. He couldn't prove Demitri's allegiance to the cartel, and even if he could, it might not matter. She'd warmed to Demitri because he was a foreigner.

Demitri took a step toward Gretchen.

"One more and I'll drop you," Ty warned.

"Are you nuts? He's helping us." Gretchen looked back and forth. She'd always preferred Demitri. If Ty didn't come up with a convincing argument, she was going to make a horrible mistake.

"He's helping us do what? Find the highway?" Ty asked. "Think about what's been happening. People have been trying to bury the team and that technology since yesterday morning. Since the press conference."

"Not people, Proctor Energy," Demitri countered.

"Listen, Gretchen. We had everything to gain from that conference. Our management flew in to take photos with Professor Whitney and the team."

"And then you killed him," Demitri said.

"We didn't kill anyone. Think, Gretchen. Why would we kill the professor? He was the goose that laid the golden egg."

"You had billions in refining revenues to lose," Gretchen said.

"Demitri's friends have trillions at stake. We can use our capital to refine oil or make Nanopanels. It doesn't matter to us."

"You're married to oil."

"We don't own the oil, we buy it. We could just as easily buy chemicals for solar paint. Think about it. Who's married to oil?"

Gretchen focused intensely. Ty waited. The conclusion was a fragile one for her. The people with the most to lose were the ones pumping the oil from the ground. The problem for Gretchen was that she deemed these countries so much more worthy than her own.

While Ty and Gretchen were focused on each other, Demitri ran four quick steps to his left and was behind Gretchen where Ty couldn't take a shot. Gretchen stood idle, consumed by her thoughts and unaware of the real threat until Demitri pressed the knife to her throat. Ty was on his feet in an instant, but his opportunity was lost.

"What are you doing?" she screamed at Demitri and struggled against the arm across her chest.

Demitri pressed harder with the blade and she stopped squirming. He kept himself behind her where Ty couldn't get a clean shot.

"You should have listened," Ty said.

He knew the skirmish would bring trouble, but he couldn't help remembering how she had treated him like a rube, snubbed him for this traitor at every turn, and never thanked him for saving her life. She deserved to be at Demitri's mercy, but Ty wouldn't abandon her. She was more than a job, but he'd never understand why she hated her own people.

How could he convince her that he was a good guy and a Proctor Energy employee?

CHAPTER FORTY-ONE

Randy bulldozed his way through a tangle that guarded the wet ground between him and his rendezvous with Cassie. The rifle opened a path into the briars but didn't protect his hands from scrapes and cuts. His Doc Martens were wet again and he was too grungy to go to the casino. So why was he rushing? He wasn't in a hurry to get out of the woods, he was rushing to see Cassie. It would take a few days to replace the McLaren. He'd spend that time moving her into the house and getting comfortable having her there.

His phone buzzed. He fought to get a hand free and answered.

Cassie greeted him breathlessly.

"What's going on?" he asked.

"I just passed the crash site. There are plenty of army or maybe national guard vehicles, but there's definitely no bus and no sign of a search party."

"Shit." Ty's pleading eyes made sense. He knew Demitri was a problem, but couldn't say so in front of Gretchen.

"Could be nothing. The bus could have—"

"Could be our guy isn't who he says he is."

Randy closed the phone and leapt out of the bushes. Branches slapped red welts across his face as he raced out of the swamp. When he was clear, he accelerated to a full run and angled south, keeping the ridge between himself and the path Ty, Gretchen, and Demitri had taken so they wouldn't hear him coming. The hillside absorbed the flare of dry leaves under each long stride and, at his pace, he closed on them fast. He kept to the open, clutching the gun and trying to remember how many bullets were left in the magazine. He ran blind to what lay ahead, the noise at his feet masking all other sound including whatever surprise Demitri had waiting.

He crossed a small hill and ran down the other side. A tractor trailer passed from left to right two-hundred yards ahead. He slowed and angled up the slope to look for the others. A string of thick pines dotted with boulders lined the ridge. Randy headed for a cluster of trees that would give him a good vantage and good cover.

When Randy was twenty feet up the hillside, a dark figure appeared among the trees and a bullet whizzed by Randy's head with a crack of energy, but no report.

He darted low along the hill. Bullets sprayed all around him.

In the midst of the attack, he remembered the chainsaws and the helicopter. He took cover behind a wide maple, unscrewed the silencer from the end of his rifle, and fired. It was a signal for help more than an assault on the man high above. The rattling report delivered a clear message to the men across the river. He fired a second time to be sure he had their attention.

The man who'd been almost completely concealed until then, shifted back in the trees and fired another burst. Randy ducked back behind the wide tree trunk and covered his head. The burst ended with the telltale clicking and scraping of a magazine change, but the man was too far away for the information to be helpful. Randy couldn't climb the hill before he reloaded. Getting caught halfway up was suicide.

Inexplicably, the man lurched forward and dropped facedown.

Ty heard two booming shots and caught movement on the ridge.

The black-suited gunman emptied an entire clip, changed magazines, and took aim. He was no cop. He was part of Demitri's ambush. Ty shifted his aim over Demitri's head to the ridge and fired a single shot. The man jerked and fell so forcefully, there was no doubt he was dead.

Gretchen panicked and dropped for the ground, thinking Ty had aimed for Demitri. Demitri was just as surprised. He loosened his grip and luckily, he didn't slice Gretchen's throat as she fell.

Without Gretchen as a hostage Demitri stood exposed.

Ty swung on him, intending to shoot.

"You don't want to do that," Demitri said. "She'll never forgive you."

Did she still love this guy after he'd held a knife to her throat? Would she curse Ty for killing him? Would she ever talk to him again?

Ty hesitated too long.

Gretchen stood up and Demitri grabbed her. What was she doing? The shot was gone, but he didn't take his eyes off the sight.

Voices shouted in a language of muddled hard consonants.

Ty glimpsed three men in black suits closing on him. They all had automatics raised. The man in the center screamed orders Ty couldn't understand.

"You better put that down or you're going to be full of holes," Demitri said, reveling in the turn of events. "You can't help her if you're dead."

Ty set his gun down and one of the gunmen took it and balanced an AK-47 with each hand. Demitri released the girl and shoved her toward Ty. Time was running out. Ty was outnumbered four to one, standing in the open with only his SW99. How could he get the girl out? He needed help. He was sure Randy fired those shots. Why hadn't he shown up?

"Couldn't you reach the clearing?" the leader asked in accented English.

Demitri pointed at Ty. "This one got smart."

"The Proctor security guard. I see. And where is the other?"

"Gone home," Demitri began.

The two-rifle man came up behind Ty and shoved him forward. Ty took a step, spun, and punched him in the throat. He dropped both guns to grab his windpipe, but fell on them.

Gretchen froze.

Ty whipped out the SW99 from his belt and had it on Demitri before anyone could move. He motioned Gretchen back behind them where the others couldn't shoot without fear of hitting Demitri.

"Let's go," Ty said and began backing the way he came, using Demitri as a shield. Two men trailed and spread out with guns raised. Eventually one of them would have a shot and take it. The other was struggling to breathe.

"Back off," Ty yelled and pressed the gun harder into Demitri's temple.

The two men spoke to each other in gibberish.

Ty did his best to drag Demitri up the slope and shield himself and Gretchen as they went. If they made the crest of the hill, they'd be out of sight for an instant. Maybe they could run for cover. Maybe the men from the crash site had heard the shots and would come to help.

Ty's next step caught on Demitri's boot. Before he could regain his balance, Demitri surged backward and the two men crashed to the ground. With one arm around Demitri's neck and the other clutching the gun, Ty couldn't stop his head from slamming into the ground. The world took two slow-motion, blurry bounces and when Ty's eyes finally refocused, Gretchen stood alone. The two men marched closer, guns raised. The choking man was also on his feet and rushing toward them.

Demitri had both hands on the gun. Before Ty could regain control, the muzzle of an AK-47 poked into his forehead. He let go of the SW99 rather than take a bullet.

Demitri was enraged. He waved Ty's handgun wildly. "Your savageness will be visited upon you. You shall taste the wrath you meant for me! I will kill you with your own weapon."

The three gunmen gave him room.

Demitri centered the gun on Ty's forehead and pulled the trigger.

The world around Ty stood still.

CHAPTER FORTY-TWO

Randy was the only one who knew the gun was empty. He'd been sent to unload it for precisely this moment. From his spot crouched in the trees, he'd save Ty and Gretchen. He identified the leader standing with an armed man on each side and took careful aim.

Demitri spouted off something dramatic, pressed the gun to Ty's head, and pulled the trigger, but nothing happened.

The group watched as Demitri checked the gun.

Ty woke to his opportunity, charged Demitri, and drove him backward. At that very moment, Randy fired a single shot from his rifle. The slug passed within millimeters of the leader's cheek, struck the cartilage in his nose, and tore out the other side close enough to stripe the opposite cheek. Three fourths of his nose ripped away. Blood spurted everywhere. The leader dropped his rifle and toppled, clutching his face. The two remaining gunmen whirled toward the report, spotted Randy on the ridge, and sensed their vulnerability in the open.

"Hisham," one of them screamed and ran to him.

Ty and Demitri crashed into the other gunman, and the three men toppled downhill, leaving an AK-47 at Gretchen's feet. Randy fired and the gunman deserted his leader for the cover of the trees. The leader knelt, clutching his face while Ty struggled for his life against two men. Randy couldn't shoot into the jumble of arms and legs, but Gretchen had time to pick up the rifle and shoot each of them point blank. Randy did what he could by keeping the only armed man pinned behind a tree.

"Pick it up," Randy yelled between carefully placed shots.

She leaned toward the gun, but recoiled before touching it.

The leader folded to the ground. He'd probably passed out from shock and blood loss. Randy had taken the shot for the psychological effect, hoping the remaining men would flee. Unfortunately, whatever held them there was stronger than their fear.

Randy yelled again, but Gretchen wouldn't move. He watched helplessly as Demitri got free and kicked Ty four times in the abdomen while the other man held his arms. Ty flopped over defenseless as the two men clambered for the rifles on the ground. Gretchen stood in the middle of the fight doing nothing to help Ty as Demitri took aim.

Randy lined him up as fast as he could, but Demetri let loose with a string of bullets that cut across Ty's midsection. At least two of them sent soil flying, but Ty's body jolted and Randy knew he'd been hit. Not satisfied, Demitri stopped the rifle and prepared to cut back across Ty's chest. At that instant Randy launched a bullet that ripped through Demitri's closed left eyelid and collapsed his lifeless body to a bed of leaves.

Ty writhed on the ground in intense pain.

Gretchen stared at Demitri's body and shrieked one continuous note.

How could she still care about him? He'd just tried to kill her.

The gunman that had been wrestling Ty, got up and fired at Gretchen, but she stood there looking stunned. Randy fired down at the gunman and missed, but the passing bullet sent him scrambling for cover in the trees.

Finally Gretchen sparked to life and ran up the slope. Randy couldn't tell if the sight of blood spurred her into action or if she finally realized that Demitri and his partners intended to kill her, but she made the ridge safely with Randy's cover.

But what about Ty? Randy couldn't get him out without help. Gretchen wouldn't cover him. Randy could provide cover, but Ty was too big for her to drag to safety. She looked to Randy for direction, but he couldn't give one. The only way to save Ty was for Randy to kill two men he knew nothing about. He couldn't bring himself to do it, and while he struggled against himself, Ty lay bleeding.

Chapter Forty-three

The two gunmen grabbed their leader by the armpits and dragged him to safety behind a cluster of wide-trunked oaks. One man kept watch up the hill while the other attended to their leader's face. Randy didn't fire a single shot during the extraction. Would they do the same for him if he went down for Ty? What then? Where could they go for help? Two shots. Two simple shots would have freed Randy to do what he needed to do, but he couldn't pull the trigger. Randy cursed himself for not shooting. These men were killers. Just like Ty.

"No man should have to choose who lives and who dies," the reverend had said.

Randy yelled, "Leave now. I won't shoot."

Neither man left the shelter of the trees. Maybe they didn't speak English. Maybe they thought it was a trap. Randy couldn't wait and make the offer over and over again. Ty didn't have that much time.

Randy snugged the rifle to his shoulder and trained the sight several inches outside the tree trunk. The next man to show himself was going down, but before either man appeared, rotors approached low over the treetops. Randy waved vigorously, but the pilot didn't see him nestled down into the trees. The helicopter flew overhead and slowed several hundred yards past. The searchers at the crash site must have heard the gunshots and sent the helicopter.

Gretchen still had matches. Before he could tell her what he was thinking, a row of heads came slogging through the brush.

Randy screamed, "Here!" with every ounce of energy.

The gunmen at the oaks heard the commotion behind them. They stood their leader upright between them with his arms over their shoulders. A white cloth, probably an undershirt, covered much of his face. They lugged their burden across the hillside, giving Randy a wide berth at the hilltop. They didn't fire to cover their retreat and Randy let them go.

Randy waited for them to begin their descent, then plunged downhill toward Ty with the AK-47 swinging back and forth to balance his undulating strides. A few soldiers broke off from the main group and followed the gunmen toward the highway. The rest continued directly toward Randy. He identified seven heads as he closed in on Ty.

"Put the gun down," one of the soldiers ordered from eighty yards away.

Randy tossed the gun aside and yelled, "We need a medic."

He kept running straight toward the advancing men, waving for them to hurry, but the soldiers approached at a cautious march.

Ty lay on his side in the fetal position, clutching his stomach and groaning in pain as Randy knelt beside him. Gretchen caught up and stopped a few yards behind. From where she stood, she could see only Ty's back. She didn't say anything and didn't move around for a look at his face or the wounds that bloodied his pale Hawaiian shirt.

"It's over. They're gone," Randy said.

Ty shook his head grimly. He was in intense pain. Speaking was a grave effort so he spoke in quick grunted phrases. "Not over."

"They're gone. We're surrounded by soldiers," Randy said.

"They know." Ty breathed with supreme effort. "Won't stop," he grunted as if he'd lose consciousness from the exertion.

Randy turned to Gretchen. "Do you know what he's talking about?"

She snapped a glance at Demitri's body a dozen feet away on the slope. He died trying to kill her and still she looked back to Ty with disdain. Randy couldn't believe she could be so ungrateful.

"What's your problem?" he snarled.

"He works for Proctor Energy, the people who've been trying to get this from me since yesterday." She waved the egg tauntingly at Ty. When she realized the soldiers were almost upon them, she shoved it back in her pocket, looking embarrassed.

"Is that true?"

Ty closed his eyes, still clutching his midsection. The desperation of knowing he couldn't convince her showed through his pain. He grunted three words to Randy. "Bodyguard. Protect. Gretchen."

The soldiers encircled them. One knelt in front of Ty, pulled his hands back, and cut his shirt open so he could see the wounds. Gretchen backed away when Ty spread his bloody hands to let the medic do his work. The wounds were low. Randy had survived two gunshot wounds of his own not long ago. He hoped Ty would fare as well.

The medic hunched over Ty, blocking Randy's view as he dressed the wounds. Randy couldn't determine what fluids were leaking out with the blood, but he hoped no vital organs were ruptured. A soldier saw Randy watching and inched into Randy's line of sight, but thought better of it and stepped out of the way. Still, there was little to see. Gretchen stared blankly at the ground. She should have felt guilty for letting him get shot, but more likely it was the sight of the wounds that gave her skin the greenish tint. Randy couldn't believe she'd taunted him with the egg after he'd given everything to keep her alive. Ty had been assigned to protect her. Maybe she didn't like being treated like an asset. She'd stolen the data from his company. She hated them, but she should have been more grateful to the man who saved her life.

A vehicle started in the distance. Voices shouted. No shots were fired, and Randy understood the gunmen were driving away and that the soldiers had been ordered not to fire unless threatened. A nearby radio crackled to life with an urgent series of commands. The troops ordered the helicopter to follow a vehicle headed south on the highway. Seconds later the copter whooshed overhead and banked east.

Randy looked up to the sky as if he could still see the massive marble tiles and white robes. He prayed for Cassie to be safe from the gunmen and for skill for Ty's doctors, but he faced a more serious problem.

Ty had posed as a student for two months to protect Gretchen. It seemed Demitri had been trying to steal the research even longer. Who was he working for? How many of those Hummers filled with gunmen would they send? If Ty was right, someone at Proctor Energy would help, but Gretchen would never cooperate. The professor had answers, but somehow Randy knew he wouldn't be found. Helping Gretchen was going to be his most difficult challenge yet.

As if things weren't bad enough, the nearest soldier ordered Randy to raise his hands. The soldier frisked him and took away the Taurus. He was unarmed, tasked with saving the most uncooperative woman he'd ever met, and in minutes he'd be surrounded by cops and reporters ready to crucify him for trying to stay alive for the last fifteen hours.

CHAPTER FORTY-FOUR

The soldier sniffed the Taurus and Randy knew the rescue had become a crime-scene investigation. The soldier pushed Randy back from the medic working on Ty. Two soldiers, their pants dripping wet from the river crossing, watched the medic work, but several others were spread around the hillside. One stood with Randy's discarded rifle at his feet. Another stood atop the ridge by the man Ty shot. A few others stood over Demitri's body, one looking back and forth from the body to the ridge as if figuring where the kill shot had come from. The rest wandered the hillside in search of evidence.

Randy shifted to Gretchen. "We need to get on the same page."

"I didn't do anything." She gave him a snarl as if she'd say what she liked.

Randy eyed her vest pocket and she straightened.

"The cops are going to separate us."

Gretchen frowned. Good. She understood he had leverage.

An indictment would send Randy to jail for good and there was plenty of evidence scattered all around. His fingerprints were all over the gun that killed Demitri. They'd seen him toss it. Gunpowder coated his hands. There were three dead men under his car and he had a trunk full of cash. Could he convince the cops it was self-defense? Maybe if Gretchen backed him up.

He'd tried hard not to kill anyone. His final shot had been fatal, but killing Demitri had given Ty a chance to live.

Two men climbed down from an ambulance and ran across the uneven slope carrying a backboard and a variety of other medical equipment. They teamed up with the medic at Ty's side, tilted Ty onto the backboard, and immobilized him with Velcro straps until he groaned in protest.

The medic produced a clear plastic bag from one of his pouches and started an IV right there in the forest. In a few moments, four men had hold of the backboard and they were ready to go.

Randy tugged Gretchen's hand and urged her to follow closely. They kept right behind the EMTs and the soldiers carrying Ty. The procession went smoothly until they reached the back of the ambulance and Randy grasped the handle to pull himself inside. A stiff arm jutted out and stopped him at the threshold.

"Can't do it, buddy. You're going to have to find your own ride."

There was a soldier on each side of Gretchen. The ranking man shook his head gravely. So much for avoiding the cops.

The ambulance lumbered over the uneven ground and left Randy precisely in the place he'd been trying to avoid all night. Traffic appeared once the ambulance cleared the wooded trail. The five national guardsmen had a clear path to lead them out. They had less than five minutes before they were handed over to the state police. Even less before the flock of television cameramen and newspaper reporters descended.

Looking back, the soldiers kept watch over Demitri's body, the gun Randy shot him with, and the perch up in the trees where he'd pulled the trigger. They wouldn't move until a crime-scene technician came to collect the evidence. Randy was sunk. He could smell the gunpowder on his hands. If charges were filed, the governor would have Randy back in a New Bedford jail before this new set of problems found its way to court.

The soldiers directed them to follow the path the ambulance had taken. Randy stepped closer to Gretchen as they followed along.

"You need to stay with me," he whispered.

"What?"

"The cops are going to try and bring you back. Don't go."

"Why not?"

"Those men aren't going to give up."

"And I'll be safer with you than the police?" she snickered.

"Yes," he said with a confidence that gave her pause.

She walked several steps before she leaned close and whispered again. "Did you and Ty make a deal? Is he paying you to keep track of me?"

"He protected you. He nearly died keeping you alive."

"He's no different than they are."

"It's entirely different." Could she really believe what she was saying? Ty had protected her. Demitri would have cut her throat for the data if Ty hadn't stopped him. Why couldn't see beyond her prejudice?

The column stepped from the trees and was greeted by a rush of traffic at the top of a grassy incline. The men turned north and when they did, a rush of activity began on the opposite side of the bridge.

"All those cameras coming at us," Randy said. "They're going to tell the world you're alive. Those men chasing you are going to see your picture. Once they do, ten times as many are going to come looking for you." The number was a bluff. Randy had no way of knowing who was chasing Gretchen or how many men they could muster, but that egg was incredibly valuable. Many men would die for it.

Gretchen balked as the photographers raced across the bridge toward them. The escorts came to a momentary stop. Randy had made his point. She was willing to stand in the face of gunfire without shooting back, but she was afraid to die on some level at least. Her courage in the face of death would make more sense if she was devoutly religious. But for an atheist who believed that death meant the end of existence, he'd expect her to fight hard for every breath. Maybe she believed in reincarnation. Randy never asked.

He helped Gretchen get her vest off before the reporters converged. The two of them held it high and ducked down between the soldiers to protect themselves from the onslaught of digital cameras. The television cameramen, lagging under the weight of their heavier equipment, lost nothing. Neither group would get pictures of Gretchen Greene today.

CHAPTER FORTY-FIVE

A trooper wrapped Gretchen in a wool blanket even though she looked comfortable in her insulated vest. The sun was fully up and the day was warming comfortably. Another trooper helped her sit on the tailgate of an official SUV. There she was surrounded by two men and a woman in state police uniform. Randy wasn't offered a blanket or the warm words of concern that Gretchen received. Instead, the officers ringed Gretchen and turned their backs to Randy, subtly separating the two survivors without acknowledging their intent.

Another Connecticut trooper gently guided Randy away from the crowd attending to Gretchen where it was difficult to hear what they were saying to her and, more important, what she was telling them. Randy wouldn't stray from the truth, but if too much of the truth came out, it would be impossible to keep Gretchen out of protective custody. Separated as they were, he felt completely powerless.

The trooper introduced himself formally and asked Randy's name. He hesitated as anyone living with a pseudonym might. The trooper sensed something was wrong and asked for Randy's identification. He studied it carefully. Randy wished he could explain, but no one on Earth would truly understand. The trooper looked disappointed that he couldn't find a problem with Randy's driver's license. He slipped it into his shirt pocket rather than hand it back.

"The guardsmen say you were holding a rifle when they found you. Would you like to tell me how you came to be in the middle of the woods with an assault rifle? You're a long way from home."

"We were pursued from the moment my car stopped until the guardsmen marched us out. I took the rifle from one of the men chasing us."

"He gave it to you?"

"I whacked him over the head and took it."

The trooper pulled out a notebook and made a notation.

Randy considered asking for a lawyer, but if he did, the interview would get infinitely more formal. He still had hope of walking away as a good Samaritan caught in the crossfire, and the last thing he wanted was to be hauled down to the state police barracks.

"You came from the college?"

"No."

The trooper backed up further still and asked how Randy knew Gretchen. When he described the accident scene and how he'd decided to stop at the last second, the trooper soured with skepticism. His eyes sharpened as if looking for the evidence that would link Randy to the start of the chaos. The mounting details in his notebook cried out for theories to confirm his suspicion. If Randy's story didn't overwhelm the damage that Walter had done in his television interview, Randy was going to spend his entire day in one interrogation after another. He hoped Gretchen was supporting him. She had no reason to lie unless she was cornered and trying to hide what she'd done in the lab, but based on the way she treated Ty, she was perfectly capable of fabricating something about Randy to save herself.

The trooper asked Randy about the accident over and over. He wanted to know precisely where he was in relation to the other cars. Randy knew they'd found at least four dead men in the wreckage and he was careful to give the trooper everything he remembered. He admitted that his car swerved and hit the three gunmen, but the trooper couldn't know Randy intentionally pinned the men without killing them. The trooper also couldn't know whether the men died before or after the Hummer slammed into the

McLaren. They were alive when the McLaren stopped and he told the trooper about the pounding on the glass, but there was no way to prove it.

The trooper went through the scenario four times, searching for discrepancies in each telling, but found none. They moved on to the forest, the escape across the river, and the gunfight that had ended twenty minutes earlier. He followed the same tactics, asking the same questions in different ways and running through events time after time to make sure the descriptions lined up. The questions came faster and faster until the final question. "Why did you shoot your friend after he protected you all night?"

Randy grinned at the simplistic attempt to trip him up. "Ty's going to be ok. Go to the hospital and ask who shot him."

"So it was these men that crashed into the Malibu last night?"

"Yes."

"And where did you get the handgun?"

"Same as the A-K. The guy I hit over the head had it on him."

"The men chasing you, how many did you see?"

"Eight, maybe ten."

That number of men could fit in the vehicles that had crashed on the road. The trooper didn't argue, but Randy could tell he was troubled why ten men would want so desperately to catch or kill three young kids. Randy didn't offer the answer. Instead he tried to listen to the lighter conversation centered around Gretchen. The police did everything to make her comfortable, ironic given that she was the center of the torrent that had swept from Cambridge to Connecticut.

The trooper radioed into the field. Randy heard him asking if they'd found any bodies out in the vicinity. He was surprised when only two were reported in. Demitri and the soldier on the ridge had been spotted before Randy and Gretchen left the woods. But what had happened to the others from the fight on the other side of the river? Randy had wounded two and tied two men up with their boot laces. Ty had done lots of shooting and his friends had clashed with the gunmen for what seemed like an hour of heavy fighting. Where were all those bodies?

Randy had a fleeting thought it had all been a deception. That both groups of men in the forest the night before were working together to get the data from Gretchen. But why go to all that trouble? She put up almost no resistance. They could have taken it from her anytime. Ty had killed the man on the roadway. Randy had seen the effects and he'd seen Ty's wounds, too. Demitri wanted that data badly enough to kill for it. Right then Randy wanted to know everything about Gretchen's relationship with Demitri and who he might be working for. She was still surrounded by police, but the mood was light as if she'd never been questioned. The cops saw her as a victim to be rescued and Randy as the villain. If nothing changed, they might just walk away.

The trooper returned with a tired-looking police officer who must have been on site since the gun battle the night before. The man asked Randy where he was in relation to the crash site. When Randy explained that they'd crossed the river, the man immediately doubted his story. Randy explained in detail how they had ventured into the swamp, avoiding the deep water, and crossed on a fallen tree. The man wasn't eager to venture back into the forest and seemed somewhat convinced by the detail in Randy's story. Whether one of them was an expert at interrogation and could tell Randy was telling the truth was debatable, but the idea that Randy had been the one shooting at the police was tabled for the moment.

The men stepped away and whispered to each other.

The weary officer walked back to a patrol car and the trooper returned alone. "One more question for you. What were you doing with so much cash in your trunk?"

"Going to Foxwoods," Randy answered without hesitation. He hadn't planned to put that much money in play, but the answer was honest if not complete.

The trooper grimaced. He didn't like the answer, but Randy could tell he had nowhere to go with this line of questioning. They hadn't found drugs in the car, which is the first thing they would have suspected. Even if they believed Walter's wild theory about a payoff to blow up the lab in Cambridge, they had no evidence.

"I was driving a four-hundred-thousand-dollar car before it got crushed." The trooper's eyes lit up when he heard this. Randy was sure he'd check it out when he could get to a phone. "I'd like to get that cash back, actually."

The trooper's eyes darkened with the last comment. Randy had crossed the line and where he'd been seconds from freedom, he'd just given the trooper incentive to keep him at the roadside for a while.

A uniformed man ran to the trooper.

"Sir, dispatch just called for all available units. Those guys that tore out of here in that Hummer—the helo lost them in the woods. Dispatch thinks they might be headed this way."

"What do they want us to do?"

"Close the northbound lanes."

The trooper glanced at Randy, barked, "Stay here," and turned away fast. He stopped abruptly, pulled Randy's license from his pocket, and flicked it before running off to his car. Randy caught the little Frisbee and pocketed it.

Moments later three Connecticut state police cruisers and three military Humvees raced away south. In minutes, they streaked back toward the bridge and stopped the flow of traffic on the other side. The police intended to hem the gunmen in with the same river Randy and Gretchen had used to escape them the night before.

CHAPTER FORTY-SIX

Davis raced down the wooded road at 70 mph with his lights flashing and his siren blaring. He'd be going faster if he wasn't stuck behind two troopers who'd probably never driven this road before. This was his backyard. He could be around that Hummer by now and have the driver cuffed in a ditch if he wasn't stuck at the back of this parade. Bad enough the lead car almost lost it on the curve by Dagget Brook.

Davis slid into the left lane. Nothing was coming all the way up to Mine Road, but he couldn't pass the troopers—the chief would ream him for days. He hung back and watched the Hummer barrel up to the intersection as a pickup came into view. The pickup driver saw the lights and slammed on his brakes. When he rolled back to block the intersection, Davis thought the pursuit was over. The Hummer had room to make a right onto Mine Road and head back to town, but he was going too fast. The driver thought too long, locked up his brakes, then lost it on the turn. He sideswiped the pickup then careened into the guardrail head on.

The troopers stopped nose-to-tail with the Hummer, one on each rear corner, blocking it in. Davis was stuck in the background for the bust. He parked behind the two troopers, out of the intersection. The troopers were flanking the Hummer when its rear window powered down. A muzzle appeared and they were caught with nowhere to take cover.

The gunman opened fire and ripped them apart before either trooper fired a shot. The gunman turned on Davis before he had his Glock drawn and he had to dive to shelter behind the trunk of the nearest state police cruiser. There were three men in the Hummer. He didn't know what kind of rifle poked out the back window, but his Glock was no match for it whatever it was. He kept his head down.

The engine revved, then the Hummer shoved the cruiser back into him. Davis popped up for a look and was met with a burst from the rifle. He kept low and stayed with the cruiser as it was shoved back until the Hummer rammed its way free and took off for town.

He waited a few beats longer than he should have then scrambled around the cruiser to the first trooper sprawled on the pavement. Fingers on the trooper's neck couldn't register a pulse. Davis repositioned his fingers twice before he realized the shots had been fatal. He radioed for an ambulance before checking the second trooper and finding a weak pulse.

CHAPTER FORTY-SEVEN

Cassie crawled along with southbound traffic. When she reached the accident scene for the fourth time that morning, the opening in the trees had widened and an excavator crawled toward the wreckage of the state police helicopter. The other drivers were busy scanning the troopers and soldiers on the side of the road, wondering what they were doing and what they would be missing when they drove away. The man in front of her stopped so long the road ahead of him cleared for two hundred yards. Cassie honked and he moved on.

There were several gaps among the military and police vehicles parked on the shoulder, as if half the search contingent had given up and gone home. Cassie continued well past the scene and pulled into the breakdown lane. This time she had her press credential in hand and her reflective vest strapped on when she stepped from the car. She left her notebook behind and joined the mob of reporters and cameramen conglomerated at the tape line. The press vest might be a hindrance this morning, but she didn't dare leave it behind.

The first person to notice her arrival stepped up and blocked her progress toward the tape. "Swooping in to do some damage control for your boyfriend?"

"Keep digging, Walter. Talked to Bart today?"

He wheezed a lungful of air. Obviously he knew how much damage he'd done in his television interview. "Why do you keep rescuing this lunatic?"

"You don't know what you're talking about."

"Maybe you should talk with my friend Pinto."

"I know what Randy did. I also went to the hospital and saw how Pinto and his friends retaliated. If the two of you don't back off maybe Randy will change his mind about the assault charges. I still have the photos and I'm sure he can get the medical records with a two-minute phone call."

Walter glared. Pinto was Walter's staunchest ally in the crusade against Randy. Both men desperately wanted to see Randy punished and their hate bound them together. Pinto fed Walter information that he couldn't admit publicly and Walter protected his anonymity. Some of Walter's articles bordered on libel, but that wouldn't cost him jail time. If Randy ever talked about the beating, Pinto would spend a few months behind bars. If Walter's blunders threatened to put him there, Walter would be fighting Randy alone.

Cassie's threat left him stinging as she walked away.

She skirted the throng of reporters until she reached the tape, ducked underneath, and strode confidently toward the investigators. The nearest officer was intent on a conversation, but the last thing he wanted was a bunch of reporters breaking his line. He sparked to attention and hurried to intercept her.

"You know the drill, lady. Press stays outside the tape."

Cassie kept walking until she was close enough to be heard over the hum of slow-moving traffic. "I'm here to help a friend. You found three people in the woods this morning. One of them called me for a ride."

This wasn't the lieutenant from the night before. The younger officer checked her up and down for a camera. It probably wouldn't be the first time he was scammed by a journalist desperate for a story. Cassie held out empty hands and took a tentative step forward.

"Their names are Gretchen and Randy." She realized their names had been broadcast all over New England the night before. "They'll recognize me," she promised.

"If this is a con, I'm locking you up, paperwork or not."

Cassie assured him it wasn't a trick and he led her to the back of an SUV where Cassie saw Gretchen for the first time. She was young for an energy researcher. She looked plain, but what woman wouldn't after spending the night lost in the forest. She must have attended at least six years of college, which would make her twenty-four. Randy sat casually beside her without a single official nearby. They talked in whispered tones as the officer escorted Cassie over. Tension rose inside her. She wasn't sure if it was the way Randy whispered to Gretchen, knowing they had spent the night in the woods together, or that Gretchen was four years younger.

Randy smiled and jumped down when he saw her. He didn't look guilty after being caught whispering with another woman. Their relationship was defined not in words but fleeting caresses and glances. They had no spoken commitment, so he was free to do what he wanted, but they were both emotionally invested. If he was caught flirting with another woman she hoped it would show on his face. Since it didn't she felt slightly better.

Randy stopped a foot away. Cassie closed the distance and wrapped her arms around his lean shoulders, nuzzled her head into the base of his neck, and held him tightly until his body responded to hers. She reached up to kiss his cheek. Gretchen watched with only casual interest.

"I was worried about you," she whispered.

"It was nothing."

"Tell that to the helicopter pilots." *And their families*, she thought.

"It's going to get a lot uglier."

She asked what he meant and he told her they needed to help Gretchen.

"Really?" Cassie wanted to get back to Dartmouth and what they started in her apartment. Forget the flock of reporters and the horde of police. Sure, the discovery was important, but why did they have to help?

Randy pulled her closer. "I'm going to give you a blockbuster story. But this time, I'm going to be looking for something in return." He nibbled gently below her ear as if his point needed illustration.

"Promises, promises."

Cassie introduced herself to Gretchen. The younger girl was polite but preoccupied. She clutched the blanket around her shoulders even though it was nearly sixty degrees. Her eyes flicked to catch any movement and she stiffened when Randy got close, as if she'd been traumatized overnight and credited Randy more with being part of the problem than the solution.

The officer cautioned them against leaving. He recommended a trip to the hospital for Gretchen and a police escort to make sure she was safe. Randy assured him they'd be fine and after ten minutes of wrangling, Cassie walked to her car and backed it through the crowd of reporters, under the police tape, and behind the shelter of the official vehicles on the shoulder.

The grassy slope to her right was so steep she stopped twice for fear of flipping over. When she arrived, she shifted to the passenger's seat and let Randy drive. Gretchen climbed in back, profusely complimenting Cassie's Corolla. No one had ever been that excited about her car, not even her parents. Later she'd realize that Gretchen saw everything through a lens of environmental impact. That made the Corolla a fantastic choice even if the back seat was a bit cramped.

The police parted the reporters so Randy could drive out. At the back of the crowd, Walter jumped clear and pointed an accusing finger at Randy. The car jerked to a stop and Randy was out on the asphalt before Cassie could argue. As he closed in on Walter, Cassie saw them together for the first time. The difference between the two men was striking. Even lean as he was, Randy was an imposing figure, six inches taller with an angry arm slicing toward Walter's face. Walter's accusing finger shriveled back down by his side and he shrank from Randy's approach.

"I've had about enough from you, Macedo."

Walter hesitated, wide-eyed.

"I don't want to read another word from you. Got it?"

"I know what you did in Westport."

"What do you want? An award?"

"I want you in prison."

Cassie could feel Randy's rage even with his back turned. A trooper moved along the front edge of the crowd, sensing Randy was about to drop Walter there on the roadway.

"Buzz off. I know a thousand ways to make you miserable," Randy snarled. Walter had interviewed the Marstons and he knew Deirdre had broken down and been hospitalized after the night with the snakes, the rain, and her gruesome discovery in Charlie's house. Surely he could do the same to the middle-aged journalistic weasel.

Panic washed across Walter's face.

Randy knew he'd made his point and turned for the car. Cassie half-wished Randy had slugged him and shut him up for good, but she didn't say anything when Randy ducked in and drove away. Soon they reached the off-ramp Cassie had taken three times that morning. He turned and followed the swamp.

"Got a GPS in this thing?" he asked, buzzing from the confrontation.

Cassie reached in the glove compartment and fixed the four-inch display to the dash.

"What do you call her?"

Cassie looked at him and shrugged. Why would she name her GPS?

"Turn her on, let's hear what she sounds like."

Cassie obliged, but without an address programmed, the machine quietly displayed a menu. "Where are we going?"

"North and east."

"Why aren't we taking I-ninety-five?"

"The cops have it blocked off."

"And you didn't tell me? I could have snapped a picture. A quick story might have made up for yesterday."

"Forget that. You're going to get an incredible story today. Whatever we do, we're staying off the highways."

Trees rushed by as they rounded the swamp where Randy and Gretchen had been forced to turn back that morning. Every so often a green patch appeared with a cape centered on the lawn. Cassie had passed these houses many times as she went back and forth waiting for Randy to appear through the trees.

Cassie clicked the GPS and expanded the map of their current location. No matter which way she scrolled, she saw unbroken swamp with as much blue as green and without a single road cutting through. She was about to ask Randy if he had a destination in mind so she could program it in when the car slowed to a stop and rushed backward as fast as Cassie would dare drive on the narrow tree-lined road.

Randy pointed into the only yard in sight and the three of them looked out the passenger's side of the car.

"Yah, I see him," Cassie said. "He's been painting that shed all morning."

"Not him. The dog. Gretchen and I talked about dogs this morning."

Cassie burst out laughing. The dog must have tipped a paint can and rolled over in it until his fur was saturated with red latex. His face was still a deep chocolate brown, but every other part of him was bright red to match the shed the man was painting. The painter had been so focused on his work that he hadn't noticed the trouble his dog had gotten into. Cassie imagined the Lab padding through the house and leaving a trail of red paw prints everywhere he went.

"Looks like this guy painted more than his shed," Gretchen said.

"Looks like there's more than one way for God to make a red dog."

Gretchen gasped.

"Looks like we're going to church."

Randy hit the accelerator.

CHAPTER FORTY-EIGHT

"You're not bringing me back to school?" Gretchen asked from the back seat, her voice wavering. Had the danger finally sunk in? Nothing he said fazed her, but maybe seeing the blood on Ty's shirt made her realize what would have happened if Ty and Randy weren't there to protect her. Demitri might have slit her throat or he might have kept her alive to interpret the research, but it was finally clear that he only cared about crude sales. She'd been duped and really slow to figure it out. She had to be gun-shy about trusting anyone.

"Relax, we're not going anywhere near Boston."

Randy had no idea where they were going. Gretchen was the most opinionated, argumentative woman he'd met. It would have been much easier to leave her with the police and she probably would have been happier with them, but they needed to stick together. She was in grave danger until they discovered who Demitri was working for. Randy owed Cassie an explanation about Gretchen, the house, and his quick exit from the hospital, but she understood the gravity of Gretchen's situation and co-piloted pleasantly.

Trees whizzed by then broke as they crossed under I-95 heading east. Randy drove quickly but with no particular destination planned, though he had a nagging hunger and would stop anywhere that served lunch.

The road forked a few miles later and across a triangle of grass sat a squat, white clapboard building with peeling paint and a Coke sign out front. Randy swung around, rumbled over the crumbling asphalt, and parked at the back. He steadied for complaints from Gretchen even before he opened the door. They wouldn't find a grease-free, vegetarian-friendly restaurant out here in the sticks and he wasn't going to drive around looking for one. They'd have some lettuce inside. Gretchen could make do. Randy needed a burger and fries to replace the energy he'd burned overnight. His half of the rabbit hadn't made a dent in his hunger and it had been hours since. Ever the good sport, Cassie led the way around front and to Randy's surprise, Gretchen didn't complain once on the way in. Before he ate anything, Randy headed for the tiny men's room and washed the night's dirt from his hands and face.

Gretchen sat in a high-backed booth facing away from the door. Anyone coming in would see Randy and Cassie sitting side by side and overlook Gretchen hidden by the top of the bench. The rundown diner and its battered tables with dented metal trim was the perfect place to stop in the lull between breakfast and lunch. They weren't likely to see another customer. Through the wide service window they saw a single cook standing at the grill waiting to prepare something. The lone waitress pretended to busy herself before coming to hand out menus and offering to bring drinks.

The burger Randy was looking for topped the second column of the menu. Gretchen made faces at the selections, bemoaned the unhealthy ingredients, and cursed the multiple sprayings of pesticides applied to the aged vegetables. She had to be hungry after eating only berries and mushrooms, but she flipped the single, laminated page over and back twice, not pleased with anything she found.

"If you don't like anything here, we can stop down the road and you can search for twigs and berries." Randy laughed even before he finished.

Cassie looked up from her menu, bewildered by the odd suggestion.

"I forage," Gretchen said. "Randy thinks it's funny."

Cassie looked even more confused. No wonder. A girl from Dorchester and then New Bedford had little exposure to wildlife. She probably knew what foraging meant, but couldn't imagine searching for things growing outside and eating them. Of course there were wild places far from the smog and pollution where this was actually a good idea. Randy watched her eyebrows tilt without offering any help.

Gretchen wasn't new to reactions like Cassie's. "Wild food was the basis for the cultivated vegetables we eat today. It might not be perfect by grocery store standards, but it's a lot better for you."

Cassie put down her menu and turned toward Randy in the seat next to her. "So what are we doing here?"

"I've got to eat. Nature Girl might not like this place, but it's low key and that's what we need more than anything. That and a greasy burger."

Cassie asked why they hadn't left Gretchen with the police on I-95. Randy detected a hint of jealousy, not so much of Gretchen, but of the time they could be spending together. The last time they'd been alone, he'd massaged her neck to help her relax after Tom's thugs threatened her. Back then their relationship was complicated. The whirlwind around Tom and Heather threatened their lives, and sleeping with Randy while writing stories about him would have tainted her objectivity. The investigation was over and Cassie's articles about Randy were printed. There was nothing between them now but Gretchen.

Gretchen didn't seem the least bit embarrassed by her imposition, nor offended by Cassie's suggestion that they'd be happier without her. It was almost as if she expected to be cast out of any social group she encountered. She was comfortable as an outsider. She didn't make excuses or accommodations to fit in. Gretchen was who she was, take her or leave her. She'd probably have been happier with the cops, too, but then she'd probably end up dead.

Randy explained how the men had attacked the college, killed the students, and hunted the professor. Gretchen seemed to be the only one of the group still alive, save Ty, who was gravely wounded and according to Gretchen, not particularly technology savvy. Capturing Ty wouldn't help anyone. Gretchen had the technology they were out to destroy and they weren't going to give up until they had her.

An idea sparked in Cassie's eyes. She rushed out to her car, returned with her laptop, and started crafting a story that would put her readers to work helping find the men who'd been chasing Gretchen.

"You're a newspaper reporter?" Gretchen eyed her as if she'd just admitted to being a serial killer. Randy had mentioned this in the woods, but she probably wasn't paying attention. He was stunned at how quickly Gretchen forgot about the gas-sipping Corolla and vilified Cassie for being a mass murderer of trees.

"Cassie can help you," Randy said. "She can make it very hard for these guys to move around. That'll give us a chance to figure out who they are and why they're chasing you without getting ourselves killed."

Gretchen gritted her teeth.

"I'm not going to print anything you don't want me to."

"It's not that," Randy said. "She has a problem with anyone who eats meat, burns fuel, or uses paper. You, lovely lady, use an awful lot of paper."

Randy narrated their escape from the car crash and the shootings in the woods overnight, details only Cassie would report. The story would be another needle in Walter's side back in New Bedford. Gretchen refused to help. She wanted no part in selling newspapers even if that meant saving herself. She was one twisted woman. Randy wondered for a minute if he'd been brought to save her from danger or to help get her head straight. Saving her might be the easier half of the equation.

In half an hour Cassie had an article that Bart could edit and print in the morning edition, but they were still no closer to solving the immediate problem. Gretchen had gotten over the idea that the story would be printed on paper and discarded within days and she even volunteered a few details. The pressure on the gunmen justified the waste somewhat, but when Randy identified the men as Mediterranean or Arabian, Gretchen's eyes went wild. She avoided Randy altogether, fuming toward the other tables. Gretchen couldn't understand that sometimes a description is just a description. She'd rather invite danger than risk offending someone from another culture. Her ideals overrode common sense. She'd stand with a gun at her feet and allow someone to kill her friend. Looking at her across the table Randy couldn't understand the unique calculus that helped her choose right from wrong.

Cassie called Bart and promised to email the story as soon as they drove to a better coverage area. Gretchen stayed focused on the empty tables when Cassie hung up the phone, but she was intent on the conversation across the table.

"Bart suggests she'll be safest with the Boston cops."

"That was my plan," Randy said, "until they shot down that helicopter. The cops can't protect her, not a chance."

Gretchen stiffened at this.

"Who are these guys?" Cassie asked.

They both turned to face Gretchen. Randy asked if she'd told anyone about the research. Slowly she opened up. She'd talked about her work with kids at school and friends she worked with on environmental campaigns, but she never expected Whitney's research would amount to anything. She had been looking for a more rigorous research program for months but couldn't find one. She was shocked when things turned around. Lately, she'd been too busy trying to keep up with Whitney to confide in anyone.

Randy wondered if one of the ecoterrorists she worked with in South America could be involved. Unlikely they'd drive Hummers. He chuckled at the mental image of armed thugs twittering around the countryside in a convoy of Priuses.

"What?" the women asked in unison.

"Nothing," he answered, convinced that Gretchen wouldn't appreciate his sense of humor. "If we're going to find who's after Gretchen, I think we need to start with Professor Whitney."

Cassie pulled a note from her laptop bag and tapped an unpainted fingernail on an address on Thames Street in Newport.

"Let's plug it into Judy and get going."

CHAPTER FORTY-NINE

Randy refused to take any major route on the trip east. Normally, Gretchen enjoyed a winding trip through the forest, but Randy hugged the corners so tight that she had to hold on to stay centered between the bucket seats where she could see the road. The car ride wasn't scary after being shot at, but going so fast and taking such a circuitous route was a sinful waste of fuel. Gretchen kept her annoyance to herself as she watched Randy talk to the GPS he called Judy. He ignored most of her advice on which way to turn. The most common thing Judy said was "recalculating," in her mechanized voice. Randy ignored her, drove across the route she suggested, and then found another road that appeared to be headed east. They were perpetually lost, but they were going fast in the general direction of Newport. Maybe Cassie would give him all the control he wanted, but Gretchen wasn't ready to hand her fate over to him.

When Randy finally turned onto Route 138 heading east, Judy and Gretchen were satisfied. When she saw how the rocky ledge had been blasted away, Gretchen understood why he'd finally listened to Judy's advice. This was his last opportunity to get on the bridge. The roadway dipped down and then sloped up sharply when it reached the water, like a Hot Wheels ramp erected on a smooth blue carpet. On the right, an old bridge paralleled them out into the water but dead ended a quarter mile from shore. As the car climbed toward the apex, Gretchen worried they were about to be trapped on an island with only one way out.

Randy seemed to read her mind and said, "Don't worry. They won't find us here. If they do, there's another bridge we can take east toward Massachusetts."

Gretchen checked her grip on the seatbacks, wondering if that had clued Randy to her unease. But why shouldn't she be worried? The gunmen attacked precisely when Whitney's discovery was being revealed. Wouldn't they know about his house in Newport? And why wasn't Randy nervous about being trapped on an island?

Randy had other things on his mind. He and Cassie were keen on each other's every movement. They didn't touch like other couples, though their interest for each other was obvious. Gretchen watched them as they crossed the small island. Randy drove more cautiously in traffic than he had in the woods, probably trying to blend in. Cassie watched calmly from her seat whether he was careening around a corner or tranquilly following the car ahead. Cassie was domesticated whether she knew it or not. The only thing left was the official ceremony.

Gretchen couldn't imagine being subjugated like that. Just seeing them together reminded her how wrong she'd been about Demitri. She'd been attracted to him from his first day on campus. He'd been cozy at first, long enough for the deep Mediterranean skin and the rich accented voice to captivate her. After that he'd been nothing more than cordial. He dangled himself in front of her for months. He kept her interested and that was all he wanted. She cursed herself for not realizing sooner.

A black Suburban crossed in front of them and Gretchen flashed back to the Proctor Energy men arriving on campus. She remembered her annoyance at the sight of the two Suburbans parked at the edge of the lot. She imagined Proctor men following her in the SUV even as it rushed away through traffic. Then she remembered the square-sided Hummers she saw on the opposite end of the campus lot. They were identical to the vehicles that crushed Ty's Malibu against the guardrail.

She hated Proctor Energy for what they represented. It didn't matter that they funded the research. She had immediately blamed them for the attack on campus and now she realized she could have been wrong about that, too.

Proctor had legal rights to the discovery. They had known the latest round of experiments were a success, but Gretchen couldn't understand how. Gretchen had only read the test results a few minutes before they arrived. Even if they had been monitoring the results remotely they couldn't have known soon enough to fly into Boston that morning. And they wouldn't be that diligent to check results every night, not after Whitney had been at it for almost a decade. She was missing something about the Proctor men, but it was beyond her grasp.

As they rushed toward the next bridge towering in the distance she pictured Ty in the hospital. She'd been completely wrong about him. He worked for Proctor Energy. As much as she hated them, Ty had worked hard to protect her. He risked his life to save hers. Demitri only wanted the flash drive and he would have killed her for it. Her cheeks flushed. Demitri was working with the men who tried to kill the entire research team. He'd gone to the woods to lead her to her death. She could still feel how much her heart ached for him. How foolish. And how horrible she'd been to Ty, treating him like a simpleton. Ty wasn't an engineering student. He was posing so he could do his job and she'd made it nearly impossible. If she'd been more helpful he'd probably be with them now. She wondered why she'd been singled out for protection. She hadn't produced the breakthrough, Whitney had. Why wasn't Ty following Whitney?

The roadway began to rise.

They sped away from a toll plaza and climbed another massive bridge. Thick cables connected two towering sets of columns. Gretchen imagined the hundreds of tons of steel that went into the construction. All the heat used to form the beams, the manpower to erect them, the paint, and the tons of asphalt poured to make the roadway smooth. It was an awesome expenditure of resources to allow man to spend time closer to the water.

CHAPTER FIFTY

Judy announced their arrival and Randy parked at a meter in front of a large two-story building of white brick. Thames was a bustling commercial street not far from the shore. The professor's house was surrounded by gift shops and restaurants, so there were people roaming everywhere. Women poked in and out of shops. Husbands stood by on the sidewalk and watched the activity on the street to busy themselves while they waited. Randy had expected the professor's house to be in a quiet neighborhood where he wouldn't be noticed slipping up to the door and working the lock. That was impossible here. Bored male eyes fell upon any movement and because the property was surrounded by a high fence, climbing it and sneaking in the back would attract too much attention. They needed to get inside without arousing suspicion so they could search without interruption.

Cassie pointed to the next building. It was set farther back and Randy had to lean over to see the bright red sign advertising the Admiral's Inn. A narrow driveway ran between Professor Whitney's fence and the inn, separating the two by twelve feet. If they could rent a room, they could stay out of sight while they found a way into Whitney's house. Randy started the car and turned down the drive. He worried about leaving the car so close to Whitney's, but the men in the woods hadn't seen the Corolla. Even if they had, it was a very popular model.

Randy stopped halfway down the drive. On the right was an inset doorway that led inside the inn. Anyone standing there would be hidden from the street and the neighbors. On the left was a gate that led to the professor's massive house. Randy parked around back, left the women by the car, and walked to the gate. The courtyard on the other side was enclosed on three sides by the professor's home and on one side by the fence. The building was oddly shaped for a private residence and Randy assumed it had been something else before the professor moved in. He rejoined the women at the inn's back door, content he'd found his way inside the professor's house.

Thames Street bustled out front, but the lot behind the Admiral was only half filled on that Wednesday afternoon. They entered through the back door and down a short entry. The original front-to-back hallway had been converted into a lobby. A reception desk ran close along one wall, which left the employees cramped behind it, but allowed plenty of room for the guests coming and going.

Cassie carried an overnight bag, but the appearance of one man and two women with no reservation and only a small bag among them brought a sour face to the woman behind the desk. The scene was reminiscent of the Piolenc farmhouse minus the alcohol and seclusion. Randy allowed himself a smile as he asked for two rooms and offered four one-hundred-dollar bills.

The innkeeper's condescension relaxed even as Randy imagined what Gretchen looked like underneath the dowdy clothes.

"Do you own the inn next door as well?" Randy indicated the direction of the professor's house after taking his change. Cassie and Gretchen perked up for her answer.

"Funny story about that," the woman said. She leaned over the desk and spoke with a hushed, scandalous tone. "It used to be one of our toughest competitors, but a science professor from Boston bought that building three years ago. Seems he was getting drunk and having trouble finding his way home. He offered to buy the Admiral, but the owners wouldn't part with it. Too much history here. It was a convent before they moved it here, you know."

"Pretty expensive solution."

"Indeed. They had forty-eight rooms before he took it over. He has no family or anything. Just him in that rambling old place. But he can afford it, you know. He's always throwing money around down here."

Randy didn't tell her that she was unlikely to see her neighbor again.

"Did he have lots of friends in town?"

"Young ladies, sure." The woman gestured to Gretchen. "About your age." She bowed her head and shook it disapprovingly. "I've seen plenty of them leaving when I was coming to work."

Hopefully the professor hadn't gotten himself into anything serious. Randy didn't want to break in and stumble across a sleeping co-ed.

Randy thanked the innkeeper, took both keys, and led the way to the stairs. Before going up, he noticed an exit that faced the professor's house, the same exit that was tucked into the exterior wall along the drive. The door wasn't alarmed and although it was directly across from the reception desk, it made the perfect passage to the professor's gate.

They climbed two flights of stairs past a gallery of sailing ships hung every few feet. Larger ships dominated the landings and their frames suggested they were painted a century ago. The two rooms isolated on the third floor landing each had a small roof deck that looked out over the waterfront a block away. A wooden gate opened to a larger roof deck for all guests. If they needed to make a quick exit, they could cross the common deck and follow a second stairway to the lobby. He couldn't ask Cassie and Gretchen to scale the building or try the leap to the roof deck next door. He felt trapped up there and cursed himself for not hiding the Taurus better.

When Randy came back in the room, Cassie had her bag open on the bed and was digging for something. Gretchen had her hand on the doorknob, ready to cross over to the other room. Randy stopped her and the two of them sat in armchairs separated by a small glass-topped table.

"Why yesterday?" Randy asked. "Why'd you take the data yesterday?"

"It's never worked before."

Cassie took notice and stopped rummaging.

"How long have you been working on this?"

"Me?" Gretchen asked. "Two years. The professor has been at it for a long time. He's been funded for about six, I think."

Randy bristled the whiskers on his chin and felt a connection with his old self for the first time since his fateful vision. If the professor truly had worked at this for six years, the odds were astronomical that on the first morning the experiment worked, his sponsors and a group of armed thugs would both show up. The hasty press conference and the attack on the lab were not coincidental. Randy just hadn't found the link.

Wouldn't it be ironic if the data in Gretchen's egg was worthless? If the whole thing was hype? The men chasing them through the night were convinced of its potential. Could they be wrong? Could the professor have been boasting and let the frenzy get out of control? Randy had no way to check. He couldn't recreate a research lab here in the inn and even if he could, he didn't know the first thing about solar energy.

"Did you tell anyone about your research?" he asked.

"I told you three times. It wasn't a secret."

"So you told people it was working?"

"There wasn't time. I checked the results as soon as I arrived. I was the first one in the lab that morning, so no one saw the results before me."

"And who did you tell?"

"No one."

Randy could see she was holding something back.

"So you were alone in the lab. What then?"

"I changed the data so it looked like it didn't work. Then I took the formulas we'd used and put them on this." She showed Cassie the egg from her pocket.

From that moment, Gretchen wouldn't have told anyone about the experiment. She didn't want anyone to know it worked, not until she figured out who she was going to give it to. Randy didn't say anything about her twisted sense of justice and he didn't ask why she wanted to give a billion-dollar technology to people who had nothing to do with its discovery. Gretchen wasn't the one who alerted Proctor Energy about the discovery, not intentionally anyway.

"Ty told them," Randy blurted.

"What?" Cassie asked.

"Ty was working for Proctor. Proctor knew everything that was happening in that lab because Ty was giving them the play by play. That's why he was there."

"Bastard," Gretchen spat.

"Bastard? He's in the hospital because he tried to save you."

Gretchen pulled back, feeling scolded, but Randy didn't let up. "I can't figure you out. Either you're really stupid or you're the most ungrateful bitch I've ever met. Proctor spent millions on you. Ty took three bullets for you. What are you going to say about me in an hour? And you want to give a billion-dollar technology to who exactly? Some primitives who couldn't win a sixth grade science fair here in the states? It's not our fault they're poor. Don't you get that?"

Cassie jumped up, angling to keep Gretchen from storming out.

Randy wanted to grab her by the throat, but he caught his breath, turned to the slider, and walked outside. Cassie tried to calm Gretchen down. Their voices muffled behind him as the glass door slid home. The more time he spent with Gretchen, the more he wished he'd never seen the Malibu against the guardrail.

He tried to focus on the men chasing her. If he could find them, he could be rid of her for good. Ty wouldn't have leaked the breakthrough. He was too much of a professional. Whitney had to be the one who made contact. Randy couldn't prove whether the technology worked, but he knew the playboy professor needed cash to fund his lifestyle. He must have contacted this second group, whoever they were, and tried to sell them his work. That egg Gretchen was carrying might be useless, but Randy needed to know who Whitney had been talking to if he wanted to help her. In a few hours it would be dark and he'd have his chance.

CHAPTER FIFTY-ONE

Dozens of reporters flocked to the hospital only to be corralled by the public relations staff. Walter was proud of his restraint. After learning which local hospital the ambulance had taken the wounded man to, Walter enjoyed a leisurely dinner and bided his time while Ty Summers was in surgery. Routine surgery would take an hour and if things went well, Ty would regain consciousness in the recovery room within another two hours. After three long hours of waiting, Walter pulled into the visitors parking area.

He tucked a small notebook inside his jacket and walked through the main entrance over to the elevators like any other hospital visitor. He recognized a few reporters from Boston and Providence bunched in a corner of the lobby but paid them no attention. Getting inside the public hospital proved almost too easy, because the security staff couldn't recognize him as a journalist if he didn't identify himself. He took the elevator to the second floor and followed the snaking hallways to the surgical intensive care unit. When he reached it, a set of locked double doors blocked the corridor. The sign above the intercom indicated he was in the right place.

He felt his empty back pocket, gathered himself, and pressed the button.

"I'm Walter Summers," he drawled. "I'm here to see my son Ty."

A nurse instructed him to come through the doors to the desk.

The lock clicked and Walter was inside.

A harried young woman met his eyes over a monitor and asked him to sign in. Behind her, two nurses spoke in hushed tones. Another hurried down the hall and into a nearby room. Machines beeped all around. Family members stood in the doorways. He guessed there were many more sitting or standing by bedsides deeper in the rooms where he couldn't see them.

He signed Walter Summers just as he'd rehearsed and when the nurse asked for his ID he clapped his empty back pocket. He frantically patted his other pockets, knowing his wallet was safely hidden in his glove compartment. He was betting they wouldn't keep a worried father from his gravely injured son, but when he told the nurse he'd just flown in and must have left his wallet in the cab, she balked. He turned and showed her his empty pants pockets.

She considered for a long moment. The other nurses had rushed off to attend to patients. She watched another flit by, raising her chin as she passed, hoping for help with her dilemma, but the nurse scurried to more important duties. Finally the woman behind the desk relented with a shrug and directed Walter to Ty's room.

Ty lay still in the dim light. A father would have stepped right up to the bedside. Walter hesitated to intrude on such a private moment, but he needed to act in character or he was going to arouse suspicion. The bedrail was cold as he inched his way around. Ty was completely in the grip of the anesthesia. He was bigger than Walter expected. Older than a college kid.

"It's ok. You can talk to him," a voice called from the door.

Walter started.

The nurse apologized, made a quick check of the equipment, and turned for the door. "He's going to be fine," she said. "The surgery went well. It'll just be a while before he wakes up." She disappeared without waiting for a response and Walter was left alone with the sleeping hero.

Words were exchanged just outside the door. Walter recognized the nurse's voice talking to a man by the door, but couldn't hear what was said. Probably a doctor. Nothing to worry about. Walter shrunk into the chair in the corner and left the room dark while he waited for Ty to wake on his own.

Nurses came in every so often. At every visit he asked them how Ty was and when he might wake up. Each time the response was the same, Ty was fine, he'd wake up soon.

Some time after ten-thirty, Walter closed his eyes as he lay back in the chair. He listened for a rustled sheet or a babbled word, but the monotony settled him to sleep in the corner, nearly invisible to the nurses as they came in to check his alleged son. By the time Ty began muttering, Walter was soundly asleep. The voice became stronger and more coherent as Walter dozed.

After several minutes, another sound could be heard in the room. If he were awake, Walter would have been alarmed by the metallic scraping at the window. The lock worked open from the outside and the window rose steadily to the hilt. The October night air filtered through the sterile hospital variety and settled over Walter, chilling him, but not enough for him to stir and give away his presence. Fortunately for Walter, he was a quiet sleeper and his wheezing breaths were attributed to Ty in the bed.

A gloved hand gripped the sash. A nylon jacket rubbed against the window frame. A boot thumped to the floor and a figure stood erect in the room. A second man moved through the window and in the tight space one of them bumped the radiator.

The clatter woke Walter and he opened his eyes to find two dark figures standing right in front of him. Light glinted off a black handgun and Walter yelled without thinking, "You don't belong in here."

The men startled hearing his voice. They hadn't noticed Walter asleep in the chair. They'd aligned themselves to shoot Ty, so only the closest man had a shot at Walter. The other was directly behind his partner.

The nearest man wheeled and snapped off a shot that buried into the wall above Walter's head as he dove for the floor.

"Security!" Walter screamed as he crawled frantically, getting nowhere.

Walter heard a man at the door command the intruders to put their guns down. Walter never saw him there. He was trapped on the floor between the chair and the bed. He tried to crawl underneath Ty's bed, but the metal frame blocked his way.

A muzzle flashed. A slug knocked deep into something wooden.

A booming report shook the room. It was so loud in the confined space, it would ring in Walter's ears for the next hour. The furthest man crashed backward and fell to Walter's eye level. Feet shuffled. The second man turned toward the door, but before he could steady himself, another booming report sent him crashing to the ground just six feet from where Walter quivered on the floor.

Not a second was wasted.

Walter still hadn't gotten up when the man from the door pounced on the sprawled figures. He kicked the guns away and checked for signs of life.

"Clear," he yelled toward the nurses outside. He yelled again when they didn't rush in. "I need some help in here."

The lights came up and there was a flurry of white, first surrounding Ty, then the men on the floor. Walter looked away but not before he registered a gaping head wound on the man closest to him.

"He's dead," Walter muttered to himself.

The man from the doorway wasn't wearing a policeman's uniform. Walter had been reporting on crime for years, but this was the first time he'd witnessed one in person. Thirty seconds earlier he'd been asleep. Now his heart raced and his stomach churned as he tried to get control of himself and capture the scene. He took out his notebook and sketched the room and mapped out the positions of the intruders, the guard, and Ty in the bed.

Walter noted everything significant he heard, though the activity for the first minute was so frantic he couldn't keep up. The nearest assailant had been shot in the head. The staff abandoned him as hopeless within seconds. The other assailant had been struck through the heart and died before a doctor could reach him. Things slowed then. Ty moved in his bed, awakened by the gunshots. A nurse stood beside him. Walter saw her look in his direction. He couldn't hear her over the buzzing in his head, but he read her lips as she said, "Your father is here."

Six people blocked Walter's exit. The nurse waved him over emphatically, annoyed he still hadn't gotten up of the floor so his son could see him.

Walter tucked away his notebook and stepped up to the bedside. "You're going to be ok, Ty," he said.

Surprise was slow to register on Ty's face. For a few seconds he couldn't make out the face at the bedside and Walter hoped he'd walk away with more than his eye witness account of the killings. If he could pass himself off to Ty for another ten minutes, the staff would filter out and he might even get a few questions answered. The anesthesia made Ty groggy, but the nurse on the opposite side of the bed understood something was wrong and didn't budge.

"Who are you?" Ty asked, struggling to focus on Walter's face.

"That's your father, Ty. It's ok, the anesthesia is making it hard to see."

"I see fine. That's not my dad," he said with effort.

The guard grabbed Walter's jacket and lifted with one hand. The other was on his holster. He didn't draw his weapon, but after seeing him fire it twice in the confined room, Walter didn't need more convincing to stay still.

"Who are you?" the guard barked.

"I'm not working for him. I'm a journalist."

"Who's him?"

"Randy Black. The guy who's trying to kill Ty. I'm a reporter. I'm trying to put him away."

The guard looked at Walter like a schoolchild. One of the nurses rushed out of the room and Walter knew he was in big trouble. Hospital security was already on its way and the local police would surely follow. He had no ID to prove he was a journalist and as he stood helpless in the grasp of a killer, he wished he was back in New Bedford where he'd know the cop who responded. The worst he could expect was a trespassing charge, maybe fraud for lying about his identity. He'd signed a false name on the register, there was no denying that. With luck he'd be out in time to get an article on the web by breakfast.

CHAPTER FIFTY-TWO

"If we get caught inside we're all going to jail," Randy said with his back to the door. The latex gloves from the hardware store were tucked in his pocket as was the mini flashlight.

Gretchen snarled, barely shaking her head side to side as if she were cursing Randy's chauvinism to herself. The sting from his rant was still fresh. She was just a few feet away, poised on the edge of the bed to rush out and follow him if he dared leave her behind. Cassie leaned against the bed beside her, also with her feet on the floor, but with a more temperate reaction to his proposal.

"You think we can't do this because we're women?" Gretchen snipped.

"I have more experience with these things. That's all."

Cassie reassured Gretchen that Randy had been incredibly clever at Heather Lovely's security complex and outside Judge McKinnon's house. "So when we're over there," Cassie continued, "make sure to follow his lead."

Randy glanced at the paint can on the floor and the paper bag beside it. He hadn't meant to encourage her, but Cassie walked over and picked up the remaining pairs of gloves and left the other painting supplies behind. She turned straight for the door, pausing only to hand Gretchen two white latex gloves. He hadn't been keen on leaving Gretchen unprotected in the room, but he liked bringing both of them along even less.

"Listen," he said. "There are dozens of people still out on the streets. We can't give them any reason to suspect something's wrong next door."

Both women gave the obligatory nod, but he felt queasy opening the door and slipping out into the hall.

Randy turned the final corner of the stairwell with the two women shadowing him like they were attached. Their hands squeaked on the railing and their shoes somehow managed to clomp on carpeted stairs. The innkeeper was looking directly at him when he descended far enough to see the long reception desk. He'd hoped to slip out into the night, hidden in the sheltered doorway where he could approach Whitney's fence without being observed. But they couldn't go out the side door with her watching. What was she doing up? She glanced at the computer as if she'd been playing a game. Was she paid to man the desk, or did she overnight here and just sit at reception to use the computer?

The three of them stepped into view.

"Evening," the woman behind the desk said.

She was younger than the woman who had checked them in. She must work the overnight, which meant she'd be there when they came back.

"Couldn't sleep. Thought we'd go out for a quick drink."

The young woman recommended a bar two blocks down.

Randy thanked her and said they'd go for a drive, primarily to cover their use of the back door. Cassie and Gretchen didn't say a word during the exchange. They followed him out with only a "good night" at the door. They looked surprised when he started the car, but he tapped his ear and signaled toward the innkeeper. She was used to hearing vehicles coming and going from the parking lot. He hoped she didn't have a camera to watch.

When the innkeeper had her chance to hear the car, he killed the engine and the three of them walked casually down the driveway and ducked into the recessed doorway. The women donned their gloves while Randy peeked around the corner until the sidewalk cleared, then he took two running steps across the drive and leaped for the top of the gate. He swung a leg up, hooked his boot on top, and then threw himself over, twirling in the air on his way down. He landed heavily on a stone walk, easily caught his balance, and opened the gate for the women to come across.

Light spilled into the courtyard from every side, illuminating a still fountain in the center and islands of perfectly manicured grass wedged between brick paths and shadowy flowerbeds. Cassie and Gretchen skirted the fountain and followed the path to a set of double doors. Randy stepped through a flowerbed and looped from patio to patio, poking his head in each window he passed. When this had been an inn, thirty rooms faced the courtyard, fifteen at ground level and fifteen above. The furniture remained in the rooms. Most were tidy, but a few looked slept in.

Across the courtyard Gretchen eyed the keyhole as if she could will the lock open by peering at the tumblers and becoming one with them. Fortunately, the bachelor had left behind a more practical opening at the corner. Randy pushed up an unlocked window and crawled into a disheveled guestroom with beer bottles in ranks on the dresser. He moved quickly through to fetch Cassie and Gretchen before they noticed he was gone and panicked. The kitchen was across the main hall, which is why Whitney would have chosen this particular room. Around the corner, Randy waved to the women through the door and welcomed them inside.

"How'd you do that?" Gretchen asked.

"Professional secret."

Gretchen instinctively reached for a light switch.

Randy grabbed her wrist before she made contact. "Not a good idea."

"Who's going to see lights in the courtyard windows?"

"Buildings overlook this place on every side."

"A few lights will make it look like he's home," Gretchen continued.

"Anyone watching this place will know he's not coming home." Randy twisted the flashlight and led the way back to the messy room. The women stayed close to the light and Randy found a small means of control.

The beam flicked over a dozen empty beer bottles arrayed on top of the dresser and night tables. Gretchen stepped right into the room and nosed around while Cassie hung in the doorway, hesitant to intrude. The bedclothes were thrown over as if someone had sprung from the bed and left them where they fell. There was no refrigerator. Gretchen pulled open every drawer in the dresser and waited for the light before pushing each one

221

closed. It was completely empty; ditto the closet. A Bible occupied the drawer in one of the night tables. Its twin was empty. There was nothing hidden under the bed. The trio faced each other and wondered out loud if it was Whitney using this room or if he'd rented it out as if it were still an inn. He certainly didn't need the rental income.

The door to the adjoining room was locked, but the door from the hall was open. Again they found empty beer bottles, a messy bed, and a Bible, but no clothes and nothing to indicate anyone had been in this room longer than overnight. When they opened the third door they found the same scenario except for a red cooler with three inches of warm water and a box of condoms in the nightstand.

"His maid only comes once a month," Randy said.

"What?" Cassie asked.

"He's an overgrown teenager with thirty bedrooms. When he has company he uses a clean one. When the maid comes, she cleans the entire place and he starts again."

The next room confirmed the pattern. It was further down the courtyard and the bed was neatly made and not a thing in the room was out of place. Randy turned toward the front of the inn.

"Where are we going?" Gretchen asked.

"To find Whitney's room." Randy didn't wait for a reply. He swept the light back and forth so the women could see the outline of the hall as it wrapped around the courtyard and turned back toward the main building. Around the corner, he found the only locked door they encountered inside.

Gretchen flipped on the light in the next room and reported she'd found the kitchen. She itemized her discoveries aloud as Randy worked the lock.

"Plenty of beer," Gretchen called.

The lock was better than the one on his parents door at home, but there was no deadbolt. It would keep Whitney's dates from stumbling into his private room, but with his tools, Randy could open it in thirty seconds. Unfortunately, he'd left those back in Dartmouth, never intending to use them again. In the kitchen he found a steak knife, peeked in at Gretchen as she surveyed the aging contents of the fridge, and went back to work on the door. It popped open easily with a little leverage from behind. Immediately Randy knew he was in the right place. The room was triple the size of the others. The twelve-inch floor tiles suggested it had been the dining room before Whitney commandeered it. The tiny flashlight did little in the large room. Since Gretchen already had the kitchen light on, Randy switched Whitney's bedroom light on as well.

An unmade king-sized bed faced him from the opposite wall. To the right, a desk cluttered with stacks of papers and mail drew him over. The envelopes were nothing but utility bills and such for the inn. There were brochures for boats and jet skis and fliers for local clubs mixed in, but nothing that resembled work. He turned all the way around and realized there wasn't a single book in the room. A man on the verge of a scientific breakthrough would have reading material everywhere. Did Whitney just vacation here? The series of single-use beds confirmed the innkeeper's playboy description. Maybe he only came here to find tourists.

Gretchen and Cassie came in from the kitchen. Gretchen went straight for the computer and turned it on. A thorough search of the computer could take hours and Randy wasn't planning to stay that long with the lights burning. Whoever was chasing Whitney would show up eventually.

A password prompt appeared and Gretchen made several guesses.

Randy suggested there might be a better way, but Gretchen rebuffed him sternly. She had a computer science minor as an undergrad and she was certain she could break in because she knew the professor better than he did.

Rather than argue, Randy started through the desk drawers. The first had a box of facial tissues, nothing else. The next was stuffed with CDs and paperback manuals for a variety of computer games and software. The bottom drawer was a tangle of wires and unwanted peripherals. The drawers on the other side of the desk were crammed with papers that had been stuffed in with no thought to organization. Back to the drawer with the tissues, he noticed deep gouges in both sides of the casing and then understood why the drawer contained only one item.

The computer powered down with a whoosh and Gretchen explained she'd locked herself out and would have to restart. Randy pulled the drawer out of the desk and turned it over. A single sheet of paper was taped to the underside. Gretchen powered the computer back on and nosed in for a look at what Randy had found. The password for the computer stood alone at the top of the page. Gretchen entered it and the computer accepted and showed a background photo of the waterfront two blocks away.

The scant list of passwords included two banks, one of them foreign, and an online poker site. If there were a bookcase in the room he would have checked for Caro and Sklansky. Anyone who made money playing poker owned a few poker books. In the drawer with the CDs there were plenty of war games and car chase games, but not a single poker game.

Gretchen yielded her seat and Randy opened the Internet and located the offshore bank. Fortunately, the browser remembered Whitney's account information and as soon as Randy entered the password, he was browsing through the professor's banking records. There was a deposit near the end of each month. The amounts varied, but they were all around four hundred thousand and they went back five years. The transfers all came from the same institution called PPP Financial.

Randy turned back to the password list. The poker site was called Poker Player's Paradise. Could Whitney make four hundred thousand a month playing online poker? Not likely. If he could, why would he waste time on solar energy research?

Randy opened the icon from the desktop and logged in as the professor.

The account showed a balance of three hundred dollars. No one could turn that into four hundred thousand, not without cheating. The machine stored some history of his playing style. The professor played No Limit Hold 'em. Before Randy could make sense of the statistics, a chat window opened and a player called WMD sent a message asking for a game. Two other players asked for games in the next three minutes and Randy knew exactly what was happening on the poker site.

CHAPTER FIFTY-THREE

Lou couldn't believe what he was seeing in the courtyard.

"Jonesy, get over here."

Jonesy slapped the cards down on the night table and hustled over, standing at the edge of the window where he couldn't be seen from outside.

"You believe this?"

"Nope."

They'd been crammed in this little room for thirty-six hours, sleeping in shifts with someone always in the chair facing the window, looking for a guy and a girl. Neither believed anyone would be stupid enough to show up at the professor's place, but as they watched, two figures followed the path past the fountain and right up to the back door. They were small and wore long hair. Two women? Women weren't big on breaking and entering. This had to be their couple. Maybe they'd picked up an extra skirt along the way, but where was the guy? As if in answer, he opened the door from the inside and let them in.

"What do we do?" Jonesy asked.

"I'll go down and wait for them to come out. Let's keep a line open until they do." Lou was thirty pounds lighter. If someone needed to be chased down, he was the one to do it, although when he caught them, he'd be glad to have Jonesy by his side.

Jonesy patted his phone. "Call me when you're down there."

As Lou closed the door, Jonesy pulled on his sneakers. Jonesy would be a terrifying figure chasing you in his huge black sweat suit and sneakers until you realized he could only run 8 mph.

Lou walked down to the lobby and straight out the front door with a story about not being able to sleep. The girl at the desk was more interested in her computer than Lou. She probably thought it was weird for two men to share a room, but then she had no idea what they were doing upstairs and probably didn't want to know.

Lou could only watch two sides of the building and settled for the front and the fence along the courtyard where they had gone in. He found a shadowy spot in the entrance to a gift shop where he wouldn't be spotted by anyone leaving Whitney's. A police cruiser drove by and when the officers saw him in the shadows they stopped a few doors down. Lou moved along Thames with his phone to his ear and luckily the cops didn't back up to question him. He settled back in the nook as soon as the cruiser was gone.

He narrated the action along Thames to Jonesy who's view was limited to the dark courtyard in front of him. Groups of four or five college kids straggled by every ten minutes or so. Otherwise, the street was deserted.

After half an hour, Jonesy warned him that they were moving. The gate swung open and a guy and two women walked out of the courtyard as if they were Whitney's guests. They closed the gate and walked down the drive directly toward him.

Lou made up a story about his night in the bar and started telling it to Jonesy to cover his loitering across the street. He stopped mid-sentence when the three of them turned and walked up the front steps and into the Admiral.

"You're not going to believe this," Lou said. "They're walking into the Admiral. Right through the front door."

Jonesy cracked open their door on the second floor and waited to see which room they went into. Lou waited outside for Jonesy to report back. A minute passed, then another. He fought the urge to follow them in. If he found them in the lobby and they left, he couldn't follow them back out without being obvious. So he stayed outside and waited five minutes. Finally, he said into the phone, "What's going on? You see them?"

"Nothing. Not a sound up here."

Lou worried it was a ruse. If he'd been spotted they could have walked right out the back door and disappeared over another fence. Jonesy never would have seen them. Lou doubted they were that smart, but he ran inside, pulling his wallet as he made the stairs. He breathed heavily as he reached the reception desk.

"Shoot. I missed him," he said out loud.

The innkeeper looked nervous behind the desk. She was the only security and probably not fond of the role. A man running in at this hour was enough to have her hand on the phone ready to dial 911, but she must have recognized Lou from his trips to the kitchen.

Lou waved his wallet. "I was just having drinks with some people I met outside the inn. The guy, Randy I think his name is, he left his wallet."

The innkeeper reached out her hand.

"I'd rather give it to him in person if you don't mind. Can you tell me what room he's in?"

The woman hesitated, but looked at the register out of the corner of her eye. She was wary, but Randy had just passed through the lobby and she knew Lou was a guest. Lou leaned heavily on the desk as if he'd just run ten blocks. "Eighteen or nineteen," she said. "Third floor. They just went up. If you hurry, you might catch them on the stairs."

Lou thanked her and headed upstairs. He pulled out his phone again when he was out of sight.

"They're on three," he said to Jonesy. "There's two ways up."

"Should we call for help?"

"I think the boss is going to want to talk to 'em before we do anything."

CHAPTER FIFTY-FOUR

Midnight came to the rented room Randy was supposed to be sharing with Cassie. Gretchen was still griping that they'd left Whitney's too abruptly and he couldn't send the caustic know-it-all to her room fast enough. It was his fault. If he'd gone alone he would have made less noise, less light, and taken less time. She'd be asleep now and he wouldn't have to listen to her. Instead he sat on the bed while she whined about how much of an idiot the professor was and how little Randy understood him. Randy's mind wandered to his lack of preparation for the moment Gretchen finally went to her own room. He thought about hopping the fence to the professor's and borrowing some protection from his nightstand. The professor wouldn't mind. He was probably dead. Even if he wasn't, with all the money he was taking down from the poker site he wouldn't miss a condom or two.

Gretchen's tone turned even more bitter and Randy tuned back in.

"...seeing a poker game on his computer. So now you think he's a genius because he wins money at poker?"

"He's lousy at poker."

"What?" Gretchen asked, frustrated she wasn't following his logic.

Cassie was intent on his answer, too.

"When I logged on as Whitney, four players asked me to play."

"So what?"

"If you're playing poker for money, do you want to play with someone who's beating you?" Randy paused. "Of course you don't. Whitney was losing money on a regular basis. That's why they were so excited to play against him. That was just a few minutes. I bet there are dozens of players who were dying to play against Whitney."

"If he's not a good player, how is he winning so much money?"

"Someone was dumping chips." Randy could see Gretchen didn't understand so he continued. "Someone was losing to him on purpose. The amounts were a little different each month because the professor was playing and losing some of the money before he cashed out."

Gretchen's head tilted as she considered. For once she held her tongue.

"It's perfect," Randy explained. "Operating an online gambling site is a bit shady, in most places at least. They wouldn't keep very good records. They might keep withdrawals and deposits, but they wouldn't record who played against who. That means there's no way to prove who was paying him off."

"That's how he afforded his place next door," Cassie said. "Someone was paying him to keep quiet. When he announced the press conference he made that someone very angry."

"So," Randy said to Gretchen. "He really *was* a great researcher."

"He was a drunk and a bastard."

"To you everyone's a bastard."

"He should have released the technology five years ago."

"Maybe. But how would you feel if I took that egg from you and told you that you could never tell anyone about it?"

Gretchen's eyes lit with the recognition that Whitney might have been a victim at some level, but there wasn't a lot of sympathy behind those tight little lips.

"You might start drinking, too," Randy continued. "Five million a year was enough at first, but eventually his conscience got to him. At some point the booze and young girls weren't enough." Randy wanted to add that he couldn't understand why, but that was the wrong thing to say in front of Cassie.

"And there's no way we can find out who was paying him?"

Whoever was paying the professor wanted Gretchen dead because she'd seen the data.

"The money's not going to lead us anywhere."

The telephone rang at the bedside.

Gretchen looked to the French doors that led to the roof deck, then flashed to the solid door to the stairway. Randy motioned for her to relax and picked up the phone. Nothing was said until he said, "Hello."

"Well hello, Mr. Black. What a delight it is to finally make your acquaintance. Do you know who this is?"

Randy walked to the French doors and pulled back the curtain. A huge man in a black sweat suit waved a semi-automatic handgun from behind the gate. There would be no escape across the roof decks.

"I know what you want," Randy answered.

"Good then. Let the girl come with us and we'll have no trouble. I assume that you and your lady friend are smart enough not to speak to anyone about what Gretchen has told you. Of course we'd be glad to compensate you for your faithfulness."

"Like you paid the professor?"

Randy cursed his stupidity for letting Gretchen turn the lights on next door. Someone had been watching Whitney's house and simply followed them back here. Why hadn't he been careful enough to at least circle the block? The men from the highway couldn't have gotten here that fast. He'd underestimated how important this discovery was and he'd made easy prey of the two women in his care.

"Not quite that much. Whitney discovered the technology after all. I'm just asking you not to talk about it for a little while. Why don't you send Miss Greene out the door and take the case from the gentleman in the hall?"

"Not gonna happen."

"How heroic. I wouldn't have expected less after reading about your exploits. You do understand that you're blocked into that room by my men outside? They are armed of course."

The man on the phone went silent to let the trapped feeling sink in. Randy might get past the guy on the roof, but it would be impossible to get the women out without someone getting shot. The guy on the phone was completely calm. He wasn't worried about them getting away. He probably had other men on the ground. Maybe even waiting by their car.

"My life's work is much more important than that Marston fellow's. I'm not going to let you destroy it. So here's how it will go. You step out into the hall and let my man put the cuffs on you. Then the three of you can come down here and we'll talk this over. We've already checked you out of your rooms. And don't try alerting the police, it will only make my men angry."

Charging the man in the hall or on the roof deck would leave the women vulnerable to the man left unoccupied. The women couldn't follow while he fought an armed man and they couldn't jump from the third floor.

He hung up the phone and faced Cassie.

"We've got a problem." Randy told them about the call and the men waiting outside both doors.

Cassie's face sank with fear. "Shit," she muttered.

Gretchen wasn't so supportive. She yelled, "Idiot!" She took no responsibility for flicking on the lights next door. Her eyes flashed around the room then she jumped from her seat and headed for the deck. When she saw the man through the glass she let out a piercing shriek.

Randy ran over and put a hand over her mouth. Fortunately, they occupied the only two rooms on the uppermost floor and the people in the rooms below made no sign of stirring. "That's not going to help."

With a gun Randy could have fought his way out and led the women to safety. Unarmed, he faced the door with a sick feeling ballooning in his stomach, but he assured himself they'd have a better chance to escape. In the car or somewhere along the way, he'd find a way out. The last thing he saw before he opened the door was a flashback to the faces of the three men pinned by the McLaren. Their friends would be very angry.

The voice from the phone is what finally convinced him to turn the knob. It wasn't some unearthly voice, but that of a placid gentleman without an ounce of menace.

The man in the hall had an entirely different demeanor. Stern and unyielding, he faced Randy from three stairs below with his gun aimed squarely at Randy's chest. There was no case on the steps, but once he'd opened the door open it didn't matter. There were only three feet of lateral play. A gunshot across the landing almost couldn't miss.

The man tossed a pair of cuffs and instructed Randy to secure them himself. When his hands were cuffed behind his back, the man holstered his weapon and frisked Randy. Rather than go inside for the women, he turned and led Randy down two flights and outside into the tiny parking lot out back. A Suburban was waiting there and another rugged-looking man with a military haircut ushered Randy into the back seat, removed one cuff, and then secured it to a steel bar mounted into the bench seat for the purpose.

In a few minutes, the man from the roof deck and the man from the hall returned with Cassie and Gretchen. Neither of them was cuffed. The guns were encouragement enough for them to behave on the way out of the building and into a matching Suburban that pulled up behind the first.

CHAPTER FIFTY-FIVE

The Suburban rolled down the narrow drive and made a left on Thames. The matching SUV followed along. Randy craned his neck to watch, but the Corolla wasn't part of the caravan. The innkeepers would eventually find the car and they'd know it was too new to be abandoned. Would they have it towed without realizing who it belonged to? Or would they know something was wrong? Randy believed what the voice said. One of the guys up front had checked them out of the hotel, but he didn't understand why they left the car behind.

They made another left and headed out of town.

"Get comfortable back there. It's going to be a long ride."

"You can't just pick us up and haul us off," Randy protested.

The men up front didn't respond. Randy shifted in his seat for a better look. They were dressed in dark suits like mafia muscle and they weren't intent on their mirrors. If they weren't going to watch him, this could be his best chance to escape. He went to work bending his thumbnail back and forth until he could tear it off.

"Were the hell are we going?" Randy said, mostly to cover the noise he made with his hands.

The men didn't look back, didn't respond.

"This is kidnapping. That's federal you know."

The men said nothing to this or the next dozen flimsy complaints Randy used to cover his work on the tiny lock. The car traveled east back to I-95 before he finally had the lock open and started easing the cuff open one click at a time.

The blond man in front turned around unexpectedly. Randy hadn't said anything in a mile and was caught completely off guard with both hands on the cuffs.

"We're not cops. You have no rights here. Our job is to get you where you're going and we're going to do that. If you're broken when you get there, no one is going to give a damn. Understand?"

Randy didn't answer. He waited half a mile before releasing the cuffs another click.

"It'll be a lot easier if you cooperate," the blond man warned.

Randy couldn't believe he knew what was going on in the back seat. The guy barely ever looked back, but Randy held still for another mile before risking another click of the cuffs. He coughed to cover himself, a lame ploy, but he was running out of legitimate-sounding complaints and the warnings from the front were making him nervous.

The guy in the passenger seat hesitated half a second then reached forward to the dash, flipped open a compartment, and pressed down hard on a button. It wasn't the solid click of the button that alarmed Randy as much as the menacing way he lifted his arm and jammed his finger down. The driver took his eyes off the road and turned back to watch.

A bright blue ark jumped from the steel bar to the cuff and latched on. The charge traveled instantaneously down the short chain and into Randy's arm. Piercing pain stabbed every muscle and forced them to stretch outward to its utmost. His entire length went rigid and he was helpless while the current pulsed through him. Thankfully the blond took his finger off the button. Vibrations played their way up and down Randy's arms and legs. A humming tune in his ears coordinated the rise and fall of the tingling sensation dancing around his body. He smelled ozone.

A grin wrinkled the driver's face.

Now Randy knew why the blond was sitting up front and not behind where he could see better. He wanted access to the switch and he didn't want to be within reach while Randy was being shocked.

"You want to click that cuff closed now?"

The chances of getting loose weren't worth another jolt.

Randy tightened the cuff around his own wrist and settled back.

They headed south for about an hour before arriving at an airport Randy wasn't familiar with. There was no commercial terminal, no signage for passengers, or even cargo haulers. The Suburban headed into a massive hangar filled with murky shadows in the predawn hours. The few visible lights shined on a custom Lear 60. The driver stopped within twenty yards of the plane. The SUV carrying Cassie and Gretchen stopped beside them.

No one in Randy's vehicle moved until the door opened from the outside. Cassie was shoved in far enough to cuff her hand to Randy's. Only then was he unlocked from the bar. When Randy stepped onto the concrete, the huge hangar doors were already closed and five men surrounded them on their short walk to the retractable stairs.

Chained together and surrounded inside the cavernous hangar, they had no choice but allow themselves to be led up the stairs to their seats. Randy was cuffed to a low leather chair in a row of three with his back to the windows. The women were allowed to sit side by side facing forward. The blond man and his darker companion from the Suburban filled the chairs on either side of Randy. The remaining three aligned themselves on the opposite side of the cabin. They allowed him no room to maneuver. He'd be hemmed in for the entire flight and zapped unconscious if he so much as stood without permission.

Cassie looked drowsy from the ride. Gretchen's eyes flicked around the cabin like she was being delivered to her executioner. That was a distinct possibility. The voice on the phone could have been a ploy to get them into the Suburban without a struggle. Once he was cuffed to that bar, the men had complete control of him. Gretchen understood how dire their situation was. She had barely looked at him on the way to the plane. She blamed him and she was right. He'd screwed up and there was nothing he could do but rest and wait for the plane to land.

The guards talked and joked for the entire flight, but after the episode in the back of the Suburban, Randy knew they were attuned to his every movement. The pilot was locked in his cabin up front. Rand had no chance to overpower five men in the confined space even if he got the cuffs off without attracting attention.

Midway through the flight Randy was allowed to use the bathroom without the cuffs. When he stepped out the door the men were on their feet. The blond stepped up from behind and crackled a hand-held stun gun. The jumping spark reminded Randy of the pain and the hopeless sensation of being completely conscious while electricity took command of his muscles. He walked to his seat and locked the cuff himself.

The sun rose on Randy's left and some time later, the jet turned and the ocean came into view. They had been traveling southwest making the water up ahead the Gulf of Mexico. They circled and continued their descent. Randy looked past Cassie and Gretchen asleep in their chairs and glimpsed the runway as the jet dipped. When it leveled off, an oil refinery came into view.

The runway and the refinery were separated by a mile of barren dirt, so a mishap on the private airstrip wouldn't set off a chain reaction of explosions at the refinery. Randy studied the squat white tanks that looked small from the air though he knew they were imposing up close. The tanks were dotted around a wide area crammed full of metallic sprouts that grew straight up in ordered rows. The sprouts were connected by a tangle of smaller pipes woven together in an infinitely confusing mess. As he looked closer, the tangle sprouting from each white tank looked similar in form to the next, although he couldn't imagine how any one person could understand the routing that connected each tank to whatever processing was happening outside on the ground.

The plane dropped further and he could make out a pair of high chain-link fences, one inside the other, both topped with barbed wire. They'd soon be headed inside that fence and he wondered if the security measures on the inside were as tight.

CHAPTER FIFTY-SIX

Standing on the lush green grass, the prince could feel the moisture rising all around him, dispatched to the heavens by the blazing desert sun. To his right, the waterfall finally achieved the thunderous rush he desired. Powered by the new desalinization plant, the two thirty-six inch pipes burrowed through the rocky landscape and dumped thousands of gallons of water on the rock face and sent it cascading down as if the prince had tapped the most vibrant natural spring imaginable. The ten-acre pond was the centerpiece of the golf course design and would be the envy of his counterparts in the cartel once the course was finished and they were invited to play.

To the west, the string of earthmovers and king-sized dump trucks filled with imported topsoil and the bulldozers that sculpted that soil into tees, fairways, and greens, sat idle waiting for his highness to survey the most recently completed hole. The circling of the sprinklers ceased and each retracted into the ground in a steady progression from where he stood all the way to the flag flapping in the gentle breeze.

Waves of water vapor immediately sprouted up all along the fairway as the life-giving water was baked away from the green carpet.

He stepped to the tee and took the club offered, addressed the ball, and swung as he'd been taught only weeks before. The ball started on target, but sliced increasingly right until it splashed down in the man-made lake.

"What now?"

"You may play it wherever you like, highness."

"Idiot. What do the rules say?"

"There, by the water's edge."

He held out a hand and found a cool glass of water as they began walking down the fairway. A young man rushed ahead, another followed, burdened by an oversized leather golf bag under the brutal sun. When they reached the water's edge, the first young man placed the ball as he'd been told, so it sat high on the grass with the prince's name aligned toward the flag.

As he readied for his next shot, an electric cart buzzed up the fairway toward him. He turned and the cart came to a stop. He swung high and the ball found a wide sand trap that lined the left side of the green. The white sand made a stunning contrast with the lush green all around. He glared back at the cart driver and called for a new ball to be placed. He struck it thin and it found the same location.

The cart rushed up as the group began to walk.

"Highness, the television people are waiting."

He stopped. He had no fondness for Western media, but this meeting was his duty.

"The new hole pleases you, highness?" the architect asked.

"The sand must go."

"It is—"

"Extend the green. I will not play from sand!"

The green was already a hundred feet wide to accommodate his slice. The architect looked confused but knew better than to protest. His highness mounted the cart next to his information minister and the driver made a wide turn and headed back to the palace. When they were clear of the course, work resumed and the sprinklers were turned back on.

Several minutes later he strode down a wide marble hall trailed by the information minister. He moved to the podium and addressed the cameras and microphones prepared for his arrival.

"Our members and I wish to express our sincerest sympathies for the attack in Boston yesterday." The speech the information minister had compiled went on for several minutes, lauding the cartel as a peaceful organization of businesspeople all over the world and described the United

States as one of its largest customers. The minister said nothing of the excesses of the Infidels, only that the cartel valued that important relationship.

When he finished, hands shot up all around the room.

He gestured to a man in Arab garb. "Highness, how do you respond to the Western accusations that the cartel was involved in the attack on the Institute yesterday?"

"Ridiculous. Our members have vast untapped reserves of energy we wish to sell to the Americans. We also have our own scientists. We don't need to steal technology from Westerners when we can barely keep up with global demand for our products. Renewable energy is an admirable pursuit and will alleviate some of our excess demand. We expect in years to come the Americans will be buying solar panels and wind turbines from our members just as they buy our traditional products now."

Hands shot up again.

He dismissed them with a wave, turned, and left the room.

When he was alone in his office with the information minister, he asked, "What is the status of our operation?"

"We have tracked the girl to Texas, highness. She will have the illusion of safety for a few hours. Then we will have her."

CHAPTER FIFTY-SEVEN

The stifling Texas air immediately brought beads of sweat to Randy's skin. The sun was barely up as he descended the folding stairs, but it already felt like a summer day in New England. Gretchen and Cassie led the way onto the tarmac. None of the three wore cuffs, yet they walked directly to three waiting SUVs, each with three men in black jumpsuits holding M4 rifles. Counting the five men from the plane, the odds of escape were turning decidedly dire. The cuffs were unnecessary because the flat land extended for a mile in every direction. They couldn't outrun the M4s.

The vehicle started with a jolt, but without any sound from the engine. The mile to the refinery passed quickly with wide open terrain on both sides. The Suburban slowed for the gate to swing open. Randy looked left and right down a line of heavy pipes buried just inside the first fence line. Filled with concrete and spaced six feet apart they'd halt any vehicle that crashed through the fence. The occupants would be kept outside the inner fence, which was twenty yards further in. The gate seemed the easiest portal whether you were an authorized guest or fighting your way out.

Further still, they passed a row of towers that rose twenty feet off the ground and were topped with a black metal ball with a ten-inch horizontal slot cut into the front. They looked like guard towers, but the opening looked too low for a person to see through.

"You really have that many guards?" Randy asked.

The men up front didn't answer. He didn't expect an answer from the blond and the dark man that flanked him. This time he didn't pepper them with questions.

Further in, they began passing the refining plant, a facility of such massive scale Randy was awed. The field of pipe and towers and storage tanks dwarfed the vineyard in Westport. What had looked like a garden of metal pipes from the air resembled cylindrical office buildings from the ground. Randy couldn't fathom the money spent to build this facility or the money that was made here on a daily basis. It was then he realized they hadn't seen a single worker since passing through the gates. The plant was shut down for their arrival. There would be no witnesses to what happened to Randy, Cassie, and Gretchen.

The driver pulled up to a large brick building. The overhead door raised and the driver pulled in and parked on the ground level. What looked like an office building from the outside was actually a garage with four rows of cars parked on the ground floor and a ramp at the far end. The space was closed off from the outside. There wasn't a whoosh of air handlers and yet the air was clean even though fifty cars were parked on the ground floor.

"We walk from here," the driver said. The four guards exited and led Randy to an elevator. The bulk of the force was following behind and didn't unload until Randy, Cassie, and Gretchen were three-quarters of the way to the wide elevator platform. Tire marks led from the garage onto a platform large enough for two of the Suburbans to park on. When the entire group stepped on, the car was filled. The operator punched an access code. Randy counted six digits, but the man shielded the pad with his body and Randy didn't see any of them.

Rather than rising up to the higher floors, the elevator descended into the earth, startling the three newcomers. The ride continued deeper and deeper until finally the earth opened up to a square-cut cavern with a dozen golf carts parked and waiting.

The carts held groups of six. Cassie and Randy rode together. Gretchen warranted her own car where she was surrounded by armed men. A hundred feet underground, sixteen hundred miles from home, their bodies would never be found. Randy regretted his surrender back at the hotel, but there was nothing he could do in the narrow corridor. He'd have to wait for an opportunity when the three of them were together and could find their own way out. He kept looking back, expecting the carts behind to veer off and whisk Gretchen away to an underground prison where he'd never find her, but the two trailing carts followed closely the entire trip.

The drivers parked side by side at an overlook that opened up to three floors of glass-fronted rooms. Air was exhausted through an open air courtyard that rose fifty feet above the sunken building. Higher up, the opening narrowed into the mouth of a massive exhaust pipe.

A suited man in his late fifties walked briskly down the platform toward the group. He extended his hand to Gretchen and welcomed her warmly. She recognized him on sight, but she wasn't pleased to see him. He shared a pleasant greeting for Randy and Cassie. This was the man from the phone. He introduced himself as Lyle Ashton and Randy knew he was the one who'd been paying for the research at the Institute.

"You may be wondering why we work so far underground."

The group nodded more out of deference than curiosity.

"Heat rises, of course, and this is Texas," he said grandly. "When terrorism became a serious concern, we moved our control center down here. No bomb can penetrate this deep and we can defend the facility exceedingly well from right here." He gestured to the rooms beyond the courtyard and for the first time, Randy saw the figures seated behind the glass.

As Ashton spoke, Randy scanned the ends of the tunnel and the offshoots that ran perpendicular every so often. The tunnels ran outward as if this underground building was just a small part of the submerged complex. If the money spent on the above-ground plant was staggering, the investment down here was astronomical.

"We're well away from the refinery operations I assure you. This location is just inside the outer fencing. Those tunnels allow us to get to any location on the surface without exposing ourselves until it is absolutely necessary. Most of our defenses are controlled from here, but the guns still need to be reloaded eventually."

The low slits in the towers meant the guns were operated by remote control. The towers could be small because there was no gunner inside. And the round shape accommodated a rotating weapon.

"What's in the towers?" Randy asked.

"Fifty-caliber machine guns. Operated from those upper rooms there." He pointed. "Come, come," he said and began walking toward the stairs. "I'll show you."

The guards stayed on the platform with the golf carts.

Ashton descended the metal stairs and waited for them at the first tier below. The nearest room housed a dozen men in black, reading books or sitting at tables playing cards. Across the open courtyard was an identical room with a similar group of men.

Ashton saw their curiosity. "The guards can't watch monitors for the entire day. We break the duty up into short shifts. When they're not monitoring the perimeter, they are in this room ready to rush wherever they are needed." They could be up the stairs in seconds, ready to intercept anyone who fought their way down here.

The rest of the first floor held small offices filled with monitors and small groups of men watching them. They descended to the next level where the rooms looked very similar, but the men were dressed in casual clothes instead of uniforms and rather than the sparse decor above, the small rooms were filled with the comforts of office life. Pictures of families lined desks cluttered with stacks of reports, coffee mugs, and desk toys. A duct at each room blew a constant rush of air out into the courtyard. The men here—he hadn't seen a single woman on the tour so far—were the workers Randy had expected to see on the surface.

"From down here," their host said, "we control the refining process above ground. Those huge towers you saw on the surface are responsible for separating the crude into various types of hydrocarbons." He reveled in teaching his short lesson. "Oil is a mishmash of decayed matter. The hydrocarbons that make up that sticky black soup come in various lengths, each suitable for different purposes. Fortunately, they all have different boiling points. What we do is vaporize them and send them climbing up those gleaming towers outside. The higher they climb, the lower their boiling point and the smaller their molecular chains. The pipe work around the towers collects the various components. As they come out of the towers, we do some purification and then cracking and unification to convert some of the lower value compounds into more useful substances—like the ones we use in gasoline."

Randy was curious about the refining works, but he was consumed with finding a way out of Ashton's stronghold. Gretchen soured at talk of oil.

Ashton continued walking along the lowest tier. "Of course, having everyone down here helps us keep our employees safe. Everything on the surface can be controlled from here and the switching gear above is encased wherever possible to shield it from damage."

Was all this security overkill for an oil refinery?

Ashton reached the end of the tier and gestured to an opening in the rock that was invisible from above. The opening narrowed into a corridor that reached deep underground and turned away from the office complex they'd just visited. Wherever they were going seemed to be outside Proctor Energy property. Randy imagined this was the end for them, a prison where they would be held until Gretchen complied with Ashton's demands. Randy's only comfort at this point was that the guards had stayed behind on the upper tier.

Just as he had this thought, two men sprinted down the corridor to them. The blond and his partner from the Suburban had changed into black jumpsuits to match their teammates. The blond whispered in Ashton's ear. The older man looked concerned. He looked back the way they'd come for a moment, but decided to press on. The guard was so surprised by the decision he reached out for Ashton's arm. Both guards eyed Ashton, intent on his instructions, and Randy saw his opportunity.

CHAPTER FIFTY-EIGHT

Ashton's decision captivated the two guards. The three Proctor men clustered together, disregarding Randy in the center of the corridor with Cassie and Gretchen at his back. The only leverage the men maintained, aside from being deep underground in a terrorist-proof bunker, was the M4 rifles they carried. If Randy could get the M4s, he could find a way to the surface and back to civilization.

Randy shrugged as if he were annoyed by the delay, then subtly turned away from Ashton and gestured toward the far wall with his thumb. Cassie complied promptly but casually. Gretchen took a giant step back.

Randy lunged forward and drilled a fist into the kidney of the nearest guard. The guard dropped to his knees and Randy followed with another fist to the back of his head. The guard fell forward smothering his weapon underneath a two-hundred-pound pile of immotile flesh and bone.

The blond turned. "Hey," he yelled, the words echoing down the corridor even as his buddy's fall shoved him backward.

Randy catapulted himself over the fallen soldier and tackled his stumbling adversary. His right hand found the muzzle of the M4 and held firm as his left shoulder drove in just below the falling man's ribs. They crashed into the rough hewn rock. The guard hit first, his head meeting the wall as the rest of his body collapsed to the floor. Randy fell on top of him, driving the blond's shoulders to the floor. His neck bent forward, his head unnaturally close to his chest. Randy ripped the gun away and kneeled over him.

The guard's eyes blinked into focus. Anger and surprise snapped across the man's face along with the intention to recapture his weapon and control of the situation. The crash against the rock could have knocked him unconscious and the fall to the floor at that awkward angle could have broken his neck, but a man with a broken neck wouldn't exhibit such fire. The guard's arms struggled under the weight of Randy's knees and the response was swift and brutal. Randy remembered the blond's joy when he pressed the button and sent the blue spark pulsing through his body. More than his joy, Randy remembered the pain. He spun the rifle and crashed the butt down on the guard's forehead, draining the light from the blond's eyes and sending him slumping to the ground.

"That's quite enough," Ashton said.

Randy ignored him, rolled the heavier guard off his M4 and handed it to Cassie.

"I don't know what to do with this," Cassie said, holding it away from her body as if it carried a communicable disease.

"You won't have to fire it, just hang on to it in case I need it."

"You've got this all wrong," Ashton interrupted.

Randy turned to him and pointed the M4 at his feet. "You kidnap the three of us and hold us here underground and we've got it wrong? Tell me how I've misunderstood the rifles and the handcuffs."

"We've got an important proposition for Miss Greene."

"You're going to pay her for the data she took from Whitney? Are you going to keep her down here and dispose of her like you did him?"

"We're going to pay her quite handsomely, yes."

Gretchen didn't care about money. Randy was certain Ashton was stalling until his guards responded to the commotion. He hadn't seen cameras along the rock wall, but with all the monitoring equipment it was hard to believe they weren't being watched.

"We don't need the data Miss Greene is carrying. It's quite outdated."

Randy heard the words and saw Ashton's forthright expression, but couldn't believe what he was hearing. "You were willing to kill for it," Randy said.

"Not us," Ashton said, "We've had that data for a very long time. Not terribly practical, but we've refined the technology and we're ready to go commercial."

"So what do you need me for?" Gretchen asked.

"We need a hero, Miss Greene. A heroine, if you prefer."

Randy laughed out loud. What a ridiculous choice. Gretchen would steal the technology and export it to Kenya or Ethiopia.

Gretchen looked back at Ashton incredulously. Even she didn't believe she qualified as a hero.

"Let me show you," Ashton said. "No tricks. You have my word."

Randy kept the rifle trained at the gray-haired executive's feet and they followed him to the end of the corridor and into a cavern ten times larger than the one that controlled the refinery. This wasn't a monitoring operation, it was a manufacturing operation.

"The vehicles you rode here in, they're built with our latest application. It's still more complicated than a typical paint job, but we've got the process refined so our electric cars are no more expensive than your Corolla, Ms. Corcoran. Certainly not as expensive as your McLaren."

"But not as fast." Randy chided himself for being drawn in.

"Touche."

The pipe work here looked like a simplified underground refinery, but Ashton explained that they were taking some of the raw materials from the refinery above to make commercial use of the professor's solar technology.

"You were paying him to keep quiet about his discovery?" Randy asked.

"Not my decision. Not our finest hour, but we had no choice."

Randy shifted the M4 and carried the weight in his crossed arms.

With the rifle pointed at the outer wall, Ashton relaxed. "We were funding the professor when he made his discovery."

Gretchen balked. "He finished the formulation this week."

"No, dear," Ashton said. "Whitney made this discovery five years ago. The problem was, he made lots of noise about it and attracted attention from the wrong people."

247

Randy looked around the room and the fortifications were beginning to make sense.

"Back then his discovery would have revolutionized energy production. Imagine how you would feel about that if your entire economy was built on paying others to pump oil out of the ground at your feet. Economies, civilizations are now built on an endless stream of wealth that just bubbles up from the ground. What would happen if that oil became worthless?"

"They'd be pissed," Randy said.

"Royally. They threatened to blow us off the map if we tried producing Whitney's solar paint."

"So you paid Whitney to keep quiet?"

"They paid us. We paid Whitney. We used our share of the payoff along with our profits to move our research underground."

"What about the press conference?"

"We've been preparing for this day for five years. We are ready to tell the world what we've discovered and we thought it fair to give Whitney credit. It's his discovery after all. Unfortunately, he couldn't keep quiet until we were ready. He bragged over drinks and helped another researcher get dangerously close to duplicating his work. The word got out and everything went to Hell."

"And that's why you want Gretchen."

"Precisely."

CHAPTER FIFTY-NINE

The cement block warehouse covered four acres. The loading dock along its backside buzzed to fill the trailers parked at every available door. Inside, containers were emptied, long rows of crates cracked open, and their contents hauled to fill the trucks from front to back. Three hundred Carl Gustavs were packed in various trailers along with hundreds of crates of ammunition, enough to lay siege to the refinery for hours and idle the operation for years. The Gustavs, shoulder-fired rockets designed as an anti-armor, anti-fortification weapon, would be devastating to the refining plant. The gasoline, kerosine, and diesel manufactured there would provide fuel to burn the facility to the ground.

Dozens of compact pickup trucks were backed into the trailers right up to the lidless cases of ammunition. Each truck had mortar tubes welded side by side at the rear of the cargo bed like crude church organs with their pipes slightly askew and cut short. Four men would ride in the bed of each truck, uncrating amunition and feeding it into the tubes as fast as they could.

Once the pickup trucks were in place, the men gathered in the center of the warehouse and faced their leader. The ball of white gauze taped to Hisham's face where his nose had once been drew the attention of every man ready to board the trucks. No hospital bed could keep him from spilling his enemy's blood. Their leader's injury would be avenged this day.

A sea of black-suited men fanned out in all directions from the table at the center of warehouse. They squeezed together around dismantled crates and wooden lids heaped together in mounds of scrap wood. Two groups of sixty men proudly quartered AK-47s in front of the trucks that would haul them into battle. This elite group would assault the inside of the compound while their comrades pounded the facility from outside the fences.

Hundreds of men in the warehouse fell silent as Hisham began speaking in a flat nasally tone that was much less powerful than it had been just a day earlier. The men at the back couldn't hear a word. Their unit leaders up front would relay the battle plan later.

A detailed map of the compound lay on the table. Hisham poked it repeatedly as he described the devastation the Carl Gustavs would wreak from beyond the fence. The fuel they produced would be spilled and turned against them in a blaze that would rage on for days. Only the highest level commanders could see the blueprint, but no one questioned the devastation their firepower would visit.

The finger traced the outline of the two fences and warned of the machine guns mounted high. Three men would be assigned to disabling the towers. "The towers are armed with fifty-caliber machine guns. These guns have incredible range and firepower, so we must keep our distance. Remember," he thundered louder than before, "there are no men in these towers. It will be difficult to get inside, but then the guns are vulnerable. We will smash them and we will have complete control of the refinery."

The leader gave final instructions to the mortar teams and the assault team, then exhorted the crowd. "We will burn this plant to the ground and dig up the men responsible for this." He pointed to his missing nose. "We will drive them into the sand and tear them apart."

CHAPTER SIXTY

"We're prepared to compensate Miss Greene handsomely for her participation because she's the only remaining link to Whitney's research." Ashton turned from Randy to Gretchen. "We're prepared to give you ten thousand acres of rainforest to preserve as you like."

Ashton had chosen the ideal incentive for Gretchen. Money would have annoyed her. She would have reviled power within the American capitalist machine, but preserving the environment was her life's work. The impact showed on her face immediately. Ashton had done nothing more that purchase a personal gift, but the choice was brilliant. Proctor Energy would make billions on this invention and they'd just landed their figure head with five words that made their payoff palatable.

"If you already have the technology, what am I supposed to do?"

"Continue your work, here with our scientists. We will have some conditions, but you will be credited for many of the advances that spring from Whitney's work."

"Why would you give me credit?"

"Because you will become the spokesman, spokeswoman, if you like."

The selection made perfect sense. What better way for an oil company to remake its image than to hire a zealous environmentalist to lead its alternative energy project. Ashton already owned the technology. They didn't need a researcher who was years behind their in-house team. They were buying a public relations boon. Gretchen's ecoterrorist pals would line up to cheer Proctor Energy if she was delivering the message.

Ashton led them further into the complex and showed them a technical wing dedicated to battery research. It was ten times the size of Whitney's lab. So far the vehicles were well-suited only to areas with consistent sunshine. In the northeast and northwest, the vehicles had significant range limitations on cloudy days and at night. This didn't dampen the potential for the technology to power homes and businesses, but Proctor Energy wanted to sweep the country with a revolutionary change. Vehicles that operated for just pennies a mile were the most visible aspect of the strategy.

As they descended the stairs to a lower floor, Ashton promised to show them the evolution of Whitney's coating system. They walked out onto the landing and a dozen armed guards lined the railing a flight above with guns trained on the four of them.

Randy had been carrying his gun cross-armed without regard to keeping Ashton under control. Until the moment the safeties clicked off on the upper floor, he hadn't considered using Ashton as a hostage. He'd been so absorbed by the conversation about the technology and Gretchen's role in it, he'd been caught completely unaware. Cassie still held the M4 and looked to him for direction, her eyes filled with panic.

Before Randy moved to calm her, Ashton stepped out in front of them, waved his hands, and ordered his men to lower their weapons. They did. A single man hustled down the stairwell toward them while the other eleven maintained their position above with their rifles pointed at the roof of the cavern.

The security guard stopped two dozen feet short. "Are you ok, sir?"

"I think we've come to an agreement," Ashton said.

Gretchen still wasn't certain. She nodded but said nothing.

"We have a situation," the man said gravely.

He motioned Ashton forward, but he balked after a few steps.

"There's a line of trucks headed in our direction. They turned off the highway. They'll be here in ten minutes."

"Any chance it's a delivery and they're just on the wrong access road?" Ashton didn't seem to believe this himself.

"Do you want to take that chance, sir?"

Ashton didn't hesitate. "Your timing couldn't have been better," he said toward Gretchen. He turned to the guard and said, "Get her and the other young lady to the secure room." Then he turned to Randy. "You can stay with the ladies, or you can come with us. Your choice, but we can use every man we can get."

Randy looked to the massive vent at the top of the cavern. That vent led to the surface and his first thought was whoever was coming after Proctor would eventually find their way down here. When they did, they'd destroy the whole place and everyone in it.

The guard read his thoughts. "That vent will be sealed once an attack begins. We've got several days' oxygen down here and alternative intake and exhaust for the ventilation system about three miles away." Randy was impressed. They were expecting a well-funded assault and they were ready.

Cassie handed her M4 to the guard, glad to be rid of it.

The old guy rushed upward taking the stairs two at a time.

Randy hesitated with his eyes on Cassie. "We'll be ok," she said. "Go." Her lips formed a kiss from ten feet away. She lingered for a second then turned to follow Gretchen and the guard to the safe room.

Randy sprinted up the stairs with the M4 and saw Ashton dash into the stone tunnel that led back to the control rooms for the refinery. Randy caught him halfway through with a half dozen guards trailing him. When they reached the lower floor of the control room, Ashton rushed to the center of the open area and began shouting instructions. "Initiate data transfer to the hot site in New York. Research data has priority.

"Soon as we have visual of hostiles on the perimeter, I want Homeland Security on the phone and I want choppers here fast. Record those calls, people. I want the world to know how fast we responded.

"All refining operations shut down now. Cool it down, people. Let's get moving and contain the volatiles on the surface.

"Non-essential personnel through the tunnel. If you're not carrying a gun, I want you through this entrance in twenty minutes."

Randy admired the discipline as the first men rushed for the tunnel.

CHAPTER SIXTY-ONE

Ashton looked over the forty men he'd hired to defend the refinery and the solar technology operation. The company had thousands of employees all over the world, but it was up to these forty to protect the livelihood of the others and to ensure the future wealth and prosperity of the firm. He wished he'd hired more men, but he never knew when the attack would come. Most of the men had been paid to wait around for the last two years. Many of the real fighters had gotten antsy and left, but the men assembled around him were ready. They were well equipped with helmets, body armor, and plenty of spare magazines. They were better trained than the men they'd face. They also had the fifty-calibers on the surface and the protection of the tunnels, but they'd be outnumbered five to one.

At that moment he wished he'd installed one monitoring station for every guard tower. He'd strung them together in groups of four. Each operator controlled four towers, one on each side of the compound. An attack against one side of the compound would be met by all ten guns at once, but an attack on multiple sides would force the gunners to choose a single tower and leave his other three unmanned. Ashton never expected they'd need to fire from all the towers at once. In the three years, the guns had only been fired during drills. If the cartel was smart enough to spread out thinly around the entire perimeter, many of them would get through in the first wave.

"Jennings," he called.

The man hurried over, gear clanking as he moved.

"I want you up on the intake tower. Don't shoot anything until it's inside the fence, understood? Anyone comes inside, it's open season."

"Yes, sir." Jennings mounted a cart and headed for the highest point in the entire complex where he'd have a view of anyone on the surface moving toward the underground control center.

A younger man carried a cordless phone and handed it to him. Ashton gestured to his ears to ask if the call was being recorded. The man nodded affirmative.

"Ashton."

"Well, Lyle, it seems you have broken our agreement."

"What agreement would that be?" Ashton couldn't admit to what his company had done, not if he wanted to share this recording with Homeland Security.

"Don't be coy with me. Send out the girl and the man who has been helping her and we can go back to working together for our mutual benefit."

He was glad the prince was smart enough not to spell it out. "They are American citizens. I can't let you harm them."

"Harm? I just want to speak with them about solar technology. It seems they have made a valuable discovery."

"They're not coming out. I suggest you tell your men to stand down. If they attempt to enter this compound, you're going to have U.S. Marines breathing down your neck."

"As if you are in charge of the Marines. Fool. You can do nothing in my country. I walk in and out of yours at my choosing. Send the man and the woman out or I will burn your facility to the ground. Defy me and I will make sure you never buy another drop of cartel oil."

In six months he might not need another drop of cartel oil. They had spent the last five years investing all their free cash into this underground manufacturing operation. If it was destroyed and the cartel refused to sell them oil, Proctor Energy would be on the verge of bankruptcy before they could ever sell Whitney's solar paint. The cartel was selling all the oil they could pump. If Proctor didn't buy it, a Chinese importer would. "You know I can't do that."

Ashton cradled the phone between his neck and shoulder and signaled with his two hands flat and slowly coming together to form a platform. His aide signaled for the exhaust shafts over the control center and the solar technology manufacturing plant to be closed.

"Fool!" the prince yelled into the phone.

Even as the prince spoke, Ashton signaled for his aide to call Homeland Security.

"You make a grave mistake. We will destroy every tank, every pipe, until you can never make gasoline again. Then we will dig you out of that hole you hide in and teach you what happens to those who trifle with me."

Ashton's breath caught in his throat. The excavation of the control centers had been a massive undertaking, but the entire project was run from the shelter of the brick parking garage that stood atop the elevator shaft. Never had they excavated open ground. There was nothing he could do to protect the plant above from a prolonged attack, but he expected the underground fortifications to be a surprise.

The men from the tractor trailers were headed to meet him where he stood and they weren't going to wait for Homeland Security to arrive before coming in.

Ashton hung up the phone and exchanged it for another. "That credible threat I told you about, it's on my front porch."

CHAPTER SIXTY-TWO

The golf cart sagged as Randy stacked the final crate of ammunition in the rear. He hadn't expected to be in charge when he volunteered to help. Loading the perimeter machine guns was about the best job he could have hoped for, but he couldn't really affect the outcome of the battle by lugging bullets around. His partner, a thin twitchy guy named Tim, explained that the carts were the fastest way to get ammunition through the tunnels to the guns that lined the outer edges of the complex. The ammunition was too heavy for men to carry to the perimeter and the guns went through it amazingly fast. They hadn't anticipated anyone getting down into the tunnels, so the golf carts had no armor whatsoever.

Tim explained the layout of the tunnels. Essentially, the tunnels formed a big square around the underground manufacturing operations. There was only one exit on the inside of the square, that was the cavernous entrance to the control center. One level higher, Randy could find the elevators and the way out. On the outside of the big square, ten tunnels led to the perimeter. Each connected to four guard towers. To get to the next set of four towers, they'd have to come all the way back to the big square and move along to the next tunnel that led to the perimeter. It wasn't efficient for delivering ammunition, but the configuration allowed the security team to concentrate its force along the square. As long as they controlled the square and the elevator shaft, they controlled the entire underground complex. The long straight tunnels also gave them a huge advantage over anyone fighting their way in from the guard towers because there was nowhere for them to hide.

Tim handed Randy a radio and showed him how to tune it for the frequencies they'd need. The cart eased off toward the station on the northwest corner, struggling silently under the heavy load. A hand banged on a fender and Tim stopped the cart and turned to face another guard who was hustling around the back.

"Careful making the corners," the man said. "We're closing the blast doors twenty percent. When you're coming in from the outside, call on the radio and identify yourself by name."

"Got it," Tim said. "Don't you guys lock us out."

The man gave a slow nod and hustled to the next cart.

They started away again. In two hundred yards they made the corner and started heading west.

"What was that about?" Randy asked.

"The guard towers are the easiest way in."

"Past the fifties?"

"There's a hatch at every tower. It gives us an exit, but if they get through they'll be running around down here with us."

Randy looked down the long straight corridor as Tim chugged along in the cart. They passed one corridor heading off to the right to the four towers in the center of the north fence. The blast door had already been closed partway, creating a small shelter for a few men to take cover where the tunnels met. Randy imagined facing an assault force in the hall. Bullets would be ricocheting wildly off the walls and even a poor shot could find its target after a lucky bounce. The straight corridor sections that made up the big box were four hundred yards long with nowhere to take cover except the intersecting corridors. A battle down here promised to be a bloodbath.

Tim reached the northwest corner and turned down the smaller corridor that angled up toward the surface. He avoided the blast shield easily and the cart struggled up the incline with its load until the corridor branched left and right.

Tim hopped down. "We've got two towers west and two north."

Tim led Randy single file along a narrower, man-sized passage that forked and then dead ended at a ladder made of metal rods bent to form the outline of a step. Tim climbed up into a metal tube that was narrow enough for him to touch both sides at once. Randy followed. It was much warmer above ground and when Tim shifted, sunlight streamed in the arced opening the gun fired through.

"How do they aim this thing?" Randy asked.

Tim pointed to a metal plate at the top of the round tower. "There's a camera on the other side of that. The lens is exposed to the outside, there's no avoiding that, but it takes a direct hit to the lens to knock it out."

"So if you lose the camera you lose the gun?"

"Not exactly. There are other cameras higher on the buildings, but they're not calibrated for each gun. It's spray and pray without the primary."

Tim called in on the radio and let them know they were in Tower 40. Then he removed a plastic hood that covered the belt-fed ammunition that ran through the machine gun. He explained that the hood kept the empties from tangling in the belt and jamming the gun. The brass would bounce off and fall the height of the tower all the way into the tunnel below. They'd be stepping over thousands of casings later, but the design insured that the empties never stopped the gun from firing.

A blast echoed over the compound.

Tim wheeled around toward the opening. "Holy shit." He depressed an override switch and the entire ball on top of the tower rotated left toward the center of the compound. The machine gun rotated along with it, maintaining its alignment in the center of the small opening. The turret jerked to a stop before it came even with the next tower down the line.

Tim gasped. Randy climbed around him and peered out. Thick gray smoke hung around one of the distilling towers in the refinery as if it had been sprayed there.

"See them outside the fence?" Tim asked.

Randy looked out beyond the fence and saw a line of movement at the edge of his vision. The terrain sloped downward and Randy could barely make out the movement of men that seemed to be arrayed along the entire west fence. The men randomly stood, fired, and ducked back down to reload.

"Let's go!" Tim yelled, but Randy was already waiting for Tim to climb down.

The last thing Randy saw before ducking into the tower was a flight of thirty shoulder-fired rockets arcing toward the refinery at once. This batch would be followed swiftly by another as the men alternated like six lines of Revolutionary War soldiers firing together and dropping to reload while the line behind them fired.

"Clear that Tower Forty!" came a voice over the headset.

"Forty clear." Tim called over the radio while Randy was still five rungs up the ladder.

The gun roared to life, the report deafening inside the metal tube. Cascading empties clinked to the ground, pelting Randy with casings that felt like knuckles rapping his head and arms.

The two retreated down the tunnel toward the cart where they could hear each other and the radio. The blasts above were barely audible through the layers of rock, but the constant volleys of rockets had to be devastating the plant. Randy had a vision of gasoline cascading down through the tunnels and the roaring explosion that would follow. The sloping tunnels would funnel the fuel back to the box that outlined the underground operation. The facility itself wouldn't be damaged, but anyone in the tunnels would be incinerated.

CHAPTER SIXTY-THREE

Jennings settled prone at the top of the ventilation tower as the first rocket hit. The volley that followed streaked in low over the fences. A dozen rockets crashed into various towers and exploded. A few skipped off rounded edges and exploded in midair. Others missed altogether and fell to the ground, exploding against scores of parallel pipes that moved raw oil and semi-finished products from process to process. One rocket splintered a trailer that maintenance workers used to escape the Texas heat. Fortunately, no one was on the surface when the hot semi-processed fuel began leaking from the tanks.

The men firing the rockets disappeared into a dip in the earth about one hundred yards outside the perimeter fence. Then another group popped up, with only their heads and shoulders visible. These men fired a second volley of rockets into the facility from positions interspersed among the first group. When the third group popped up, Jennings called the command center. "We've got trouble up here, sir."

"We're hearing it. How many men?"

The fifty-caliber machine guns began firing in rapid bursts.

Sand kicked up short of their target and the guns adjusted and fired again.

"Could be a hundred."

"A hundred?" Ashton sounded hopeful as if he were expecting a much larger assault.

Jennings' rifle lay next to him flat on the platform as he used the binoculars to focus in on the enemy. The men with rockets were in range, but he was ordered not to shoot until they were inside the fence. They were inflicting so much damage on the refinery from outside the fence, Jennings had a fleeting hope that they'd stay out there rather than risk the wrath of the fifties up close. Unfortunately, based on the arc of their rockets, he was well within their range even one hundred feet above the facility.

Ten rockets flew in from the east and slammed into the tower nearest the garage. The coordinated strike about halfway up ripped a jagged hole in the plating. Flames licked the outside and then rushed inward, following the rising vapors higher into the tank until the explosion buckled every seam. The tank ruptured and folded over on itself where it had been gashed, collapsing in a fireball within a hundred yards of Jennings.

The destructive power could level the entire plant.

"Sir, sir. We've got men firing in from the east fence."

"Shit. What are you doing up there, Jennings?"

"Observing, sir."

"Fire at will, Jennings. Fire at will."

The men in the west were directly ahead of him. Rather than turn around and expose himself, he shouldered his rifle and chambered a round. The fifties were peppering the sand along his line of targets in the west. They were still able to get the rockets off and soon some of the gunners would have to shift around to control their towers in the east.

Jennings lined up his first man, but he dropped back down before he could fire. The second wasn't so lucky. He lingered over the rocket he launched as Jennings released his shot. The man saw his rocket explode inside the refinery, but paid dearly for lingering.

Something new appeared in the sand.

A group of pickup trucks came into view about fifty yards apart. Jennings zeroed in on one and watched four men hustle to hang mortars the instant the truck came to a stop. He nailed two men out of the first truck before the other two ducked for cover. The other trucks sent arcing flights of mortars just over the first fence. He thought they were aiming for the bomber barrier, but the mortars filled the fence line with smoke. Jennings leveled on another truck and picked off another mortar hanger, wondering how they planned to rush the compound. They couldn't be simple enough to rush the fifties on foot.

Jennings fired. Chambered. Fired. Chambered. Fired.

Replacements sprung up into the bed of the truck, but Jennings wasn't the only one focused on them. The fifties zeroed in and ripped two of the trucks apart.

The men with the rockets came up again, but this time they took precise aim at the buildings just inside the wall. After the first barrage hit, Ashton was barking on the radio again. "What the hell is going on up there? We're blind down here."

The rockets had hit the backup cameras. The guard towers were enveloped in smoke. With the higher cameras out on the east and west walls, the control room was blind to the attack and helpless to do anything but fire randomly over the fence.

"They've got mortars firing smoke. East and west walls are socked in. Looks like they hit the secondary cameras with rockets."

The men were attacking like they'd been there to help build the facility. They were coming in. When and where he couldn't tell.

"How many of those trucks do you see?" Ashton asked.

"Ten west, sir. Estimate the same east."

More rockets crashed in, focused on the towers flanking the gate.

"Fire control, you hearing this?" The men at the monitors were instantly on the line. "Put some fire out there and let Jennings get you on those trucks."

One of the fifty-calibers opened up with a burst. Jennings adjusted them north and twenty feet higher. The second burst ripped through the pickup, killing three of the operators and probably anyone who had been in the cab.

"On target. Next."

Another burst ripped into the sand and Jennings guided it onto a truck. This time he didn't hesitate to move on. Once the first bullets hit target, Jennings ordered them to keep on and gave instructions to the next operator.

The barrage of mortars slowed, but with no wind, the smoke hung over the fence line.

Two tractor trailers appeared on the access road but stayed well back. Jennings began guiding one of the towers toward the first rig and then the alarm went up on the ground. Jennings saw the scurrying in his peripheral vision, but he was too focused on spotting the impacts and communicating adjustments. A professional soldier might have done it faster and slowed the incursion, but Jennings had never been in the military. He was a guard who could drop a buck at three hundred yards. Everyone knew it. That was why he was on top of this tower. His proficiency with a rifle was what got Jennings killed.

The assault force didn't bother with automatic weapons fire. Not a single AK-47 had been fired in the attack. It was as if they knew there would be no men on the ground. They did have Carl Gustavs and when they finally spotted Jennings on the tower directing fire from his vantage point above the smoke, a squad of men took aim and fired.

Four rockets crashed into the western side and exploded at various heights. Filled with air, there was nothing inside the tower to burst into flame, but the impact ripped gaping holes in the tower and rocked it so furiously that Jennings was bucked off. He lost his rifle about halfway down as he plummeted one hundred feet to the rooftop below.

CHAPTER SIXTY-FOUR

The gauze-faced leader stepped out from the pickup truck and climbed the bank until he was standing tall with nothing to protect him from the machine guns except the smoke that blinded the cameras. The guns remained silent. He waved one of the men cowering below the bank to bring him a Gustav. He stood there waiting as the man climbed the slope and handed him the weapon.

A burst rattled in the distance. He flinched but quickly saw the sand jumping fifty yards to his left. The men inside the fortress were blind. The breeze was so slight the smoke would hang on the towers for several minutes. Long enough, but when he was done with the Gustav, he'd give the order for another round of smoke.

He aimed the Gustav at the fence and fired. The explosion shattered a metal post and tore a wide hole in the chain-link. Seeing the result, he ordered a single volley from each side of the compound focused on the two perimeter fences. The rockets flared and ripped gaping entrances all along the east and west fences.

Immediately he ordered his men to take cover. The sensors inside the control room registered the intrusion and the guns on the towers dropped their sights low over the fence and fired a steady spray that buried into the sand up and down the entire fence line. Had they been charging to get inside, half the force would have been cut down in the rush.

When the guns silenced to reload, a process that would take many minutes, he gave the signal for the trucks to move in. The two tractor trailers tugged ahead then rolled forward one behind the other, increasing their speed toward the gate. The first driver pushed his rig through gear after gear. The second kept his rig on the bumper ahead, eager to get through the gate before the guns came back to life. Even if the men monitoring the towers saw them coming they were defenseless. With their guns empty, nothing would stop the assault team from driving right into the refinery. They'd fight their way below ground and have control of the compound in twenty minutes. The entire facility would be destroyed before the army arrived.

The lead truck reached 50 mph when it crashed through the first gate. What happened next was a shock. The countermeasures weren't in the blueprints. The driver saw the massive pipes shoot up from underground before he reached the second gate, but he was helpless to stop before the pipes slammed against his bumper. Most things the big rig hit would fly out of the way, save a train or a massive boulder. The pipe barrier buckled and bent, but the cab took most of the abuse. The driver catapulted from his seat and crashed headfirst through the windshield. As the nose of the cab dropped and the back wheels left the ground it looked as if he'd been dumped from yesterday's coffee cup and spilled out over the ground. He skidded across the asphalt and stopped thirty feet in front of the cab at the base of the fence. His slide proved to be about fifteen feet too short.

There was no stopping the momentum of the trailer even lightly loaded as it was with soldiers and gear. As the barrier bent and gave, the cab and its payload bucked skyward. There was no warning to the driver of the second rig and the abrupt bounce of the trailer took him by surprise. He rammed the underside of the trailer, sending it into a cartwheel that flipped the trailer over its cab and landed it squarely on the driver sprawled on the pavement. The rear door of the upside down trailer ripped through the fence, providing an entrance, only after the roof crushed the driver. The assault force was flipped over and tangled with each other on top of the sheet metal roof. The second driver locked his brakes and lost control of the trailer, but fortunately for the men inside, the second trailer slapped sideways into the barrier, rocked with the impact and halted upright, the men inside badly shaken.

Smoke obscured the trailers from Hisham's view. Curses roiled through his mind, not thoughts of defeat, but murderous rage at the unexpected obstacle and the traitor responsible for gathering information about the compound. He held his anger and in several seconds he was rewarded.

Doors creaked open. Voices shouted. Feet stamped on asphalt. The men in the trucks had been jostled, but they continued toward their objective. It was then he decided to improvise and deal the ultimate devastation to the American Infidels.

From his radio he ordered three quarters of his men to carry ammunition for the Gustavs into the compound. The others would bring their weapons. Together they would bring the refinery to its knees from the inside even as the battle raged below. They'd assemble in the center of the compound to avoid crossfire and to inflict maximum damage from close range.

Four others he assigned an imperative task. To blow open the access hatches to the guard towers along the west fence and to disable the guns by cutting the communication wires.

The horde descended on the refinery, while the men below scrambled to load guns that would be useless as soon as the attacking force streamed through the holes in the fences and gained the refinery grounds.

CHAPTER SIXTY-FIVE

Sixteen bolts rammed home in unison, securing the vault door and filling Cassie with dread at being locked in. The resin coating that made the walls and floor airtight reflected muted voices over the crowd of white-collar refugees. Plush furniture broke the single room into smaller spaces where research and refinery employees gathered to pass the time as if this were a scheduled break from their normal workday. They watched television, played video games, and used computers. A dozen clustered on the floor with remote control cars, trucks, and even a helicopter. Their intensity suggested these toys were a future product line. Other employees wore headphones and bobbed to music. The electronic comforts belied the panic Cassie felt not only for being locked up underground, but also for the fight playing out on the surface. The employees showed little concern for the outcome. They certainly knew about the security measures that protected the compound, but she assumed they knew little about their adversary.

Time passed slowly for Cassie. Blind to the world above, she could only wonder what Randy was doing and wish they'd left Gretchen with the police and gone home. Every employee around them burned electricity one way or another, but Gretchen didn't seem to mind. The solar researchers routinely stored and burned power and Cassie wondered if their work earned them special status in Gretchen's eyes.

A tremor shook the couch Cassie shared with Gretchen. She clutched her knees to herself and imagined one of the massive oil tanks exploding.

"You all right?" Gretchen asked.

"I wish I knew what was going on up there."

"So you could *print* the story?"

Gretchen emphasized "print" like a ten year old trying out a four letter word. No matter what Cassie said, Gretchen would never understand the important messages printed on those pages. Cassie's work was as worthy as Gretchen's, whether she wanted to believe it or not. Cassie understood Gretchen wasn't trying to be snotty, she just couldn't turn off her disdain for anything contrary to her beliefs.

"I was thinking about all the people up there," Cassie said.

"Randy?" she asked as if caring about another person was illogical. Gretchen sniffled and pulled a handkerchief from her pocket. She'd never seen a twenty-something carrying her own handkerchief, but Gretchen wouldn't abide the waste of paper if she could prevent it.

"Nice color. Where'd you get that?"

"Blackberries."

Had she really used blackberries to die her handkerchief?

"Everything you do is about conservation," Cassie said almost to herself. It was a pathology as much as a life choice. She wondered aloud, "How can you care so much about the world and so little about people? Don't you have a family and friends you care about?"

Gretchen looked confused and detached as if the idea of personal relationships was foreign, as if she'd never had a real friend in her life.

Cassie regretted her words but couldn't pull them back. She expected a hail of insults but Gretchen said nothing. She wasn't ugly. Why was she such an outcast? In that instant Cassie realized what had driven her to such extremes. She should have seen the contrast the moment she read the newspaper account of the accident. When Cassie was researching Gretchen back in the hotel, she'd stumbled across an account of oil-tanker captain Richard Greene.

"The kids gave you a hard time, didn't they?"

Gretchen frowned cautiously.

Cassie rested a hand on Gretchen's. "How old were you when the spill happened?"

Gretchen tensed. For the first time Cassie struck a vulnerability that Gretchen couldn't defend. She understood then that Gretchen had remade herself to compensate for her father's mistake. Gretchen didn't answer, just stared back looking wounded.

"It wasn't your fault. You had nothing to do with it."

One of the researchers turned to face them, but seeing the tension immediately turned back.

"Twenty thousand tons," Gretchen said. "He spilled twenty thousand tons." She hunched forward. Cassie imagined her downcast eyes were recalling images of the devastation along the coast.

"You need to stop punishing yourself. It's not your responsibility to fix his mistake. That's absurd."

That was exactly what Gretchen had been trying to do since elementary school. She'd been trying to conserve so much that she erased the damage her father had done when he'd run the tanker aground.

Somewhere on the wall behind them, a phone rang and was answered. Cassie heard a single word above the chatter. "Inside?"

She spun. The man at the phone scanned the room to see if he'd raised a panic. A few savvy workers tuned in anytime the wall phone rang, but most were focused on their entertainment as if this was well-earned time off to be enjoyed. The man at the phone coolly hung up and returned to his armchair, but Cassie could see the hesitancy in his walk.

Cassie pictured armed men outside the vault door. Inside could mean inside the fence or it could mean inside the buildings on the surface. At least he hadn't said underground. Cassie tried to focus on Gretchen but couldn't shake the image of armed men storming the tunnels.

CHAPTER SIXTY-SIX

Randy crawled through the hatch of Tower 40 and stepped outside into the smoky chaos to see what had just happened above ground. If Ashton knew Randy would be brazen enough to open the hatch from the inside, he would have locked him up in the solar research area with the women. Voices shouted. Men ran. The smoke was lifting from the ground, but he could see only a dozen yards from the metal tower. Moving around it, he ducked through a gaping hole in the chain-link. Crawling low between the fences and getting ever farther from the tower and the hatch to safety, he found that by hugging the ground he could see in patches down the fence line. He crawled through a hole in the outer fence and could see clearly across the expanse of sand and scrub outside the complex.

He gasped at what he saw and reached for his radio. "Thirty to thirty-five. You got anything left?" He'd just finished reloading Tower 40 and he knew Tim was busy with Tower 39.

"Thirty-two's ready to rock," came the first response. The others were loaded except Tower 34.

Randy asked how close in they could shoot. They could shoot through the outer fence but were ordered to avoid doing so.

"I've got a hundred bad guys waltzing in down there. Drop down just above the fence and I'll tell you when to light 'em up."

A string of readies followed.

The men moved sluggishly through the sandy scrub, sagging under heavy burdens Randy assumed to be explosives. Some men moved faster than others and Randy let the first dozen stream in through holes in the fence until the bulk of the group moved to where the guns were aimed.

"Go! Go! Go!" he yelled.

The guns sprung to action all at once and the area outside the fence danced with thousands of impacts that ripped through men, sand, equipment and sent rocks flying, men collapsing and a chain reaction of rockets exploding. The guns raked back and forth and decimated the core of the group. A few turned and ran, the rest streaked toward the fence. Some made it through to join their faster comrades inside; many dropped in the sand outside the fence.

When there were no more targets he called, "Hold your fire. Nothing left to shoot at. Ashton be advised, you've got bogeys inside the fence."

They asked how many, but Randy could see nothing in that direction. He asked Ashton to hold on and crawled back into the smoke, through the gap in the fence and past Tower 40 where he began. A low brick building provided cover and a view toward the refinery. What had once been a glistening, organized mass of pipes and valves was now bruised and smoldering. Thirty men moved toward the refinery operation, one with a white-bandaged face stood out. He gave orders, assembling a group to take aim at certain points in the refinery.

Randy remembered something he'd read, *Strike the shepherd and the flock will scatter*. He lay prone, lined up, and fired.

The report barked and the leader dropped face down on the asphalt. With the tower guns silent and the men yet to launch against the refinery from the inside, the report gave away Randy's position. The men swung around from the pipes and towers to his position by the little brick building.

He dove backward to shelter behind the wall. He landed before a single bullet chased after him. He scrambled crablike over the asphalt, kicking his feet, pushing with one hand, and clutching the M4 with the other.

Rockets demolished the tiny building behind him, sending crumbled bricks and mortar raining down over his head. Randy got up to run, standing just as another explosion blew a hole in the asphalt ahead of him. A stabbing pain in his chest dropped him to the ground on all fours. The M4 bounced out of reach. He thought he was dead when he hit the ground. He'd killed two men in less than twenty-four hours, surely he'd worn out God's patience.

The men were lining up on him again. If they had rifles he'd be dead by now, but fortunately all they seemed to have was rockets and had to reload after every shot.

The stabbing pain in his chest turned out to be a softball-sized chunk of gooey black pavement torn up by the rocket. The whole side of his torso lit up with intense pain at any movement, but he couldn't stay outside. He willed himself up through the blinding pain, hobbled to the tower without his M4, and slammed the hatch.

Another explosion chased him in, slamming high against the tower. The reverberation knocked his wobbly legs off the metal rungs and sent him plummeting down below ground where he fell in a tormented heap on top of spent casings.

He keyed his radio. "Thirty five. They're right behind you. Spin around."

"No can do."

"What?"

"Safety. They don't let us fire inside the compound."

"Screw that. Light 'em up."

The controller explained that a pin stopped the turret from rotating into an unsafe direction. That way they couldn't accidentally shoot coworkers inside the refinery and no one could break into the control room and use the machine guns against the equipment or personnel on the surface.

CHAPTER SIXTY-SEVEN

Two men with AK-47s leaned into the doorway and opened fire, spraying their entire magazines at the three men huddled behind the concrete barrier that fronted the elevator to the complex below. When the defenders' heads ducked down, three men hustled in the opposite side of the overhead door and turned sharply right, darting for the cover of the parked cars beyond. Wesley swung on the last of the group and reeled off four shots before he connected. When his man dropped, Wesley lined up a headshot and finished him before dropping back down.

The concrete all around him flashed to life as another group of men entered the door and sprayed in his direction. He knew another group was running inside to flank them, but there was nothing he could do about it. If he stood up he'd be dead. They were outnumbered eight to one and while the men outside the large door had to share time in position to fire, there was always a group of men with a full clip ready to blast away. Wesley's men were pinned. Every time they came up for a shot, they were met with a barrage of automatic fire. They'd already dropped twelve men in the huge doorway, but they kept coming and now they were scuttling around the parked cars. When they found a flanking position, they would take dead aim and pick off Wesley's men one by one.

"Big problems up here, sir," Wesley said into his radio.

When Ashton asked for status, Wesley told him they were facing nearly eighty men with automatics. The barricades kept them safe with a sixty-foot killing field in front of them, but that wasn't going to last now that they were flanked. Ashton needed to send help up the elevator or the men with the AK-47s would be coming down.

"Are they inside with you?" Ashton asked.

"Some. Most are outside."

"Can we get them flanked?"

"Working on that," came another voice.

"Who the hell is that?" Wesley asked.

"An honored guest. I'm in tower thirty-five," Randy said.

"How many men have you got?"

"Just me. But I've got something for you. Give me a minute and push 'em back outside if you can."

Wesley shook his head and popped up for a burst at the door. When he focused he saw seven men side by side firing full auto. He leveled and drilled a horizontal burst through the group chest high, emptying his magazine and dropping three of the seven. Every other head on his team was down and for a second he thought he might be the only one left alive. In answer, two guns fired from the bunker to his right.

Push them outside. Ridiculous.

A series of explosions rocked the far wall and the reverberation inside was deafening. He thought for a second the men outside who'd been pelting the refinery with rockets had come around to the garage and, not knowing what it was, set to leveling it. The rush of bodies at the opposite end of the floor told him it wasn't so. His adversaries had just created an entrance that was impossible for him to defend.

CHAPTER SIXTY-EIGHT

"Shit. Shit. Shit," Randy screamed into his headset. "I need help on thirty-one, thirty-two, thirty-three, and thirty-four."

"What's going on up there?" came the reply.

From where he struggled inside the turret nearest the gate, Randy glimpsed the team setting charges to the hatch doors. They were blowing the hatches one by one and soon they would have a wide open door to the subterranean research center where Gretchen and Cassie were hiding. Randy explained this while he struggled against the massive pin that refused to budge. If someone didn't respond, those men would be in the tower with him in two minutes. If the explosion didn't kill him, he wouldn't last thirty seconds with machine-gun fire coming up at him from the hatch.

He remembered the override Tim had used to get a view in Tower 40. He found the button and turned the turret until it banged to a stop against the pin that kept the gun aimed safely. The wrench he'd found below was too short. It didn't give him enough leverage to move the pin, but the vibration from the turret helped jiggle it upward. He kept pressure on the wrench and rocked the turret back and forth. Each time the turret banged home, the pin gave in to the pressure from the wrench and lifted a fraction. Randy kept on, and the further the pin was removed, the more work the turret and the wrench accomplished with each strike.

Outside, a blast rocked one of the towers. He heard the metal door swing open during a lull in the rocket fire.

When the turret hit the pin again, it popped loose. The wrench flew from Randy's hand and clanged down through the tower to the floor of the tunnel. His eyes blurry from the pain, Randy blurted, "You're free," into his headset.

He let himself down the metal rungs left-handed, allowing his right to hang by his side. The hydraulics whined as the turret turned backward to face an enemy it was designed never to engage. The adjustments became smaller and smaller until Randy knew the gun was on target. He called into his headset even though he hadn't reached the foot of the tunnel. "Go thirty-five."

The gun roared to life.

Shell casings kicked off the inside walls of the turret and splashed down, thudding off Randy's head and shoulders as he descended.

The smoke cleared as the turret turned toward the compound. The gunner had never imagined seeing so many targets presented all at once. A long line of men launched rockets at the refinery from the main drive. Behind them, an even larger group stood in support of each rocket launcher, passing ammunition in an assembly line of destruction. The men stood upright and admired the damage their rockets inflicted. No men were put in reserve to guard the flanks or even watch for action to the rear.

The gunner passed up this group for a contingent of men standing outside the entrance to the garage. These men were the immediate threat even if the rockets could disable the gun he was now aiming.

Ashton stood directly behind him and saw with amazement the troops on the ground above. He gasped at the number of men, the damage they'd inflicted on his plant, and the revelation that he could use the awesome firepower along the perimeter to annihilate them. He ordered the men working Tower 23, Tower 24, and Tower 25 to follow Randy's lead and remove the pins that limited the turrets' rotation.

When the gunner opened fire the devastation was awesome. The assault team had bunched up against the garage wall and the fifty was dead-nuts on when he opened fire. Single shells ripped through three and four men each.

He kept it wide open, nudging it barely left and right, keeping the pattern of fire slamming into the concentrated group. As they thinned, shells skipped off the asphalt and ripped through the attackers bunched on the other side of the wide doors. The men turned to run for the far corner of the building and the gunner chased them there with the remote, dropping more than half of the men before they reached shelter.

When the rest of them disappeared, he wheeled for the men with the rockets in the center of the compound. There was no cover for them to run to. They were so far out in the open only good luck could save them from the fifty. A few crouched and fired rockets at the tower. The gunner targeted them first. The rest scampered, a few for the flaming refinery, a few for the fence, and a few for the cover of the garage.

The gunner trailed them all over the open compound.

Behind him he heard the operators of the other towers reacting to the astounding array of targets.

"Get our guys out of the garage," one of them yelled.

Others opened fire along the back edge of the garage where the gunner had chased the intruders seconds before. The men from Tower 24 and Tower 25 scorched the open asphalt that ran from the gate all the way across the compound to the garage.

When Wesley and his men cleared the upper level and rode the elevator down underground, Tower 22 opened up through the hole the invaders had blown in the garage wall. Bullets ricocheted all around the cement structure. Cars parked that morning by the staff were ripped open, gas tanks ruptured. Some of the invaders were cut down by the bullets, the rest were killed or chased outside when the gasoline ignited and set off a chain reaction of automobile explosions.

CHAPTER SIXTY-NINE

The celebration reached Gretchen and Cassie in the research station. Randy had rigged one of the towers so the gun could fire inside the fence. Others followed suit and soon the refinery was ablaze with machine guns answering the barrages of rockets. The attackers inside the compound were cut down en masse. Twenty minutes later Apache helicopters arrived to cruise the perimeter and kill or capture the remainder of the force.

Ashton came in personally half an hour later to tell them the assault was over and that they were safe, but this didn't soothe Cassie's nerves. She hadn't stopped pacing once she'd heard Randy had been hurt. The two women followed Ashton through the complex and back to the elevator. When they reached the surface, the devastation was awe inspiring. What had been a pristine brick garage now had gaping, soot-covered holes opening the building to the weather. Several gasoline-powered cars had exploded and burned. Water from the firemen's hoses drained down from the parking area and pooled where the overhead doors had been.

The scene outside was doubly gruesome. The first thing Gretchen noticed were the flames and black smoke rising from the refinery. The whole complex was shaded by an ocean of black smoke that hung overhead. Further away, bright sunshine lit up the landscape on all sides as if to emphasize the tragedy that occurred within the chain-link. What had been an ordered, if hopelessly complex, arrangement of parallel pipes was now a tangle of oversized scrap metal that covered dozens of acres. The entire plant would need to be demolished and rebuilt if it would ever return to service.

Even more horrifying was the human toll still being arranged on the tarmac. A handful of Proctor Energy men lay still at the foot of the garage wall and Gretchen was forced to walk by the uncovered bodies, some burned, some dead of gunshots or rocket blasts. A group of helicopters waited on the tarmac between the garage and the refinery. They were ringed by a circle of guards to prevent sabotage by any remaining militants. Toward the center of the complex, soldiers and Proctor Energy guards were dragging bodies and aligning them in a horribly long row of uncovered corpses. As she scanned the terrain, she saw dozens of men spread out around the complex, checking bodies for signs of life and collecting the dead.

Ashton pointed and Cassie turned and ran in the direction he indicated. Gretchen saw the ambulance parked just inside the gate and the men working on someone at the base of a guard tower. Gretchen wouldn't have known it was Randy but for Ashton's indication and Cassie's sprint. She saw other ambulances scattered around the complex and paramedics attending to the wounded. It was strange of men to shoot each other one moment and then work to save each other the next, but the irony was overshadowed by the sheer savagery splattered all over the grounds.

Walking toward the ambulance, Gretchen saw the men carefully pulling down Randy's shirt, and as she approached she spotted blood stains over his ribcage. Cassie kneeled by his side, captivated by his every movement as if it were a gift. Randy minimized his reaction to the pain, though he stayed seated on the ground with his back against the metal tower.

The ambulance driver told him he needed X-rays to make sure there was no internal damage. Ashton arrived behind Gretchen and spoke up strongly. "Make sure he gets whatever he needs."

The paramedic looked inquiringly at Ashton and he introduced himself and assured him that any medical expenses would be taken care of by the firm. He gushed over Randy's role in saving the manufacturing plant and thereby his company.

"Anything else I can do?" Ashton asked.

"I could use a new ride," Randy joked.

"Done. I've got something perfect. A concept car. Too ostentatious for me. Needlessly fast. It's so fast no one will believe it's solar powered until you sneak up on them without a sound. Something you just might be able to put to good use." Ashton turned on his heel and went off in search of others to help and damage to inventory.

Cassie and Randy faced her once Ashton left. Gretchen didn't quite know what to say. She had played a role in the disaster all around her, but it wasn't entirely her fault. Proctor and the cartel were destined to clash. Randy couldn't blame her for that, but she'd made his last two days a nightmare. Looking at the two of them on the ground, she saw what Randy had given to help and how painful that was for Cassie.

Gretchen felt a micro seizure in her chest, as if the world she'd organized stopped spinning for a second to realign itself with the universe in a new way. She'd convinced herself that she was doing her utmost to save the world. Just then she considered that maybe it was something else. A way to separate herself from the world and maybe an excuse to vent her anger on anyone who came near.

She couldn't face the two of them then. She turned from Randy and panned across the refinery. "Amazing what people will do."

"These are your people," Randy chided. "South Americans, Africans, Middle Easterners. The cartel is big business and they can't afford to lose us as a customer."

He was smiling when she turned around. Not a smug I-told-you-so smile. It was playful, rounded with a bit of hope. She wouldn't give in and tell him she understood how wrong she'd been. But looking at him it was clear he already knew. She'd underestimated Ty and Whitney because of who they were and she'd foolishly trusted Demitri because she was looking for anyone different. Without Randy the misjudgment would have been fatal.

"I'm going to make sure we buy as little oil as possible," she said. She'd been doing that her entire adult life, but now she had the power to make a real difference. Three days ago no one could have paid her to take the job of big energy spokeswoman, but that's precisely why she was the ideal candidate for the job. Proctor was giving her a platform and for the first time in her life, her father's mistake would help her accomplish her goals. She could tell the world about the twenty-thousand tons and that would only inspire them to embrace Whitney's marvel.

"So you're not going to run off with that egg?"

"No," she said.

Two paramedics lifted Randy onto a stretcher, wheeled him toward the back of the ambulance, and lifted him in. Cassie followed.

"Watch out for red dogs," Gretchen said. "I hear they're forced to run down slow-moving prey."

She caught his grin as the door closed.

CHAPTER SEVENTY

Two weeks later one hundred seventy-seven journalists gathered on the tarmac in the shadow of ruined distillation towers to hear Lyle Ashton talk about the future of Proctor Energy now that the company's flagship refinery had been destroyed and its relationship with the cartel had been severed in favor of a new direction for the firm. Television cameras rolled where earlier heavy machine guns and rockets had battled to destroy each other.

Ashton stepped to the microphone. "This refinery was destroyed by greed. Greed of those desperate to keep us enslaved. Greed of those who believe they can control the world economy and ideology by controlling our energy supply. Today we have won the battle against men who would rather pollute our world and line their pockets than work to preserve it for future generations."

The audience was filled with financial reporters ready for a story on the bankruptcy of one of the nation's premier firms. Ashton's optimism took them by surprise.

"One hundred thirty years ago our economy was revolutionized by the introduction of commercial electric power. Small, clean electric engines soon separated the use of power from the generation of power. This revolutionary change allowed workers to use power wherever they needed it. Our economy boomed. I look around and I see cameras, phones, digital recorders, all sorts of devices running on clean electric power. But this clean power is a mirage. Power plants sprung up to provide all this power. Their tentacles, these wires we see along our roadsides, they reach deep into our communities. If you find the source of these wires, you will see the real cost, the environmental cost, required to feed our energy habit.

"Just as we separated workers from the rotating shafts that delivered power to our ancestors, today we cut the cord from dirty power plants fueled by coal and oil, for a new power plant that looks something like this."

Ashton gestured off to his left and on cue, an electric car, covered with Whitney's solar technology silently rolled toward the podium. This wasn't an ordinary electric car, it was an eight-passenger sport utility vehicle, the kind Gretchen spent years railing against as excessive and wasteful.

"This is the new power plant. It not only generates enough power to get you where you need to go, it will charge your laptop, your cell phone and anything else you want to plug into it. Just don't park it in the garage."

The crowd laughed.

Ashton went on to describe how homeowners and business owners could turn their buildings into clean power plants and sell electricity to their neighbors. He cautioned that breaking America's dependence on fossil fuels and their foreign producers wouldn't happen overnight, but the technology was ready. Ashton introduced the two people who would work to apply it to every community across the country.

Gretchen Greene stepped up to the podium with her counterpart from Ashton's team. Cameras flashed as Ashton shook hands with each in turn. Questions erupted about Whitney, the attack in Boston, and how they kept this technology secret. The questions went on for thirty minutes. Ty Summers watched from his wheelchair in the third row, not unaware that Gretchen's eyes fell to him a bit too often.

Ashton eventually stepped in and called an end to questions. Then Gretchen led the group, through the bombed out shell of the garage and down the elevator to the manufacturing facility below.

When they finally reached the railing that overlooked Gretchen's new office, she began explaining how the factory was built and dedicated to the memory of her brave professor. Standing there she realized that for the first time in her life she was in a position to help make big changes in the world. She'd help make them and for the right reasons.

CHAPTER SEVENTY-ONE

A week later, halfway around the world, three men clambered into an inflatable boat and motored away from the shore just as dawn broke over the horizon. The outboard labored over the waves to rendezvous with a faster boat that raced them out into the shipping channel. The men were hoisted aboard a massive oil tanker and escorted to the bridge. They listened as the call was placed from the United States.

The servant who answered took several minutes to finally reach his highness and give him the phone.

"Enjoy your last round of golf today," was all his highness heard.

The explosion ripped simultaneously through the island's only power plant and the massive desalinization plant installed to supply the fresh-water demands of the lush golf course under the blazing desert sun.

The phone line went dead as the power plant went offline.

The water gushing from the two massive pipes slowed to a trickle. The waterfall ceased as the sun went to work evaporating every last bit of moisture from the manmade pond and the fairways it supported.

The sun would soon do more than burn the grass on this hundred-million-dollar golf course. It would smash the power the cartel wielded all around the world.

CHAPTER SEVENTY-TWO

Walter walked to his car after work and dropped inside. He slammed the door angrily after losing another round with Bart. He would never understand why Cassie went to such lengths to save a hoodlum like Randy Black. Walter's articles painted him realistically, showing the terror he wreaked on innocent families and the devastation he'd caused in that Connecticut hospital. Bart refused to print it.

There was no response from the car when Walter turned the key. Not a whimper or a click, nothing. He whacked the steering wheel with his palm and grabbed for the door handle. The door wouldn't budge. He removed the key and clicked the remote. Still the door refused to unlock.

Walter swore and bashed the steering wheel with both hands this time. It was getting dark. His car was dead and he was locked inside with no one nearby to help.

Just then he saw a white sheet of paper stuck into the vent above the radio. The note didn't belong tucked in behind the plastic trim. He yanked it out, sending the vent cover falling to the floor.

I asked you nicely, the note said. *Now buzz off.*

Walter trembled. With the reading of the word "buzz," the car was suddenly alive with a swarm of yellow jackets pouring out of the vent and stinging him repeatedly. He swatted, screamed, and pounded on the windows, but the car refused to let him out. His arms burned. He screamed louder and swatted wildly with the note in a futile attempt to protect himself.

Miles away the sleek electric car raced silently down Route 88. In the short time he'd had the car Cassie had taken to calling it the Black Mobile, for its color and its owner's penchant for fighting injustice. At 102 mph, only the tires announced their hasty approach toward the beach on that October afternoon.

They parked beside a gray van in the beach parking lot. Cassie had swooned when he gallantly kissed her hand and asked her for their first official date. After careening around New Bedford together, burgling a house in Newport, and surviving a military-style assault in Texas, this first date would be hard pressed to avoid being a letdown, but the arrival at the deserted beach was a good start. Walking the beach in a strapless dress and heels however, wasn't her idea of a good time, but he'd said formal and he was as sharp as she'd ever seen him. A little stubble added to the cache.

A gentleman in a tuxedo opened Cassie's door and led her around to Randy's side of the car. He still favored his right side as he walked to the carpet laid out over the sand. She took a skeptical first step but found there was a solid foundation beneath the carpet and was amazed he could have such a thing installed on a public beach. As their table came into view, her worries about the formal attire and the cool October air faded.

Red-carpeted steps led up to a platform trimmed in glossy black with a checkerboard tile floor. Heaters fired in each corner and as she stepped up to her chair, she gladly handed her jacket to the attendant. They faced each other across the table. She had a view of gentle waves that would soon fade into a starry night, yet continue to provide a gentle rhythm for the remainder of their dinner. Randy faced her and the dunes behind.

As the first attendant breezed away with their coats, a second arrived with a tray of various breads. Without prompting, the attendant plucked a squat, brownish muffin and placed it on the small plate at Cassie's right. The waiter asked Randy to select his own bread, left the tray, and headed back toward the van.

A young woman delivered a bottle of Marston Vineyards sparkling and poured two glasses. Randy raised his glass and toasted saviors large and small. She felt the redness blossoming at the base of her neck as his eyes fell on her, thanking her for all she'd done.

The evening couldn't have been more perfect until she sipped the sparkling and bit into the muffin. The sparkling was dry and sweet, which made the bitter muffin a nasty surprise. She labored to finish the single bite and when she looked up, she saw Randy reveling in her culinary distress.

"What?"

He told her that particular muffin was from Gretchen's recipe. The waiter brought some Autumn Olive and a wild salad that was actually tasty. Her appetite improved when the waiter delivered something Gretchen would never eat, a boiled lobster. Randy had a small roasted animal she didn't recognize. She didn't ask what he'd chosen for dinner or why.